PRAISE FOR
Witchling

"Reminiscent of Laurell K. Hamilton with a lighter touch . . . a delightful new series that simmers with fun and magic."
—Mary Jo Putney, *New York Times* bestselling author of *The Marriage Spell*

"The first in an engrossing new series . . . a whimsical reminder of fantasy's importance in everyday life."
—*Publishers Weekly*

"*Witchling* is pure delight . . . a great heroine, designer gear, dead guys, and Seattle precipitation!"
—MaryJanice Davidson, *New York Times* bestselling author of *Undead and Uneasy*

"*Witchling* is one sexy, fantastic paranormal-mystery-romantic read."
—Terese Ramin, author of *Bewitched, Bothered & BeVampyred*

"Galenorn's kick-butt Fae ramp up the action in a wyrd world gone awry . . . I loved it!"
—Patricia Rice, author of *Magic Man*

"A fun read, filled with surprise and enchantment."
—Linda Winstead Jones, author of *Prince of Swords*

The Otherworld Series

WITCHLING
CHANGELING
DARKLING

CHANGELING

YASMINE GALENORN

BERKLEY BOOKS, NEW YORK

THE BERKLEY PUBLISHING GROUP
Published by the Penguin Group
Penguin Group (USA) Inc.
375 Hudson Street, New York, New York 10014, USA

Penguin Group (Canada), 90 Eglinton Avenue East, Suite 700, Toronto, Ontario M4P 2Y3, Canada
(a division of Pearson Penguin Canada Inc.)
Penguin Books Ltd., 80 Strand, London WC2R 0RL, England
Penguin Group Ireland, 25 St. Stephen's Green, Dublin 2, Ireland (a division of Penguin Books Ltd.)
Penguin Group (Australia), 250 Camberwell Road, Camberwell, Victoria 3124, Australia
(a division of Pearson Australia Group Pty. Ltd.)
Penguin Books India Pvt. Ltd., 11 Community Centre, Panchsheel Park, New Delhi—110 017, India
Penguin Group (NZ), 67 Apollo Drive, Rosedale, North Shore 0745, Auckland, New Zealand
(a division of Pearson New Zealand Ltd.)
Penguin Books (South Africa) (Pty.) Ltd., 24 Sturdee Avenue, Rosebank, Johannesburg 2196,
South Africa

Penguin Books Ltd., Registered Offices: 80 Strand, London WC2R 0RL, England

This is a work of fiction. Names, characters, places, and incidents either are the product of the author's
imagination or are used fictitiously, and any resemblance to actual persons, living or dead, business
establishments, events, or locales is entirely coincidental. The publisher does not have any control over
and does not assume any responsibility for author or third party websites or their content.

CHANGELING

A Berkley Book / published by arrangement with the author

PRINTING HISTORY
Berkley edition / June 2007

Copyright © 2007 by Yasmine Galenorn.
Excerpt from *Darkling* by Yasmine Galenorn copyright © 2007 by Yasmine Galenorn.
Cover illustration by Tony Mauro.
Cover design by Rita Frangie.
Interior text design by Stacy Irwin.

ISBN: 978-0-425-21629-3

BERKLEY®
Berkley Books are published by The Berkley Publishing Group,
a division of Penguin Group (USA) Inc.,
375 Hudson Street, New York, New York 10014.
BERKLEY is a registered trademark of Penguin Group (USA) Inc.
The "B" design is a trademark belonging to Penguin Group (USA) Inc.

PRINTED IN THE UNITED STATES OF AMERICA

10 9 8 7 6 5 4

To Bast, mother of all Catkind,
and her four-legged children everywhere.

ACKNOWLEDGMENTS

Thank you to: Meredith Bernstein, my agent. With you behind me, I have no doubt I can achieve my goals. To Christine Zika, my editor, who encouraged me to take these books and run with them. I'm going to miss your help! Thank you to my husband, Samwise, my chiphead who looks like a bad boy.

Thanks to so many friends: Lisa D., Brad and Tiffany, Linda R. W., Thera and Jeremy, Margie, Siduri, my sister Wanda, Maura, my Witchy Chicks, and so many more. Thanks for being in my life, and what a journey we're all taking!

To my cats, my little "Galenorn Gurlz." To Ukko, Rauni, Mielikki, and Tapio, my spiritual guardians.

Thank you to my readers, both old and new, for spreading the word about my books, for continuing to follow me on this trail of words I leave, for reading in a world filled with other entertainment options. You can find me on the net at Galenorn En/Visions: www.galenorn.com. Come join us in our Reader Forums or you can contact me via the e-mail listed on my site, or write to me via snail mail (see Web site for the address or write care of the publisher). Please enclose a stamped, self-addressed envelope with your letter if you would like a reply.

Those who will play with cats must expect to be
   scratched.

                                    —CERVANTES

We have to distrust each other. It is our only defense
   against betrayal.

                          —TENNESSEE WILLIAMS

CHAPTER 1

~~~

The moon was high overhead, rounded and full like one of those snow globes human children like to play with at Christmastime. I could barely see her up there watching over me as I slipped through the thick grass, padding lightly on the frost-shrouded ground. The night was clear but bitterly cold, and my breath formed little puffs of air as it spiraled out of my mouth.

I was freezing, but it was better than staying inside where Maggie could get hold of me and slobber her kisses all over my fur, or where Iris could trap me into that stupid cat bag and forcibly clip my claws. Her manicures always left me with stubby nails the next day. And nobody but nobody was going to ruin the French manicure that I'd just paid fifty bucks for down at the local salon.

As I rounded the gazebo near the path leading to Birchwater Pond, a movement from within the trees alerted me, and I paused midstep, listening. The noise repeated itself: a ruffling of leaves, the snapping of brittle twigs on the forest floor. Oh great Bast . . . please don't let it be Speedo, the neighbor's dog. That little pisser was the most tenacious basset hound I'd ever met. The *only* basset hound I'd ever met, to be honest. He delighted in chasing me whenever I showed up on all fours, baying like a drunken troglodyte. While I could easily outrun the mutt, I didn't trust him. Of course, to be fair, he wasn't a Were, just a regular old dog. Probably a good thing, now that I thought about it, considering that he was shy a few bolts in the bucket, but still . . . I glanced around, looking for the nearest tall tree. It never hurt to be prepared.

When Speedo didn't break through the undergrowth but the noises continued, I reconsidered. Possum, maybe. Or skunk. Skunk would be bad, but *this time* I'd fight my instincts and leave it alone. Skunk me once, shame on the skunk. Skunk me twice, and I'd be the butt of my sisters' jokes for weeks.

As I searched my gut, something told me that my stalker wasn't an animal. At least not your everyday furble running through the woods. I might not be a witch like my sister Camille, but I had my own set of instincts, and they were whispering loud and clear that somebody was out there. I raised my head and sniffed, inhaling deeply. *There.* The faint scent of big cat, but behind that, something stronger. And then I knew what it was that I sensed: *cat magic.*

Cautiously, I made my way to the gazebo and loped up the stairs. I didn't want to be caught in the grass unarmed. There wasn't much I could do in this state if a demon happened to pop out of the woods to attack me. Turn into a ball of fur and razor blades, maybe, but considering my size, fighting back promised a quick and painful end to my existence. Once I was in the gazebo, I'd be able to scramble up on the railing, which would give me a better vantage point from which to observe.

I lowered myself into a pouncing position and wiggled my butt, preparing for the pounce and leap, but as I sailed into the air toward the third step, my big old fluffy tail decided to play tease and tickle with a patch of spiny cockleburs that were growing near the edge of the gazebo. *Oh shit!* I thought as I went thudding to the ground, belly first, feet splayed out like some cartoon cat from *Tweety and Sylvester.*

I blinked as my dignity took a direct hit. As I shook my head and pushed myself to all four feet, I found—much to my dismay—that the tufts of my tail fur were knotted up in the prickly plants. I let out a little growl of frustration. Why did I have to have such long fur? Granted, I was the prettiest golden tabby around, but sometimes looks were overrated. I tugged, trying to free myself, but no luck. The fur was stuck and not coming loose.

An insect that hadn't bitten the dust during the cold snap buzzed around my head, and I twitched my ears, resisting the urge to bat at it. *Nope, leave it alone,* I thought. *I've got bigger concerns than a flutterbug. Like getting loose from this fucking plant.* When I was in cat form, it was always harder to control my urges. Beetles distracted me, and spiders . . . leaves flying in the wind, a dandelion going to seed . . . oh yeah, I was a sucker for anything that promised to offer a good chase.

I tugged again, but a sharp pain at the base of my tail told me that maybe that wasn't the best idea in the world. Now what? I couldn't transform back while the moon was full, not until morning. And with Camille off racing with the Hunt as it streaked through the night woods, and Menolly in town at a Vamps Anonymous meeting, my family sure wasn't going to come to my rescue.

With a little huff, I tried again and almost ripped out a wad of fur. Well, shit. Frustrated, I crouched, trying to avoid getting any more entangled than I already was. This night was just getting better and better.

First, I had to miss my late-night fix of trash TV, and a night without Jerry Springer was a night without a chance to force Menolly to sit and visit with me. We did our nails, I ate tons of popcorn, and we gossiped about Camille and her lovers until it was time for Menolly to go to work.

And then I'd been all set to take out a mouse that was gnawing at Camille's comfrey plant. I had the rodent down, under my paw, when she began spieling out a sob story about a litter of munchkins at home. Camille always said I was too softhearted, and I guess she was right. I let the mouse go, albeit with a grumpy "Get out of here before you're toast."

My sisters didn't know that I could talk to animals when I was in my Were form. This was my own special world, one they couldn't enter. Camille had her connection with the Moon Mother, and Menolly had her bloodlusts . . . although that was a rather recent addition to her life—the Elwing Blood Clan had turned her into a vampire against her will. It wasn't like she'd *asked* to be turned into a bloodsucker. But all my life, I'd kept my ability a secret. It was all mine, and I didn't feel like sharing.

After the mouse ran off, I stopped to groom, and damned if I didn't find that I'd picked up a thriving patch of fleas. Now I'd need a flea dip or some Advantage, and both clashed with my tea rose perfume and left me with dry skin and a mild rash.

Which brought me to the present: host to a flea circus, stuck to a cocklebur plant, with an unknown intruder watching me from the woods who was packing a butt load of cat magic. We were having some big fun now! Big whoop. It pissed me off that a lot of people assumed that all of us Weres spent the nights of the full moon partying hearty and getting down with our bad selves. If this was party central, give me a good book and a mug of hot milk any day.

Another crackle from the woods caught my attention. Whatever I was going to do, I'd better get on with it. I gingerly tested the burrs again. Nope, the prickly heads were holding me prisoner. It would hurt like a son of a bitch, but I'd have to yank myself free. I couldn't risk hoping whoever was lurking in the woods was friendly. I closed my eyes, steeling myself for the rip, when a noise to my left startled me. Nerves jangled, I whipped around.

There, illuminated in the light of the moon, sat the mouse that I'd released. She rose up on her hindquarters, her nose and whiskers twitching as she stared at me. I swallowed every instinct in the world urging me to bat her a good one and tried to exert a pleasant, how-you-doin' smile.

"You need help?" she squeaked.

"What do you think? Do I *look* like I need help?" I said.

She gave me a pained look. "I don't have time for this. My children are hungry. Do you need help, or don't you?"

Oh Great Mother, the gods save me now. It was bad enough I'd been softhearted enough to let her go, but to be forced into accepting a favor from an entrée? "Beggars can't be choosers, I guess," I muttered, ego shot to hell.

A twinkle raced through her eyes, and she tittered and puffed up her chest. "Say it, then."

"Say what?"

"Mice rule, cats drool."

I huffed. "What? You expect me to—wait!"

She turned tail at my outburst and was sauntering off.

"Come back. Please!"

"You going to say it?" she asked over her shoulder.

I squirmed. With no choice, I hung my head and hoped to

hell nobody ever caught wind of this. "Mice rule, cats drool." That was it. Utter humiliation. My night was complete.

She sniffed, satisfied, then slowly examined my tail. A nibble here, a nibble there, and she broke through the twigs attached to the cockleburs entangled in my fur. I swished my tail back and forth. The weight of the burrs threw off my balance a little, but I was free, and that's all that mattered. I grudgingly thanked the mouse as she skittered away.

Another shuffle from the woods, and I made tracks, too. I had the suspicion there might be a Were hiding in the forest, but I also knew some demons had the ability to use cat magic, so I wasn't about to count on whatever was stalking me to be feline-friendly. Taking a deep breath, I loped across the lawn toward the house.

The back door on the porch was locked, but I'd installed a cat door. Camille had warded it to match my aura, so the alarms would be set off by anybody who crept through except me.

Once inside the enclosed back porch, I scratched at the kitchen door until Iris opened it. She picked me up and chucked me under the chin, and I gave in without a fight. Iris loved cats and treated me like her personal puss. The Talon-haltija was short and stocky, milkmaid pretty, with a smile that would melt a glacier. She'd been bound to a family in Finland until they all died out, and then the house sprite joined the OIA—the Otherworld Intelligence Agency—for which my sisters and I worked. They assigned her to remain Earthside as our assistant.

At first, she just worked in Camille's store, but after a nasty encounter with the demon Bad Ass Luke, Iris moved in with us. She took care of the house and helped us out when we needed it. It was kind of like having our favorite aunt around.

"Poor puss. You have a rough night?" she asked, examining my fur. "What do we have here? A tail full of stickers? And fleas?" She wrinkled her nose. "What have you been doing, girl? Come on, Delilah, we'd better get you cleaned up. I'll have to cut these burrs out before you shift back, but I think you'll still end up with one seriously sore ass."

I squirmed, wanting to tell her about the presence I'd felt, but she couldn't understand me. I could hear and understand both the Fae and humans while in Were form, but we hadn't been able to figure out a way to make the communication a two-way street.

As she carried me over to the counter and held up the scissors, I quieted down. As long as she didn't try to clip my claws, she could pamper me all she wanted. When Camille or Menolly returned, they might be able to pick up a bead on whatever it was I'd been sensing and do something about it before the magical signature faded away.

By the time the moon went to bed, I was curled up by the fire, purring heavily as I drifted in and out of my nap. I'd tried to wait up for Camille and Menolly, but the pull from the flames was too strong. The minute I snuggled up in my cushioned slumber ball Camille had bought for my birthday, I slid right into the arms of Morpheus. Which is why I woke up with one paw still furry and the other rapidly shifting into a hand.

Nobody ever believed me when I told them it wasn't painful. Oh, it might be if you weren't a Were but had a shape-shifting spell cast on you, but for us, it was as simple as changing clothes. Speaking of clothes, my collar had disappeared and was just as quickly transforming back into my sweatpants and tank top. And Iris had been right. My butt hurt.

"Seems my Kitten is back from her journey." Menolly's voice echoed in my ears as I rolled off the slumber ball and thudded to the floor, fully transformed as the last whisker vanished.

I blinked, squinting at the window. First light was about an hour away. "Cutting it thin, aren't you?" I said, my throat a little raw. My stomach rumbled, and I discovered that I was a little queasy. What *had* I eaten during the night? Definitely not Miss House Mouse. A little less engaged in the feline mind-set, I decided to drop off some cheese nips where I knew the mouse and her family lived. Poor thing. I must have given her a good scare, even if she had taken advantage of my situation.

"You don't look so hot," Menolly said. She was sitting on the sofa with Maggie in her lap. The baby Crypto was slurping away at the contents of the bowl of cream, cinnamon, sugar, and sage that Menolly held.

The pair had become inseparable since Camille had first rescued the calico gargoyle from a demon's lunch box, and they had bonded in one of the strangest friendships I'd ever seen. It would be years before we knew whether Maggie would develop past the stage of a smart cat or a slow dolphin, but that didn't matter to us. She was a rambunctious little sweetheart, and we all adored her.

"I've got a good excuse," I said, rubbing my backside. "I ended up with a butt full of thorns last night."

"Delightful. I didn't fare much better. No bellyful of blood here, and I'm hungry." I grimaced, but she waved away my protest. "At least I'm always beautiful," she said, looking over my bedraggled state. "Even after a hunt. But you look like something the cat dragged in."

I shot her a nasty glare.

"What's the matter? Your sense of humor vanish overnight?"

"Give me a break." My stomach rumbled. Yeah, I needed food, all right. "I'm hungry, I stink to high heaven, and Iris had to cut off a pile of fur when I came home." I was never a pretty sight the morning after the full moon, and usually I just wanted to head upstairs for a shower and spend the day in my Hello Kitty pajamas. "I'll bet you aren't all that pretty to your victims," I added, feeling snarky.

Giving me a wicked grin, Menolly said, "Most of my meals are so enthralled, they come on demand. Trust me, they love it." Even though Camille had convinced her to join Vampires Anonymous, Menolly's cutting sarcasm had remained intact. Sister or not, Menolly was one scary badass chick. Gorgeous, but she could be a real freak show when she wanted to.

"Yeah, they love it till they realize you sucked them dry." I shook my head, reaching for the doughnut box sitting on the coffee table. Chase, who fancied himself my boyfriend because we had sex once a week, had sent them to me. When the box of thirty-two gourmet doughnuts had been delivered along with a dozen red roses and a catnip toy, a little thrill ran through my heart. He really did understand me.

"So what happened? No pervs out last night?" I winced as I stretched. My muscles needed a good workout. I'd head down to the gym toward evening. They loved me there and had given me a free lifetime membership because men signed up just to watch me work out. Being half-Faerie in a world enchanted with our presence had its perks.

"Not that I could find. I drank a little, then wiped the guy's memory and sent him on his way. I only took enough to stave off the worst of my thirst, but I'm going to need a real hunt in a few nights." Her frost-blue eyes flashed against the copper of her Bo Derek braids. As she shook her head, the ivory beads she'd had woven into the braids clattered like the bones of a dancing skeleton. Menolly made no noise, except when she chose to. The beads reminded her that she had once been alive. That she hadn't always been a vampire.

"You mean a full kill," I said. The phone rang, but it stopped after one ring. Iris must have picked up.

"You nailed it." Menolly shrugged, but I could hear the craving in her voice. A young vampire, she still needed to drink deep and often.

Looking at her, it was hard to believe my sister was a vamp, except for that Butoh dancer complexion. Petite, she barely made five three, if that, but she could toss a dead demon over one shoulder and carry him like a child, and she could drain a person of blood without blinking. She was the youngest, but sometimes she felt old as the hills to me.

Camille, the oldest, was a buxom and curvy five foot seven witch. Long waves of curly black hair cascaded down her back, and her eyes were violet with silver flecks. She was the practical one, although you wouldn't know it by the way she dressed, which was one step shy of a fetish bar.

And me? I was the middle child, though both Camille and Menolly annoyed the hell out of me by treating me like the baby. At least I had them both beat in the height department. I topped six one, and my body was muscled and lean. No couch potato kitty for me, except during my late-night TV binges.

My hair would have been called flaxen by a poet, and until recently had fallen almost to my waist. Tired of the constant upkeep, I'd marched into a salon and asked for a layered shag that barely skimmed my shoulders.

The three of us looked about as much like sisters as we did like goblins. Our mother had been human, and our father was one of the Sidhe. We fell at odd points along the spectrum. Unfortunately, our half-breed status upset the status quo with Father's relatives. Worse, it upset our internal balance.

Camille's magic proved chaotic and was as erratic as her choice in men. Menolly could climb a hundred-foot tree, but she fell off a simple perch when spying on a rogue clan of vampires. They, in turn, tortured and turned her into one of them.

As for me . . . my shape-shifting was unpredictable, and I couldn't always control it. And even though I was a Were, no gorgeous lioness appeared when I transformed. Just a golden, long-haired tabby, whose tail occasionally got stuck in the briar bush and who ended up with fleas. Damn it. I smelled like Advantage and the beginning of a rash was climbing up my back. It seemed Iris had dosed me a good one. I needed to take a shower before I broke out in hives.

"Where's Camille? I have to talk to her about something I felt out in the woods last night." I glanced around, looking for signs that she might be home. No stilettos, no corsets lying around, no stench of sulfur from misfired magic.

"She said she was stopping off at Morio's before coming home," Menolly said.

Just then Iris appeared in the doorway. "Camille just called. She's on her way home. I'm going to take off for the store. She should rest for a while before coming in," the house sprite said. "Tell her I'll expect her in around one?"

I nodded, watching as Iris bustled off. Camille ostensibly owned the Indigo Crescent, a bookstore in downtown Belles-Faire, a grimy suburb of Seattle. In truth, it was a front for the OIA—the Otherworld Intelligence Agency—for which we worked. They'd sent us Earthside because, bluntly, they thought we were a bunch of bumbling bimbos. Klutzes we might be, but a pack of vacuous T & A? Never. We had brains! We had looks! We had . . . the worst record in the service. However, thanks to the bureaucracy, instead of getting us out of the way, the OIA had put us right on the fast track to Hell.

A few months ago, we'd had a nasty bit of business with a Degath Squad, a trio of demons from the Subterranean Realms who were on a scouting mission. They were looking for the spirit seals—ancient artifacts that, when joined together, would open the portals and allow Shadow Wing and his minions to take over both Earth and Otherworld.

We'd barely managed to squeak through the assault alive.

When we returned to Otherworld to prove that things weren't so hunky-dory back on Earth, we found our home city in an uproar with a full-scale civil war going on. We reconsidered our options and showed up on the doorstep of the Elfin Queen.

When we dropped the dead demons and other assorted goodies at her feet, Queen Asteria promptly proclaimed that, like it or not, as of that moment we were now working for her. Oh, and one other thing—a little thing, really—just don't tell the OIA about this arrangement. When a millennia-old magic-wielding queen tells you to do something, you don't argue.

One thing we knew for sure: Where there was one demon, there were bound to be more. Where there was one Degath Squad, other Hell Scouts would follow, and eventually, with an army to back them up. And even with the help of Camille's boyfriends, Trillian and Morio, a gorgeous hunk of dragon flesh we knew only by the name of Smoky, and my boyfriend Chase Johnson, we were a pale wall of defense.

The door opened, and Camille blew through. She was in full getup: flowing plum chiffon skirt, black lace bustier, black PVC boots that laced up her calves, their heels a mile high. Her eyes sparkled with silver. She'd been running magic, all right. Her glamour was so strong that I was amazed she didn't have a pack of men following her home.

Of the three of us, she had the most appeal to full-blooded humans. Her very scent invited them to come play, and her voluptuous curves left little to the imagination.

Camille had another side, though. She'd taken care of us after our mother died. Menolly was off in her own little world by then, though not yet a vampire, but Camille held it together for our father and for the three of us.

"Something tripped the wards," she said. "I can feel it. Anything happen tonight I should know about?"

I jumped up. "I've been waiting for you to get home." I glanced out the window. First light was only moments away. "I want you to come out back with me. I smelled cat magic last night, and I think we might have a Were prowling around, but I'm not positive. I was in cat form, and the full moon can cloud my senses."

She ruffled my hair, a habit that I both loved and hated. "Let's go check it out, sweetie." With a glance at Menolly, she added, "You need to get downstairs. The sky's clear, and the sun will be up soon. I'm surprised you aren't already feeling the pull."

Menolly brushed her eyes. "I am, actually. I'll put Maggie in her box and go to bed." Unlike most vampires, Menolly slept in an actual bed, and her nest—very Martha Stewart— was hidden in the basement behind a secret entrance we'd fashioned to keep out intruders. No one else but Iris knew that the bookshelves in the kitchen actually opened up to reveal the staircase leading to Menolly's apartment.

Camille followed me out to the backyard. I grabbed a trowel on the way. Everything looked so different from this height, but the minute I saw the cockleburs, I felt my dander rise. I stopped, kneeling down to root them out.

"What are you doing?" Camille asked.

I grunted. "These suckers got stuck in my tail last night. I'm going to hire a gardener to come in and clear the yard of thistles and thorns and other nasty crap like this." Managing to get the point of the trowel under the root, I levered the plant out and tossed it in the compost pile.

"Oh yes, *that's* going to do the trick. The seeds will just spring up again, you goober. Just make sure you don't get rid of my belladonna or wolfsbane," she said, choking back a snort as I led her to the path where I'd sensed the intruder. "I take it your butt's sore?"

"Worse than diaper rash," I said. "So are the wards sounding an alarm, or were they just tripped by accident?" They were Camille's spell, and she was the only one who'd be able to sort through the variances of disruption that happened when they'd been detonated.

She closed her eyes. "No demons at play, but that doesn't mean much, considering how Bad Ass Luke conned Wisteria into working with them." Stopping suddenly, she blinked and said, "Did you know that Trillian is going to be staying with Chase until he can find an apartment? He moved in with him last night."

I blinked. Chase hadn't mentioned anything of the sort the last time I'd talked to him. "No. And just how long do you think that arrangement will last?"

Trillian was a Svartan, one of the elves' darker-souled cousins, and he'd been stringing Camille along for years. They were lovers, though at times she wasn't sure if she even liked him.

"I don't know, but it's better than what Menolly suggested," Camille said, shuddering. Our lovely troublemaker of a sister had put forth the idea that Trillian might want to room with Morio, which would have been the mother of all disasters. Of course, she'd been sporting a smirk when she made the suggestion, but both Camille and I knew that Menolly had a hankering for havoc. Her idea of fun was a rousing fight down at the Wayfarer.

"I think I've been forcing her to watch too much Jerry Springer with me," I said, rolling my eyes.

Morio, a youkai-kitsune from Japan—a fox demon-slash–nature spirit—was Camille's other lover. They had hooked up when they accidentally tripped a lust spell out near

Mount Rainier, and that was all it took for the two of them to start hitting the sheets. Camille had a weakness for bad boys.

Trillian and Morio kept a cautious truce because of their shared interest in Camille, but they were clear rivals for her affection. It was a good thing that the Fae weren't monogamous by nature, or there would have been bloodshed by now, considering the amount of testosterone involved.

"Well, he isn't likely to kill Chase, since Chase is *my* boyfriend, but still . . . I hope for both their sakes—and ours—that Trillian finds an apartment soon." With a wicked grin, I added, "Bet you the arrangement lasts less than two weeks," I said, fishing a twenty out of my pocket and waving it at her.

"You're on." Camille snorted. "I'll give it three at the most." She suddenly stopped and raised her head.

"Hold on, there's something here. It's faint . . . but definite . . ."

She plunged into the bushes and knelt near the base of a large oak that watched over the wooded acreage that spread out next to our land. As she examined the tree, I scouted around the path, finding a line of footprints. The night had been clear with no rain to wash them away. They led up to the tree, then away from it again and disappeared in the middle of the tangle of huckleberry, brambles, Oregon grape, and fern.

Just then, a Steller's jay dive-bombed me from the branches of a fir, scolding at the top of its lungs. *Little bugger,* I thought as I waved it away. It could smell the cat on me. I wrinkled my nose and let out a little hiss, and it screeched even louder. Another jay joined it on the branch, and both perched there, eyeballing me.

"Don't you dare, unless you want to become my breakfast," I muttered.

"Delilah!" Camille's voice brought me out of my sparring match. Her expression was a mixture of disbelief and wariness. "I know what was here."

"What? What was it?" I leaned against the oak, waiting. *Not a demon. Please don't let it be a demon,* I thought. I was tired of demons. While I could kick ass with the best, I didn't like conflict. When my sisters got into arguments, the stress turned me into a pussycat.

"You were right, there was a Were around here," she said, her eyes flashing with silver. "And unless I'm off my game, I think he's a werepuma." She looked up at me. "He's marked the tree."

"Eww . . ." I wrinkled my nose, hoping he'd been in Were-form when he'd taken his territorial piss.

A werepuma? I stared at the trunk, then at our house, which you could just barely see from this vantage point. Why had he marked the tree? He didn't own this land, we did. Was he in league with Shadow Wing and the demons? Or was he a free agent? And if he wasn't aligned with our hellion friends, just what did he want?

CHAPTER 2

My sisters and I lived in a funky three-story Victorian in the suburb of Belles-Faire, one of Seattle's seediest districts. Sure, it was a crummy neighborhood, but we had the necessary acreage to provide us with the privacy needed for our work. Menolly's apartment was in the basement, Camille had the second story, I had the third, and we shared the main floor as a common living area. We'd given Iris a spare room near the kitchen. It was small, but so was she, and we let her live there rent free in exchange for her help around the house.

A couple days after the full moon, I was putting the finishing touches on a three-cheese omelet when Camille sashayed into the room.

"Food ready?" she asked, her eyes lighting up.

I nodded. We took turns with Iris making breakfast. "Omelet. Toast is on the table." I divided the eggs and dished them out onto the waiting plates.

"That smells good," Camille said. She was dressed to the hilt in a crimson halter dress with a low V-neck. A silver belt slung low across her hips, and she was wearing fuck-me pumps to die for. I gave her the once-over.

"New guy?" I asked, grinning.

She laughed. "As if I didn't have trouble enough with the two I've already got. No. If you want to know, the Faerie Watchers Club is meeting at the store today. I play it up for them when they come in. They like the show, and it gives me a chance to dress up."

I could never pull off the outfits that Camille wore, even if I wanted to. My closet of choice included plenty of low-rise jeans, camis, turtlenecks, and sweaters. Ostensibly, my cover for the OIA was that of a private eye, and since I took on real cases, I had to be able to move. Sneaking through bushes and climbing fire escapes in a tight silk dress just wouldn't cut it. Not to mention that, at six one—a good six inches taller than Camille—I didn't *need* stilettos, though I owned a few pairs. My taste in footwear ran to motorcycle boots.

Iris joined us at the table, and I pointed to her plate. "Food's on."

She scrambled up on the barstool that allowed her to easily reach the table. At barely four feet, she didn't look intimidating, but she packed a wallop that could take down a grown man. Or beast. A pissed-off house sprite was nobody to mess around with.

"What do you need me to do today?" she asked.

Camille flipped open her Day-Timer. "I'll need you at the store this afternoon while the FWC members are there. They're coming in around three, so if you could show up around two forty-five, I'd appreciate it."

"No problem." Iris had a photographic memory, not only for visuals but for conversations. "What else?"

"Would you take Maggie outside to play for a while this morning? I think she needs some fresh air," I said. "But be careful. Whoever that strange Were is, he's still hanging around the borders of the property, so stay close to the house."

"Done," she said. "By the way, Delilah, I don't mean to complain, but you haven't cleaned your litter box yet."

"I noticed that, too," Camille said. "Remember, no maids, so we clean up after ourselves." She ruffled my hair.

I grabbed her hand and gently bit her thumb, leaving a mild impression from my fangs. She yelped, and I grinned.

"I didn't even leave a mark, so don't try to play me for sympathy. You mess up my hair every time you do that. Anyway, I'm sorry about the box. I can't believe I forgot. I'll get to it first thing when I get home."

When we'd been unceremoniously dumped Earthside by the OIA, we'd made a pact. Without servants to look after us, we agreed to clean up after our own messy lifestyles. Thinking about the number of hunts Menolly had been on, I was secretly grateful that I only had to contend with kitty litter. I glanced at the bookcase that was hiding the entrance to Menolly's lair. The last thing I wanted was to clean up her blood room where she hosed herself off after feeding. Washing the love stains off Camille's ridiculously expensive sheets was child's play next to the mess Menolly left. I resolved to do better in keeping up my end of the bargain.

Camille snorted. "I can tell what you're thinking. I'm glad I don't have to clean her lair either, though I have a better stomach for it than you do."

"Hey, you said it. I didn't." I was still working on accepting Menolly's transformation, while Camille had managed to overcome any revulsion she might have had. I didn't like being squeamish, but I couldn't help it.

I jerked my head toward the door. "Let's head out. Iris, have a good day. You know where to call us if anything happens." I scooped up Maggie from where she was playing in the corner and gave her a big smooch on her fuzzy forehead. Camille crowded in, and after a moment, Iris had to wrestle the gargoyle away from us.

"Get moving, you two. I'll take care of the little one here," she said, tucking Maggie back in her playpen.

Camille shrugged into a flowing black opera coat and marched out the door into the frostbitten morning. I slipped on my leather jacket and checked to make sure my long silver knife was safely snapped inside my boot sheath. I'd carried a gun for a while, but the iron had proven too much for me, even what little there had been in the specially formatted Glock that Chase had bought for me. I'd never had to shoot it, and it wouldn't work on demons anyway.

Chase, on the other hand, had special bullets made for his gun. Some were embedded with iron in the center for taking down rogue Fae who might be breaking the law. Others included silver and would kill lycanthropes, the only type of Were affected by the metal.

The December morning was overcast as I clattered down the porch steps, the clouds glimmering with a luminous sheen that warned of impending snow. While Seattle wasn't exactly the winter wonderland of the world, on occasion we received a coating of the white stuff.

Camille blew me a kiss, then jumped in her Lexus and headed down the driveway. I crunched my way across the frost-covered grass to climb into my Jeep Wrangler. As I warmed up the engine, my thoughts went back to the Were who'd been stalking our land. Since we'd discovered his tracks, the three of us had walked the borders of our acreage each night. We could still smell cat magic, but neither Menolly nor Camille could sense demon energy. Just because we couldn't smell it didn't mean it wasn't there, though.

With Shadow Wing on the rampage and most likely pissed out of his mind, my optimism had been tempered by brutal reality. Maybe this was what growing up meant. I couldn't play Bubbles on *The Powerpuff Girls* anymore. The trouble with life was that it always interrupted our best-laid fantasies.

The Indigo Crescent sat smack in the middle of the Belles-Faire business district. My office suite was in the same building on the second floor, and from there I played private eye in between assignments from the OIA. An outside stairwell provided an alternative entrance, so clients could come and go after bookstore hours.

I managed to find a parking space a block away, but the air was so cold it sucked the breath out of my lungs as I jogged down the street. Camille's Lexus was parked smack in front of the store, as usual. I knew her secret though, and it wasn't dumb luck. She had some nasty dirt on the parking gods, and they never failed to give her a good place. I'd been after her to make me a charm for the past month, but she kept putting it off. I was beginning to think she was holding out on purpose.

As I strode into the store, my breath still visible, I was greeted by the sight of Erin Mathews, president of the Faerie Watchers Club, and her friend Cleo Blanco. I broke into a wide grin. Cleo and Erin were two of the coolest humans we knew, and I loved hanging out with them. Especially Cleo.

Erin owned The Scarlet Harlot, a lingerie store a couple blocks away. Cleo was a female impersonator–slash–drag queen. In his alter ego, he was Tim Winthrop, genius computer student and the father of a young daughter with whom he spent every weekend, no matter what else he had on his plate.

Erin and Cleo were complete opposites. Despite owning a lingerie shop, Erin dressed in jeans, flannel shirts, and hiking boots, which matched her down-to-earth personality. On the other hand, Cleo's tastes—and his nature—ran to the flamboyant when he was out in drag.

Nearly my height, he teetered in five-inch platform PVC boots, fire-engine red and almost hugging his crotch. They clashed in full Yuletide splendor with his hunter green buttcupping leggings and striped sweater tunic. Beneath the sweater he was either wearing a massively padded bra or he'd recently gotten implants. Cleo's wig was bleached blond, and he sported Tammy Faye eyelashes.

Camille was discussing something with Erin, so I parked my butt on the counter next to Cleo and high-fived him.

"What's shakin', babe? Besides that rack of yours?" I pointed to his chest and grinned. "Where on earth did those come from? Boobs R Us? Are they real, or is there a whole lot of stuffing going on?"

"Well, if it isn't Delilah the Dick." He arched his back and shimmied his shoulders. "You can thank Erin for my makeover. She whipped up this little number for me. I'm trying it out before the show tonight."

Erin turned at the sound of her name, and Cleo winked at her. "Just giving you credit for my lovely cleavage." He turned back to me. "By the way, did I ever tell you how much I love your teeth? They are *so* hot. I bet the boys flock for miles to get a love bite from you."

My fangs were permanently visible, unlike Menolly's, which retracted in standard vampire fashion. "All part of my nature, dude. Although they can be a hassle if I get too excited. I've punctured my tongue a couple of times."

I didn't mention that I'd also punctured Chase's tongue once or twice. And after one disastrous attempt, I'd decided that giving him a good blow job was out of the question, and he hadn't been in a hurry to suggest another try. That little escapade had cost us two weeks of unhappy—and for him, painful—celibacy. Unlike Camille, I'd been a virgin, except for when I was in cat form. But after a rocky start to my sex life, I'd finally discovered what all the hoopla was about. Now it was getting harder for me to hold my hormones in check.

Shaking myself out of my thoughts, I focused on Cleo's chest again. "Erin did you proud. I'd grade the girls at least an F."

"Meow. Do I detect a hint of envy, Cat Woman?" Cleo grinned to show he was joking. He still wasn't used to us, but I had to hand it to him. He had more guts than most of the humans we met.

I snorted. "Trust me, if I was jealous of anybody's boobs, it would be Camille's. They're the real thing, and they're double-D."

"Hey, I heard that." Camille sauntered up and slid her arm around Cleo's waist.

He gave her a lecherous grin and bent over to flick his tongue along her neck. "Well hello, little Miss Witch. You know, I might think about making an exception to my no-chicks rule just for you, girlfriend."

"Don't turn in your queer card yet, babe," Camille said, stretching to plant a kiss on his chin. "My bed overfloweth."

Cleo laughed, a rich and throaty sound that made me smile. "Jason would kick my butt anyway. He's delightfully possessive."

"He's also gorgeous, my dear," I said.

Jason was Cleo's boyfriend, and they made quite a striking couple. As dark as Cleo was fair, Jason owned his own car repair shop and had more business than he could handle. The pair seemed to have a bright future in front of them.

"Any chance we'll be hearing wedding bells soon?" I pointed to the hunk of ice Cleo was sporting on his left finger.

He winked. "You never know."

Camille glanced at the clock. "Okay, time to open shop. Delilah, are you going upstairs to work, or do you want to hang here for a bit?" She had that look in her eye that told me she'd put me to work if I opted for the latter.

"I'm going, I'm going." I slid off the counter, reluctant to leave the warmth of the shop for the upper regions of my office. "It's so damned cold up there. The heat never makes it upstairs." I'd been reduced to using space heaters to take the edge off the chilly suite. Luckily, the OIA footed the bill. Considering how pissed we were at them, I took a perverse delight in sticking it to them any way I could.

"You could stay down here and help me shelve books." Camille thrust a stack in my direction, but I shook my head.

"I'd better get to work. I've got an appointment with a new client in ten minutes. If he comes through the store, send him up."

"Later, babe." Camille waved as I took the stairs two at a time.

At the top of the steps, a short hall led to three doors: a bathroom, a janitor's closet where we kept our cleaning supplies, and my suite. The OIA wasn't about to spring for a custodian, and we couldn't take a chance hiring an outside service to clean, so we'd lucked out when Iris volunteered to play maid. We paid her by the hour, and she came in once a week to mop floors and dust and take out the garbage. I dreaded the day she met somebody, got married, and settled down to raise a house full of little sprites.

I opened the main door leading into my office and glanced around before entering. Caution didn't run in the family, but I'd lucked out and picked up the habit somewhere. Someday, that fraction of a second might come in handy and save my life.

My waiting room was sparsely furnished with an old sofa, two chairs, and a table on which rested a handful of magazines, a lamp, and a bell. I flipped the sign that I posted on the main door from Closed to Open—Please Ring the Bell for Service. As I glanced around the grimy room, I thought once again about how lonely I felt at times, being stuck Earthside. Sure, I solved the occasional case, ferreted out secrets for heartbroken wives and cuckolded husbands, but was that really helping anybody?

If we were back in OW . . . Hell, when I thought about it, I had no idea what we'd be doing if we were back in OW. With civil war on the horizon, most likely we'd be pressed into military service. Especially considering our track record. At least we knew how to fight and live to tell about it.

I opened the door to my office and slipped off my jacket, then turned on the heater. A large oak desk that I'd found at a thrift shop filled the room, along with a leather chair patched with duct tape and two padded folding chairs for clients.

The one thing my office was abundant in was plants. Plants that could survive chilly weather and shade. They made me feel like I could breathe. A huge print of a forest glade on one wall reminded me of home, and Iris had managed to find enough knickknacks to provide a little sparkle here and there. She'd also polished the one window in my office to a high shine. At least I could see the sky in this brick-and-mortar jungle.

I paused by a side table where a statue of the Egyptian goddess Bast sat on a gold and green cloth. Around the statue I'd arranged a necklace of turquoise beads, a vase of fresh flowers, a sistrum, and a cobalt-blue glass pyramid. A bronze candle holder held a tall green taper, and I let out a long breath as I lit the candle.

"Lady Bast, guide my feet. Guard my path. Know my heart resides with you." The simple prayer was one I offered up every morning and every evening. She guarded all of catkind and was, to me, what the Moon Mother was to Camille.

Somewhat comforted, I slid into my chair and flipped through my mail. A couple bills. An invitation to a seminar on police procedure and the private eye, a reminder that my Jeep was due for servicing . . . nothing important. As I tossed them on the desk, the bell in my waiting room chimed.

Shaking off my growing depression, I glanced at the clock. My new client—potential client, rather—was right on time. I was totally unprepared for the wave of dizziness that slammed through me as I headed for the door dividing my office from the waiting room. What the hell? I blinked and tried to focus as I opened the door.

The man in the waiting room stood a good four inches taller

than me. Trim in the waist, he was wearing a leather jacket adorned with studs, and I could tell that his shoulders were broad and his arms muscled. Golden hair grazed his collar. As I looked into those luminous topaz eyes, I knew what he was.

He held out one hand and tilted his head ever so slightly. "Zachary Lyonnesse at your service."

I caught my breath at the touch of his fingers on mine. The warmth of his body heat sent a crackle of cat magic racing up my arm, and a familiar scent told me everything I needed to know. Well, maybe not everything, but enough to start with. I straightened my shoulders and motioned him in.

"Delilah D'Artigo. So, Zachary Lyonnesse, perhaps you'd care to tell me what the hell you've been doing spying around my property?"

He leaned his head back and let out a short laugh. "I knew you'd finger me. I told Venus the Moon Child that you would, but he wasn't so sure." He dropped his voice as he said, "I'm glad that I didn't underestimate you."

Well, at least he'd admitted that it had been him. I cleared my throat. "So, are you going to answer my question, puma-boy?"

As I heard the challenge ringing in my voice, I knew I was in trouble. I circled him, instinct urging me to let loose and transform, to teach him whose territory he was in. Thank the gods I managed to retain enough control to know that a golden tabby was no match for a puma.

The light in Zachary's eyes flared, and the corner of his lip flickered into the tiniest smile. "Don't fluff your tail at me, girl. I'm not here to hurt you, and regardless of what you might think, I'm not a voyeur. You want to know why I was watching you? Because I want to hire you. But first, I had to get a feel for the situation. I'm not sure who to trust anymore, and right now, *trust means everything*."

I licked the tips of my fangs. His arrogance irritated me, but he was bigger and more dangerous than I, at least in Wereform. And I recognized hierarchy. "What do you want?"

Zachary let out a sigh, his shoulders dropping along with his cavalier attitude. "I'm from the Rainier Puma Pride. We need an investigator at our compound. Someone who can understand our special . . . situation. This is a delicate matter. We heard about you and your sisters through the Sub-Cult network. I know you're half-Fae, and a Were. It only made sense to ask another shifter for help." He pressed his hand to his forehead, squinting.

"You have a headache? Would you like some aspirin?" I wasn't about to let down my guard when it came to an unknown Supe, but he looked so worried that I couldn't help but feel sorry for him. "Why don't you sit down?" I reached for his arm and guided him to the chair opposite my desk.

That did it. The light faded from his eyes, replaced by a dark and shadowed look, and he slumped into the chair. "Someone is killing off members of our pride," he whispered.

Hell, no wonder the guy looked so upset. I moved to my desk, motioning for him to continue. "Tell me about it."

Zachary rubbed his chin, and it flashed through my mind that the five o'clock shadow he had going looked pretty good on him.

"We need to know who's killing our people. We've tried investigating on our own, but nothing . . . We're always too late, always a step behind. Five of our members have been murdered in the past few weeks, and I don't mind telling you, we're running scared."

"Have you gone to the police?" I asked but already knew the answer.

"This isn't a police matter. They have no idea how to handle affairs of this nature. The victims weren't killed by any human, that I can tell you." He stared at the floor and scuffed the carpet with the toe of his boot.

It occurred to me that Chase's Faerie-Human CSI Squad might be able to help out. I scribbled a memo on my notepad to ask him if he could do anything.

"Would you like some tea?" I asked. I kept a microwave on a table along with a variety of zap-and-eat noodle dishes, teas, hot cocoa, and other treats. I popped two mugs of water in the oven and nuked them for two minutes.

"Thanks," he said, struggling to cover up a sudden yawn. "I feel like I haven't slept in days, and I probably look it, too."

I flashed him a quick smile. "You look just fine," I said, dropping the tea bags in the mugs of steaming water. "Here, let this steep for a few minutes. The mint should help perk you up." Returning to my desk, I picked up my pen. I'd type up notes on my laptop later. "Tell me everything, and don't leave anything out, no matter how minute."

Zachary picked up his cup and held it to his nose, letting the steam rise to fill his lungs. He let out a long, slow breath and relaxed into the chair. "The first murder happened last month. Sheila didn't come home the morning after the full moon."

"Sheila?" I asked. "She have a last name?"

"No. I'll explain in a minute," he said. "At first we thought she'd just fallen asleep out in the woods, but by noon, we started to worry. We sent out a search party, and they found her next to a stream. She was still in puma form and very dead."

"That means she was killed before sunrise."

"Right." He leaned forward, his voice cracking. "Her blood had been drained and . . . everything was gone—inside. She was dry as a bone. But it also looked like her heart had been ripped out. We never did find it."

I winced. What could you say to a story like that? *I'm sorry* wasn't going to cut it. I opted for a question. "Do you have any idea who killed her? And how did you explain her disappearance to authorities?"

Zachary shrugged. "Not a clue. None of the victims had any real enemies. All were well-liked in our community. As for the police, some of our pride still live outside the confines of society. They keep to the compound while others—like me—have Social Security cards, get jobs, pay taxes. We finance the land and supplies. Those who choose not to pass in society contribute in other ways. Sheila had no birth certificate, no Social Security card. She's not listed in any computer anywhere, so who's going to miss her?" He rubbed his temples. "Except those of us who loved her."

I jotted down a few notes. This was far more serious than anything I'd run up against before. And it was the first time an Earthside Supe had approached me for help. "Give me the names of all the victims, please."

"Well, I told you about Sheila. Her parents came down from the mountains years ago and joined our clan. They're both still alive. Then there were Darrin and Anna Jackson, newlyweds. They vanished while they were camping."

"Camping? At this time of year?" I asked, glancing out the window that overlooked the back alley. The clouds shone silver, and the temperature was hovering around thirty-three degrees.

"Werepumas are strong. We're the Rainier Puma Pride." There was a sense of self-esteem in his voice that made me want to sit up and salute.

"We're used to cold weather," he continued. "So camping this time of year doesn't bother us. Anyway, we found their bodies near where we found Sheila's—near an old mining arrastra by Pinnacle Rock."

"What's an arrastra?" I wasn't familiar with the term.

"The prospectors used mills that were usually built in a stream to grind the ore down enough so they could pan it for gold. You'll see, if you come out to take a look around." Zachary looked like he could be a prospector himself; he was rugged enough. I found my mind wandering from the problem at hand to the muscle under his jacket. Just how buff was he, anyway?

Hastily reining in my thoughts—they were rapidly veering in a direction I wasn't prepared for—I asked, "So, were all of the bodies found near the stream?"

He nodded. "The creek flows alongside the hill. And Todd Veshkam disappeared while he was out cutting deadwood for kindling. Again, we found him near the arrastra. The bodies were all in the same condition: dry as a bone, hearts missing."

"Sheila, Darrin, Anna, Todd . . . you said there were five victims?" I paused, my pen poised above the notepad.

He closed his eyes. "Yes. The last was Hattie . . . Hattie Lyonnesse."

As he spoke, I felt the rush of anger in his voice. I jerked my head up and looked into his eyes. They glittered, dangerous and feral. "*Lyonnesse?* Isn't that your last name?"

Zachary nodded. "Hattie was my sister. And I want you to find the bastard who killed her so I can put an end to his miserable life."

CHAPTER 3

"Your sister?" I set down my pen, feeling terrible. Instinctively, I leaned forward, reaching for his hand. "Oh, Zachary, I'm so sorry. I didn't realize—"

He stared at my outstretched palm for a moment, then lightly brushed my fingers with his. "Don't. Please don't. There's nothing you can say. She's gone, beyond our help. What you *can* do is find the son of a bitch who did this. Closure isn't all it's cracked up to be, but it's all my family can hope for."

Unsure of what to say, I cleared my throat. "What was she like? Hattie? Tell me about her."

He smiled then—just a glimmer—but enough to break through the dark shadows crowding his face. "Hattie was one of those women born to be a mother. You know the type? She didn't have kids of her own yet, but everybody who knew her knew that she'd settle down and raise a litter. Hattie lived with our mom. Father's dead. He was shot by some idiot on a full moon three years ago. The best we can figure is that the stupid ass got between Dad and a good meal and probably thought my father was coming after him. He shot him with three bullets. Dad managed to run into the bushes, where he hid until he died. No doubt the guy didn't look back, just ran off, probably thinking he escaped with his life."

"Who found your father?" I asked, staring at the desk. It seemed that life was harsh everywhere. I'd thought it bad back in OW, but here, even with more societal rules, the art of living was pretty damned rough.

"Hattie and I did, the next morning. He'd bled to death." Zachary let out a long sigh. "Anyway, Hattie stayed on with our mother after his death. She was dating one of the compound boys. Nathan Joliet's his name. Nate's never learned to pass, either, and I don't think he wants to. He takes care of repair work for a lot of the folks around the compound, and they give him food and supplies . . . whatever he needs."

"So she was engaged," I murmured.

"Yeah. Hattie never aspired to anything grand. She was content with a simple life. She was proud of who she was. A member of the Rainier Puma Pride. And she was dedicated to preserving bloodline and heritage." He stood and crossed to the window, staring down on the back alley. "She was due to get married next month, but then the murders started. Sheila was first, then Darrin and Anna. And then Todd."

"And then Hattie died, and you decided that whatever's happening can't go on any further." I doodled a circle on the paper, wondering if he'd be sitting in my office if the latest victim hadn't been a member of his family.

He turned, a wounded expression creasing his face. "Is that what you think? That I'm only here because of my sister? That doesn't say much for your opinion of me, does it?"

Feeling about two inches high, I shook my head. "I'm sorry. I didn't mean it like that." I had, but I wasn't going to admit it. A lot of selfish people had crossed my threshold, and it was easy enough to make a wrong assumption.

Zachary grimaced. "I didn't mean to jump down your throat. I'm just so tense the past few weeks. I know you didn't mean it that way. Anyway, the answer to your question is no. I wanted to come to you right after we found Anna and Darrin and realized that Sheila's murder wasn't an isolated incident. The elders overruled me. I took over my father's spot on the Council after he died, and while I have some input, they still consider me too young to take seriously."

Ah. The hierarchy again. Zachary was low cat on the totem pole, and he'd have to work his way up the ladder by claw and fang.

"When Todd died," he continued, "they began talking about bringing in somebody from the outside. And then Hattie went out for a walk one day and never came back. That's when the Council finally agreed that we need help. Somebody's murdering our people, and we *have* to find out who's doing it and stop them. It's too late for Hattie, damn it," he said, slamming his hand against the oak desktop, "but maybe it's not too late for the next victim."

I leaned back in my chair and swiveled, propping my feet on the edge of the windowsill. "You need someone with experience. What makes you think I'm the best choice? I have to tell you, I'm still a little green in the business."

Zachary gave me a soft, slow grin. "I think your business goes further back than you let on. I doubt that you spend all your time chasing wayward spouses. I've heard rumors that a skin-walker took a nose dive somewhere near your house. And demon scent was tracked to your door, but no demons ever came out again. I've been watching the three of you. You don't go as unnoticed as you think. Tell your sister Camille that her wards are working fine, though. Our shaman can't negate them."

Holding my breath, I wondered who'd spilled the beans. But then again, it was hard to hide the deaths of a harpy, a Psycho Babbler, and a demon like Bad Ass Luke. Especially over here, Earthside. We were on the A-list of tabloids. The Fae were hot, and we fit the bill.

He seemed to take my silence for assent. "So, will you at least come have a look?"

I sighed. A gnawing pit in my gut told me this case ran deeper than a local hunter out to nab himself some mountain lions. For one thing, serial killers usually worked to an MO, and that sure seemed to be the case here. All the victims were found in one area, and all had been destroyed in a bizarre fashion. From the condition of the corpses, there had to be something at work beyond just a simple murderer gone over the edge. Perhaps a rogue Corpse Talker? The missing hearts would line up with that idea.

"All right. I'll come have a look, but I'm not promising results." Now came the hard part. I had trouble asking for money, especially when it came to other Supes. But Zachary stepped in before I could hem and haw my way toward settling a price.

"Will a five-hundred-dollar retainer do for a start? You come out and take a look. If you think you can do anything, then we negotiate the rest of the price. If not, then consider it a good-faith fee for your time today and for the visit." He swept his bangs back from his face, and I caught my breath as a wave of his scent washed over me. Aroused, I swallowed as he tossed five bills on the desk.

Managing to keep my cool, I said, "That works. Mind if I come out on Saturday? Say around sixish? I'm bringing my sisters, by the way." If I set the time late enough, both Camille and Menolly could come with me. I wasn't about to go without backup. This wasn't just some ticked-off little pissant. Whoever was stalking the Puma Pride was dangerous and all too deadly.

"No problem," he said. "I'll call with directions later. By the way," he said, his voice throaty, "You can call me Zach."

As I wrote out a receipt, I kept one eye on him. He wasn't wearing a ring, but that didn't mean anything. I wasn't sure how their clan handled relationships and marriages. Cats weren't monogamous, but these were Earthside Supes who had lived near humans most of their lives, so who knew how they ran their interpersonal lives?

As he reached for the receipt, he lingered, his index finger slowly stroking the top of my hand. Shaken, feeling sucked under in a whirlpool of emotions I hadn't planned for, I glanced up, my Fae glamour shining through before I could stop it. He caught his breath and leaned forward. As my lips parted, he paused, his face hovering an inch above my own.

"You have the most beautiful eyes I've ever seen, Delilah D'Artigo." And then, silent as snow falling on water, he slipped out of my office and was gone.

By the time I arrived home, Camille was curled on the living room sofa with Trillian, her main squeeze. By main, I mean *overriding obsession*, and by squeeze, I mean *Svartan*—the king of Tall, Dark, and Dangerous. With jet-black skin that shone with a faint glow, long silver hair, and eyes the color of an ice floe, Trillian was more gorgeous than any man had a right to be. And he knew it.

Camille belonged to him, bound by a lust oath. As she'd found out the hard way, there was no breaking away from sexual bondage with a Svartan. He gave her free reign on whoever else she might want to spend her nights with, but in the end, she belonged to him, chained by magic as old as time.

I didn't really like Trillian, but I was beginning to see that beneath that cold, aloof nature, he really did care about my sister.

"Is Menolly awake yet?" I asked, grabbing up a bowl of corn chips and stuffing a handful in my mouth. I loved junk food, I loved trash TV, and I was coming to love much of human culture, as homesick as I was.

Camille nodded toward the kitchen. "She's feeding Maggie. Iris made a huge pot of spaghetti, and there's plenty left if you're hungry. I already ate."

I coughed. By the look on Trillian's face, I could guess what she'd had for dessert.

"Back in a minute," I said, and dashed down the hall. Menolly, with her Bo Derek braids the color of burnished copper and her vamp-pale skin, was rocking Maggie by the stove as she fed her a bottle of gargoyle formula. She cooed to the little calico Crypto. Damn it, where was my camera? If I could catch the scene on film, it would give me something to hold over her head for years to come. Then I remembered; Menolly wouldn't photograph. Some of the wives' tales about vampires were true.

Instead, I leaned against the cupboard and cleared my throat. "How's our baby girl today?"

Menolly jumped, her eyes shifting to bloodred, then back to their usual pale frost. "Damn it, Kitten, will you make some noise when you enter the room? Both Camille and I've warned you about sneaking up on me! I could hurt you. Or Maggie."

Oh hell, I'd done it again. I was one of the few people who could actually surprise Menolly, but I risked my health doing so. Camille had the scars on her arm to prove what happened when our sister was startled. But I hadn't thought about her hurting Maggie.

I scowled and stared at the floor. "Sorry."

She tucked Maggie back into her playpen. "Camille and I've scolded you about that before—"

That did it. I yanked off my jacket and tossed it on the

table. "And I'm so sick of you two *scolding* me! I screwed up—I'm sorry. I'll be more careful, but you have to quit acting like I'm your stupid little sister. Damn it, Menolly, *I'm* older than *you*. I may not be a badass like you, or able to throw lightning like Camille, but that doesn't mean that I'm naïve. I thought I made enough noise when I came in the kitchen. *Stop.* Apparently I'm quieter than I thought. *Stop.* I'll make sure it doesn't happen again. *Stop.* So quit treating me like I'm an idiot. *End of Message.*"

"You're in a mood, aren't you?"

I let out an exasperated sigh, and Menolly shrugged.

"All right, all right," she said. "I'm sorry, I didn't realize we hurt your feelings, Kitten."

She didn't get it, and she probably never would. Sometimes sisters were a pain in the butt. "Never mind." I frowned and popped another corn chip in my mouth. "Listen, I have some interesting news for you and Camille. Come into the living room, would you?"

It was Menolly's turn to grimace. "Trillian's in there," she said, as if she had a bad taste in her mouth. I shot her a warning look, and she backed down. "Oh, all right. Let's go."

Before following her into the other room, I dished up a plate of spaghetti and grabbed a fork and napkin. Menolly sat atop the upright piano in the corner, shooting nasty looks in Trillian's direction. She made no bones about her feelings—or dearth thereof—about him, though neither Trillian nor Camille paid any attention to her.

As I slid into a chair, ready to tell them about Zachary, the doorbell chimed. Menolly went to answer it and in a moment came back, a guarded look on her face. Behind her walked a cloaked figure, so silent that even my acute hearing couldn't pick up the sound of his footsteps.

"May we help you?" I asked, setting my dish on the coffee table as I stood. This was no FBH—full-blooded human. Nor any regular Fae. We could all feel the strong and tangible presence of earth magic in the room.

"On the contrary, it is I who can help you," a soft voice said from within the robes. The figure pushed back the hood of his cloak, and we found ourselves staring at an elf. He was fair and reed thin, with pale hair the color of early sunlight. He wore a headband bearing a crest that we recognized as being a symbol of Elqaneve, Queen Asteria's court. It was Trenyth, the Queen's assistant. We hadn't heard from him in a while.

I caught my breath. Had something happened to the spirit seal? Or Tom Lane?

"Please, sit down," I said, motioning to the nearest chair.

Trenyth inclined his head but remained on his feet. "Thank you, but I'll stand." He kept his gaze on Menolly as he spoke. "I can stay but a few moments, for Her Majesty has need for my services at home. But I bring you a gift from the court— from our wizards. Queen Asteria commissioned this to be made for you." He pulled a small forest-green pouch out of his pocket and handed it to me.

I stared at the bag. The material was as soft as anything I'd ever felt and radiated magic—heavy magic born of the soil and rock and bone and crystal. The Queen's seal had been embroidered onto the cloth. I silently passed the bag to Camille.

She opened it, and a brilliant spike of polished crystal rolled out onto her hand. Inclusions radiated from the center outward, like a sunburst caught in ice. "What is this?" she asked.

"A fire-and-ice charm." Trenyth pointed to the sun caught within the quartz. "This crystal will detect the work of spies: traps, guards, wards, and listening devices, both technological and magical. If the sunburst within the center glows brilliant red, you'll know that you're near such a device. The Queen set our mages to work on this shortly after you left her audience two moons ago, and this is what they came up with."

Camille let out a relieved sigh. "Oh thank you, and please thank her. We haven't much to report at this moment, but we're keeping watch."

"Don't thank me yet. I also bear a warning," he said. "Our Earthside informants notified us that a Degath Squad passed through one of the Elemental portals a few days back. The guardian of the portal was mortally wounded. She lived long enough to tell Pentangle, the Mother of Magic, about the attack. Pentangle tried to track the assailants but lost them.

However, she has reason to think that they're heading in the direction of Seattle. So keep your eyes open."

"Oh Great Mother, another Degath Squad? And they've already made kills? Do you happen to know what kind of demons we're talking about?" A knot formed in my stomach. We were on the edge of another battle.

Trenyth shook his head. "There's a problem. We're not even sure all of them *were* demons, but they all bore Shadow Wing's sigil on their shields, and they carried the mark of the Hell Scouts. We know that at least one was a Jansshi demon, but the guardians of the portal had a hard time scanning the other two."

I racked my thoughts but couldn't find any reference hiding back in the corners of my brain. "I don't think I know anything about the Jansshi."

Camille cleared her throat. "They're similar to the Jiangshi, but I don't think they've ever taken human form. The Jiangshi are known as hopping corpses," she said. "They originate in China."

The elf nodded. "The Jansshi are worse, though. Rather than zombie, they're full demon, but they're stupid and vicious. They demand the hearts of their victims as an offering, which they eat. Consider them the thugs and pawns of the Subterranean Realms. Shadow Wing must have sent this one out to be the muscle behind the group. The Jansshi look human, but with grossly distorted bellies and sunken chests."

"Hearts?" Zachary's friends had been missing their hearts. Maybe it wasn't a rogue Corpse Talker after all. But what would the Degath Squad be doing out on the Puma Pride's land?

"Yes, and the guardians of the portal who were killed were missing theirs," Trenyth said.

My stomach lurched, and I held up my hand. "Tell me one thing, were the bodies dried out? As if all their internal . . . as if they were mummified?" There was such a thing as being too graphic.

Trenyth shook his head. "No. Why?"

"I don't know . . . it may be nothing," I said, feeling queasy. As I looked at my plate of spaghetti, my stomach threatened a revolt, and I ran into the kitchen, where I splashed cold water

on my face. As I watched the water swirl in the sink, any re-
mote hopes that Bad Ass Luke and his cronies had been a fluke
vanished with the last drops. Down the drain, into the sewer.

Camille was right. We were on the brink of a war, trying
to forestall wholesale destruction. We could probably do it if
Shadow Wing sent one team at a time, but what would we do
when he elevated the stakes?

By the time I returned to the living room, Trenyth was
ready to leave. "Keep the crystal safe, and Queen Asteria will
contact you again soon." He paused by the door. "You won't
receive much help from Y'Elestrial, I can tell you that," he
added but would not elaborate. Within seconds he had passed
into the night like a ghost.

The four of us stared at one another, unsure of what to say.

Finally, Camille spoke. "Okay, so we have another batch
of demons to mop the floor with. At least we know ahead of
time. I'll strengthen the wards tonight before I go to bed.
Menolly, report anything unusual at the Wayfarer to the rest of
us immediately. Everybody keep your cell phones handy."

"I think I might have already found a connection, but I
don't know how it ties in," I said, crossing my legs as I settled
into one of our huge, overstuffed chairs. "Today, I met our
Were from out near the woods and found out why he's been
watching us. He's my new client."

Camille frowned. "Really? What's his name? What did he
want?"

I told them about the conversation I'd had with Zach.
"Whatever killed the five victims ripped out their hearts."

"But I thought the demons came through the portal only a
few days ago. This sounds like it's been going on for several
weeks," Menolly said. "We can't let our paranoia drive us to
jumping at shadows."

With a frown, I shrugged. "True. It also crossed my thoughts
that we might be dealing with a rogue Corpse Talker, because
of the missing hearts. As for the mummification angle, I have
no idea what's going on with that."

Camille frowned. "That's an interesting possibility. Corpse
Talkers always take the heart."

"Yeah," I said, shuddering. We'd witnessed the creatures in action. Each time, I was left feeling vaguely nauseated and afraid. "One thing's for sure. Somebody's brutally killing the Weres in his clan. I'd like both of you to go out there with me Saturday evening."

"Of course," Camille said. Menolly nodded. Trillian pouted until I told him he was welcome, too, and then he declined.

"I just wanted to feel welcome," he said, blinking those icy cold and taunting eyes at me. Camille slapped him, and he gave her a look that would have frozen me cold in my tracks but just set her laughing.

"We'd better start researching everything we can find out about Jansshi demons. We have to know their vulnerabilities, if they have any," Menolly said. "What worries me is that Trenyth said they're stupid. If the Jansshi demon's the brawn, who the hell is playing the brains of the squad? I'm not looking forward to finding out who else we're up against."

"You and me both," I muttered.

Just then, a peal of chimes echoed from upstairs. They could only mean one thing.

"The Whispering Mirror," Camille said, jumping to her feet. She raced toward the steps and up to her study, the rest of us hot on her heels.

The Whispering Mirror had been set up by the Wizards Guild and served the same purpose as a video telephone, linking us to home. Considering that our city was on the verge of civil war, we hadn't been surprised that news was barely trickling out from Y'Elestrial. The OIA had been out of touch with us for over a month, Earthside time. We were worried enough that we'd been discussing making a trip back home to see if Father was okay.

A member of the Guard, he was faithful to Court and Crown, but his loyalty had been put to the test by our troll of a Queen. Well, not a *real* troll. She was prettier and didn't live under a bridge. But Lethesanar was an opium fiend and had a particularly cruel taste for torture. Last we heard, our father was doing his best to play it neutral, but the time was coming when his loyalty would be tested. If he chose to follow his conscience, then he'd be in danger. The Queen treated traitors as kindly as Menolly treated the pervs she called a Happy Meal.

Camille slid into a chair in front of the Whispering Mirror, which was mounted on the wall beneath a desk and covered by a black velvet cloth. She yanked away the velvet as Menolly and I leaned over her shoulders. Trillian rested himself against the doorjamb.

Framed by the magical silver mined from deep within the Nebelvuori Mountains back in Otherworld, the glass shone with a faint bluish light and the mist within whirled, a chaotic vortex waiting for the right voice to open the link from one dimension to another.

"Camille," she said. The mirror worked on principles much like vox software for computers. After living Earthside for a while, I was beginning to think that the FBHs were gaining on us. I'd developed a fascination for their technology—well, ours, too, considering our mother was human—and I had taken to the computer like a cat in a field of catnip.

After a moment the mist in the mirror began to swirl, then cleared, and we found ourselves staring into our father's face. He and Camille were spitting images of one another. I favored our mother, and Menolly's looks were a genetic throwback to some unknown ancestor.

Medium height, of trim build, Father's hair was the same color as Camille's—raven black—though he wore it in a tightly bound braid. His eyes were the same as hers, too. Violet with silver specks. He was out of uniform and, by the scene in the background, he was at home. Most of the guards who had been in the Des'Estar any length of time had Whispering Mirrors in their homes.

I leaned in and blew him a kiss. "Hey, we were worried about you. What's up?"

He blinked once, then a soft smile grazed his lips. "You remind me so much of your mother, rest her soul." He scanned our anxious faces, his brow lined with furrows that hadn't been there a year ago. "Menolly? How are you doing, child?" He still hadn't fully adjusted yet to the fact that she was a vampire. His long-standing hatred for the undead was tempered only by the reality that his own daughter was one of the afflicted.

She gave him an affected nod, but I could tell they were glad to see one another. "Can't complain. Not much, at least."

Camille cleared her throat. "It's so good to hear from you," she added, relief flooding her voice. "We were thinking of making a trip home to see you."

"What's going on?" I broke in. "Are you okay? Is the war going to be over before it even begins?" Ever the optimist, even I knew the answer to my last question. But hey, hope made living worthwhile.

"Over? No, my girls, it's just beginning. The sides are drawn. The goblins have forged a treaty with Lethesanar and are sending in troops. The Svartans and elves back Tanaquar's claim. The Elfin Queen has officially forged a truce with the King of Svartalfheim, offering manpower and weapons. As you can imagine, her decision has turned heads."

"No doubt," I murmured. The Svartans and elves were born enemies, both lines springing from a single race millennia ago. Somewhere along the line, the race had divided, and the Svartans moved into the shadows while the elves stayed in the light. For them to join forces meant the shit really had hit the fan.

Father didn't know that Queen Asteria had drafted us into her service. Technically, we were traitors to the Court and Crown, but when caught between a cliff and a demon, jumping over the edge starts to look like a damned good idea.

He let out a slow, long breath. "I have little time today, and there are things you must know. Your lives may depend on it."

That sobered us up. "Don't tell me they managed to resurrect Bad Ass Luke somehow," I said. "Demons and zombies and ghouls, oh my!"

"This is serious, Delilah," Father said, glancing over his shoulder. I could see the glass bell clock Mother had taken with her to OW when she married our father and crossed between worlds for good. "My shift starts soon, so listen and listen good."

"Yes, sir," I said, staring at the ground.

He cleared his throat. "Word has it that Lethesanar is about to mount a direct attack on the city of Svartalfheim. My conscience won't allow me to take part. I'm a loyalist to Court and Crown, not to a drug-addled, power-crazed warmonger who no longer can see what stands before her. If we go to battle against Svartalfheim, then . . ." His expression said everything. Our father was gearing up to desert the Guard, and he'd be skewered if he was caught.

"What are you going to do?" I asked.

With a shake of the head, he said, "To be honest, I have no idea. I'll find a way to get in touch with you. I've already moved your things into storage where they will be safe. Your aunt Rythwar knows where to find everything. She was forced to flee the city and is living well outside Y'Elestrial's boundaries. There's a death threat on her head."

Camille gasped. Both Menolly and I stared at our father, slack-jawed. Our aunt had been a close friend of Lethesanar's and had lived in the inner courts.

"Holy crap. What happened?" I asked.

"She was working for Tanaquar." Father took a deep breath and let it out slowly. "Lethesanar found out. She put a death threat and a bounty on your aunt's head. Rythwar is hiding out. And . . ." He paused, looking uncertain. "I'm not sure how to say this."

"Just say it," I said. Whatever the news was, I had a feeling it wasn't going to be a happy picnic in the park.

"Because of Camille's involvement with Trillian, you may shortly find yourselves unemployed. If so, hightail it back through the portals before the Queen takes it into her head to close them entirely. You don't want to be stranded Earthside."

I coughed. "There are always the Elemental portals, like the ones belonging to Grandmother Coyote and Pentangle. They aren't under the OIA jurisdiction." Which immediately reminded me of the demons headed our way. "There's another Degath Squad running loose over here."

Father closed his eyes for the briefest of moments. "I'm so sorry, my girls. I have the feeling it will be a long time before things are back to normal." He wiped his eyes, older and wearier than I'd ever seen him look.

"You'd better kiss any help from the OIA good-bye," Trillian said grimly. "Maybe you'd best do as your father suggests and go home."

"We can't just leave," Camille said. "Shadow Wing is too great a threat. He'll find the rest of the seals, and both Earth and Otherworld will be doomed. There's no place to hide."

"She's right." I snorted. "What makes you think OW will be safe much longer if Shadow Wing is allowed free rein in Earth? Let's face it, we're all screwed and pretty much alone in this mess."

Father coughed. "Not entirely. You said Queen Asteria believed you about Shadow Wing."

I glanced at him, wondering just how much he knew. Camille must have been thinking the same thing, because she gave me one of those *should we tell him* looks. I shook my head. As much as I wanted to, we couldn't take the chance. Too much rode on secrecy.

"Yeah, she does." I let out a soft breath, then asked the question we were all thinking. "Can't you join us here? We could use your help."

He shook his head. "No, I can't." There was a noise on Father's side of the mirror. "Someone's at the door. I have to go. I doubt if I'll be able to contact you for a long while. Remember, your aunt Rythwar knows what's happening. She's living in a small house on the Riellsring River, en route to the Nebelvuori Mountains. There's a glade of oak trees shortly before you reach Sandstone Falls, and behind that glade, a wild berry patch. She lives a mile or so farther toward the mountains. Don't look for a path; there isn't one. And don't tell *anyone* where she is."

The noise grew louder; we could hear pounding on the door and then a voice echoed into the room. "Captain, the Queen requires your attendance in her court. We're moving against Svartalfheim tonight, *sir*!"

Father gave us one last desperate look. "It's begun," he said. "If something should happen to me, never forget that I love you. And your mother loved you. Keep to your conscience and do what you know is right, regardless of the outcome. I'm so proud of you."

"Father—" Camille cried out, reaching toward the mirror.

I could only stare as the glass grew dark and then, once again, clouded over with mist. "Oh Great Lady Bast, either he marches to war or will be marked as a traitor. What are we going to do?"

Menolly sighed. "We'll do exactly what he said. Follow our conscience. Delilah, there's nothing we can do right now back home. We'd end up tossed in prison. We'll do what we can here and pray that the gods protect Father and Aunt Rythwar. Meanwhile," she said, glancing at the clock, "we'd better stick to our routines in case we're being watched. It's time for me to go to work." Menolly ran the Wayfarer Bar & Grill, working the night shift.

I frowned. How the hell was I supposed to focus on work when all this crap was happening? When we'd first been assigned to our Earthside posts, it had been a pain in the butt. Now it was a full-scale nightmare. But Menolly was right. As much as I longed to race home and try to put everything to rights, I knew there was nothing we could do there.

"If I ever get my hands on Lethesanar . . ." I grumbled, leaving the thought unfinished.

Camille rested her hand on my shoulder as we turned to go back downstairs. "Everything will work out. Wait and see. Father's smart, and so is Aunt Rythwar. And hey, if we get fired, well, hell, there are dozens of things I'd rather be doing than working for a bureaucratic nightmare."

I gave her a faint smile, then laughed. "And you call *me* an optimist? But thanks, I can use a good dose of happy-ever-after." We went back downstairs, but I knew that all of our thoughts were focused on the family we held most dear.

CHAPTER 4

Things weren't any better the next morning. We were all on edge, and it didn't help matters that before I managed to make it to the breakfast table, Trillian stopped me in the hallway.

Meticulous as usual, he was wearing a pair of black jeans, a pale gray turtleneck, and high-heeled motorcycle boots. His leather jacket hugged his waist and was decorated with studs and buckles. He and Camille made quite the pair, all right. Crossing the boundary between pirate and urban ninja, Trillian was a hunk. An arrogant bastard, but a hunk nonetheless.

"Morning," I said, yawning. As usual, I'd stayed up half the night and was planning on a nice little catnap in my office later on. I sniffed the air and was greeted with the aroma of sausage and hotcakes drifting down the hall. "Ready for breakfast? By the smell of things, Iris has been at the stove again."

"She's a talented cook," Trillian said, stopping me with the barest of touches on my arm. "Before we eat, I want you to promise to do something for me, Delilah." His eyes were liquid, molten ice, and if I was any weaker, he might have cajoled a "Sure thing" out of me without further explanation. But I knew Trillian too well. Any time he wanted a favor, it was bound to be for his benefit alone.

"What do you want?"

"Still don't trust me?" he said, a slight curve to the corner of his mouth. That curve turned Camille into mush, but it just made my skin crawl. He was cunning and crafty, all right. "I want you to convince Chase that I'm not going to rob him blind, tie him up, castrate him, or tear up his apartment." He clasped his hands behind his back and rocked on his heels, giving me an insider smile that came across as crocodile-in-waiting. "Your boyfriend won't let me stay there alone."

I snorted. "That sounds like Chase, all right. I take it this little arrangement isn't working out so well? Why don't you just hurry up and find an apartment?"

Trillian huffed impatiently. "I have standards."

"You mean you can't afford anything but a dive," I countered. "Sorry, I'm not about to get in the middle of your quarrel. Camille and I both told you this was a stupid idea, but no, you two had to go ahead and take the plunge. Now you've only been there a few days, and you're already whining."

As much as I wanted to be done with this conversation, curiosity got the best of me. "Tell me, Trillian, just how did you get Chase to let you stay with him in the first place?"

I couldn't figure it out. Chase was a smart man who liked his privacy. He wasn't a pushover in any way, and I knew he didn't trust Trillian. How the two ever ended up as roomies—even temporarily—confounded me.

Trillian said nothing, turning to go into the kitchen, but I caught a glint in his eyes. I grabbed hold of his shoulder and spun him around.

"You bewitched him, didn't you? You blasted him with that damned magnetism you Svartans ooze from every pore, and he didn't stand a chance!" Hands on my hips, I leaned down—I was a little taller than him—and let him have it. "That's the most low-down, arrogant trick in the book and—"

"Might I remind you of one thing?" he said mildly, inspecting his fingernails. "Your detective is head over heels because of your half-Fae blood, my dear, so don't even *dare* try to guilt-trip me. Just what did Camille say when she found out you charmed our illustrious detective?"

Abruptly, I shut my mouth and took a step back. So he'd figured out that I'd turned up my glamour that first night Chase and I'd been alone. And Chase still didn't know about it. I'd been so ashamed afterward about using it on an unsuspecting FBH that I hadn't told Camille. She thought Chase had made the first move, and so did Chase. So did Menolly. And I was determined to keep them all deluded.

Trillian let out a short bark of laughter. "She doesn't know, does she? You didn't tell her that you enchanted lover boy, did you?"

I glared at him. "Chase was bothering Camille, and she wasn't interested in him so I . . . just—"

"Took him off her hands for her? This is absolutely priceless," he said, grinning from ear to ear. "Come on, pussycat. Let's eat breakfast. You and I are more alike than you'll ever admit. Camille can be ruthless when she chooses, but she's up-front about it. You put on a good front, but behind that facade, you're no meek little puss-in-boots, are you?"

I gritted my teeth and said nothing. Trillian might be an absolute ass, but he called the shots as he saw them. And he saw through me clear as crystal. I'd been interested in Chase, even though I wouldn't admit it, because I was curious about sex and the whole orgasm-with-people thing. He was cute and available. But I knew that he'd go on dogging Camille, even though she didn't want him, so I turned on the charm the first chance I was alone with him. I was as guilty as Trillian was in using my glamour to get what I wanted.

"I didn't tell Camille because . . ."

"Oh, you don't have to explain your reasons to me. I don't really give a damn. But from now on, maybe you won't fuss about my relationship with Camille or my use of a little bewitchment here and there."

I wanted to wipe that smug look off his face and protest that we were nothing alike. That I would never stoop as low as a Svartan might. But I'd only be lying to myself.

"I didn't even know I was interested in Chase, not until I knew for sure that Camille didn't want him," I said. "I was as surprised as anybody when he actually responded to me."

Trillian stood back to let me by. Shaking my head, I pushed past him into the kitchen, where Iris was fixing pancakes and sausage.

As he swung in behind me, I turned so quickly that he bumped into me. I whispered, "If you have a bone to pick with Chase, do it yourself. But listen and listen good: if you hurt him, I'll sic Menolly on you. She doesn't like you, and she's just waiting for the word. Trust me on that one."

Trillian snorted but said nothing. He pushed into the kitchen and leaned down to plant a kiss on Iris's cheek.

She handed him a plate and motioned to the table. "Fatten yourself up, boy," she said. "Breakfast is ready, and there's more on the griddle."

Trillian settled himself at one end of the table and speared a hotcake with his fork, loading it thickly with butter and honey.

Iris flashed me a wicked grin. She was the only one who could keep him in check. He usually settled down after Iris gave him a direct order. Camille had formulated a theory that Iris must remind Trillian of his mother. I thought that was probably stretching it, but who knew?

I piled a plate high with hotcakes and sausage and poured myself a large glass of milk. Iris looked gratified as I dug into the breakfast. "So, what's on your schedule today?" I asked her.

She flipped the last pancake onto the stack, then unplugged the electric griddle and scrambled up on her barstool. A noise on the stairs told us that Camille was on her way. As she swung around the corner, dressed to kill as usual, a smile broke over her face.

"Food," she said, eyeing the table as she gave Trillian a light kiss. As her lips met his, a flare of sparks showered between them, and for a fleeting moment, I could see the flicker of cords that bound them together.

Iris broke in. "If you'll eat and get out of here, I can get started on cleaning. It's almost Midwinter, and we have to prepare for the holidays."

I glanced at Camille. "Midwinter won't be the same without Father. Should we even bother?"

Camille shrugged. "I thought about just forgetting it this year, but it's tradition, Delilah. Mother would have wanted us to hold Yule, and frankly, I could use a taste of home for the holidays."

Back in Otherworld, on Midwinter's Eve, most of the city showed up at the Erulizi Falls, which poured into Lake Y'Leveshan. The lake and the falls would both be iced over, sparkling like crystal under the snow-showered night. Everyone gathered around the shores for the midnight ritual to celebrate the ascension of the Snow Queen and the Holly King. Magic flowed like honey, and by morning, when the sun rose, the frozen fields would shimmer under the weight of the newly fallen snow.

Our mother had taken Y'Elestrial's traditions and blended them with her own. We not only attended the citywide celebrations but decked our house in holly and evergreens. She'd even convinced Father to bring in a tree every year so we could decorate it with charms and crystals. The house had been so beautiful during those days.

All of a sudden, I wanted nothing less than to re-create the Midwinter festival here in this world that had been forsaken by the gods. "Maybe . . . maybe we can hold a ritual down by Birchwater Pond?"

Iris glanced at me, a smile crinkling the corners of her mouth. "I think that's a lovely idea," she said. "We'll decorate the house tonight. I'll have everything ready, if you girls trust me."

Camille leaned back against her chair, looking relieved. "Thank you. You're part of our family now, you know."

"Speaking of which, Delilah, do you have time today to stop at the Fairy Tale and pick up my outfit?" Iris glanced up at me. "It's paid for already. Jill called to say it's done."

I nodded. "No problem. I'll have it for you tonight."

Camille glanced at the clock. "Ugh. We'd better get moving. While I'm at work, I'll see what I can find out about Jansshi demons, if anything."

Trillian followed her into the living room, and I tagged along behind. As we slid into our coats and headed for the door, he gave me one last look.

"You'll talk to Chase?" he asked, a look of triumph in his eyes.

I glanced at Camille and sighed. Despite my threat to sic Menolly on him, he had me, and he knew it. "Yeah, when I get the chance."

As we stepped out into the breath-snatching chill of the morning air and headed down the driveway to our cars, I couldn't help but feel vindicated when Trillian slipped on an icy patch of frost-covered leaves and went sprawling at Camille's feet. Snickering, I delicately stepped over him and headed to my Jeep.

The windchill factor had sent the temperature plummeting to below freezing by the time I reached my office. I dropped my purse on the desk and flipped open my Rolodex as I swiveled in my chair to look out the window at the overcast skies. Silver . . . snow weather, Camille said. She could smell it on the wind, and if there was one thing she knew, it was the scent of lightning, snow, and rain.

I found the name I was looking for and picked up the phone. I knew one well-placed Were who lived in the city. She passed, still hidden in the broom closet, but she had scads of information on the Were community in Seattle. If anybody knew about the Puma Pride Clan, Siobhan would.

I punched in her phone number. Siobhan Morgan was a selkie—a wereseal, and she lived near the Ballard Locks on Thirty-ninth Avenue West in a condo on the shoreline. Near the juncture where Shilshole Bay met Salmon Bay, she was able to slip down to the water whenever she needed.

Siobhan had a breathy voice and always sounded like she'd just finished working out or running a marathon. "Speak to me," she said.

"Meow."

She laughed. "Delilah, good to hear from you. What's up?"

"I wondered if I could drop by and talk to you about a Were clan out near Mount Rainier. I was hoping you might know something about them." A fly landed on my nose, and I batted it away. Even in the midst of a cold snap in December, our building had flies and rodents and all sorts of delightful beasties.

"Who are we talking about?"

"The Rainier Puma Pride," I said.

After a brief pause, she said, "Yeah, come on over in about ninety minutes, if you would. I know a little about the Puma Pride. A very close-knit bunch. They seem fine by what I know, so far, but there have been rumblings in the Were community.

Vague, but you might want to catch up before getting tangled up with them."

I made sure I had her address right, grabbed my coat and purse, and hit the bricks. I'd slip down to Pike Place Market and take care of Iris's errand before heading out to Siobhan's house. As I climbed into my Jeep, I wondered if the rumblings she had spoken of had anything to do with the dead Weres, and if so, just what was going on.

Pike Place Market was jammed with holiday shoppers. A semi-open market that was the pride of Seattle with over two hundred little businesses, a massive number of vendors who rented space by the day, street musicians, mimes, magicians, and a plethora of artists, it reminded Camille and me of home. While Menolly never really got to see it—it usually shut down by the time she was ready to go out—Camille and I loved to come to the market and shop. I just had to make certain to avoid the fish throwers. Way too much temptation there.

I maneuvered my way through the vegetable stalls, sniffing in the scent of fresh herbs—most of the vegetables were out of season—and freshly woven wreaths. As I rounded a corner, three young girls came racing across the wooden floor of the mezzanine, and the youngest, who couldn't have been older than seven, ran smack into me. The girls screeched to a halt. The one who'd plowed into me looked up, and her eyes grew wide as she hurriedly backed up.

"You're one of the Faeries!" she whispered, her voice almost too soft to hear.

I gave her a wink. "Yes, I am. My name's Delilah." I didn't extend my hand; friendliness was too easily misconstrued with Earth children, and I understood why, though it made me sad to think about.

She held her hand to her mouth, her little friends equally in awe. Finally, one, a girl with short red hair and more freckles than bare skin, said, "Hi. My name's Tanya. Are you a Faerie princess? I always wanted to meet a Faerie princess!" She sniffed a red carnation that she was carrying.

Hating to disappoint her, I shook my head. "I'm sorry, Tanya, but I'm not a princess. I'm just a regular old Faerie. Most of us aren't very special."

"You're a bad woman," said the one who'd run into me. "My mommy says that you Faeries are all sluts and that you're the reason Daddy left us."

Oh great gods in heaven. How the hell was I supposed to deal with this? And did the girl really even know what the word *slut* meant? Hoping she didn't, I let out a long sigh and said, "Some Faeries cause problems, and some don't. Just like people . . ." I stopped, not sure how to explain what I was trying to say, or if I should even bother trying.

Tanya, the redhead, beamed me a huge smile and turned to her friend. "Janie, it's like the bullies at school. Just 'cause Billy yanked my hair doesn't mean all boys are bad."

"That's right," I said, stopping as a tall, thin woman strode up. Janie, the girl who'd decided I had broken up her home, backed up against her. Mother and daughter, that much was obvious. Her mother looked like she wanted to drown me right then and there.

"Get away from my daughter, you bitch," the woman muttered, just loud enough for me to hear. I glanced at Janie, thinking it was a shame she was going to grow up so angry. How could she help it with a role model like that?

"I didn't mean to interfere—" I started, then shut my mouth. It wouldn't do any good. But as I turned to walk away, Tanya tugged on my jacket. I looked down at her as she handed me the carnation.

"I still think you're a Faerie princess," she whispered.

I winked at her. "Maybe I am, but I'm in disguise, so don't tell anybody, okay?" She giggled and ran off, beaming. I watched her go. So I told a few white lies now and then. What could it hurt, if I could make somebody's dream come true?

The Fairy Tale, a clothing shop, catered to the renaissance crowd, and the owner, Jill Tucker, was an accomplished seamstress. She did a good business in both custom and off-the-rack clothing, and Iris had hired her a couple times over the past few months to make her custom outfits. I leaned on the counter, smiling at the pewter dragons that paraded across the shelf next to the register. Camille should buy one for Smoky, I thought, but then nixed the idea. It would probably seem stupid to someone as old as he was. Hell, he probably had solid gold statues tucked away somewhere in his barrow.

"May I help you?" Jill swung around, her smile infectious. She was holding a measuring tape and a piece of cloth that looked like the weaver had caught the Aurora borealis midripple.

"I'm here to pick up an outfit for Iris? Iris Kuusi." Iris used the Finnish surname that had belonged to the family to whom she'd been bound, until they all died out. She often told us stories about her days with them, usually when we were curled up near the fireplace with a big bowl of popcorn.

Jill tossed the tape on the counter along with the material. "Oh yes, she mentioned someone would be coming in today to pick it up. We've met, haven't we?" She extended her hand, and I took it, shaking lightly.

"Once, I came in with Iris when she ordered several custom-made aprons. I'm Delilah D'Artigo."

"Right! Her dress is ready to go. Hold on, and I'll be right back." She ducked into what looked like a back room the size of a closet and returned with a white box tied with a big red ribbon. A pewter unicorn charm dangled from the bow. "Here it is. Tell her to let me know if she needs any alterations. It was nice meeting you," she said, picking up the measuring tape again.

I could sense the busyness emanating off of her and picked up the box. The holidays had most people I'd met lately in a frazzle. "Have a lovely day," I said, meaning it.

"You, too," she called as I left the shop and headed out of the market.

The drive to Siobhan's condo took me right by Discovery Park, which consisted of over five hundred acres of protected meadows, thickets, and woodland situated on Magnolia Bluff. The park included two miles of shoreline designated as protected marine reserves.

Camille and I often came here to walk and think. The call of the gulls echoed along the tide flats, and it always seemed as though we could breathe easier while looking out over the bay toward the Olympic Mountains. I preferred to stay up in the woods, while Camille liked walking on the shore. The park was one big playground.

I navigated through the winding streets skirting the park, until I pulled to a stop in front of a two-story building. It had originally been a large house and was now divided into four different condominiums. Far from the chrome-and-glass towers going up around the city, Siobhan's home retained the flavor of an era gone by. The building had a homey feel, almost like a boardinghouse.

Jumping out of my Jeep, I headed toward the staircase on the right side of the building. There were two apartments on each floor, with stairs on either side of the building leading to the upper two residences.

The building needed a new paint job, that was for sure. Weathered from the winds and rain, paint flaked off the walls, but overall the place didn't look run-down so much as tired. Large shrubs and bushes surrounded the house, and ivy twined up the walls. Around back a patch of open lawn overlooked the bay.

I dashed up the stairs and knocked at a faded white door marked with the gold letters B-2. After a moment, the door opened. Siobhan stood there, tall and thin, with long black hair and pale skin. She was black Irish, and it showed. Dressed in a pale gray linen skirt and turtleneck, she reminded me of a shaft of moonlight streaming through the window on a cool autumn night.

"Hey, come in," she said, ushering me through the door. Siobhan moved like a shadow; one moment she'd be there, and the next she'd be on the other side of the room.

Her house was a reflection of her nature. Paintings of the sea, wild and foaming ocean waves, graced the walls. The sofa and love seat were a soft silver suede, and the wood gray and reminiscent of driftwood. Even the flowers she bought mirrored the colors of the ocean. All whites and pale violets with an occasional spray of pink interspersed among the roses and orchids.

"Would you care for something to eat?" she asked, holding out a tray of smoked salmon and crackers. My stomach rumbled, and I eagerly bit into an hors d'oeuvre, then wiped my mouth with a paper napkin. As we sat in the living room, overlooking the bay, I wondered how long she'd lived in the city. Earthside Fae were as long-lived as the Fae from Otherworld. Siobhan could be a hundred years old or five hundred.

"When did you first come to Seattle?" I asked, watching as the wind picked up, whipping the waves into white frenzied lines of sea foam.

She gave me a half smile. "I came over to Ellis Island a long time ago. I was barely into my maidenhood then, but I was ordered to leave my home and start new here."

I gave her an inquisitive look. "Why?"

"Our bloodline was, and is, wearing thin. Inbreeding has caused problems, and so the elders of the pod chose fifty of us, all younger members, to immigrate to the New World. They wanted us to establish a new life, to bring our bloodline across the ocean, and strengthen it with the blood of the North American Pacific selkies. They have the largest pods here in the world, you know."

I nodded. I knew all of the Earthside Weres were having problems due to inbreeding. As the human population grew, their own population shrank. Add in the difficulty in finding open territory, and it was causing havoc on their numbers.

"It's hard being an Earthside Were, isn't it?" I asked.

She nodded. "We don't have many options. Unlike other Fae, selkies have to mate with our own kind in order to produce offspring. It's not like the movies, where you're bitten by a werewolf and take on all the characteristics."

I nodded. Earthside, bitten Weres were sterile and far fewer in number than legends hinted at. In OW, it was the same way. And I, myself, would never bear a Were child because of my mixed blood, though I *would* have a child who was part Fae. My being a Were was a quirk of genetic scrambling and considered a birth defect among my father's people.

"So, our elders sent us across the ocean," she continued. "And I made my way over to the coast. But they should have sent someone else in my place. I can't get pregnant, and there aren't any healers here for my kind. Not of the caliber that I need." She sighed and raised her eyebrows. "I hoped to have pups, and my boyfriend has been patient, but there doesn't seem to be a family in the cards for us."

The catch in her voice made me want to put my arm around her and give her a hug. A thought occurred to me. "Listen, would you like me to talk to the OIA medics and see if they can examine you? They might be able to find out what's wrong. Your cover wouldn't be blown, and perhaps we could find out why you can't conceive."

Siobhan's eyes lit up, and for the first time since I'd known her, the faint ghost of a smile broke wide open. "Oh Delilah, that would mean so much to me. I love Mitch, and I hate to think of him finding another woman. Our numbers have dwindled to the point where all fertile selkies—of either sex—are expected to do their part to enlarge the gene pool. Mitch will be expected to impregnate another selkie if I can't have a child, and then he'd have to take her under his protection. Perhaps my association with humans is intruding on my nature, but I don't want to share him with anybody else."

"I can't promise anything, but I'll do everything I can," I said.

She settled back, beaming. "Now, what did you want to know about the Rainier Puma Pride?"

I finished off another salmon cracker and leaned forward, bracing my elbows on my knees. Staring at the floor, I said, "Zachary Lyonnesse came to see me at my office. I can't tell you why—that's confidential—but I just want to know a little bit about the reputation of the clan. What are they like? Do they have any enemies?"

Siobhan frowned in concentration. "The Rainier Pumas are an old clan. They stick to themselves a lot and are highly respected in the Were community. I can't think of anybody who doesn't like them, unless . . . There are two possibilities. There's a lesser Puma Pride over in eastern Washington. They resent the Rainier Pumas, but they aren't strong enough to challenge them. It's all about strength and cunning."

"Do you know their clan name?"

She squinted, staring out the window. After a moment she said, "I think they're the Icicle Falls Pride, but I'm not certain. But there's another possibility. There's one other group who consider the Pumas their enemies, though I haven't the faintest idea what they could have to argue about."

"And who is that?" I asked, pulling out my notebook.

She leaned close and whispered. "The grapevine has it that there have been some skirmishes between the Rainer Pumas and the Hunters Moon Clan. From what I understand, the antagonism has led to several deaths over the years. I don't know if they have a vendetta going on or not."

"The Hunters Moon Clan? Doesn't ring a bell. I assume they're Weres?"

She shivered as she crossed her arms in front of her. "They call themselves that, but they aren't natural Weres. There are rumors that say they derive their power from the evil shaman who created them over a thousand years ago. They're dark and treacherous and refuse to heed the rules of the Supe community, but they're so dangerous that nobody really wants to enforce the covenants between the tribes."

The room seemed to darken as she spoke, and a tingling in the back of my neck warned me that we were on slippery ground. We'd been so busy with getting adjusted to being Earthside and then with fighting Bad Ass Luke and his cronies that I'd ignored my inner promptings to collect information on the local Supe groups and build a database. In fact, Chase had given me the go-ahead and had promised full access to his files.

"A touchy situation, then. What are they like?"

Siobhan motioned for me to wait, then went to the door and peeked out. After a moment, she closed it and locked it behind her, inhaling deeply as she leaned against it. She glanced around the walls and at the ceiling, then returned to the sofa.

"As you might gather, I don't like talking about them. I try—all members of the Puget Sound Harbor Seal Pod try—to steer clear of them. They can be deadly in more ways than one." She leaned forward. "The Hunters Moon Clan is a nest of hobo spiderlings."

"Spiderlings? You mean werespiders?"

She shrugged. "As I said, they aren't natural Weres, but yes, they are shape-shifters of a sort."

"Oh shit," I said. My stomach twisted. We had werespiders back in OW, and while some of the nests were fine and respected society's rules, others were twisted and cruel, holing up in the depths of the forests, where they could build vast hidden cities. If the Hunters Moon Clan were an unnatural offshoot of the Weres, then they might be far more difficult to get a sense for.

And to make matters worse, hobo spiders were a venomous species that had infiltrated the Pacific Northwest with a vengeance. In their natural form, they waged war against other spiders for territory, eliminating the competition. I could easily see them trying the same tactic with the other clans.

"Where do they nest?" I asked as it dawned on me why Siobhan had taken a long look at the ceiling and walls before speaking. Any shapeshifter or Were who could change into something as small as a spider would have a much greater ability to spy on their enemy and go unnoticed.

Siobhan shook her head. "I don't know," she said. "I suppose somewhere in the woods, but don't take my word for it."

I bit into another salmon-topped cracker. "These are delicious. So, anybody else seem to be on the bad side of the Rainier Puma Pride?"

She gave me a thin smile. "You might try the Loco Lobo Pack, a group of lycanthropes up from the Southwest. Wolves and pumas don't mix all that well. So, how are you getting along? Do you have plans for the holidays?"

As I launched into a vague description of what we were planning, the tension in the room slowly dissipated. Siobhan was scared stiff of the Hunters Moon Clan; that much was obvious. I chatted for a while and promised again to call her as soon as I talked to the medics working with the OIA.

When I left, the wind coming off the bay was harsh, and

the smell of snow rich and vibrant to my nose. The afternoon sky glowed with a silvery light, and I felt a stab in my heart, as if an icicle had broken off the roof and plunged through me. I had no idea what was making me so afraid, but suddenly the only thing I wanted was to be safe at home, to call Zachary and tell him I couldn't take the case. But that wasn't an option, not as long as the Degath Squad might be involved.

As I hopped in my Jeep and started the engine, a tickle made me jump. A spider, just big enough to cover my little fingernail, had crawled on the top of my hand. I stared at it for a moment, then without a second thought, I smashed it flat and flicked it out the window.

"So much for you," I whispered. "If you were a spy, then you've just found out what the D'Artigo girls do to their enemies." Wiping my hand on my jeans, I eased out of the driveway onto the road. I decided that when I got home, I'd ask Iris to fumigate my Jeep.

CHAPTER 5

By the time I stopped at McDonald's for a Coke, it was almost three. I checked my messages on my cell phone. Nothing. I punched in number four on speed dial and waited until Chase picked up.

"Hey babe," he said, his voice smooth and fine. "What's going on?"

"Wanted to run a few names by you for you to check on," I said. And then, because his voice made me feel strangely comforted, I added, "I'd like to see you this afternoon, if you have time. I'm busy tonight, but I miss you."

He cleared his throat and then, with a catch in his voice, said, "I want to see you, too. The office is slow today. I can get away for an hour or two. Meet me at my place?"

"See you in half an hour, traffic willing."

Chase lived in Renton, south of Seattle, where the rents were a little cheaper and the neighborhoods a little shadier. It helped him afford the designer suits he had a penchant for. As I navigated through the confusing array of one-way streets and construction projects, I thought about our past few months together.

Chase was an enigma to me. I couldn't say I loved him, not really. At least I didn't think so. But I was fond of him, more than just about anybody else in my life. He had earned my respect by his devotion to his work, and that was a hard thing to do.

He'd also surprised the hell out of me by dragging out an unexpected loyal streak that hid just beneath the surface. Now, *that* worried me. I wasn't really down with the concept of monogamy, though I wasn't as sexual as Camille, at least not overtly. I'd warned him that I wasn't looking for anything serious, and so far, there had been no problems.

The first time we'd slept together the sex had been so-so. I'd been mainly interested in finding out what all the sex-with-people hoopla was about. I'd already lost my virginity in my cat form to a gorgeous long-haired silver tabby named Tommy, but let's face it, male cats are pretty self-centered, and Tommy-boy wasn't a werecat, which meant that any hope of a relationship was highly limited. He mainly talked about chasing mice and butterflies, and the neighbor dogs that he wanted to take out but was too afraid to go near. I'd grown fond of him, but after a while, our different perspectives on the world wore thin.

After a few romps with Chase, however, something had shifted. Maybe my hormones kicked in, or the Fae blood. Whatever it was, sex had become so intense that it threatened to overwhelm me. It was like a hidden riptide, waiting to drag me out into deep water once it had gotten hold of me.

As I pulled into the driveway leading into his complex, the first flakes of snow came drifting down to kiss my eyelashes, flickering like diamonds floating on the breeze. I hauled ass up the stairs, shivering from the chill.

Chase was waiting for me, wearing nothing but his boxers, a chocolate-brown velvet smoking jacket, and a smile. He leaned against the wet bar, dark eyes smoldering, and I caught my breath. For an FBH, he washed up damn good.

"Hey, baby," he said, his voice as smooth as the skin on his face. "What's your pleasure?"

I wanted to talk to him about Trillian. I wanted to tell him about the case. I wanted to pour out my worries about the De-gath Squad and the Hunters Moon Clan, but all of that faded away as he arched one eyebrow.

"Fuck me," I said, dropping my purse on the floor, along with my jacket. I began to tingle as he slowly walked to me, and then, in a single blur of motion, he wrapped one arm around my waist as his other hand tangled in my hair.

He propelled me to the bedroom, where he pushed me against the wall, his hands sliding under my cami to cup my breasts through my bra. He was my height, and our gazes met and locked. I loved matching my strength against his, and though I would win if it came to a fight, he was no slacker.

Picking me up, he tossed me on the bed and pulled off his smoking jacket and boxer shorts. I leaned back, leisurely brushing my hand across my stomach. He stared down at me, muscled and erect, rigid with desire. The gleam in his eye made my stomach lurch.

"Leg up," he commanded.

I lifted one leg, languorously allowing him to slide my boot off, and then the other. I held my breath as he leaned over me, tracing a circle around my belly button with his lips before slowly unzipping my jeans. The only sound in the room was that of the denim sliding down my thighs and then to the floor. I caught my breath as he grabbed my hand and pulled me up to sit on the edge of the bed, quickly sliding behind me, wrapping his legs around my hips as he snuggled his chest against my back.

I shuddered and raised my arms, and he lifted my cami over my head. As he unhooked my bra, I leaned against him, feeling the silken brush of his chest hair against my skin. He reached around, softly squeezing my breasts before he gave the nipples a sharp pinch. I let out a yelp, growing wet as his fingers traced their way down my stomach, as his hand trailed over my abs to gently play with the curly golden hair nestled between my legs.

"Oh, good gods, don't stop," I said, my voice low and throaty. "You're driving me crazy."

Chase laughed. "That's the idea, baby," he whispered in my ear. "Get you all hot and bothered and then take advantage of you."

"You, take advantage of me?" I whispered back, and quick as a cat, I whirled around, pressing him back on the bed. I straddled his pelvis, holding myself just above him, grinning as I brushed my fingers over my breasts, lingering over the nipples. "You want me, Detective? You want to play with the pussycat?"

He let out a snort and folded his arms under his head. "Baby, you know what I want."

"Say please, then," I taunted him, circling my hips above his rock-hard shaft. He looked so luscious it was all I could do to hold back.

He gave me a coy grin, just enough for me to know that I

had him. "Come on, give it to me, girl. I'm so hard I'm going to explode."

I slid down the length of him, slowly, wet with anticipation as he thrust up to meet me, driving him deep inside my waiting body. I arched back as we matched thrust for thrust. Chase reached down between us, one finger gliding over my clit, massaging me as I rode him. With the other hand, he reached up to caress my breast.

"Oh, Great Mother, don't stop," I whispered as wave after wave of dizzying need swept through me. "Harder, please, fuck me harder."

He rolled me over then, bearing down on me as his hips ground against mine, driving himself so deep that I wanted to scream. I opened my mouth to beg for sweet, merciful release.

And then I blinked and found myself staring at Zachary Lyonnesse, his golden-boy good looks gazing down at me as if he'd just woken from a wonderful dream. I could hear him panting as he furiously pumped away, his thick staff driving itself farther and farther into my core with each thrust.

"What the hell?" I shouted, but then I blinked again and found myself staring up at a very startled Chase. But we were both too far along to say anything else and, teetering on the edge, ready to drop over the chasm into the realm of darkness and fire, I shook off my confusion and pulled him down to part his lips with my tongue, staving off any doubts. We kissed, connecting again in our rhythm until everything faded but one single moment of ecstasy.

As we sprawled on his bed, cheese, crackers, and peanut butter on a tray, I stared pensively at the bedspread. Chase tapped me on the shoulder. "Something wrong?" he asked. "Do you want more?"

I gave him a quick smile. "I'm fine. It was wonderful. I'm just a little worried." That was the truth. Whether my flash to Zachary had been fantasy or a psychic connection, I didn't know. We were both Weres, so there was a possibility that we'd somehow homed in on each other's energy.

Whatever the case, I felt vaguely guilty, because I knew that it was the sight of Zach that had propelled me to a climax more intense than I'd ever felt before. It had been feral. Primal, even.

The thought came to mind that this must be what it was like to make love to one of the Fae, and I suddenly understood their reluctance to involve themselves with humans. But how could I possibly tell Chase what I was feeling?

I sighed and pushed my hair out of my eyes, putting the incident on hold for now. We had serious matters to discuss. No more procrastinating. I told Chase about Zachary's visit— omitting any hint of the attraction I'd felt—and my subsequent talk with Siobhan.

"So, first I need you to run Zach's name through the computer and see what you come up with, along with the names of the victims. Ten to one at least three victims won't show. I don't think there's a record of their births. And then, could you scour your informants for any mention of the Hunters Moon Clan?"

He jotted down the information, then leaned back, pulling a long sip of sparkling water. As he raised his arm, I spotted the fresh nicotine patch on his shoulder. Cigarette smoke— almost all smoke, really—was hard for both Camille and me to be around. It caused our senses to run amok. Menolly didn't care. She was a vampire, and Chase could have smoked like a chimney around her without any complaints. But he'd given it up for me and hadn't had a cigarette or cigar since the first night we slept together. He went through a lot of chewing gum and patches, but he'd been true to his word. Just another reason I didn't want to say anything that might hurt him.

"Not a problem, baby. Anything else?"

"Yeah. Would you mind asking the OIA medics if they'll examine Siobhan? She really needs to find out what's going on with her infertility problems. And she was so helpful, even though it was obvious she was scared out of her mind."

"Sure thing. Hey, I've got something for you," he said, his eyes excited.

"What?" Chase was forever buying me little trinkets. Not once had it felt like a bribe or a plea.

"Here—open it." He handed me a small box with a red rose attached to the top.

Curious, I carefully opened it, setting the flower to one side after inhaling a long whiff of its rich scent. I popped the top on the box and peeked inside. "No, you didn't!" I started to laugh.

"Hey, nobody knows my girlfriend like I know her," he said, grinning.

I pulled out the bag of catnip mice and snorted. "Have I told you lately how great you are?" I said. And sitting there naked in his bed, staring at the plastic bag that contained four overstuffed toys, I meant every word. Anybody could buy me diamonds. It took a real sweetheart to think about what I might really like to play with.

As I was getting dressed, I remembered my other promise. I let out a long sigh. "Listen, Chase, Trillian was over at our place this morning. He said you won't let him stay here alone, and he's pissed." I slid my cami over my head and shimmied into my jeans, holding my breath as I zipped them up. As I ran my hands through my hair and checked my makeup, Chase raised his eyebrows and sat down beside me on the bed.

He had carefully pulled on his creased trousers and was buttoning up his shirt. I still couldn't believe that he preferred suits to jeans, but that was Chase, Armani on the outside, muscle shirts on the inside.

He snorted. "You actually think I'd trust Trillian here alone? I don't even know what possessed me to invite him to stay with me. I must have been out of my mind." He adjusted his tie and brushed his wavy hair back.

I bit my tongue. I could have told him why he let Trillian stay here, but that would just drive another wedge between the two men, and right now we needed both of them to cooperate. And if Trillian found out I had spilled the beans, quite possibly he'd find it a delight to tell Chase that I'd charmed him, too. And I knew that finding out he'd been duped by both of us wouldn't make Chase a happy man.

"He'll find a place soon, I'm sure of it. I think he wants to be able to bring Camille here—to get her out of our house now and then." As soon as the words came out, I knew I'd said the wrong thing, but there was no going back.

Chase blanched. "You mean he wants to bring her over here to fuck her? I . . . I think I'd feel weird knowing Camille had been . . . I mean Trillian and Camille—"

I raised an eyebrow. Just what I thought. Chase was still attracted to my sister. "You can talk about her if you want," I said, slowly, realizing that I meant what I said. "I don't mind that you're attracted to her. But seriously, don't even think about suggesting a three-way, because it's not going to happen."

Chase stared at me, an unreadable look on his face. "Have I ever asked you to consider a ménage à trois? No. And would I ever ask you? No. After all," he said, giving me a faint grin, "you two could probably tear me apart if you were pissed. Tell me, what does she see in him, anyway? He's a creep, as far as I'm concerned."

I frowned, trying to think of how to best explain the complicated workings of my sister's love life. "Trillian is Svartan. Isn't that enough? Fae and Svartan sexual ethics are complicated at best, murky and cruel at worst. The dwarves and elves are far more human in their approach to sex than we are."

"What makes Svartans so special, and is it just their men?" Leading me out into the kitchen, Chase retrieved two bottles of mineral water from the refrigerator and twisted the cap off of one and handed it to me, then opened the other for himself. "I asked Camille once, but she brushed me off. I got the distinct impression she thought I was trying to compete with Mr. Suave, there."

I leaned against the counter, sipping the San Pellegrino. The bubbles tickled my nose, and I sneezed. "It's not just the men. The entire Svartan race possesses an innate sexual magnetism. When you actually *have* sex with one of them, the bond forged is harder to break than any contract humans could ever think up. Camille *belongs* to Trillian—they're bound by magic so strong that I doubt if anything except death could break it."

"You mean, they're linked on a magical level that also happens to be sexual," Chase said.

"Precisely. When she ran from him, the separation drove him crazy, and it almost tore her apart. Normally, Trillian should be able to break the bond and walk away."

"Then why doesn't he? Does he love her?"

I shrugged. "Hard to tell. But I don't think he can leave. I think that there's something about her—maybe the combination of her Moon magic and her blood turned the tables. Trillian's as hooked on her as she is on him. I can just about guarantee that he'll never let her go again." I could tell that Chase was trying to wrap his head around the whole mess, but it was a struggle. "Why do you care so much?"

"Because I want to know, so just tell me."

"Why? What could it possibly matter to you how Trillian looks at Camille?" The thought that I was playing substitute crossed my mind, and I didn't like it.

But Chase put that worry to rest. "Because she's your sister, Delilah, and she matters to you, so she matters to me. The same with Menolly, though I don't even pretend to be comfortable with the fact that she's a vampire. But I'm trying. I'm trying to understand your world, and that includes everything that touches it. I'm doing my best to fit into your life."

Taken aback, I stared at the bottle in my hand. That was an answer I hadn't expected.

"I'm sorry. I didn't mean to sound abrupt." I reached out and gently touched his arm. He gave me a long look, and I smiled. "I guess I'm just touchy. Okay, here's the thing. Trillian's an odd duck for a Svartan. He doesn't play by the rules, and he's done a lot of nasty things in his lifetime. But when it comes to Camille, he melts. He doesn't seem to care about her mixed bloodline, which is really strange, considering how elite the Svartans consider themselves. I guess he really does love her. And *love* isn't a word that applies to many Svartans."

Chase chewed on his lower lip. "It sounds like the Fae connect on a sexual level in a way that humans don't fully understand." He took on a pensive look. "What about you? Do you miss . . . being with your own kind?"

So that's what this was all about. Chase was fishing to find out whether I wanted to sleep with someone from Otherworld.

Someone not human. Which meant he really did care about me. Otherwise, it wouldn't matter.

When I thought about my reaction to Zachary, it occurred to me that perhaps Chase had a right to be worried. Shit, I so didn't want to think about all this today. I wanted to just shake it all off and say, "Relax! Does it have to be so complicated?" but I knew Chase would never go for that spiel. He wanted answers. The question was, would it matter to him what those answers turned out to be?

Frustrated, I tried to dodge the inevitable.

"Sex *is* a powerhouse of energy for the Fae. But when you talk about Svartans, it goes deeper than that. Sex is part of their very essence, and anybody they sleep with is in danger of becoming hooked. Camille willingly bound herself to the addiction. It suits her nature. It wouldn't work for me or Menolly. Then again, we have our own quirks when it comes to the bedroom."

I hadn't told Chase that I had sex with tomcats when I was in Were form. Somehow, I didn't think he was ready to hear that yet. As for Menolly, neither Camille nor I knew how she satisfied herself now that she was a vampire. I wasn't sure I *wanted* to know. The answer might scare the hell out of me.

I paused, then softly said, "Chase, you know I'm new to sex. You know I haven't slept with my father's kind yet. That may happen, and probably will. But for now, I'm with you. For now, I'm happy with that fact. I can't promise to be a one-man woman. Not yet. But I *can* promise that I'm being honest when I say I love being with you. You're a good man, and sexy, and I enjoy what we have together."

He grunted. The conversation had run its course.

"So, how do I get the varmint out of my house without getting skewered?" he said. "He makes me nervous."

"You could help him find an apartment. Trillian's brilliant, but he has no idea how to look for a place that both suits his needs and his coffers."

Chase snorted. "I love it when you talk all archaic, woman. *Coffers*; I haven't heard that in years. But you're probably right, though I don't know about the brilliant part. I'll get a copy of the classifieds and help him look. Maybe I can get him out of here in short order. Since he's Svartan, he can damned well turn on that charm and convince potential landlords to lower the rent."

I started to say, "What are you thinking?" but then shut my mouth. Chase and Trillian would be much happier when they ended the roommate shtick.

"I'd better get home," I said, looking at the clock. "And aren't you due back on duty soon, Detective?"

He flashed me a guilty grin. "Yeah, but it's been slow lately. Everyone's behaving themselves as far as I know. I'll run those names through the computer and give you a call later tonight when I see what I come up with. Oh—and what's your friend's name again? And her number? For the medics?"

"Siobhan Morgan. Her number is 555-7325."

He wrote it down. "Siobhan, that's right. I'll have one of the OIA medics give her a call and see if they can help her out." He kissed me gently on the forehead, then pulled me to him and full-on Frenched me.

After I came up for air, he walked me to the parking lot. The snow was starting to fall in earnest. I shivered. Winter was a harsh season, following the frozen lacework of frost trailing from the Autumn Lord's wake. I glanced at the ground, which was covered with a thin layer of white.

"I wonder how long this will keep up," Chase said.

"Camille could tell you. She's tied into the weather. Lightning, snow, anything that comes in on the winds, she's tuned into." I opened the door to my Jeep and swung into the driver's seat. "Talk to you later, babe."

Chase waved as I eased onto the road and headed for home. As the flakes fell from the sky, I had a nasty feeling that the storm presaged a bigger one just over the horizon.

When I pulled into the driveway, Camille's Lexus was already there, which meant that she'd closed the shop early. As I dashed up the steps and into the house, laughter echoed from the living room. I peeked around the corner to see Iris and

Camille decorating a tree that was at least twelve feet high. It almost reached the ceiling, and they were bedecking it with crystal moons and golden sun faces and ivory balls with glittering gold trim.

"Iris, I have your package from the Fairy Tale." I held out the box.

"Wonderful!" She motioned to the recliner. "That's my Midwinter gown. Put it on the chair, would you? What do you think?"

As I laid the box on the chair, I gazed around at the brilliantly decorated living room. A garland of strung cranberries wound around the tree. Swags of evergreens held together by big burgundy ribbons and gold garland scalloped their way around the ceiling. Iris stood back, a beatific look on her face. She clapped her hands, and an ornament rose up in the air, hovered for a moment, then carefully flew up to attach itself to one of the upper boughs.

"You and your hearth magic," I said, grinning. "That stuff sure comes in handy."

She nodded. "If it's related to tending the house, chances are I can enchant it."

Camille was beaming. She held out her arm, and I walked over and wrapped my arm around her waist as she leaned her head against my shoulder.

"I wish Mother was alive . . . that she could be here to see this," I said, wistfully. "It's so beautiful. You know she'd love it."

"That she would," Camille said. "Father, too. I just wish we had some word from him. I don't like worrying like this. Trillian took off for Otherworld to see if he can find out anything. He's going to hunt down Aunt Rythwar and make sure she's okay, and see if she has any information for us."

My irritation faded. Trillian was all right, if you overlooked his natural tendencies. He'd helped us out more than once, and in fact almost lost his life for us. And it looked like he would continue to stand by our side.

The light outside the living room window faded, and the sound of a door closing echoed from the kitchen. Sure enough, after a moment Menolly came gliding in to join us. She never needed more than a moment to fully wake, and another to dress. Her alarm clock was set for the moment dusk hit. She was wearing a pair of black cargo pants and a cobalt-blue long-sleeved V-neck. She looked absolutely gorgeous.

"I see you've been busy while I slept," she said, giving us a toothy grin. I swallowed a queasy feeling when I saw her fangs were partially extended.

"Your tips are showing," I said.

She blinked and ran her tongue around her teeth. "Oops, pardon me. I'm hungry tonight. I'll probably leave early to feed."

Camille nodded, but my attention had turned elsewhere. One of the ornaments on the tree was a beautiful ivory-colored peacock with a long, glittering tail. Something about the feathers made me catch my breath. My nose twitched. Oh hell. I tried to turn, to warn Camille, but was too late. The room began to swirl and, dizzy, I fell into the waiting vortex. A swirl of chaos, a nexus of bodies and forms, spun out of control as I folded into myself, crossing realities, crossing dimensions.

Flash. Tall and blonde on two feet, neither human nor Fae but some strange blend that became a third race unto itself. Hands shrank into paws, nails to claws. Spine lengthened, ears shifted. A wave of sensuality flowed through me as I rolled my head back, reveling as the transformation sped me along a current against which I could not fight.

Flash. Golden fur on four feet, neither cat nor true Were, but a mixture of bloodlines and magic converging into flesh. Everything shifted, and the room grew larger as I grew smaller. Color faded as I entered a world where the only constants were shades of gray. The air became saturated with scent. Camille's perfume, Iris's cinnamon gum, the fir tree's needles, the smell of dinner cooking in the kitchen . . . Everything smelled so incredibly strong that it sent me reeling.

And then I blinked again, and all was done.

I glanced down at my feet, at the golden fur that quivered in the slightest breeze. I was home again. There were times I wished I never had to change back. Life was easier, choices more simple, and the world seemed clear-cut. *Changeling*, the children at school used to call me. *Changeling*, they taunted me. And *Changeling*, they envied me, because they knew how much I reveled in my alter ego, and how much I hated coming back each time.

And then instinct took over, and I shook off my memories. The room loomed large with the promise of excitement as I focused on the bright, shiny toys dangling just out of reach. The swags were so tempting, looping down on the walls. And the tree—oh the tree! It was a glorious mountain, beckoning me, a medley of toys awaiting the chase. My nose twitched, and I let out a half purr, half mew.

Unable to stop myself, I took off, racing around the room in a frenzied dash that seemed to be just the right thing to do at the time.

Camille lunged at me, but she was huge and clumsy, and I let out a *purp* as I dodged to the side, a blur of orange fur. No way in hell was she putting a stop to my plans, whatever they might be. I'd know what they were when I got there.

I dashed between her legs and as she stumbled, I heard a vague "Oh fuck!" The floor shook as her shins made full-body contact with the coffee table, and she went sprawling across it with a loud "Oof!"

Menolly jumped in my path. Her reflexes were better than mine, so I jagged a hard left, and my tufted feet slid across the floor as I hit the brakes, spinning and heading directly for the tree.

It was Iris's turn, but a four-footed wonder like me could outrun any house sprite. I sprang over her head, landing on the lower limbs of the tree. The moment I felt the boughs beneath my feet, I scrambled, climbing through the branches, disregarding the sound of breaking ornaments.

As I frantically climbed—no longer sure just what my original plan had been—the sap and resin began to stick to my fur.

Oh shit, everybody was going to be pissed as hell at me. Amid a growing panic, I made my way into the upper regions of the tree, where I found a spot in which to snuggle, right under a delicate five-pointed star that lit up the room like fireworks on the Queen's birthday. Nervous, I peeked out of the branches. I felt safe in my little cubbyhole made of fir branches, and I could see the entire room from my vantage point.

Dizzy with accomplishment, I began to purr.

Down below, Camille and Iris were in an uproar. Iris was grumbling what sounded like obscenities in some obscure Finnish dialect, while Camille was shaking her finger at me.

"You come down here this instant, Delilah! Do you hear me? I know you understand what I'm saying!" She rested her hands on her hips and glared at me.

Vaguely irritated, I let out a loud yowl. Just then, a noise startled me, and I swung my head, only to see Menolly hovering near me.

Damned . . . silent . . . vampire . . . whatever it was . . .

As she reached for me, whispering, "Here, Kitten, come with me," I decided to forgo the assist. If they wanted me out of the tree, I'd get out of the tree, but I'd do it *my* way. I gingerly pawed my way out on the branch, but it was too thin, and the next thing I knew, I lost my footing and went sliding down the slopes of Mount Fir in a wild ride, taking any and every ornament with me that was in my path.

Iris yelled something, and I heard Camille give a loud shout. The next thing I knew, I landed hard on the floor, and the shock jolted me so much that I abruptly began to shift back. Too quickly, it seemed, because I was still caught up in the tree limbs, and when my legs lengthened, I twisted wrong.

"Oh shit, look out!"

Menolly's voice cut through my brain fog. I blinked amid the pile of broken glass and boughs that I was lying in and looked over my shoulder just in time to see the twelve-foot fir sway as it gracefully toppled in my direction.

"Out of the way!" Camille screamed, and she and Iris ran for the hall. Menolly lurched midair and fell to the floor in a heap, her concentration broken. As for me, it was like being caught in a nightmare where I knew something horrible was about to happen but found myself paralyzed, unable to move as events played out in slow motion.

I ducked my head under my arm and pressed my face into the rug as the thundering fir, complete with decorations, landed across my back, covering me in a pile of scratchy branches and broken glass. The tub of water the tree had been sitting in tipped as well and streamed along the floor to soak my legs and feet. I breathed very slowly while I waited for the fallout to settle.

"Delilah! Delilah, are you okay?" Camille's frantic voice spiraled into a throaty shriek from the left side of the tree.

"Kitten? Kitten?" Menolly peered through the branches on the right side, though she was cautious to avoid any pointy limbs that might act as a natural stake. "You alive?"

I managed to croak out a reply. "If I wasn't, what would you do? Turn me into a vampire?"

"I couldn't if you were already dead. Maybe Camille could manage to zombify you, but—"

"It was a joke, damn it!" I struggled to pull myself out from under the tree. So far, nothing seemed to be broken. "Help me get out of this mess."

Menolly lifted the tree, while Camille pulled me up and dusted me off. Covered with sap and scratches, I gingerly moved each leg and arm, then rolled my neck and shrugged my shoulders.

"Nothing broken," I said.

"Maybe we should have thought this out better," Camille said, looking woefully at the downed tree.

"Didn't Mother used to attach the tree to the top of the ceiling when we were girls?" Menolly asked.

I blushed, both embarrassed and yet defiant. I couldn't help it if bright, shiny toys were so tempting. When I'd been a little girl, it had been a lot worse. "Gee, I guess I'd better avoid shopping too much during the holiday season, or things could get really ugly, really fast."

The thought of passing by dozens of decked-out trees was a little more than I could handle. At least this had happened at home, where I could slink off to my room without having the good citizens of Seattle pointing at me and yelling, "Grinch!"

As we surveyed the mess—Iris with a few tears in her

eyes—the phone rang. She went to get it, and I sighed as Menolly righted the tree. Camille found a sturdy length of wire and a large screw hook and handed them to Menolly, who floated up to the ceiling and began anchoring the fir—which wasn't terribly worse for the wear—against any further mishap. I was about to fetch the broom and dustpan when Iris peeked around the corner.

"Phone for you, Delilah. I'll clean up. And tomorrow I'll buy new ornaments," she said. I could tell she was pissed. She'd worked her butt off on decorating the living room, and I'd just destroyed her winter wonderland in under five minutes. My track record was getting better. Or worse, depending on how you looked at it.

"I'll take the call in the kitchen," I said, hurrying past her with a gentle, "I'm sorry." As I picked up the phone and peered out the kitchen window at the still-falling snow, I was surprised to hear Zachary's voice on the other end.

"Delilah?" He sounded out of breath, unusual for a Were who was as fit as he'd looked.

"Yep, it's me. What's up?" His voice sent chills up my spine, and they weren't unpleasant. The thought that maybe he was calling to ask for a date flickered through my mind, but I quickly pushed it aside.

"You'll still be coming out here tomorrow, won't you?"

"Yeah," I said, and the urgency in his voice told me something was wrong. "What's wrong? What happened?"

"There's been another murder," he said. "One of our guards patrolling the compound's been killed. He was found near the arrastra, just like the others. Delilah, we have to find out who's doing this before everybody's dead."

As I stared at the phone, I spied a spider crawling up the wall and, without missing a beat, slammed my hand against it, squashing it flat.

"We'll be there," I said, staring at the blood and guts on my skin before wiping them on a paper towel. "Zachary, don't let anybody go out alone. In fact, I'd call everybody in for the night."

"Yeah," he said, sounding frustrated. "I just hate leaving

our borders unprotected. But we'll just leave the guards at the main gate and up the ante to four instead of two." He paused, then added, "I'll see you tomorrow night then."

"Until then," I said and hung up. We had to find out more about the Hunters Moon Clan. And I knew one sure way, though the thought scared the hell out of me.

We could pay a visit to the Autumn Lord, who ruled over the season of sacrifice. The lord of spiders and bats, of crisp autumn leaves and mists that rose in the night, he was Jack Frost's master. The Autumn Lord lived in a palace of frost and flame high in the Northlands, only reachable by traveling on the north wind. But if anybody could tell us about the were-spider clan, it would be him. And there would most likely be a steep price to pay for his help.

CHAPTER 6

I peeked back into the living room, my stomach twisted in knots. The thought of traipsing off to visit one of the Elemental Lords scared the crap out of me, and I already knew what Camille and Menolly would have to say about the idea. The Autumn Lord was bound to this world, but he also lived in the world of the Elementals. He was related to the Lord of Flames, who ruled a large city in the realm of the dead, though I wasn't clear on their connection.

Then again, when I thought about it, tripping into the arms of somebody bound to the underworld was a lot more appetizing than coping with the denizens of the Subterranean Realms. At least the underworld could be a beautiful and peaceful place, depending on where you were hanging out. The Sub Realms were just nasty.

Iris was sweeping up the mess in the living room. Or rather, the broom was doing the work while she supervised. Menolly had anchored the tree to the ceiling, and they were all debating on what kind of ornaments to redecorate with.

"What do you think will have the least chance of setting you off, Delilah?" Camille asked, turning as I entered the room.

I blinked. Now there was a thought I hadn't even entertained. Anxious to forestall the inevitable fireworks when I told them about Zachary's phone call and my idea, I gave it some thought.

"I tend to go for dangly, shiny things. How about those satin balls? They aren't that sparkly, and they don't break. At least not unless you step on them."

Iris piped up. "Good idea! I also am thinking resin ornaments might work. Of course, I could just erect a barrier to keep animals out, and that might do the trick."

"You can do that?" I asked.

She nodded. "It was a spell my family originally used to keep household dogs and cats out of the larders, but I could easily adapt it to just surround the tree. It won't hurt you. I promise. Consider it a mild deterrent."

"What about when I'm not in cat form?"

"I doubt that it will affect you out of your Were-form," she said, frowning. "I can't promise, but I'm fairly certain."

The broom finished its work and fell to the floor, the dustpan landing beside it after emptying debris into the trash can one last time. I stared at the remains of the blown glass baubles and balls and sighed.

"I really mucked it up this time, didn't I? Iris, why don't you put the delicate ornaments up top, get some satin and resin ones for the lower branches, and then go ahead and use your spell. I'll try to keep myself under control." I didn't want to destroy the holidays, and when I thought about our childhood, this was pretty much the way our mother had taken care of the issue.

Iris relented. "Okay. Just be good, please? I'll go put the kettle on for tea. We've had quite enough excitement for one evening," she said, bustling out of the room, taking the trash can with her.

I motioned for Menolly and Camille to join me on the sofa. "If only Iris was right, and the excitement is over, but it's not." I glared at the tree.

"What's going on?" Camille turned down the music—Tchaikovsky's *Nutcracker*—and curled up on my left side. Menolly snuggled up on my right, and we held hands like we had when we were little.

I told them about Zachary's call and my visit to Siobhan. "So, the Hunters Moon Clan is a nest of unnatural werespiders. *Hobo* werespiders."

Camille looked ready to swallow her tongue. "I'm not afraid of spiders, but this isn't exactly Charlotte hanging out in the barn, is it? Spiders don't think. Werespiders have all the natural cunning of regular spiders *plus* intelligence. And if they're an abomination, who knows what other abilities they have? Yuck." She shuddered.

"Tell me about it." I was about to bring up my idea about visiting the Autumn Lord when the phone rang again. I grabbed the cordless phone in the living room. It was Chase.

"Hey, Puss, got the info you wanted. Or what I could dredge up," he said.

"Let me get a pen," I said.

"If you want, but I didn't find out that much."

"I'm putting you on speakerphone," I said, motioning to Camille and Menolly to listen in. I punched the button and picked up a notebook and pen. "Can you hear me? Go ahead."

Chase's voice sounded tinny coming over the speaker. "Okay, here it is. I got a hit on Zachary Lyonnesse. He was arrested two years ago for a bar brawl. He blamed the other guy for starting it, but when neither one would press charges, the case was dropped and they were both let go with a warning."

"Who was he fighting with?" I asked, writing down the information so I didn't forget it. It was better to err on the side of caution; I didn't want us making any mistakes we couldn't undo.

"Geph von Spynne."

"Spell it, please?"

Chase spelled it out and then continued. "He's a tall, gangly dude with short, spiked brown hair. He and Lyonnesse were really going at it. Zachary took a nasty knife wound to the shoulder. Doc counted thirty stitches to sew him up, but apparently Lyonnesse refused anesthesia. Didn't want any pain pills afterward, either. The witnesses in the bar say the two were out for blood."

Geph von Spynne. I didn't recognize the name, but it sounded oddly familiar, like I should know it but had just forgotten. "Your informants have anything on the Hunters Moon Clan or this von Spynne character?"

Chase cleared his throat. "Uh, no. The minute I mentioned his name—and the Hunters Moon Clan—all three of them clammed up and wouldn't say a word, even for the promise of a twenty-dollar bill. And these are guys that would rat out their mother for a shot of whiskey. My bet is that they know something, all right, but are too afraid to say anything. If you can find out anything more, I suggest you do. We should probably add this information to our database."

I blinked. "We'll do what we can. Did anybody talk to Siobhan?"

"On that score," his voice lightened, "we have better news. Jacinth set up an appointment to give her a thorough examination. With a little luck, we may be able to solve your friend's problem."

With a little luck . . . "Thanks, sugar," I said. "I'll talk to you tomorrow." As I hung up, I realized I'd developed a lump the size of a baseball in my stomach.

"Well, not much to go on," Camille said, frowning. "Where do we start?"

"I can comb the dregs at the Wayfarer for information," Menolly offered. "Somebody there might know something."

"Hold on." I raised my hand. "Something crossed my mind earlier this afternoon. The Hunters Moon Clan are spiderlings. They could have spies hiding out anywhere. In the corners of the bar. Or the house," I said softly, eying the ceiling.

"We aren't even certain they have anything to do with the murders out at the Puma Pride enclave. Why would they have spies in the Wayfarer?" Menolly floated up to the ceiling and tinkered with the guy wire holding the tree in place. "There, that should do it," she said and returned to the floor.

"I have a hunch about this," I said. "Trust me; they're involved. And I know who we can talk to in order to dig deeper into their secrets, but I don't think you're going to like it. It's risky, but I think we have to chance it."

"Who are you talking about?" Camille said. "What risk?"

Menolly gazed at me, her eyes a pale frost that burrowed into my heart. "I know who you're talking about, and you're out of your mind."

I stared back at her, straightening my shoulders. "I know perfectly well what risks we'd run, but, Menolly, there's a lot more going on here than just a serial killer out to knock off the Puma Weres. *I know it.* I wish you'd believe me and show a little trust in my instincts."

"Kitten," she said softly, her gaze piercing right through me. The fact that Menolly seldom blinked still freaked me out. I turned my head to shake off her stare. It was a vampire thing; she'd never had that effect on me before. "It's not that we don't trust you, it's just that—"

"That's enough! I've had it." I stood, hands on hips, and faced down the both of them. "You both think I'm just a naïve blonde bimbo, right? That I'm the baby of the family who can't think for—or take care of—herself?"

Camille sputtered, trying to backtrack. "Delilah, please. We never said anything like that. Neither one of us thinks you're stupid—"

"Just shut up and listen to *me* for once. Okay?" Fretting, I could feel the edges blurring. I closed my eyes and tried to keep control. The last thing I needed was to shift twice in one night. I took three deep breaths while they waited.

"Okay. Here's the thing," I said. "Both of you act like I'm full of bubbles, all happy-happy joy-joy. But that's not true. Not anymore, at least. Make no mistake about it; I *liked* believing in the good in people. I *love* sunshine and flowers and chasing mice. But all that's been cut short, thanks to Bad Ass Luke. Wisteria didn't help nurture my delusions, either. And I am so fucking pissed about it."

I still had a scar from where the renegade floraed had bitten my neck, trying to sever the artery. She was securely locked up back in Otherworld in the Elfin Queen's dungeon, however, so I tried to put her out of my mind.

Camille broke in. "Heard and noted, Delilah." She turned to Menolly. "I trust her hunches. She has cat magic. If her instincts are telling her this is the way to go, then I say let's do it. I wish I had half as much gut reaction as she gets. I have prescience thanks to my magical training, but it's not inborn. And you . . ." She stopped, then closed her mouth. Menolly had never had a sixth sense, unlike Camille and me.

"And I . . . don't have anything of the sort except my reflexes. And, thanks to being a vampire, my hearing and undead-detector." Menolly gave her a toothy grin. "It's the truth; don't be shy about it. You're right. I tend to forget that cats can pick up on things we can't. In fact, I'd be surprised if Kitten here didn't have some other tricks up her sleeve that we haven't seen yet."

She flashed me a knowing look, and I glanced away. She'd hit the nail on the head, but I wasn't ready to talk about it yet. I was only now discovering the faint whisper of new abilities, too new for even *me* to understand. They'd shown up after I slept with Chase and fought the demons.

"So what is it you think we should do?" Camille asked softly. She leaned over the back of the sofa, placing her milk-white hands on my shoulders. I could feel the surge of the Moon Mother working within her. We were all changing, I thought. Changing and evolving. Camille's power was different. Not much, but enough so that I noticed.

I took a deep breath and let it out slowly. "We should travel to the Northlands to visit the Autumn Lord. He rules over everything that creeps in the autumn, including spiders. If anybody knows anything about the Hunters Moon Clan, he would. Siobhan told me that rumor has it an evil shaman created the clan a thousand years back. If that's true, then they've had a thousand years to nest and grow strong. What I want to know is, why haven't they attacked before now? What's kept them in check? If they're behind these attacks, what set them off? Could it have anything to do with Shadow Wing?"

As my words spilled into the room, Iris entered, carrying a tea tray with a floral pot on it that was steaming, and three cups. She also had added a goblet of blood for Menolly, and a plate of cookies.

She carefully slid the tray onto the coffee table and then, hands on her hips, stared up at me. "Are you daft? You think you can just waltz into the realm of the Autumn Lord and say, 'Hey, dude, tell me about the spider nests . . .'?"

The word *dude* sounded so out of place coming from Iris that we all cracked up laughing. She arched her eyebrows and, with a haughty look, said, "Be good, or I'll scatter pixie dust in your beds and you'll be itching for weeks."

"Yes ma'am," Menolly said, a flicker of a smile on her face. Iris was one person to whom she never talked back, yelled at, or was short with. Camille and I suspected that Iris and Maggie gave Menolly more stability than she'd had since her initial transformation. She relied on the innocence of the baby gargoyle and the domesticity of the house sprite to remind her of what her life had been like.

I accepted a cup of tea and sniffed the steam rising off the surface. It smelled like honeycomb and orange blossoms. "Mmm, Richya blossom tea?"

Iris nodded. "I made a quick trip back to Otherworld last week to pick up a few things. I knew you girls like Richya blossom tea, so stocked up while I was there." Our unspoken question hung thick in the air, and Iris sighed and sat down with her own cup and saucer. "I didn't go to Y'Elestrial, girls, so I can't tell you what's happening there. But your father is right; war has surely broken out by now. The signs were everywhere."

All talk of the Autumn Lord was shoved to the side for a moment as thoughts of home filled our hearts.

"Where did you go?" Camille asked, her face a mask of longing.

"I went to Aladril, the City of Seers. They remain neutral in the fight between Tanaquar and Lethesanar. They refuse to take sides, and they've enough magic to frighten off anybody even thinking of trying to force their hand." Iris blinked and sipped her tea.

Aladril was magnificent, a city of spires and minarets that rose halfway to heaven. Sculpted from gleaming marble, no one knew how long the city had existed, only that it had come through the mists into Otherworld shortly after the Great Divide, intact and already ancient. It was a magical city, and while visitors were welcome, the majority of business went on behind closed doors. Whether the seers in question were human or Fae, no one knew. They certainly *looked* human, but the fact was they were far too long-lived to *be* human, and they kept to themselves except for the vendors and the guards of the city.

We settled in with our tea, and Menolly with her goblet of blood.

"Back to the matter at hand. So, you think we should go to the Northlands," Menolly said, raising her glass in a toast.

"It's a difficult journey. How would we get there? The portals won't take us. At least, I don't think they will."

Iris shook her head. "You girls are messing with powers that you're better off leaving alone. The Autumn Lord is an Elemental Lord. His kind are dangerous at best. Robyn, Prince of Oaks, has led both Fae and human alike to believe that all of the Elemental folk are kindly toward flesh-and-blood beings, but it's simply not true." A whimpering from the kitchen stopped her. Iris stood and set down her cup of tea. "Maggie's awake. I'll go fetch her."

As she left the room, Camille took a deep breath and let it out slowly. "I think I know how we can get to his realm, but we're going to owe, and owe big, if I'm right."

"How?" I said, leaning back and curling my legs beneath me. Between the warmth radiating off the flames from the fireplace and the tea, I was starting to drift. Almost time for a nap.

Camille cleared her throat. "Smoky could probably take us on his back."

That stopped traffic. Menolly sputtered as I shot up in my chair.

"Holy crap, Camille," I said. "You do realize that he could ask *anything* from us for that kind of a favor? Smoky might be honorable—as honorable as dragons can be—but he loves to play games. He won't miss out on the chance to keep score on this one."

Camille shrugged. "If we need to talk to the Autumn Lord, then Smoky's our best bet to get there. He lived up in the Northlands years ago, he told me. Maybe he can fly between the worlds to reach there."

I knew she was right. Menolly must have, too, because she drained her glass and set it back on the tray. "How about a compromise? We'll have a look at Zachary's land and get a feel for what's going on, and then we make a decision. If there's any sign this Hunters Moon Clan had a hand in the murders, then we ask Smoky for a ride." As an afterthought, she added, "Grandmother Coyote wouldn't be able to help us, would she? She's a safer bet."

"Safer my ass. Remember the price I had to pay for the information on Shadow Wing?" Camille said. "But I think Delilah's right. The Elementals may be more apt to get involved with world affairs than the Hags of Fate."

I mulled over Menolly's proposal. "Okay, we'll do it your way. I guess we don't want to run off half-cocked until we actually know what we're dealing with. I just . . . it's just this feeling." And when I searched the corners of my thoughts, there it was: the sense that the Hunters Moon Clan was involved. The moment Siobhan had mentioned them, it was as if an alarm went off in my head, screaming, "Beware, Beware!"

"If that's all, I'm for bed," Camille said, glancing at the clock as she pushed herself to her feet.

"No Trillian? No Morio?" Menolly said, grinning.

"Not tonight. Trillian's back in OW, remember? And Morio . . . I opted out for the night." Camille gave her a hug, then reached for me. I held her tight and rubbed her back. "I'm too tired to think, let alone spread my legs," she added.

"I'm going to nap for a couple of hours," I said. "I'll be down in a bit," I told Menolly, who reached for her jacket. "Are you headed for the Wayfarer?"

She nodded. "Yeah, I'm on shift tonight. I'm leaving early, though, to catch a bite of supper before I get there."

Trying not to cringe, I shot her a wink. "Don't drink too much," I said. "And call if there's any problem. We'll have our cells with us."

As Menolly vanished out the door and we heard her Jag pull out of the driveway, Camille yawned.

Iris returned from the kitchen with a full and happy Maggie. "I took her outside, so she's done her business for the night. Are you girls turning in already? I thought we might have a game of Trivia Mania: Fae Facts." She shifted Maggie, who *moophed* at us twice, to one hip and held up a box.

It hadn't taken long after we came out of the Otherworld closet for consumerism to catch up, and now there was a host of games, outfits, action figures, and other merchandising capitalizing on our appearance. The Trivia Mania people actually took the time to talk to us in order to get their facts right. As a result, several of the more prominent Fae who'd settled Earthside and were rapidly becoming well-known figures in the community had given the game their seal of approval.

Camille gave me a look that said we were in for a late night and started clearing off the coffee table. Maggie took turns sitting on our laps. Her soft fur felt good against my hand as I stroked her head, scratching her between the ears, and her cinnamon-scented breath helped ease some of the tension out of my body. Even though I was tired, it was nice to take my mind off of murdered werepumas and the Hunters Moon Clan for a while.

The next night, everyone was fairly quiet on the drive out to the Puma Pride enclave. The day had been long, Camille hadn't heard back from Trillian yet, and we were all worried about Father and Aunt Rythwar. Menolly had learned nothing at the Wayfarer on her shift last night about the Hunters Moon Clan, Geph von Spynne, or Zachary Lyonnesse. And none of us were any closer to finding references to the Jansshi demons or how to kill them.

Chase had been short with me on the phone when I called him after lunch. He was working on a case that threatened to blow wide open. An OW dwarf had been murdered down near the Seattle docks. Chase confided in me that he was worried the Guardian Watchdogs had finally crossed the line from rhetoric into action. If so, the shit was about to hit the fan.

The Fae wouldn't stand by if they thought some selfrighteous, paranoid bigots had gunned down one of their own. Chase didn't have much time to find the murderer and bring him to justice. And the OIA hadn't put in so much as a peep on the subject. My gut told me that we were on our own over here, Earthside.

Civil war in Otherworld, demons marching from the Sub Realms, and Earth hanging smack in the middle. What a *delightful* year it had turned out to be.

Camille drove, while Morio sat beside her. He was looking good. I liked Morio, though I didn't find him attractive in a sexual way. But today his shoulder-length long hair was sleeked back in a smooth ponytail, and his goatee and pencil moustache were neatly trimmed. He looked sleek but not effeminate.

"Everybody ready for this?" Camille asked.

"Yeah," I said, shifting in my seat. I'd worn a pair of leggings under a tunic that reached my upper thighs. A pair of soft leather boots laced up to my knees. Like the skirt and tunic Camille was wearing, my clothes were woven from spider-silk and would keep me warm and yet leave me free to glide through the undergrowth without a problem.

When we reached the junction leading to Elkins Road, Camille turned left. It was five thirty and already dark. The sun was setting around four thirty nowadays, well on its way toward the longest night of the year. Menolly relished winter, with its dark nights that seemed to stretch on forever, giving her extra time in which to walk the world.

As I used a pocket-sized flashlight to read the map that Zachary had given me, I glanced out the window. The moon had yet to rise, but I could still feel her there. Camille and I were bound to the pull of her tides, and I found myself dallying, wondering what the nights of the full moon must be like at the Puma Pride compound with everyone shifting. A sudden longing to be with others who understood what it was like to be twice-natured hit me, and Zachary's face appeared unbidden in my thoughts.

I let out a long sigh and stared ahead, suddenly feeling isolated. Attempting to return my focus to the map, I looked up to find Morio staring over his shoulder at me, a knowing look on his face. He, too, was a shape-shifter, though not a Were. But while he could understand on some levels, he wasn't at the mercy of the Moon and her monthly demands.

"There's the turnoff," Camille said, interrupting my thoughts. To the left side of the road twin posts buttressed a gate between them, and standing beside both posts were hefty men carrying shotguns. We pulled to a stop by the gate, and I jumped out of the backseat and approached the nearest.

"I'm Delilah D'Artigo, and these are my sisters. Zachary's

expecting us," I said, wary of the arsenal they carried. The men didn't look friendly, and they were dressed in camouflage, which made me even more nervous. I'd brought my knife, but I didn't think it would do much good, especially against two burly bullet-wielding musclemen. Nope, especially when both of them were Supes.

They looked me over, then peered in the car. "Who's that?" the taller one sporting a buzz cut asked.

"Our friend, Morio. He's an Earthside Supe," I said. I thought they were going to pat me down, and I would have put up an unholy fuss if they did, but the man just grunted, then nodded me back into the car.

"Go through the gate and keep driving straight until you see the big house on the hill. Park in the driveway and knock on the front door. Don't go anywhere else without permission, you hear me? That goes for all of you," he added.

I blinked. *Not so friendly, are we?* I thought. Of course, they'd just had several murders in their Pride. It only made sense to be cautious.

"Got it," I said.

Camille gave them a slow smile, Menolly stared out the window, and Morio just kept his mouth shut. He wasn't much of a talker except when it came to Camille.

The guards stood back and let us through. Camille eased the car onto the dirt road, and we headed for the heart of the Rainier Puma Pride. My pulse raced when I thought about seeing Zachary again. I tried to visualize Chase's face to keep me grounded but couldn't ignore the feeling that Zach and I'd met for some reason. Some nexus point in fate had drawn the werepuma to me.

Along the road, other houses dotted the land. Some were small affairs—cottages really—while others were full double-decker farmhouses. How long had the Puma Pride made their home here? No doubt the cougars around the area found it a safe haven away from hunters and poachers.

Ahead, the road wound up a slope and to the right onto a dirt driveway, where several cars and trucks were parked. Camille eased into an open spot, and we turned our attention to the house that loomed over us. Three stories high, it was huge, a mansion really, and looked like it had been crafted by artisans rather than construction workers. The newel posts and railings leading up to the porch were hand-worked and freshly oiled. The door and walls were solid hardwood. As we sat there, staring at what seemed a palace totally out of place, Camille sucked in a deep breath.

"There are wards embedded in those walls," she said. "Magical protection. Somebody here knows their spell work."

We slipped out of the car and started for the steps just as the door opened. Zachary came running out to meet us, his face a mask of care and concern. He put his hands on my shoulders and stared at me, his eyes blurring with tears.

"Delilah, I'm so glad you came. We lost another member. Shawn, one of my cousins. You have to help us find this psycho."

CHAPTER 7

Zachary leaned against the porch railing as three men followed him out of the house. Fear emanated off of them like heat waves in summer.

All the men had a similar look, which made me wonder just how far inbreeding had worked its way through the Puma Pride. With golden hair and eyes the color of topaz, all the men had broad noses and were tall and muscled. The others appeared older than Zachary, and one had a nasty limp. I shivered, wondering what was setting me on edge, and then I realized that my body was responding to being near a pack of male Weres. They might be puma, and I might be tabby, but we were all felines, and like recognizes like.

Camille, Menolly, and Morio stepped up to shield my back. I locked Zachary's gaze, then nodded over my shoulders at the others. "My sisters, Camille and Menolly. And Morio. He's a good friend of ours."

Zachary composed himself and shook his head. "Thank you for coming."

"I'm sorry about your cousin," I said, my words thin comfort in the cold and snowy night. The storm had settled in, and we had several inches on the ground by now.

Camille reached out her hand, and Zachary hesitantly took it. "It's a shame, meeting under these circumstances. Is your cousin . . . is he still where you found him?"

Zach nodded and dashed his hand across his eyes. "Yes, I persuaded the Council to leave him there until you arrived. I thought maybe you might notice something we overlooked."

"Why don't you take us there?" I said.

He motioned for us to follow him around the side of the house. The three men who had followed him out of the house swung in behind us, taking up the rear. One gave a little hiss at Menolly, who merely shot him a long, studied look. He closed his mouth and stared at the ground the rest of the way.

The mansion was huge, and we walked for several minutes before it vanished from sight. Zach led us along a trail that entered a widespread copse of trees. As we passed into the forest, he trekked on a few yards ahead of the rest of us. I caught up to him.

"I wish we could have arrived sooner, but we had to wait until sunset. I wanted Menolly to be able to join us. She has incredibly acute senses."

"She's a vampire, isn't she?" he asked, staring at the snow-lined trail. The moon would be up in another hour, but by the looks of the weather, she would be obscured by clouds. The light from the snow reflected off the cloud cover, and the sky flickered with that shimmering light that always presaged a snowfall. With everyone in the group being a Supe of one sort or another, we were able to make our way by only the twilight glow that illuminated the night.

I let out a long sigh. "Menolly's still considered a newborn vamp; she was turned twelve Earthside years ago, but she's undergone rigorous training in order to control her urges. She's safe to be around unless you piss her off bad enough, or unless you're a pervert. Camille and I have her back, by the way, so make your men aware of our feelings, especially if you think there might be a need. Any upraised hand against Menolly will net the offender a hole in the ground."

Even though Zachary sparked off a hidden flame inside me, my loyalty and oaths to my family always won out.

"Understood," he said. "No one will bother her, though I'll tell you now that Tyler doesn't like vamps. He'll behave himself, though." As we came to the edge of the wood, he raised his hand, gesturing for us to pause. "We'll be back in just a moment," he said, motioning for his friends to join him off to one side.

"What's that all about?" Camille asked.

I gave her a veiled grin. "I think he's warning them to keep their paws off of us—all of us. I heard the hiss," I said, glancing apologetically at Menolly. "I reminded Zach that sneering wasn't considered a polite way to treat guests whom you've asked for help."

Menolly let out a snort. "As if those puny Weres could frighten me. But thank you, Kitten," she added softly. "You know I've got your back, too."

"You're growing up, babe." Camille sounded pleased.

"I told you, I'm not the little sister you think I am." I winked at her and then turned as Zachary returned with the three men.

"I forgot to introduce my colleagues. This is Tyler Nolan, Ajax Savanaugh, and Venus the Moon Child."

Venus was the one with a limp. I had the feeling he didn't go out in public much. He looked more feral than the others, more like an OW Were than an Earthside one. I could see the hint of fangs when he smiled. Earthside Weres had evolved so that their teeth changed when they did, during the full moon. OW Weres, like me, retained some of our animal aspects, even during the periods we weren't in Were-form.

Tyler, the one who had hissed at Menolly, gave us a guarded nod. Ajax followed suit. Venus, on the other hand, broke into a troubled smile.

"Welcome, Fair Folk, and we thank you for coming to our aid," he said, bowing. His gaze was fastened on Menolly, even though he spoke to all of us. "When Zachary first broached the idea of bringing you in, not all were in favor. Now, I think it's safe to say we welcome your help, if you're willing. Please, feel at home on our land."

As he stepped forward, the others backed away, including Zachary. Obviously Venus commanded some stature in the community. His authority was almost palpable. I wondered if he was the chief, or whatever they called their leader, but then I felt a sudden probing in my aura, a seeking of sorts, as he stared at me, and I knew what he was.

Venus the Moon Child was the leader of the Rainier Puma Pride, all right, even if he wasn't their king. He was their shaman, and he wove magic like Camille did, wrought from the moon like a silver arrow.

Camille sensed the same thing I did. She gently inclined

her head as he approached her. "Old Father," she said, "you run with the Moon Mother, don't you?"

He broke into a crinkled smile and reached for her hand, which she gave without hesitation. "Yes, child, I run with the Moon, as do you. But your connections to her are bound within your soul. The Moon Mother has always been with you, since long before you were born."

"That's what my goddess-mother said at my birth, when the runes were cast for my life path," she said, a wondering look on her face.

Venus nodded. "See? Now me, my oaths are bound by Were blood and the magic I learned at my father's knee. The Moon allows me to carry her magic for the Pride, but I am not her son in the same way you are her daughter." He leaned forward and placed a gentle kiss on her forehead; a faint glow remained where his lips had grazed her brow. "You are protected as a friend on our land unless you break that honor."

She nodded and curtseyed as Venus moved on to Morio. "Brother Fox, we are of different natures, and yet you are one of the shifting folk. You understand the nature of the change. Be our guest and friend as long as you abide by our customs." Once again, he leaned forward, this time placing a kiss on Morio's forehead. There was a shimmer of light that passed from his lips to the youkai-kitsune's skin.

"Old Father, I'll do my best to be worthy of the charge," Morio said, his usual nonplussed self. But his voice quaked just enough to tell me that he could feel Venus's power. And that Venus the Moon Child's magic could rival all of our abilities combined. Yet, that he couldn't solve the murders told me that we were in a heap of trouble.

Venus reached for Menolly's hands, and she hesitantly offered them. He turned her palms toward the sky, then pushed the sleeves of her turtleneck up to reveal the scars that had been embedded on her arms by the Elwing Blood Clan when they tortured her. They would never fade, having never had the chance to heal before she died. Her entire body was crisscrossed with the marks.

"Oh girl, what did they do to you?" Venus glanced up to

meet her oddly patient expression. "You are a demon, and yet you are so much more. Fae, human, vampire . . . none of your titles fully carry your story, do they?"

As he spoke, his words seemed to weave a tapestry of music around us. I could hear the thundering of dark clouds as they raced across fields and forests. The swirl of snow grew thick, coiling around us like a whirlwind of white dancers desperate for one last kiss before they melted into oblivion.

Menolly seemed caught off guard, but instead of saying something that would get us all blacklisted from the land— which I halfway expected her to do—she surprised me by remaining silent. Instead, she merely allowed Venus to kiss her forehead. Her nostrils flared, and I knew that she must smell his blood, hear his pulse, but she remained still, a porcelain statue as the snow clung to the chill of her flesh.

"Walk our lands as a guest and friend, Midnight's Daughter, but do not feed on our people or our animals, or we will have to stake you down. You understand this?" The shaman held her gaze, and she nodded, still silent.

Lastly, he came to me. As he took my hands in his, I felt a deep spark of recognition run through my body, grounding me deep into the earth and then looping up again to meet and bond with his own aura. I had a sudden flash of Venus when he was younger, wandering through the hills, shifting from puma to man to puma again, searching for something so intangible there were no words for it. He had taken lovers where he would, both male and female, and danced naked through the Indian paintbrush that grew in thick patches along the mountain.

Wild and feral, he was part of the essence of Mount Rainier, belonging to the very land. I began to understand why the enclave had bought up so many acres and developed their own community. They belonged to the volcano, bound by ties born in the blood.

"Changeling, you are lost, aren't you? You have no true Pride. You have your family but no clan, no single place to call home." He wove his words in a soft cadence, catching me up in his whispers. "Don't be afraid of being a Windwalker."

I flinched. *Windwalker* . . . how I despised that name, and how I'd hated the children who had taunted us with it when we were young. Windwalkers walked the world, never settling down, always alone and roaming. The thought of becoming one of them had terrified me. When our mother died, I'd clung to Camille like white on snow, but no matter how much love she gave me, she could never take our mother's place.

Venus caught my hands, squeezing them gently. "Don't fear your path, sweetheart. Some are bound by fate to walk the winds, to serve the gods, to serve destiny. You and your sisters straddle two worlds . . . more, truth be told, but that we will save for later. Leave worry behind. For now, you are a friend of our Pride, and you may wander our land freely. And, if the urge takes you, you are welcome here when the Moon Mother is pregnant, to prowl the woods safely with our kind, even though you are but a kit compared to our size."

His lips brushed my forehead, and I felt a surge of power race through me. He winked and squeezed my hands again. "There is more to you than meets the eye, my tabby cat. I think you'll be surprised just what you find when you look deep within your soul."

Wondering what he meant but feeling that I'd find out sooner than I wanted to, I forced my attention back to the group. Everyone was waiting, and it was obvious that Zachary, Ajax, and Tyler had been witness to this sort of ritual before. They were standing at attention, solemn, with palms pressed together in front of them.

Venus stepped back. "We're ready. Let's take them to Shawn's body."

Zachary looked on the verge of breaking down, but being Were—and male at that—he had to maintain composure in front of the others. I had no idea if Ajax and Tyler belonged to the elders of the Pride, but it was obvious that Venus's commands went unquestioned.

I reached out to Zach and slowly took his hand. We walked forward in silence. Behind us, Camille and Venus were conversing in low whispers, and for once, I didn't bother to eavesdrop on the conversation. Menolly and Morio trailed behind them, followed by Ajax and Tyler.

The Douglas firs were thick with snow, their trunks over-grown with huckleberry and briar bushes, and they closed around us as we entered the copse. Life abounded in the woodlands at home, but Earthside forests made me nervous. They were secretive, never reaching out to touch those who passed by; primeval and chaotic compared to the forests in Otherworld—except for some of the darker thickets, which most of the city Fae avoided. The woodlands here existed on their own terms, considering humans unnecessary. The wood spirits and dryads were tolerated, but only the animals were ever truly safe.

Then again, perhaps these old sentinels had reason to be suspicious, to keep their secrets hidden within their trunks and rings. They were at war with big business, with developers committing genocide against the ancient giants. No wonder they had distanced themselves from the two-footed creatures of the world.

The gleaming eyes of a hundred woodland creatures gazed at us from behind the dark bushes and deadfalls, and I could hear the faint cadence of a beating drum as we passed through the thicket. Up ahead, a babbling stream cut through the silence.

The faint outline of the arrastra sat in the middle of the stream. Stone mills driven by burro power, arrastras had been used to grind the ore in order to release the precious gold that fueled the hopes and dreams of the miners. Not that they would have found much in this area, I thought, but from what I understood, the hills had been rife with prospectors a hundred years back. Though the Fae valued silver more than gold, we understood the allure of precious metals.

Camille and Venus fell silent. The hairs on the back of my neck stood up; we must be approaching the scene of Shawn's murder.

Zachary nodded toward an opening in the forest. "We follow the stream into that glade ahead. That's where we found all of the bodies. We've laid traps, we've set up guards to watch. In fact, Shawn was on guard duty, and something surprised him."

"I thought Delilah said you were going to limit your guards to the front of the compound," Menolly said from behind us.

"We were," Venus said, answering for Zach. "But Shawn convinced us that he'd be safe if he took another man with him. Apparently Jesse had to take a piss, and while he was off in the bushes, the killer got poor Shawn. By the time Jesse found him, Shawn was dead."

Zach shook his head. "We've reached our wits' end. The Council has finally admitted that we can't handle this on our own. If it keeps up, there won't be a Rainier Puma Pride after a while. We're getting ready to send the women and children to the Blue Road Tribe up on Mount Baker until we've caught the whack job who's offing our people."

"Blue Road Tribe?" Camille asked. "Another werepuma group?"

"Bears, actually," Venus said. "A Native American group. We forged a formal alliance with them, just in case one of our mountains decides to blow. We learned the hard way when St. Helens erupted and decimated the Elk Herders."

"If we're going to do this, let's get it over with," Ajax said. "I want to take my son home and lay him to rest." His voice was rock steady, but in that moment I understood why the older man was so distant. If Shawn was Zachary's cousin, then Ajax must be Zach's uncle, and that was his son lying out in the snow, dead.

Camille started to say something but then shook her head as Zachary led us out into the glen that opened up near the stream. The water was still running, but the rocks near the banks were slippery with snow and ice. A large fire pit sat in the center of the glade, and the surrounding land had been smoothed out. Zach had mentioned that the newlywed couple had been camping. This area must be used for campouts and get-togethers.

A gust of wind blew past, and I could smell traces of blood. I looked over my shoulder at Camille and Menolly. It was obvious they could smell it, too. The look on Menolly's face was one of raw desire, and I was grateful she'd fed recently.

Near the stream, next to a large boulder, rested the body of a young man. Or what had been his body. Hair the color of wheat was splattered with dried blood, and his skin was the texture of old leather, parched as if he'd been mummified. His throat had been slashed, and his head lolled back. I winced and looked away, not wanting to see the terrified look frozen forever on his face.

A gust of wind sent a swirl of flakes into a frenzy, and then the clouds parted for an instant, and the moon shone through, gleaming down on the freshly fallen snow and the face of young Shawn. He and Zach looked a lot alike, but he couldn't have been more than a teenager. Now he would never grow up, never marry, father children, take a trade. I sucked in a deep breath and tried to keep my composure.

"Who could do this to him in such a short time? You say his partner was in the bushes, peeing? That shouldn't have taken more than a few minutes, and yet every ounce of moisture that was in his body seems to have been sucked out of his cells." Menolly knelt beside the body, shaking her head. "Not even a vampire can do *this*."

"All the victims have been like this. At first we thought maybe some odd natural process was at work, since we didn't find the first few for a while," Venus said. "You can see why we're so frightened. Whoever is doing this has the power to sneak in, drain their victims, rip out their hearts, and vanish before we can catch them. Or even catch a glimpse of them."

He sat on the ground, in the snow, and gently took one of Shawn's hands in his own. "I've tried dreaming the murderer, but I can't seem to get through a fogbank that always obscures my way. All the spells and magical traps I've set have been in vain. Nothing is working."

Ajax stood beside Menolly, staring blankly out at the rippling stream. "If you can find out anything—anything at all to help us—you'll have my undying gratitude," he said gruffly. "I'll pledge service to you and your sisters; I'll pay any cost. Just find out who murdered my son." The big man broke down then, and tears coursed down his cheeks as he silently wept under the glittering moon.

Camille squatted beside Venus and leaned close to Shawn's body, sniffing his shirt. "There's some sort of scent here that I don't recognize."

"We noticed that, too," Venus said. "I thought I knew the

scent of most of the creatures around here, but this one is new to me. And yet, it strikes a warning bell. I keep thinking I should know where it's from."

I sat down beside Menolly, shivering as my butt hit the snowy ground.

"It's not the scent of any undead that I recognize," Menolly said after a moment. "As for demons . . . almost a hint, but not quite. What do you think, Camille?"

Camille leaned down and stared into Shawn's glassy eyes. "I wish Corpse Talkers worked on Weres, but unless he had Fae blood—even a few drops—it's no use to bring one in." She glanced up at Zach, who shook his head.

"No such luck. Pure Earthside Were."

"Thought so," she said, going back to examining Shawn's body. She traced his lips with her finger and held it up to her nose, inhaling deeply. "You're right, Menolly—a faint smell of Demonkin, but there's something more—something over the top of it. This is very strange."

I looked around at the clearing. My attention wavered, and I found myself wandering over to the bank where it dropped directly into the stream. The shore ended, but the curve of the bank led up a steep incline to a mesa above. Pinnacle Rock, overlooking the creek. An inner nudge pushed me to examine the embankment, and the moment I touched the rocky face— what had probably been an ancient alluvial deposit—I knew that I had to climb it.

"Where does this lead?" I called back over my shoulder. Zachary and Tyler joined me, Menolly close behind them. Venus, Camille, and Morio were preparing Shawn's body for transport back to the enclave. Ajax just continued to stare at the endless currents flowing by.

Zach looked up. "I don't know. I don't think I've ever been up there."

"What about you, Tyler?" I asked.

Tyler shook his head. "I don't think you should bother."

"Well, I think otherwise," I said. "There's something up there."

Menolly stepped forward. "Let me go with you, Kitten,"

she said. She immediately started to climb, and it was like watching the old Menolly, before she'd been killed and changed. She lithely scampered up the bank, digging in with nails to find the barest of handholds.

I took a deep breath. I was athletic; I should be able to make it. "Okay, here goes nothing," I said.

"Are you sure you want to try that? You'll most likely end up in the drink," Tyler said. "Why not let me go get some gear and go up first, to make sure you aren't hurt?"

"No need. I'll be careful. I don't like water, but I love heights." I followed Menolly's path, feeling my way up, using my instincts to guide my feet and hands. The smell of frozen earth loomed rich in my nose, and I pressed my body against the embankment. One foot at a time, one hand at a time. Feel for a handhold. Here, a rock. And there, a slight indentation. Scramble for any foothold, a branch, a stone, a small twig poking out on which to rest my heel as I used sheer muscle to keep my body pressed against the mountainside.

As the snow began to fall in earnest, all I could see were flakes of white and the dirt beneath. I glanced up, but Menolly was nowhere to be seen; she was one with the embankment. She could have easily floated to the top, but she chose instead to take the harder route—to test herself, to cling to the person she'd been in life rather than the vampire she was now. No angst, just a choice.

We all made choices, I thought as I scrambled for a moment until my foot found an outcropping on which to rest. We all made decisions and lived with them. Aunt Rythwar had made a decision to turn her back on Lethesanar. Father was making a choice to stand by the Crown, not by the Queen. And my sisters and I had made the choice to stay Earthside and protect both this world and our own as best we could.

"I found a ledge." Menolly's voice cut into my thoughts.

"How much farther?" I called.

"Another three yards, and you're home free," she said.

And she was good to her word. A couple of minutes later, I reached over the stone ledge, and she grasped my wrist. With one heave, she pulled me up and over the edge.

Panting, I sprawled on the ledge and looked around, trying to figure out where we were. A good ten feet wide, the lip of the outcropping extended only a few inches from the embankment. Standing below, it would be almost impossible to see that there was a ledge up here, even during the day. The stone shelf continued back a few feet to the side of the mountain, which was covered with vines and brambles. I peered closer. There, beneath the snow-covered foliage, gaped the mouth of a cavern.

"A cave?" I asked.

"By the look of things, the opening's been covered for years by vegetation," Menolly said. "But see, here the brambles have been moved. And there," she added, pointing to a small opening. "Something's definitely tampered with it. We should take a look inside."

She brushed the snow away from the leaves, and we slowly pulled aside the branches blocking the way. A few came willingly, and I could see that she was right. Their stems had already been bent and broken.

I peered inside. "I wish we had a light. I can see to some degree, and so can you, but it would be nice to know if we're missing anything."

"Stay here and don't go in without me," she said and lightly stepped over the edge. Like a kite caught in the wind, she was buoyed up by a gust and then began to fall like a feather in the breeze. Menolly couldn't really fly, not unless she was trying to turn into a bat, but she hadn't mastered that part of vampirism to any great use, yet. However, she *could* float and hover.

Unless she was startled, she would drift slowly to the ground. There were limitations to the ability, and she was still learning how to use it, but it came in handy. Like when she anchored the Yule tree to the ceiling, or when I climbed the curtains and she had to haul me down by the scruff of my neck, no less.

A few moments later, she reappeared with Camille holding on for dear life, her arms wrapped tightly around Menolly's waist. They landed with a soft thud in the accumulating snow.

Camille turned on her flashlight and pointed it toward the cave. "What have we got?"

"I'm not sure," I said. "Let's see what we find."

And with that, I ripped back the branches and stepped into the cave.

Something sticky landed against my face, and I jumped, startling Camille, who was right behind me.

"What happened? Are you okay?" she asked.

I brushed my hand over my face. It was covered with silken strands. Shit.

"Yeah, but I don't like this," I said, stepping fully into the room.

Camille followed, her light flickering around the room, and Menolly brought up the rear. The cavern glistened in the beam from the flashlight, shimmering under the weight of a thousand spiderwebs. Pristine, crystalline in color, they'd been woven into a frenzy of patterns, a chaotic vision in silk. There was no symmetry here, only a kaleidoscope of beauty gone mad.

"Spiders," Camille whispered. "Are these . . ."

Menolly slid through the webs, brushing them off like she might brush away a gnat. In the center of the cave, she leaned down to look at something, then motioned for us to join her. I found a stick to bring down the webs as Camille and I made our way over to Menolly's side. She was kneeling beside what looked like a dried husk, only it was far too big for corn or any other vegetable.

"You'd better ask Zachary if they've had any other members of the pride go missing lately, ones who haven't been accounted for," she said.

"Uh," I didn't want to ask but I had to. "Is it—"

"Yes, it's another body, like the others. I think we can safely say that we're looking for the Hunters Moon Clan, and that they're turning the Puma Pride enclave into their private feeding grounds."

CHAPTER 8

❦

I stared at Menolly, trying to comprehend what she was saying. And then it all flashed together. The Hunters Moon Clan members were feeding on Zachary's people. What better way to conquer your rivals?

"Oh Great Mother, that's demented." I shuddered, quickly looking around the cave. But we were alone, at least as far as I could see.

"A good way to take care of your enemies—very old-world tribal. Not exactly cannibalistic, but damned close," Camille said. "The question is, what set them off? And why now?"

A sudden movement in the webs to our right alerted me, and I held up my hand. "Shush." As I leaned forward, I saw something scuttle off through the strands. I jumped up. "Let's go. Bring the body with us, and let's get the fuck out of here."

"Spiders?" Camille whispered. I nodded. Menolly picked up the body, and we hurried toward the front of the cave. On the way, I caught my heel on something and went sprawling.

"Shit." I sat up, rubbing my shin, pretty sure I'd roughed up the front of my leg. Camille offered me the flashlight. I'd tripped over a shield woven of bones that were tied together using leather strips. I grimaced and picked it up. "I think we'd better take this along with us," I said. "We might be able to learn something from it."

Camille nodded, grabbing it from me. She was less squeamish than I. "You're right," she said, making a face. "Let's get the hell out of here now. I don't want to end up like . . . well, whoever this poor fellow was."

Once we were back on the ledge, we faced the problem of getting down, but down is always easier than up. At least it's quicker. Camille slung the shield over her shoulder and clasped her arms around Menolly's waist.

"I hate heights," she muttered, closing her eyes, but there was no room for argument. We didn't know who—or what—had been in that cave besides us. There could be a pack of spiderlings on the way to shut us up right now.

"Tallyho and all that crap," Menolly said. Holding the corpse at arm's length, she stepped off the cliff, dragging Camille with her. Camille let out a little shriek, but the three of them floated down, albeit a little faster than if it had been Menolly alone. Watching Camille's pained expression, I found myself relieved that we hadn't brought Chase along. He handled our quirks better than most FBHs would be able to, but this little adventure might have been a bit much, even for him. It was almost too much for me.

Menolly guided them to the ground safely, however, and laid the body out. Her strength was growing, I thought as I skittered down behind them, half sliding, half rolling down the embankment. With every month she grew just a little bit stronger, a little bit edgier.

When we reached the bottom, we found Zachary and Morio waiting for us. Venus, Ajax, and Tyler had taken Shawn's body back to the enclave.

"We need to talk," I said to Zach, nodding toward the path. "Let's get the hell out of here and into somewhere that's protected and light. You've got a real problem on your hands."

Zach was staring at the body that Menolly was holding. "Another one?" He swayed and reached to steady himself on a nearby boulder.

"Looks that way. You have any idea of anybody who might be missing? Somebody who hasn't already turned up dead?" Camille asked.

He shook his head, lips pressed together. "No. Let's get back to the main lodge." He offered to take the body from Menolly, but she waved him off.

"I can carry him . . . her . . . whoever it was, but Delilah's right. We need to get out of here *now*. It's not safe, even with all of us together." She set off toward the path, and we hurried behind her.

By the time we got back to the lodge, the snow was really piling up. I had the feeling that we were in for one hell of a winter. That in itself was curious. The weather around here was wet but not usually all that cold, and with all the global warming going on, winters should be getting milder, not worse. I hoped to high heaven we weren't in for some cockeyed version of Ragnarok.

Pushing thoughts of the weather aside, I focused on the task at hand as we hurried up the stairs and through the doors, into the warm light that shone down from the chandelier in the hallway.

The foyer was spacious, with brown marbled tiling that ran throughout the hallway. A large staircase of wide, smooth steps led up to a second, third, and fourth story. The railing was glossy white and trimmed with gold leaf. For all of their rough exterior, I had the feeling that the Puma Pride was an old moneyed clan. Towering fig trees graced both sides of the staircase, nestled in gigantic stoneware urns. A hall to the left and one to the right both led to sets of heavy double doors.

"Bring the body this way," Zach said. "Just be quiet. I don't want anybody knowing about this yet. We'll examine it in the den."

Menolly hurried behind him, carrying the dried shell. Camille, Morio, and I scurried behind, as Zach led us down the hall to the left set of doors. He peeked inside, then gestured for us to pass through. We found ourselves in another hallway.

"Through the door at the end," Zach said, rushing us along the corridor. He slid past to open the door for us. After making sure the room was empty, he stood back and let us enter.

The den was a library in every sense of the word, with floor-to-ceiling shelves lining the walls, a gigantic desk, a leather sofa, and several scattered recliners and ottomans. The wood was heavy, cherry by the look of it, and the craftsmanship detailed. Morio sat down on one of the footstools next to Camille.

Menolly laid the body on the sofa, while Zachary locked the door. He turned up the lights, and as we made ourselves comfortable, he slowly approached the dead man. Kneeling beside the sofa, he took a long look at the face. After a moment, he shook his head and turned back to us.

"I have no idea who that is. He isn't from our enclave, that I can tell you straight up."

"Well, hell. Maybe he was just cutting across your property? Is he wearing a hunter's vest?" We hadn't found a gun near him, but whoever killed him could have made off with the weapon, if there was one.

"No, it's a Windbreaker, but you could mistake it for one," Zach said. "We used to be forever chasing hunters off our land. By now, only strangers make the mistake of climbing our fences. He doesn't look like any of our neighbors. Damn. I haven't got a clue who he is. *Was*." He scratched his head and sat down behind the desk. "So, what did you find up there? What's that thing on your back?"

Camille pulled the shield off her back and laid it on the desk so we could take a closer look. The bones looked humanoid, most likely leg and arm bones, and they were laid out in a pattern that formed some sort of sigil. The dried leather straps were a familiar color that set my stomach to churning. I had a feeling it had come from the same source as the bones.

Morio glanced at it and flinched. "Is that what I think it is?"

"I don't recognize the mark," I started to say, but Camille held up her hand.

"I do," she said. "The past couple of months, I've spent a lot of time rereading old magical texts." She gave me a worn-out look. "I figured they'd come in handy, so I had Iris pick up some titles for me on one of her trips back to OW."

Her face clouded with worry, she glanced at Zach. He was staring at the body. She lowered her voice and continued, "One of the texts has to do with the Demonkin. This sigil is the mark of a Degath Squad. Trenyth was right; we've got a new batch of Hell Scouts to contend with. And the stench of Demonkin is strong on this shield. Shadow Wing's hand is in this, and it's my guess he's connected himself to the werespiders."

"Who the hell is Shadow Wing, and what's a Degath Squad?" Zach paused, then looked at us sharply. *Hell*, his hearing was as good as mine. "You said werespiders? Are you talking about the Hunters Moon Clan?"

I tried to gauge how much we should tell him. "So you've heard of the group?"

His face went dark. "Yeah, all too much. You think they're behind this?"

"Yeah, we think so," I said slowly. "Listen to me. When was the last skirmish between the Hunters Moon Clan and the Puma Pride? And it would help if we knew why you guys are feuding."

He closed his eyes, thinking. After a moment, he said, "I don't really know. Last time there was an attack was . . . well, the last actual attack was when I was a boy. We routed them off our land when we found a small nest in the woods. But that was over twenty years ago. As to *why* we're enemies, I have no idea. Nobody ever mentions the Hunters Moon Clan unless absolutely necessary. We're taught from birth to listen and obey and to keep our mouths shut. I can try to find out for you, though, but it may take a little prodding."

"Do that. Meanwhile, maybe you should tell us why you were fighting with Geph von Spynne a couple years ago." I leaned forward, holding his gaze.

"You know about that?" His shoulders tensed. "We had a brawl, true, but it didn't lead to anything more than a few broken bones."

With a glance at Menolly and Camille, I nodded. "Yes, we know—and don't ask how. What happened?"

Zach winced. "He attacked one of our women, tried to rape her. I was assigned to administer punishment, but he was stronger than I thought. Wiry and thin, but strong. He knifed me, but I managed to get in some pretty nasty blows. He disappeared shortly after that. I thought maybe I'd managed to kill him." He gave the body on the sofa a sideways glance. "So you're saying that the Hunters Moon Clan is mixing it up with a bunch of demons?"

I let out a long sigh. "We aren't sure, but it's looking more and more like that might be the case. Don't tell anybody, though. Not yet. We don't want to cause a panic if we're wrong, and we've been known to be wrong a lot."

"Yeah, sure." Zach pressed his lips together, as if he were mulling over what we'd said. "It wouldn't surprise me if they are in cahoots with a bunch of demons. They're a freakish bunch. I was taught from the time I was little to be careful of them. I guess my father was right; they're up to no good."

"Well, don't go around stirring up trouble until we're certain of what we're dealing with, okay?"

"But why would the demons get involved with the Hunters Moon Clan?" he asked, looking confused. "Granted, they're a bunch of freaks and weirdos, but aren't demons rare? What could they possibly get from the Hunters Moon Clan to make it worth their while?"

"That's the million-dollar question," Menolly said.

I glanced at Camille. "Looks like you'll be talking to Smoky after all," I muttered. She jerked her head toward Zach, warning me not to say too much. She was right, I thought. We really didn't know enough about him and his people to fully place our trust in them. I gave her a slight nod, then turned back to Zach. "Listen, until we make sense of this whole mess, I highly suggest that your people avoid the woodlands. Don't go out unless you're in groups of at least three, armed to the teeth. We'll see what we can find out and call you back." I stood up, brushing off my jeans.

Menolly drifted over to join us. "I suggest you summon your shaman and ask if he recognizes who this man might have been." She pointed to the body on the sofa.

Zachary brushed past me. After he'd left the room, Morio held his finger to his lips and sidled a look-see toward a corner in the room. We glanced over in the direction in which he had nodded. Sure enough, there behind a vase of flowers, I could barely make out a surveillance camera.

We kept quiet until Zach returned with Venus the Moon Child, who examined the body. After a moment, Venus stood up and began to pace back and forth. "This is the guy we hired to inspect the pumping station near the stream," he said.

"Where we pump the water from in order to irrigate the orchards."

"An FBH?" Camille said. "That complicates matters."

"That's the understatement of the century," I said. If it had been a Supe, we could have taken care of this quietly, without bringing anybody else into it. But a human had been killed, and that made everything problematic.

"We have to tell Chase," I said. "We can't cover this up. This man might have a family who's looking for him. If he had the compound's name or address written on his schedule, then the cops are going to come looking for him. I think you'd better let us contact the Faerie-Human CSI team."

"She's right. When did he arrive?" Morio asked.

From Venus's expression, it was clear he understood precisely what danger the Puma Pride was facing. Exposure, for certain. Possibly worse. "He was scheduled to arrive around three this afternoon. I showed him the main orchard, but I never dreamed he'd wander off the path. He must have followed the pipes to the stream. I thought he'd finished his inspection and left."

Camille did a quick calculation. "So you have a couple more hours, one night at best, before the cops come knocking at your door. And even if you say he never showed, you know they'll come back. Do you really want this getting out to the population at large?"

She could be persuasive, that was for sure.

With a shake of the head, Venus said, "Call in whoever you need to. We can't have it spread around the community that a human was killed on our land. More importantly, we can't have it get out that we're Weres. Especially considering the shape he's in. Damn it, this mess is hip deep in shit and getting worse. I wish we'd called for help when Sheila died," he added.

Zachary grunted. "If you had backed me up in Council, we would have, and everybody else might still be alive. Including my sister and my cousin."

"Stop squabbling," I said. "It's too late for that now."

Camille nodded. "She's right. Delilah, call Chase. Unless you want me to do it?"

I let out a long sigh. "No, I will." But when I pulled out my cell, there was no available signal. Call it a hunch, but I had the feeling that they'd rigged it so all communication to the outside was limited to a strictly as-needed policy.

"I need access to a telephone, please," I said, shoving my cell back in my pocket.

Zach pointed to the far side of the desk. "There. Dial nine to get a line out of the compound."

"You have quite the setup here, don't you?" I asked, picking up the receiver. I punched nine, then dialed Chase's number. His answering machine picked up, so I hung up and tried him at work. Sure enough, he was still at his desk, but he sounded happier than he had earlier in the day.

"We caught him! We caught the dwarf-killer! Or should I say killers? A couple of teens from one of the local gangs. Damned bastards killed the dwarf as an initiation stunt to some weird cult. Have you ever heard of Freedom's Angels?"

"Can't say that I have," I said.

"They seem to be some offshoot of the Guardian Watchdogs, but I'm not sure how the two are connected. I've got a man on the case to find out, though. I've filed a report with OIA, but there's no word from them yet. We're holding the creeps until we get word on what HQ wants to do. They may demand extradition rights, which would open up a whole new can of worms. But at least we got 'em. What's up, babe?" he said, abruptly stopping to catch his breath.

Hating to put a cramp in his happiness, I briefly filled him in on what we'd found out. "The Weres want to take care of their dead, and considering what we're facing, that's probably best. But this guy . . . he was an FBH." I gave him the name Venus the Moon Child had given me. "We're figuring it's a good bet that he was killed by a werespider."

"Werespider? Not that damned Hunters Moon Clan you told me about?"

"Um-hmm," I said, not wanting to say anything since they

might be listening in. "Listen, save everything else until you get out here. And make it quick, please."

Chase seemed to catch my drift. "Any sign of . . . you know what?" he asked, lowering his voice.

"Unfortunately, yes. But we'll talk about it *later*. Bring the FH-CSI medics. We may be dealing with Earthside Supes, but they're probably the best group to tackle this. We need to know several things about this man's body, and somebody's going to have to find out if he has a family, who to notify . . . stuff like that." If the gods were on our side, he would be a loner, unmarried, with no kids and parents who had already passed away.

While we waited for Chase, Venus asked Zachary to bring us something to drink. I wasn't sure that I trusted the Puma Pride just yet, so I declined, and of course Menolly didn't want any. But Camille and Morio accepted hot chocolate. I noticed they both sniffed their mugs carefully before tasting. The chocolate must have been fine, because they both began to drink the steaming cocoa.

I wandered over to the bay windows overlooking the path to the woods and pulled back the velvet drapes. The snow was still coming down, but now it was mixed with sleet. Before morning, rain would be in the wash, and we'd have a soggy mess to contend with.

Zachary moved to stand in back of me. Even though I liked him, I didn't like having someone hanging over my shoulder, so I turned just in time to clip his head with mine as he bent down.

"Oops," he said. "Sorry."

I forced a smile, not feeling at all confident about what was going on. Part of me just wanted to walk away and forget the compound existed.

He leaned close to my ear and whispered, "Are you seeing anybody?"

I shivered at the kiss of his breath on my neck. "Yes . . . yes, I am." Then, not knowing what propelled me, I added, "But I'm half-Fae. We aren't exactly exclusive." I was opening myself up to trouble, I knew it, especially with Chase on his way. A twinge of guilt nibbled at the edge of my conscience, and I added, "The detective on his way here is my lover. He's a good man."

Zachary paused, then nodded. "I understand. We'll talk more, later."

Venus called to him then, and he hurried over to talk to the shaman, but I could still feel him in my aura and my thoughts.

By the time Chase and his team got to the compound, we were itching to go home. Camille and Morio were curled up in one of the oversized chairs. He was tracing her cheek with delicate kisses while she sat on his lap, whispering in his ear. Menolly had found a corner in which to float near the ceiling, waiting and watching.

Tyler led the FH-CSI team into the room. Chase glanced around, starting when Zachary introduced himself. He stared at Venus with a curious look but merely said, "Where's the body?"

Suddenly, I found myself very happy to see him. He was safe territory, a known factor. I hurried over to his side, grateful for something to focus my attention on. Menolly lowered herself to the ground and hopped on the front edge of the desk, crossing her legs precisely, folding her arms across her chest. She didn't like Chase very much, but at least she was polite enough not to hover like a bat in the rafters when he was around.

As the medics examined the body, I leaned close to Chase and whispered, "Don't say anything you don't want overheard here. Something here isn't quite right, but I can't put my finger on it. Yet."

He nodded and planted a peck on my cheek. Out of the corner of my eye, I saw Zachary watching, his golden eyes now dark and tinged with irritation. I pulled away with an uneasy feeling that none of us were safe here. Not my sisters and me, not Chase and his team, not even the Pumas who belonged here. The night was fraught with danger, and we were all walking targets.

A few minutes later, one of the medics, Sharah, an elf, came over to talk to us. "The man was an FBH, all right. It looks as though every drop of liquid in his body, every internal organ, has been—"

Chase interrupted her, holding up his hand. "I know you need more time to do the autopsy and come to any *real* conclusions," he said in a pointed tone. Sharah blinked, then took her clue and nodded. "Take the body back to HQ and do what you need to. Have the report on my desk by morning at the latest."

"Yes, *sir*." Sharah motioned to her men. "You heard the detective. Get a move on, boys, we don't have all night."

Under the watchful eyes of Tyler, Venus, and Zachary, the EMTs body-bagged the man and carted him out to the waiting medic unit. My sisters, Morio, Chase, and I headed for the door as soon as they were through. Chase wrapped his arm around my waist as we approached the three Pumas.

"We'll let you know what we find out," I said.

"Fine." Zachary gave Chase a pointed look. "Thank you for coming out here on such short notice, Detective. Especially when we're so far outside your jurisdiction."

It was barely there in Zach's voice, but I could hear it: a challenge. I didn't know whether Chase would pick up on it, but apparently testosterone speaks its own language, superseding species and race.

Chase stared him down. "I'm sure your local sheriff wouldn't mind me stepping in. Would you like me to stop by his office, tell him about the case? While I'm at it, I can tell him the reason I'm here is because y'all are Supes and needed an FBH to run interference. As it is, I'm going to have to come up with a good reason why we removed an FBH murder case from your land."

Zach cleared his throat. "No, that won't be necessary," he said, frowning. After an icy pause, he motioned us toward the door. Tyler fell in beside him as they escorted us to our cars.

"I'll call you later tomorrow," I told Zach, keeping my voice as neutral as possible.

Zachary nodded, silent as the night. But I could feel his

gaze fastened on my back as I climbed in and shut the door. Tyler, on the other hand, glowered the entire time. I had the distinct impression he appreciated neither our help nor our presence.

Camille waited until Chase was headed down the road, then she put the car into gear, and we eased out of the compound. On the way home, before anybody had a chance to say anything, I scribbled a note for them to read.

"Don't make anything other than innocuous conversation," it said. "I have a feeling the car may be bugged. I'll go through it tomorrow." And so that was how we came to discuss the impending holiday dinner the entire way home.

When we pulled into the driveway, we saw that Chase had arrived before we did. He was already inside. We spilled out of the car.

"Great gods, that was nerve-racking," Camille said as she wearily climbed the porch steps, carrying the shield that we'd found. She dropped it next to the door. "Let's leave this damn thing outside. I don't like the feel of it and don't want it in the house," she added. "So, you really think my car's bugged?"

I nodded. "Ten to one, somebody was listening. Tomorrow, before you go anywhere, remind me, and we'll scan the car with the crystal that Trenyth left us."

"Good idea," she said. "Queen Asteria is one sharp cookie. We'd be as adrift as a glacier without her help."

Morio opened the door and stood back, allowing us to enter first. Menolly popped in the kitchen while the rest of us dropped into whatever seat we could find and stared at one another. Chase was shaking his head.

"That body . . . what happened to that man?" he asked.

"External digestion," Morio spoke up. We all stared at him.

"External digestion?" I said. "Yuck."

"How do you know that?" asked Chase.

Morio tugged at his collar. "Hey, I can't help it if I majored in biology when I got my degree online. My guess is that they'll find some residue of a digestive enzyme in his body. If the Hunters Moon Clan got him, they probably envenomated him with a paralyzing neurotoxin, which also broke down his internal tissue. Then they sucked it out through . . . well . . . wherever they could find—or make—a hole on his body."

"Gee, thanks for the visual. *Not.*" Chase turned green. "Why did you have to tell me that? Now I'm going to have nightmares. It was so much easier before you all came through the portals. I hope you know that!"

I laughed, my first real laugh of the night. "Chase, the werespiders were here long before we came over from OW. As were the Puma Pride members and Morio and his kind. Get used to the idea that you had plenty of Supes here all along. You just didn't know about them."

"I still wish I didn't," he muttered but returned my smile. "Strike that. Then I wouldn't know about you, either."

Menolly came bounding back in the room. She'd changed into a clean pair of jeans and a pale blue sweater set. She wore stiletto heels, and her braids clicked gently as she pulled on her leather jacket.

She glanced at the clock. "I've got to get down to the Wayfarer. This took far longer than I'd planned. Remember, tomorrow night is my V.A. meeting. I expect at least one of you," she looked pointedly at Camille and me, "to go with me. You promised Wade you'd do what you could to drum up more family support."

"You're just trying to get a grant to help fund the organization, and you can't unless you have actual living members," Camille said. "Yeah, yeah, at least one of us will be there, and happily so."

Menolly snorted. "You know me too well," she said. "Iris left a note in the kitchen. She fed Maggie, and your dinner's in the fridge. She made a beef stew. I checked. There's enough for Chase and Morio," she added.

Chase looked up, surprised. "Thanks for the offer."

Menolly shrugged off his comment. "Hey, I'm not going to be here," she said but gave him a rare smile. She was out the door before we could say "Good night" or "Be careful."

She'd barely closed the door behind her when a noise from

the kitchen told us Iris was stirring. She peeked into the living room. "I see you finally made it home. I just finished my bath and was about to go to bed, but now that you're here, I'll heat up dinner for you before I hit the sheets."

"We can do that, Iris—" Camille started to say, but Iris waved her off.

"Nonsense. You know I don't mind. Plus, you all look like you could use a good shower. Go on and get cleaned up, and by the time you're done, dinner will be on the table." She looked around. "Did Menolly leave already?"

"Yeah," I said. "She had to go in to work."

Iris nodded and disappeared back into the kitchen. I looked at Camille, Morio, and then myself. We all looked like we'd been through a mud bath.

"Okay, she's right. We're all a mess, except for Chase. Let's meet in the kitchen after a quick shower. Chase, why don't you keep Iris company until we come down?" I thought about asking him into the shower with me, but to tell the truth, I was way too tired for anything other than hot water and soap.

Camille and Morio headed up to her room. No doubt that he'd be joining her under the faucet. "Make it quick, you two," I said as I turned the corner on the staircase, heading up to my own suite of rooms.

My apartment was the third floor of our old Victorian. It wasn't as big as Camille's suite, nevertheless it was mine, and I loved it. Three rooms and a bath. I'd set up one room as the master bedroom and the second as a workout and sitting room. The third was a kitty cat's playground, for when I felt like—or couldn't help—transforming. I'd filled the room with high-quality cat furniture: condos and climbing posts and slumber balls. In fact, sometimes when I catnapped, I preferred to change into my tabby form and curl up in one of the slumber balls. They were more comfortable than my bed.

The bathroom was filled with bath gels and supplies. I wasn't as girly as Camille, but I loved my bubbles and powders and creams. Stripping off my clothes, I tossed them in the laundry chute and climbed in the tub. No time for a lengthy bath, but the hot water was wonderful. I scrubbed my backside with the bath brush, throwing caution to the wind around the area of my butt that was still sore from the cockleburs. The scratches had scabbed over, and the bristles of the brush were soft enough that they didn't open them up again.

Stepping out of the tub, I dried off and shook my hair into place. After slipping into my favorite PJs, a terrycloth robe, and slippers, I padded down to the kitchen.

Iris and Chase were at the table. Chase nursed a cup of tea with Maggie sitting on his lap, while Iris was telling him stories about her life when she was bound to the Kuusi family in Finland. Chase liked Iris. Actually, most men did. She was witty and bright, pretty and friendly, and she had a way of making a guest feel welcome enough to take off his shoes, prop his feet up, and make himself right at home.

I poured myself a cup of tea and joined them, pulling Maggie into my arms. The gargoyle looked surprised, then wrapped her arms around my neck, gave me a nose lick, and rested her head on my shoulder, her downy fur tickling my chin.

Chase leaned his way past Maggie's head and pressed his lips against mine in a long, slow kiss. Not demanding, just welcoming. I shivered. How would I ever talk to him about Zachary? Did I even want to bother?

A burst of laughter from the hall told us Camille and Morio were on their way. Camille was wearing a purple peignoir set, and Morio was dressed in a calf-length blue smoking robe over a pair of dusky pajamas. They settled in at the table and poured their tea while Iris bustled about, heating up our dinner and quickly whipping together a batch of baking powder biscuits.

"Well, we have a lot to discuss," Camille said finally. "Tomorrow, I want to take a closer look at that shield. I'd like to know what the Hunters Moon Clan was doing with it. The thing's rife with demon energy."

"There are a lot of things we need to know," Chase said. "I called Sharah while you all were showering. The victim's name is Ben Jones. We lucked out. No immediate family to question where he's at. He worked for the Retro-Fit Plumbing Company, so we'll let them know that he won't be coming back. He was, as Morio suggested, drained dry of his innards, but his heart appears to have been removed first. Ripped out, you might say," Chase added softly. "This is a pretty gruesome case, guys. Do you think there's any chance the OIA will get involved? I know the Pumas are Earthside Supes, but . . ."

"But we could use all the help we can get," I said. "I have no idea if the OIA will be doing anything to help any of us. Trillian should have more information when he returns from his visit. When's he supposed to get back, Camille?"

She shrugged. "I thought today. Apparently I was wrong. But considering what Father told us the other day, I think we can count out any involvement on the agency's part."

"Why, though, is a Degath Squad picking on the Puma Pride? And why use the Hunter's Moon Clan to do their dirty work? Shadow Wing doesn't seem like one to stand in the shadows and play the puppet master." I leaned back in my chair, absently stroking Maggie's fur. "I still think the Autumn Lord is our best bet for information. We have to know everything we can about the Hunter's Moon Clan, and he's the one who can tell us."

Camille stared at the table. "I may not like it, but I think you're right. When demons are involved, we're involved. I'll talk to Smoky tomorrow night while you attend the V.A. meeting with Menolly. He's our best chance. I just hope he doesn't set the price so high we'll regret it."

CHAPTER 9

By the time I woke up, the sun had already risen. Hell, I'd overslept. I pulled myself out of bed, grateful that it was Sunday and I didn't have to worry about going to the office or anything like that. Actually, since I made my own hours, I was a lot freer than either Camille, who was bound to the bookstore unless Iris helped her out, or Menolly, who was in charge of the Wayfarer. I could arrange my days as I chose. Of course, I made less money than either of them, but I didn't really care.

A peek out the window told me that the day was dry and chilly, though not freezing. The temperature hovered around the thirty-eight degree mark, and what snow we'd had was slowly melting off, turning to slush.

I ran through a series of stretches, arching my back, rolling my neck, then slipped into the shower for a quick rinse-and-go. Rooting through my closet, I found a pair of cozy black sweatpants and a cute T-shirt that said, Fae is the Way on the front over a picture of Tinkerbelle standing in a Betty Boop pose. Poor Tinkerbelle had suffered a setback once we started coming through the portals and people got a glimpse of what the Fae were *really* like.

I ran a brush through my hair, washed my face, and brushed my teeth, then headed downstairs where the smells of breakfast floated through the air. Iris and Camille were filling the table with blueberry hotcakes hot off the griddle, maple sausage, a mess of scrambled eggs, and chilled applesauce with whipped cream. Iris had my milk all ready for me—warm with a dash of cinnamon and sugar sprinkled in it.

I licked my lips. "You two have been busy this morning. Feeling rather domestic?" Camille flashed me a pale smile, and the weight of last night's excursion encroached on my perky mood again.

"Thinking about last night?" Pulling up a chair, I tasted my milk, then, satisfied it was just right, chugged it down. Maybe I *had* lost a lot of my optimism and naïve everything-will-be-okay attitude since we'd landed Earthside, but werespiders or not, nothing was going to come between me and my breakfast.

"That and the fact that I haven't heard from Trillian yet," she said.

I frowned. "Maybe the Svartan king kept him there. Maybe Tanaquar? I've never been quite sure just how Trillian's connected to the war, and he's never really explained it to me." I hadn't bothered to ask, but that was beside the point.

Camille deposited the last of the hotcakes on the table, and she and Iris settled in their chairs. We were alone—no boyfriends at the table—and Menolly was sleeping soundly in her lair. Maggie crawled around the floor, content to pound on a plastic bowl with a wooden spoon Iris had given her. She giggled as she drummed out a chaotic medley of beats.

Gargoyles were primarily bipedal, but when they were young, their wings unbalanced them, tiny as the appendages still were, and so they crawled like human children. We'd had one of the OIA medics examine her and, while he wasn't a specialist regarding Cryptos, he said he thought she was developing normally. Or as normally as she could, given her background.

"Trillian runs messages between Tanaquar and the Svartan King. I think the King's name is Vodox," Camille said. "When I thought Trillian had returned to Svartalfheim after I ran away from him, he was actually sneaking back and forth between his city and Y'Elestrial. Now that Svartalfheim has packed up and moved to Otherworld, it makes his job easier, although if Lethesanar catches him, he's as good as dead."

Iris shook her head. "He's a hard one, that boy, but he's true to his word. I wouldn't trust being within a hundred miles of him if I were his enemy, but as a friend? I want him by my side." She glanced up at Camille. "I'm surprised the OIA has let you stay employed this long, considering your relationship."

"So am I, and it worries me," Camille said. "I keep waiting for the ax to fall. Anyway, back to Trillian's job. He has high connections, but they're all unofficial. He has no title, he's paid under the table, and very few realize just what he's doing."

That sounded about right. Trillian had the makings for a first-class spy. "What's on your schedule today?" I asked Camille.

She shrugged. "Wait for him to return, I suppose. Morio's coming over later this morning so we can examine the shield. Then we're going to drive out to see Smoky." She sobered. "We'll be gone all afternoon."

"I know he's going to demand a high price for his help, but there's really no other way that I can see to get there. Considering what we found last night . . ." I thought of the cave and the body of the plumber and shuddered.

She shook her head. "I know. The spiderlings sure did a number on that dude. I hate thinking about them creeping around. Can they also morph into larger sizes?"

I shrugged. "No idea, and I don't want to find out."

Camille frowned. "Neither do I, but since they can take the size of a regular spider, I'm not sure how safe I feel. I think I'll see if I can find an antipest spell."

"You could just use an insecticide," Iris said, glancing up, a twinkle in her eye. "It might be more reliable."

I repressed a snort.

Camille gave her a withering look, but both Iris and I saw the smile creeping around her frown. "The spray might hurt Maggie. And I know my magic's erratic, but Morio's doing his best to help me harness the wayward energy that plagues my spell work."

"You sure you don't want company—besides Morio—this afternoon?" I didn't really want to tag along and beg Smoky for a ride, but I'd go if Camille wanted me there.

To be honest, the dragon scared the hell out of me. Granted, he was gorgeous in human form, and awe-inspiring in dragon form, but he was also ancient enough to have more power than he knew what to do with. One step out of his good graces meant a chance of ending up on the dinner menu. Camille pushed his buttons, but he seemed to enjoy sparring with her. Anybody else try it, and he'd swallow them whole and burp later.

She shook her head. "Thanks, but since Smoky seems to respond most to me, I'll go. Why don't you help Iris around here? Take a little time to relax. I have a feeling we're all going to be praying for some downtime soon enough."

Relieved, I decided to offer an olive branch to Iris. "Sounds good. Iris, why don't you let me take you out shopping this afternoon? I owe you big for all the broken ornaments."

Iris perked up. "Shopping? Did you say shopping? Just promise me you'll hold on to your tail and not change in the middle of the mall?"

Blushing, I nodded. "I'll do my best. Can't make you any guarantees, but forewarned is forearmed. I'll keep up my guard around the decorations."

Iris sniffed. "You mean it's up to me to keep you distracted? Rather like keeping a child's attention occupied while strolling through the toy section."

"Yeah, kind of." I glanced up at Camille. "Okay, I'm done with breakfast; I'll go look through your car." I shrugged on my jacket and stepped out into the mind-numbing chill of the day.

The yard was barren, but come spring it would be ablaze with dizzying color. Iris had been out and about, spreading garden spells and planting bulbs and flowers that would spring to life next year. Yet, even amid the frozen slush that muddied the parking area and turned the front and side yards into wading ponds, our land had a feral beauty to it. We'd never manage manicured gardens and well-formed hedges—those were the province of elves and humans—but the Fae were known for their wild places. And we had enough of our father's blood in us to bring out that aspect in any place we lived.

I glanced at the woods down by the edge of the expansive lawn. The path to Birchwater Pond beckoned to me, but I had work to do, much as I wanted to go wandering. I wasn't an alley cat, happy to prowl the city streets. No, I preferred the country, and I'd rather be scampering down the back roads, whether in two-legged or four-legged form. I pushed aside the craving for a quiet walk and turned my attention to Camille's car.

The Lexus was a beauty, and she kept it in pristine condition, much to the consternation of her bank account. At least she put her ability to charm the pants off just about any human male to good use. She always managed to get a discount on services and parts, and both Menolly and I took her along when we needed work done on our own vehicles.

I pulled out the crystal Queen Asteria's messenger had given us and closed my eyes as I grasped it in my hand. The magic pulsated, a steady rhythm warming my skin. I wasn't a witch, but the energy had an oddly familiar cadence to it.

Elfin magic went back far before that of most wizards. Camille was tied to the Moon Mother, and her magic had roots extending far into the haze of history, but the elves . . . their magic was that of tree and wood, and deep dark caverns, and ancient rivers running wild through the land. They walked the paths of the forests, and even Elqaneve, their city, was grounded firmly in the soil of Otherworld, though it had first taken hold in the body of the Earth Mother.

Slowly, with an even pace, I circled Camille's car, watching the crystal carefully. It flickered softly, pale blue, frost white, and then, as I reached the trunk, a blush of rose began to form inside the sunburst. Bingo. I popped her trunk, and the crystal flared. And then I paused. I don't know what stopped me—instinct perhaps, or perhaps a gut feeling—but I pulled my hand out of the trunk and turned on the flashlight that I'd been carrying in my pocket. I flicked it on, and what I saw made me grateful I hadn't reached into the dark.

Toward the back, a metal disk the size of a quarter was fastened to the floor of the trunk. A bug, no doubt. But guarding the disk were two brown spiders with jointed brown legs. They could have been house spiders, but I knew they weren't. They might have been Weres, but again, I knew they weren't. They were guardians, magically enhanced to withstand the cold weather. Sentinels. And they would have bitten me if I'd reached in without looking.

I slowly withdrew my hand, not wanting to alarm them. If

they scuttled off behind the liner in the trunk, there'd be no finding them. They'd have the advantage, and their target would most likely be Camille. I shut the trunk gently and bolted back up the stairs into the kitchen, where Camille and Iris were putting away the dishes out of the dishwasher.

"There's a bug, all right," I said, "and two guards to make sure it's not disturbed. I think they've been enchanted, which means insecticide probably won't work on them. We need to catch them or kill them. We can't let them get away."

Iris frowned. "I have a spell that might work," she said. "But I need a feather from a scavenger bird and a bit of spiderweb."

"I have the spiderweb," Camille said. "What kind of feather are you talking about?"

"Crow, raven, something along that line." Iris folded the dish towel. "I'll go get my wand."

As she disappeared into the room off the back of the kitchen, I looked at Camille. "Iris is coming in more and more handy. I'm glad she's here."

"Me, too," Camille said grimly. "I wonder how many of those things are in my car. I'm not too sure that I want to drive all the way out to Smoky's in it. Who knows what else they have hidden in there?"

"The Hunters Moon Clan must have spies planted all over the Puma Pride compound, and I'll bet they wanted to find out what was going on with us being there, so they planted the bug last night while we were searching the land. Thank the gods we kept our mouths shut on our way home."

I frowned, looking at the ceiling. My skin crawled, and even though I knew it was psychosomatic, I scratched my arm, thinking about the eight-legged creeps. "And you have to wonder, if they've traced us back here, are they planting spies in our house right now? I'm getting the heebie-jeebies big time, Camille."

She wrapped her arm around me. "It's okay. Everything will be okay," she whispered. "The wards haven't been set off." She paused. "That's odd. The wards didn't trip when we came onto the land last night, and those spiders are enemy enough to set them off. I wonder what happened?"

"I dunno, but I'm liking the Hunters Moon Clan less and less the more we find out about them."

"When Trillian gets back, we'll ask his advice," Camille said. "He's good with dark magic. I have a feeling that the werespiders are into some pretty nasty stuff." With a sigh, she let her arm drop and picked up the phone. "I'll call Morio and ask him to bring his SUV. Chances are it's clean, but leave me the crystal so I can check it out. Meanwhile, why don't you go run it around your Jeep and Menolly's Jag? Safe is better than sorry. I'll go get the feather and spiderweb for Iris."

Once again, I clattered down the porch steps, and this time went through the routine again with the crystal and my Jeep, and then Menolly's Jaguar. So far, so good. Nothing. I glanced back at the house just in time to see Camille and Iris appear. Iris was wearing a thin green robe that showed off her curves. She might be old enough to be our aunt and a good deal shorter than we were, but she was still as sexy as a maid on a summer morning.

As they headed down the porch steps, I tossed Iris the keys. She caught them and quickly unlocked the trunk, then lobbed them back to me. Camille handed Iris the spiderweb, which the house sprite immediately ate, and then the feather, which she held up to the winds. Without fanfare or pomp, it vanished as Iris mumbled something I couldn't catch.

And then she leaned forward and blew into the trunk in the direction of the spiders and the bug. A shower of frost shot forth with her breath, freezing everything in sight and startling me so much that I almost fell on my butt. The inside of the trunk looked like it had been through an ice storm. The spiders were frozen in place. Iris held out a quart jar and, using the end of her wand, tapped them into it and shut the lid.

She walked over to where Camille and I were watching, both of us thoroughly impressed, and held up the jar. The spiders were frozen, but I had the feeling they weren't dead. "Got them! Now, take care of that bug while I give these fellows a one-way trip to the Underworld. Then I'll just tidy up and dress for our shopping trip."

As she climbed the porch steps, I shook my head. "She's a

wonder. What did we ever do without her? I bet the OIA is paying her substandard wages, too. They always shortchange the sprites and their kin."

Camille frowned. "Yeah, and I know that she's absolutely refused to go to Otherworld to stay. Of course, she's a member of the Earthside Fae. She loves it here." She kissed me on the cheek. "Thanks for finding that bug."

I gave her a quick hug and walked over to my Jeep, where I swung into the driver's seat and stared at the dashboard.

Camille followed me and climbed in the passenger side to wait. "What's going on? You have something on your mind?"

"No, not really," I said, staring through the windshield. "I guess this whole mess just has me shook up. I'm worried about Father and Aunt Rythwar. And I'm attracted to Zach, yet he makes me nervous. The whole Puma Pride makes me nervous. They're hiding something, Camille, but I can't put my finger on what it is. It's something big, though."

Even as I spoke, I knew that's what had been nagging at me since we first set foot on their land. The Puma Pride was hiding a secret buried so deep that it would take a bulldozer to unearth it. A secret they were dying for.

"Do you think the Puma Pride's in league with the demons? With Shadow Wing?" Camille asked.

I thought about it for a moment. "No, it doesn't track. I don't think they're the bad guys. That shield wasn't from their clan. I think it's from the Hunters Moon Clan. And I think that they're after the Puma Pride, and we'd better find out why before the werespiders have killed everybody there." Trying to shake off my fear, I shook my head.

"The Were clans and tribes over here Earthside are a lot more territorial than the clans back home in Otherworld," Camille said. "Maybe this is all about revenge. Maybe this has nothing to do with our Degath Squad. Maybe the Degath Squad has nothing to do with us. Could the Hunters Moon Clan have summoned them to help them wage war against the Puma Pride for their own twisted reasons?"

I hadn't thought of that. "It's a possibility, I suppose. The clans at home seem to get along better. They can be dicey around the full moon, but they aren't so tightly wrapped up in their own little worlds as they are over here, Earthside. Of course, in OW they're accepted as normal members of society, so maybe they don't have to be so clannish."

Iris reappeared at the top of the stairs, dressed in a skirt and sweater set. She was carrying a velvet blazer and slipped it on as she hurried down to my Jeep.

"I dispatched the spiders. They weren't Weres, but they were magically enhanced hobo spiders. They're pretty much toast, so don't worry about them."

I had a sudden flash and glanced at her. "Uh, you didn't put them in the oven, did you?"

"I wouldn't do that," she said, shocked. "That would be cruel and unusual punishment. I nuked them."

Blinking, I stared at her. Camille opened her mouth to say something, then shut it again.

Iris shrugged. "What? Squashing won't work very well; they might be able to be reanimated later. I wanted them out of our way for good. Microwaves and magic don't mix all that well, so it seemed the perfect solution. I made sure they were in a bag first, though, so they didn't mess up the inside of the oven."

I admit that I ate the occasional mouse or rat or butterfly, but suddenly breakfast seemed a little too close to the surface. Camille had a look on her face that told me she felt the same way I did.

"Yes, well . . . thank you." Camille hopped out of the Jeep. "I'll make sure Maggie's downstairs with Menolly before Morio and I leave, if you're not back by then," she said, heading for the house.

I waved, then reached over to help Iris hop in, but she clambered into the Jeep without my help and fastened her seat belt. "Okay, let's roll. I want to hit the sales before it gets too late in the day," she said.

Thinking that I was very glad Iris was on *our* side, I pulled out of the driveway, and we took off for Belles-Faire Town Square, one of the bigger shopping districts in the area.

* * *

Two hours later, I coasted the car to a stop in front of the house. I glanced over at Iris, who was still glaring.

"Still not speaking to me?" I asked with a grin. "I told you I'm sorry."

Iris jumped down to the ground and yanked a handful of bags out of the Jeep. I scurried out behind her, trying to placate the furious sprite.

"I didn't mean to! It wasn't my fault," I said, trying to help her with the parcels. She tore one particularly shiny bag out of my hand.

"I can't believe you actually did that," she said as she stomped up the porch steps. I followed more slowly, carrying the bags she'd left behind.

"Listen, maybe someday I'll manage to gain better control over my nature, but until then, you're just going to have to accept that I'm not always in the driver's seat." I tried to keep pace with her. For such a short woman, she was surprisingly fast.

She dropped her bags on the porch and whirled. "And just how would we have explained it to those poor children if you'd killed that turkey? As it was, you practically scalped the poor thing. I may like a good roast bird for Thanksgiving or Yuletide, but at least I make sure mine's *dead* before I try to eat it! And look at you—you've got feathers all over your shirt. You look a mess." She slammed her way through the door.

Miserable, I glanced down at my shirt, where a few stray and bedraggled feathers clung to the fabric. *Oops.* I picked them off, sighing. It wasn't my fault that there had been a petting zoo in the middle of Gosford's Plaza. And it really wasn't my fault that the rather large turkey in the pen had been so appealing.

"Look, I'll make it right with the store," I said, hurrying in behind her. "I'll call them and tell them it wasn't your fault and that you shouldn't be banned from there because of me. Okay?"

"That's another thing! Gosford's is my favorite place to shop. Being forcibly evicted from there is just not an option." Iris let out a little huff and set her purchases down on the kitchen counter. "Whatever. Just . . . oh just nothing . . ."

I saw a tiny crack of a smile trying to break through her frown. "You have to admit," I said, "it was pretty funny."

"Not for that damned bird," she said and then let out a stifled laugh. "Oh, *all right*. It was funny, but there aren't enough laughs in the world that will make up for getting me expelled from shopping Nirvana."

"Hey, you yourself said we managed to get everything you wanted. And I paid for it all, so you shouldn't be so pissed at me," I mumbled as I poked through the refrigerator. I wanted poultry, and I wanted it now. A container on the top shelf held some leftover KFC, and I grinned as I pulled it out and dug in. "Want a piece?" I asked, offering her a drumstick.

"I do not, thank you very much!" Iris snorted and went to work unpacking our loot. At least she was smiling again. She spread out the decorations and candles, then folded the bags and carried them out to the back porch to put them away. The next thing I knew, she let out a piercing shriek. I dropped the chicken leg and raced to the door.

Iris was standing frozen, gazing at a large web strung across the porch. It was thick and ropy, unlike any spiderweb I'd ever seen. In the center, held by strands as strong as steel, was a grumpy old tomcat who prowled the backwoods. My friend, Cromwell. And he'd been drained dry, a folded paper tucked between a rubber band and his neck.

I shuddered and stepped forward, a slow burn building in my heart. I quietly disengaged the cat, carrying him over to the counter where Iris kept her gardening supplies, and removed the paper from beneath the band, wanting to kill whoever put it on him.

Cromwell was a stray who'd been through a lot of fights in his life. We'd chatted several times when I'd been out prowling under the full moon. He'd been on his own since he was a kitten and didn't much like people, but he made his way from house to house. Most of the neighbors left out a handful of food for him every night. Sometimes the raccoons got it before he could, but then he'd just move on to the next house and eat there.

He was old, and he was sick and probably dying, but he'd stubbornly clung to life, fueled by the will to survive, to fight against the odds.

"He didn't deserve this," I said, fighting back tears. I clenched my fists as I stood over his body, wanting to teach whoever had murdered him just how it felt to be sucked dry of both life and dignity.

Iris came up behind me and gently rubbed my lower back. "I'm so sorry. I've seen him around the neighborhood. He was a buddy of yours, wasn't he?"

I glanced down at her, wondering how much she knew about my life as a cat. Nodding, I reached for a burlap sack to cover him up, but she stayed my hand and said, "I'll be back in a minute. You stand guard over him."

While I waited, I unfolded the paper. In looping Spenserian script—thin and spidery and written with precision—it said: "Curiosity killed the cat. Keep away from the Rainier Puma Pride, or you and your sisters might end up joining your friend."

Iris reappeared with a silk pillowcase embroidered with tulips and daisies. I recognized it as one of her own and gave her a grateful look.

Quietly, I slipped the note into my pocket, then picked up Cromwell and slid him gently into the waiting folds of his silken shroud. Iris tied the end of the pillowcase shut with a purple velvet ribbon and looked at me, waiting for my lead.

I turned back to the web and let out a loud hiss. Iris pushed me out of the way. With a flicker of her hands the web froze and crashed to the floor, breaking into shards as it fell. I picked up the shovel and motioned for her to follow with Cromwell. We carried him out to the backyard and there, beneath a young oak, I dug a hole.

Iris laid him in. "Do you want to say a few words?"

I thought about it but then shook my head. Cromwell wasn't one for ceremonies. He wasn't a lap cat. He'd been a fighter, a true tom. If he had been human, he would have been a soldier or warrior. Cromwell wouldn't have wanted pretty words or flowery good-byes. I just pressed my fingers to my lips and blew him a kiss. "May Lady Bast take you into her arms, my sweet friend," I whispered before filling in the grave.

On our way back inside, I showed Iris the note.

She shrugged off the warning. "You're not going to let this stop you, are you?"

I snorted. "They chose the wrong girls to pick on and the wrong cat to kill. Iris, we've faced down demons and won. A nest of spiderlings can't hold a candle to that kind of fiend." But still, when we returned to the back porch, I couldn't help but glance at the walls, the ceiling, the corners of the room to make sure we weren't being watched.

CHAPTER 10

At precisely four thirty, Menolly woke. She brought Maggie up with her from her lair and sat in the rocking chair playing with the baby while Iris and I filled her in on what had happened. Camille and Morio were still out, but a message on the phone told us they'd be late and not to worry.

"I suppose that leaves you to come to the meeting with me," Menolly said. She didn't say much about the spiders and Cromwell, but I could tell she was taking it all in, listening and thinking as we spoke.

I nodded. "Let me change first. I still have feathers from the turkey stuck to me."

"Turkey?" Menolly asked, darting a look at Iris, who stifled a chuckle.

I arched my back and nodded. "Oh go on and tell her. You're dying to anyway." I left the room, but all the way upstairs, I could hear Iris and Menolly laughing away. No doubt at my expense.

I tossed my dirty clothes into my hamper and decided to take a quick shower. The meeting was at eight. During the spring and summer, they started around eleven P.M. to avoid any chance of sunlight, but during the late winter nights, especially in December when everybody was busy with holiday plans, Vampires Anonymous held their meetings during the early evening to allow their members time enough to ensure their loved ones made it home safe before going out to feed.

By the time I had changed clothes and was back downstairs, Menolly had changed into a long-sleeved sweater and calf-length linen skirt, both in shades of blue green, and a pair of high-heeled brown leather boots. Her burnished braids stood out against the teal, and she'd attempted to put some color into her cheeks, though it wasn't her best look. Even the palest blush stood out like clown makeup against her alabaster skin. I gently reached out and began spit-cleaning her cheeks. She rolled her eyes.

"All right, all right, I get the message. I'll go wash it off," she said.

"The lip gloss looks great, but the blush . . ."

She plunked Maggie into my arms and took off for the bathroom. When she returned, she looked normal again. I handed Maggie to Iris, and Menolly and I took off for town.

The night was clear and cold, with the temperature dropping rapidly. I zipped up my jacket, but the air rippled around me, the breeze sapping every ounce of warmth from my body. Menolly didn't bother with coats. The weather didn't affect her. Unless it was raining or unless the jacket went with her outfit, she'd given up outerwear.

She insisted on driving, so I hopped in the passenger seat and leaned back against the headrest, thinking about Cromwell the cat, and Zachary, and the Hunters Moon Clan. The last thing I felt like doing was attending a support group for a bunch of vampires. Drinking blood from a Happy Meal on legs seemed only a step or two above sucking out their predigested internal organs, but since Menolly was willingly accepting our support, far be it from me to make waves.

"Okay," I said as she climbed in and buckled her seat belt. "Let's get this show on the road."

She put the car into gear, and we eased out of the driveway onto the road and into the night.

The meeting was in full swing by the time we got there, and my mood started to pick up a little. Most of the vampires who attended Wade's group were doing their best to coexist peacefully with the living. Contrary to their nature, they chose to continue their life—unlife?—in the best way they could.

Some had jobs, a few were married, others continued on with their social lives and volunteer work. Most had been FBHs. And yes, they all drank blood but did their best to be careful, and the lion's share of their meals walked away to live another day, albeit a cup or so low on red octane.

Over the past two months Menolly had worked together with Sassy Branson, a socialite-turned-vamp, to instill a little decorum and tidiness in the patchwork cluster of living dead that came to the meetings. The Goth boys and girls who'd been coming to the meetings covered with grime and dried blood were now clean and tidy, if still attired in their ever-present black.

There were a couple of Microsoft nerds in the group, but now their hair was brushed, and they wore fresh T-shirts. Tad Radcliffe was a cutie with a ponytail down to his ass. He'd brought along his very-much-alive girlfriend, and she looked more nervous than a cat in a dog kennel. The other geek, Albert, was a pudgy young man who reminded me of the Comic Book Guy off *The Simpsons*, and was constantly bemoaning his bad luck.

He actually had a point, when I thought about it. Never again able to eat his favorite foods—Budweiser, Whoppers, and nachos—neither would he ever be able to shed the beer belly he'd put on before his death and rebirth. Something seemed inherently unfair about the situation. He, too, brought his touchstone with life: his best friend, a gnarly-looking dude wearing a Red Dwarf sweatshirt.

Still others kept to the shadows: a young woman who seemed terribly unsure about what she was doing there, an old-school vamp who liked to terrify his victims and insisted on wearing the full Dracula getup, cape and all, and an arrestingly beautiful woman who looked like a Scandinavian ski bunny. None of them talked much, and all looked either angry or bored, but they came week after week, drawn by the social life they could no longer have in the regular world.

Sassy Branson was always there, too. She air-kissed us the moment we came through the door. "You haven't forgotten about my Christmas party, have you?" she asked, her voice rich and thick and intoxicating.

A chic socialite from Seattle's upper crust, her friends still thought she was alive. She kept to her house in the daytime, cultivating the image of eccentric recluse, and only went out and threw parties at night.

"We have it on our calendar," I said, grinning. "The twenty-second, the night after the solstice, right?" We'd have time to celebrate both her party and Yuletide.

Menolly greeted Sassy with a smile, but even as she exchanged a few words with the older woman, she was scanning the room. I knew who she was looking for. Wade Stevens, the organizer of Vampires Anonymous. He and Menolly had been dating on a casual basis since their first meeting.

She perked up, and I glanced over by the podium. There he stood, hair forever spiky, forever bleached blond. Wade was around five foot ten and solid but trim. He wore glasses—not that he needed them anymore—and was dressed in a pair of tidy jeans, a white tee, and over the top, an unbuttoned Hawaiian shirt.

"Uh-oh," she said softly.

"What's wrong?" I glanced around. Everybody seemed to be behaving themselves. There were no fights, no hissing or extended fangs anywhere. Since this was the monthly family-and-friends night, all the vampires—even the Vlad wannabe—were on their best behavior.

"Look over there. Standing beside Wade." She stared. Hard.

I glanced in the direction in which she was looking. Next to Wade stood a woman who was clearly a vampire, but unlike any I'd ever seen. Her hair had been back-combed into a huge, coppery-colored bouffant. She was short and stout and wore a polyester pantsuit. Her handbag was big enough to slam-dunk a mugger with. And Wade had her nose and her eyes.

"Oh great gods, is that his mother?" I asked, unable to tear my eyes away from the pair. "Don't tell me she's—"

"A vampire, too? Yes, she is. I was hoping to avoid meeting her, but I guess she decided it was time to get a look at what Wade's been doing here." Menolly frowned.

Wade seemed a little irritated, too. His usual cheer had taken on a strained quality, and he looked even more pale than usual. But when he glanced up and spotted us, the gloom disappeared, and he waved us over. Menolly let out a long sigh as we maneuvered through the rows of chairs.

"Let's get this over with," she said. "This might just be the deal breaker."

"*I'm* the one who has to worry that she might bite. What's wrong with you?" I teased her.

"You don't understand," she said. "You've never heard Wade talk about his mother. I can't believe somebody went and turned her into a vampire. I'd like to rip the balls off of whichever idiot did it."

I choked, and she thumped me a good one on my back, but it was too late. Wade's mother heard me coughing and turned our way. Within seconds, she'd reached our side and was rooting through that giant handbag of hers. She finally found what she was looking for—a menthol cough drop—and shoved it my way.

"Here, dearie, you sound like you're catching a cold. Take this—go on, take it!" she insisted as I shook my head. "I have plenty, and you—you're still among the living. If you don't take it, you might end up with pneumonia, and let me tell you, a pretty girl like you doesn't want to take to her sickbed. You don't have our natural protection against disease, you know. Go on, now, it'll soothe your throat. Take it!" As she pressed the cough drop into my hand, she turned to Wade and gave him a little swat on the arm. "Well, don't just stand there. Introduce us."

Wade closed his eyes briefly, as if trying the old *I'm asleep and when I open my eyes this will all be over* ploy. When he blinked and saw that she was still there, he forced a smile.

"Mother, this is Delilah D'Artigo. And this is her sister Menolly. I told you about Menolly, remember? Girls, this is my mother, Mrs. Belinda Stevens."

Wade's mother looked us up and down as if we were stray cats that her son had dragged home. Especially Menolly. She flashed us a bright smile, but her eyes were cold. Whether her reserve was from her being a vampire or not, I wasn't sure. She held out her hand languidly, almost as though she didn't really want to touch us.

Menolly accepted her hand and shook it with a squeeze that brought a little gasp from Mrs. Stevens. I gave Belinda a nod.

"So nice to meet you, girls." She peered closer. "Wade tells me you're both half-Faerie." The word *Faerie* came out with a horrendously nasal twang, making it sound like some dread disease. "You have another sister, yes? She's the one who wears the corsets so tight it's a wonder that her boobs don't pop out over the top, am I right?"

Menolly let out a little cough as if she were about to say something, but I jabbed her in the ribs, and she turned her head.

Belinda Stevens walked among the rolls of those most dreaded of all women, both Earthside and in Otherworld, whether you were Fae, a vampire, a Were, or human: *the boyfriend's mother.*

"Camille is a force unto herself," I said, stepping in. "She's dynamic and vital, and without her, we'd be lost."

Wade edged closer to his mother, tapping her on the elbow. "Pull in your fangs, Mother. These are my friends."

"And Menolly here is more than just a friend, so you say." Belinda arched one eyebrow in a fair imitation of Mr. Spock and transferred her purse to a nearby chair. "So tell me, girls, how long have you been on Earth?"

"We prefer the term *Earthside* to *on Earth.* We aren't, after all, aliens from another planet," Menolly said, her words crisp. "Otherworld and Earthside were linked together in the past. Long ago."

"I see," Belinda said. Quite clearly, she didn't. "And so how long have you been *Earthside*?"

"About seven . . . maybe eight months." Menolly's eyes were taking on a shine that I didn't like. I'd seen that look before, when she was staring at something that she considered a blight on existence. Trillian, for example, or wine spritzers or cockroaches.

"And how long have you been a vampire, dearie?" Honey would have oozed faster than the saccharine sweetness flowing off the woman's tongue.

Menolly let out a loud sigh. Obviously, Wade had not

warned his mother about touchy subjects, or she wouldn't be so nosy. "Twelve Earthside years, Mrs. Stevens. And you? How long ago were you killed and raised?"

Blinking as if surprised to be asked such an intimate question, Belinda shrugged. "Two years now. I'm actually grateful, though. I can watch over my little boy forever," she said, patting Wade on the arm.

He grimaced, and I heard Menolly suck in a deep breath—purely reflex since she didn't need to breathe. I grabbed her by the shoulder, gripping her tightly. She stiffened, then relaxed.

"Isn't that so incredibly *sweet*?" she said as Wade gave her a hopeless look. Nothing he could do would stop his mother from her appointed task to gather and assimilate personal information.

Belinda paused for a moment, then, "Twelve years? You must have been a young girl when it happened. So little life experience; what a pity."

Menolly snapped then. "Actually, I'm probably almost as old as you were at the time of your death, though *I* look a damned sight better. I'm the youngest of my sisters, so right now—including the twelve years I've been a vampire—I'm about fifty-five years old, counting by your calendar. Is there anything else you want to know? How many men I've slept with, or maybe my bra size?"

Uh-oh. Wanting out of the way of any resulting fireworks, I edged my way toward Sassy Branson. She liked me. She'd protect me if anything happened. Because I knew there was no way in hell that I could fight my way out of a room of bitchy vampires.

As I took one step too many and ended up in Sassy's lap—she was sitting right behind me—she put her arms around me and pulled me against her to whisper in my ear. "I'm betting that Menolly wishes she could take his mother down and stake her right now. Too bad she can't. At least, not here. Listen, if the going gets rough, you just stay by me, okay?" She let out a shuddering sigh. I realized she could hear the pulse of my blood, and even though I wanted to break away and run, I knew better. I just nodded. Vigorously.

The rest of the room seemed to pause, the other—living—guests warily backing toward the exits. The last thing we needed were for the vampires to get set off because of a cat-fight. Even though Belinda wasn't exactly model material, the sight of two women rolling around in a wrestling match might just do it for these guys, and the fact that there were a few meals-on-wheels like me around would only serve to heighten their excitement.

Wade eased his way between Belinda and Menolly. He gently pushed them apart. "Mother, Menolly, back off. We don't want a fight here." He glanced at each one in turn.

Speak for yourself, psych-boy, I thought. Menolly loved a good fight. And it looked like Belinda was no slouch in the rough-and-ready category herself, though I'd wager she'd deny it.

"Please, Mother," he added, whispering so low that I could barely hear him. Only my cat's hearing helped me pick up what he was saying. "This is my group. Don't embarrass me in front of them."

She gave him that icy stare that only irate mothers can give and then sighed and sat down, shaking her head. "Have it your way. Ignore the fact that I gave birth to you and spent thirty-two hours in labor. Ignore the fact that I put you through med-ical school when that no-good father of yours disappeared and that I made sure you had enough to eat and all the clean clothes you could ever want. You're an adult now. But all I ever wanted was for you to be happy. I just try to find out a little bit about this girl you've fallen for, and you both nearly stake me for my questions. Don't mind me—I'm just an old woman, and my feelings don't count—"

Wade pressed his lips together and shook his head at the ceiling. "I'm sorry, Mother. You know I appreciate all you've done for me—"

"And I keep on doing for you, and it looks like now I'll be your mother forever, or until you drive me into the sun with your lack of consideration!"

Menolly bit her lip so hard I could see the tooth marks. She touched Wade on the arm. "I think we'd better get the meeting started." Ignoring Belinda entirely, she turned and walked away, effectively slapping the woman in the face.

I turned, wildly looking around for something to focus my attention on so I wouldn't break into hysterical laughter. Sassy noticed my expression and did the last thing in the world I was prepared for. She grabbed me and planted her lips full on mine as one of her hands reached up to caress my breast.

Shocked by how good her kiss felt, how exquisite her touch felt, I let her lock lips with me, swooning as I wondered languidly if she'd take me home with her and do delicious things to my body all night long. But, amid the lingering kiss and ensuing fantasies running through my mind, I realized my danger. Trying to keep panic at bay, I did my best to push Sassy back. Menolly had beat the warnings into my head: *Vampires Are Not Safe. Do Not Mess Around with the Undead. Do Not Offer Yourself As a Willing Slushy Machine.*

Don't get me wrong, the concept of having sex with another woman wasn't the issue—that had occurred to me before, and I expected one day I'd act on it—but Sassy was a vampire, not an FBH anymore, and her tongue in my mouth was a little more than I could handle at the moment. I had no designs, past my immediate carnal reaction, on being her love bunny.

As I was starting to get afraid that I hadn't objected quickly enough, Sassy broke it off. Staring at me with glittering eyes, she grabbed my hand and dragged me to the back of the room.

"Sorry about that," she muttered. "I just didn't want you to laugh. That might have caused problems. Most vampires take themselves way too seriously, and the laughter thing kind of gets to them."

"And you don't?" I couldn't help but ask.

"Heaven help me, no." She grinned at me and patted her hair back in place. "My dear, I didn't reach the age I did by taking myself seriously. You have to let go and laugh. It's a lesson I learned the hard way during life, and it's one that I hope never to forget in death. *Undeath.*"

"Thank you," I murmured, still shaken by my reaction to her. "I think." Once I made sure we were well away from the melodrama playing out with Wade and his mother, I added, "I thought for sure there would be bloodshed between Menolly and Belinda."

Sassy stifled a laugh. "I think it's funny. Menolly's just trying to be accepted by Wade's nest, my dear, and her way of doing that is to earn the respect of his mother through asserting herself."

Somehow I didn't think Menolly gave a rat's ass about being accepted by Belinda Stevens, but I kept my mouth shut.

"I do pity the poor boy," Sassy continued. "I gather somebody got pissed off at him and turned his mother into a vampire in retaliation. Wade and his mother never got along in life. Now she's going to be on his back forever, because I can guarantee you, women like that do not give up control over their sons."

I glanced over my shoulder at the trio and shuddered. Just another reason why I never intended to marry. My family was warped enough, but add somebody else's family to the mix, and the possibilities were nightmarish. I turned back to Sassy.

"So, we really are looking forward to your party next week," I said, striving for some sense of normalcy.

She beamed. "My dear, it's simply going to be the event of the season! I'm glad you're coming," she added, reaching out to sweep my bangs out of my eyes. "You really are a lovely girl," she said in a husky voice, and I realized that Sassy was hiding more than the fact that she was a vampire. She was definitely a woman's woman. My stomach lurched as she swept her gaze up and down my body. The scary thing was that I found myself responding to the invitation. Vampires could charm Fae, but not as easily as they could humans.

"My boyfriend thinks so, too," I said, deciding that Chase had uses I hadn't put to the test. Deflecting interested vamps might just be one of them.

Sassy gave me a curious look, then after a moment shook her head and turned away. "It looks like they're ready to start the meeting," she said. "By the way, at my party, please remember that most of my old friends don't know I'm dead, so mum's the word."

With a giggle, she brushed a stray strand of her gray hair back into the tidy chignon she wore it in. Sassy's brilliant plum dress and sable wrap seemed lushly out of place in the basement meeting hall, but when I looked in her eyes, I realized how alone she must feel, hiding in the closet for so many reasons. She was a lonely woman, and it was obvious that she still had quite the conscience. Sassy Branson was a misfit, as were we all. And perhaps that is why I liked the woman.

By the time Menolly and I pulled into the driveway, she was willing to talk again. After the meeting, the moment I opened my mouth to say something, she shushed me, telling me to shut up. She fumed all the way home, driving a good sixty miles an hour, though I kept asking her to slow down. She didn't even notice when I plugged CCR into her CD player, a group she usually detested.

Morio's Subaru was in the yard, though, and so was Trillian's Harley. We'd jumped out of the Jag and headed for the house when she stopped me.

"Kitten, I'm sorry I was so snippy on the way home. It just took me some time to calm down. I never expected Wade's mother to be such a bitch."

"She is rather Jerry Springer, isn't she?" I said, giggling.

That cadged a smile out of her, and she wrapped her arm around my waist. "Yes, she is at that, Kitten," she said. "And that's precisely why Wade and I are going to just be friends. I don't think I could subject myself to frequent visits from his mother, even if he was the best lover in the world. And he's not. I like him, and I'll help with the group, but dating? I don't think so. Now, come on, let's go see what bad news the terrible trio have managed to dredge up."

Camille and her lovers were curled up on the sofa. Trillian sat on her left side, his arm draped over her thigh, and Morio was on her right, his arm resting around her shoulder.

"Have a party while we were gone?" The words were out of my mouth before I could stop them.

Camille flashed me a snarky look, but beneath her grin was

a subdued look I seldom saw from her. Both Morio and Trillian were frowning. Actually, Morio was frowning, but Trillian had a scowl a mile wide.

Menolly pulled up the ottoman, while I dropped into the recliner. "Okay, Father—the war—the shield—Smoky . . . Spill it," I said.

Trillian snorted, then said, "Your father is safe, as far as I can tell. He disappeared into the woodlands near where your aunt is living. There *is* a price on his head, but he hasn't been caught. Your aunt is safe for the moment, too."

Relief must have shown on my face, because he added, "Don't get your hopes up. The war is in full swing. Y'Elestrial has moved on Svartalfheim, and the actual battle's begun." Trillian let out a long sigh, and I realized that he was as unhappy over the situation as we were.

"What about the OIA?" Menolly asked.

"They've been put under military rule. There isn't a chance in hell the cavalry will be coming to your rescue if something happens."

It was as bad as we feared, but at least our father and our aunt were both safe. I glanced at Camille. "And the shield we found at Zach's? And Smoky?"

As I spoke, a shadow flickered over Trillian's face, enough to tell me that somehow the dragon was the source of his irritation.

Camille bit her lip. "As we thought, the shield has demon energy behind it. My bet is that it belongs to one of the Hell Scouts. We left it out at Smoky's in his safekeeping. I don't want it in our house."

I stared at my hands, not wanting to think about the answer to the next question. But it had to be asked. "What did Smoky say about all this?"

She pushed herself off the sofa and walked over to the window, staring out into the darkened night. "An ill wind is blowing, and our names are riding the currents. I can feel it, as sure as I can feel my heart beating." She turned. "Smoky will help us, but he said we don't need to fly to the Northlands; he knows how to open a magical gate that will summon the Autumn

Lord. He agrees that it's our best decision and our only real course of action."

"What's the price?" Menolly asked. "There has to be a price. We're dealing with a dragon and an old one at that."

Trillian jumped up and stormed into the kitchen. By the sound of it, he was rummaging around in the refrigerator. That was odd. Trillian never threw tantrums. He was a scary-ass cold-as-ice dude who rarely allowed his feelings to show. Menolly and I glanced at one another, then at Camille.

She cleared her throat. "In return for his help, I've agreed to become his consort for one week. We'll make the arrangements later, after we've taken care of this matter with the Puma Pride. I'll do whatever he wants, so long as it doesn't interfere with my oaths and allegiances to you two and to the Elfin Queen."

Concubine. While she didn't say the word, it echoed in my head. Yep, Smoky was going to have his way with Camille one way or another, and he'd just found the perfect excuse. Clever of him, but then again, he was a dragon, and we didn't dare ever forget that little fact.

A crash from the kitchen followed by "Gods almighty, where's the damned ketchup?" told us that Trillian was well and truly pissed.

Morio shook his head. "The price is high, but it's your decision. It can't be easy, being a dragon's mistress, but I believe he'll be honorable to his word. As much as he can be. That being said, he made it quite clear as to just what sort of services you'll be providing. I'd rest up before your week, Camille," he said with a soft smile. "You're going to be a very busy woman."

Startled, I turned away. Morio almost sounded like he was enjoying the fallout. As I caught his eye, he winked, and I hastily jerked my attention back to Menolly, who simply gave Camille an accepting nod as if it were a done deal, no further thought needed on the subject.

"And in return? What exactly did he promise?" Menolly asked.

"In return, he will open the barrier to the Northlands. And

he'll summon the Autumn Lord. Menolly, you'd better not come with us. The spell has to be cast in the afternoon. Smoky insisted that Delilah, Zachary, Morio, and I come out to his land. He didn't invite Trillian, however." Camille let out a small grin. "I think he doesn't like the idea of—"

"He doesn't like the fact that you belong to *me* and that I'm only loaning you to him. And then, only if he returns you in one piece," Trillian said, stomping back into the room. He carried a large sandwich that looked far too messy.

I marched over to where he stood, holding the sub over the coffee table as he tried to keep the mustard from dripping. "Honestly, I know you're pissed, but this is ridiculous. Let me take that and I'll go make you another. I expect that Iris is in bed, or she'd do it."

Trillian gave me a blistering scowl but surrendered the massive hoagie, and I ran it into the kitchen, holding it out in front of me so it wouldn't drip all over my shirt. I dumped it in the garbage, then washed my hands. Before I set about making another for him—and one for myself—I took a quick peek in Iris's room to make certain she and Maggie were snuggled in for the night.

When I returned to the living room, Trillian was taking potshots at Smoky and berating Morio for allowing the deal to be struck.

"What was I supposed to do?" Morio said. "She's not *my* property. If she wants to fuck a dragon, I'm not going to stop her. And bluntly put, after what we felt on that shield today, I wouldn't bother to try. If it takes a roll in the meadow with Smoky to net us some much-needed information, then that's what it takes. Since Camille doesn't mind, why should we?"

Camille didn't look like she minded at all. In fact, she was blushing, and I had the feeling my sister was looking forward to the encounter. Knowing Smoky, he'd make sure she'd enjoy their liaison.

Trillian let out a growl. Menolly flashed him an exasperated look. "Oh for the sake of the gods, will you just deal with it? You don't care if he hurts her, you're just worried she'll like his package of goodies better than yours. And frankly, I think that, even in human form, you can count on Smoky having some pretty elaborate—and impressive—equipment. So you'd better prepare for some *hard* competition."

"I don't recall asking for your opinion, O Fangstress. Why don't you go stake yourself?" He sighed as he accepted the sandwich I'd made for him. Menolly hissed at him but kept her ground.

I shook my head. "Stop fighting, all of you. We have to do this. There's no other choice, and since Camille holds the key, that's simply the way things are. Do you think we should take Chase with us?"

Camille shook her head. "No, Smoky was specific about who he wanted there. But he did insist Zach come along—said something about since it's his people being slaughtered, he owed it to them to play his part in this journey."

That brought me right back to Cromwell and the threat. "Before we decide anything about who else is going, there's something you have to know. Did Iris tell you already? When we got home today—"

"She told us about the cat and the note," Morio said. His eyes were glistening. "I'm sorry about Cromwell," he added.

"Thank the gods Maggie was downstairs with Menolly," Camille whispered, giving me something new to worry about. "We need to make sure we never leave her unattended, even if it means she spends some of her days down in Menolly's lair or with Iris at the shop."

"So what do we do next? Tell Zachary he's expected to go along with us?" Menolly looked at Camille, then me. "Is there anything else we need to know about you traipsing off to meet the Autumn Lord?"

Camille frowned. "I'll ask the Moon Mother. I'll be back in a moment." She headed outside. As one, Morio and Trillian rose to go after her. Before they could reach the door, Menolly shoved them back into their seats.

"*I'll* make sure she's safe," she said, slipping out to the foyer as they glared after her. They weren't stupid enough to try anything, thank the gods.

The phone rang while we were waiting, and I picked up to

find Chase on the other end. I quickly filled him in on what
we'd discovered. He wasn't thrilled with the idea of us including Zachary on the trip out to Smoky's and leaving him behind, but he was trying to play it cool. Honestly, I thought.
Men were more trouble than they were worth sometimes, be
they FBH, Svartan, dragon, or Earthside Supe.

"I'll contact you as soon as we know more. Meanwhile,
don't bother contacting the OIA for a while. It's a mess back
in OW right now. If we need help from home, we'll contact
Queen Asteria."

"Who?" he asked.

"The Elfin Queen. I told you, remember?" I made a kissing
sound and hung up as Menolly and Camille returned to the
living room.

Camille paced the length of the room. "The Moon Mother
isn't talking, but I know this is the right thing to do. There's
something to be learned . . . and something to be gained, but
I can't tell what."

I closed my own eyes, searching the depths of my psyche.
And there it was: the same whisper on the wind. We had to go.
I had to go. This might be Zachary's story, but for better or
worse, we were part of it.

"You're right," I said. "I'll call Zach." I picked up the phone.

"Wait," she said, "there's something else."

I set the receiver down.

"The wards around the land were broken by whoever it was
that killed Cromwell. I was too preoccupied to notice when I
first got home, but now I can sense that they were negated. Not
triggered but eliminated, which accounts for the lack of immediate warning. Whoever was here has strong magic behind
them. After midnight, when the moon is strongest, I'll reset
them and see if I can find out anything more."

"Negated? That means a butt load of trouble."

For someone to deactivate Camille's wards meant they
wielded strong magic indeed. She might have her ups and
downs with her spell crafting, but if there was one thing she
was good at, it was warding the house and land. I flashed back
to Zachary's first visit to my office. He'd mentioned that his

shaman couldn't negate the wards, so whoever had deactivated them had to be stronger than Venus. Which meant big trouble for us, since Venus's magic seemed pretty damned potent.

I picked up the phone again. "Since Menolly's not going, we'll leave as soon as we can. When did Smoky say to come out?"

"He said to show up around three tomorrow," Camille said. "I'll go wake Iris and tell her she'll be watching the shop by herself. And she'd better take Maggie to work with her. If you could ask Chase to check in on them throughout the day, I'd appreciate it."

I nodded as I punched in Zach's number. The vision of Cromwell spread out in the web and sucked dry haunted me. Zachary's friends mattered, but I hadn't known them. But Cromwell, he was an innocent, caught in a dangerous game. Wrong place, wrong time. And I'd do everything I could to make sure that nobody—human, Were, or animal—ended up in that situation again.

CHAPTER 11

The next morning as I came downstairs from a late start—and an even later shower—Zachary knocked at the door. He had a five o'clock shadow that wouldn't quit. The beard gave him a rugged look, and I couldn't pull my gaze away. I wasn't sure exactly how I felt about the man, but I had to admit that he was gorgeous in a lumberjack sort of way.

My pulse quickened as he brushed against me on his way into the living room. I held my breath. Zachary smelled like warm musk and vanilla and cinnamon, and I wanted to reach out and touch his arm, to spend a lazy morning inhaling his scent.

"I'm not sure what good I'll be," he said. "I've never even heard of the Northlands or the Autumn Lord." He took off his coat and slid into a chair. "You got any coffee?" he asked. "I'm sleepwalking here."

I sniffed the air. Sure enough, the aroma of fresh-brewed coffee drifted out from the kitchen. "I think Camille's making a pot. Cream and sugar?"

"Nah. As black as ink and as thick as mud. Thanks." As he stretched his arms overhead, his T-shirt clung to the muscles that spanned his chest, framing his narrow waist. I tried not to stare but found myself mesmerized. The scent of his sweat hit my nostrils, and I quivered, not sure what to say or do next.

He squinted at me. "You look different this morning," he said.

"How so?" I asked, blushing. His gaze was almost palpable, like warm fingers tiptoeing over my skin on a cold morning.

Zach let out a low laugh. "I'm not sure. A little older. Alive and vibrant. Maybe I'm just tired, and everything seems vivid but . . . you just look . . ."

After an awkward moment, not knowing what to say or do, I forced myself to stammer out, "I'll be right back with your coffee. By the way," I added at the door, "the Northlands aren't on any map. They aren't in OW, either. They exist outside of both realms, through one of the sky portals. But that doesn't matter. We won't be going there. Smoky's invoking the Autumn Lord to come Earthside."

Leaving him to contemplate that, I headed into the kitchen.

Camille was standing near the stove, drinking her coffee. She'd dressed in a calf-length walking skirt, a plum cowl-necked sweater, and a pair of knee-high leather boots that had buckles on the side and a good tread for walking, even if the heels were three inches high. I never bothered to ask her how she could manage heels in the woods; it just seemed to come naturally to her. Meanwhile, I'd opted for my comfortable go-for-a-hike jeans, a turtleneck that was as turquoise as tropical water, and a pair of sneakers.

I leaned against the sink next to her, squeezing my eyes shut as I tried to figure out what to do about Zach. There was some sort of mutual attraction between us, that much was obvious, but I had no idea where to go from there. Or if I should go there at all.

"You okay?" Camille gave me a worried look.

"Yeah, I guess. Zach's here. He asked for some coffee."

Whether it was the hesitation in my voice or whether she was just observant, Camille set down her mug and faced me, a knowing smile on her lips. "You want him, don't you?"

I shrugged. "That's just it. I don't know. I wasn't sure at first whether it was just hormones or whether I was really attracted to him. I'm still not certain, but whatever it is, the feeling is getting stronger."

Camille sighed and poured him a mug of coffee. "He take cream and sugar?" I shook my head, and she continued. "I think you inherited a lot of your emotional reactions from Mother."

"Maybe, but it's not that I feel guilty because of Chase . . ." I stopped, searching my feelings. What I'd said was true, to a point, but there was something else there, something that made me hesitate.

I tried again. "Zachary's sexy and a Were and he seems like a good guy. I *should* be attracted to him. It makes sense. But I keep thinking, am I attracted to him because I think I'm supposed to be? What I have with Chase isn't logical. Chase isn't a Supe, he's possessive even though he tries to pretend he's not, he'll age and die a long time before I will. But . . . there's just something about him that I've grown comfortable with."

"Maybe you're more like Father than Mother," Camille said.

Letting out a long sigh, I jumped up to sit on the counter and swung my legs back and forth. "Zachary makes me feel awkward, like I'm not in control of myself. I don't feel very confident around him. And I don't know why."

"Want a little advice?" At my nod, Camille said, "Don't sweat it. Don't force it. Right now we have more important things to worry about, and I'd say just put the whole issue on the back burner for a while. If Zach and you are meant to come together as lovers, it will happen in its own time."

I stared at the coffee. The dark liquid was steaming, and a light froth of foam coiled on top. "I guess that's all I can do." As I reached for the mug, I noticed something on a paper plate near the microwave. "What's that?"

"Something important. I was going to tell you, but we got off track. This is another reason I suggest you wait to act on your feelings for Zach."

I glanced at the paper plate. It held a sticky pile of spiderweb, the web that had been Cromwell's final stand. "What's wrong?"

"I did some scrying on this web before dawn. I woke up early and couldn't get back to sleep, so I went out to make sure the new wards were holding. And then I checked the back porch—which I forgot to do last night in all the excitement." She paused, looking worried.

"And?"

"And . . . of course I found spider energy on the web and porch. But there was something beneath it—as if there'd been two magicians here, not one. So I did some more scrying to find out who was with the spiderling."

I nodded. "What did you find? Demon energy? The Jansshi demon?"

"That's the tricky part," she said, shaking her head. "Not demon energy, Delilah, but werepuma. Cat magic."

I tried to comprehend what she was saying, and then it dawned on me. "You're kidding! Couldn't it be some residue from me or something?"

She shook her head, keeping her voice low. "No. And to make sure, I checked Cromwell's body. There was a strong vibration of cat magic on him."

"But how do you know? I buried him." She couldn't be right about this; it meant . . . it meant too many bad things to think about. "Maybe the werepuma was following Cromwell's killer? Maybe he tried to stop him?"

She frowned, leaning back against the counter. "After I sensed the cat magic energy on the porch, I exhumed Cromwell's body." She looked at me, pleading for understanding. "You have to believe me—I wouldn't have done so if I hadn't needed to, but we have to know. It was the only way I could trace the energy."

Stunned, I leaned back against the counter. She dug up Cromwell's grave? A werepuma in league with the spider clan? I jerked around, looking over my shoulder at the archway that led to the hall.

"Could it have been Zachary? Is he setting us up for some reason? Do you think he's in league with the spiders? Or the demons? Maybe this is all a trap?" I began to shake. What if this was all a setup? What if we were being herded right into Shadow Wing's plan?

But Camille rested her hand on my shoulder. "I don't think it was Zachary. Otherwise, Smoky wouldn't have suggested bringing him with us. When I reset the wards, I targeted them to trigger if those same energies returned, and they're quiet this morning, so Zach can't be the one."

"Maybe it's a Were from a rival puma clan," I said, thinking. "There are others, though the Rainier Pride is by far the most active and respected, as far as I can tell." I let out a long sigh, wondering how much deeper this mess was going to get. "Did you . . . is Cromwell still . . ."

"He's buried again, with a ring of flowers around his body, and coins on his eyes so the boatman will ferry him across the river to the western shore to rest with Lady Bast. Trust me, I said prayers for his soul, and he's safe back in the arms of the Cat Mother again." She paused, then added, "About Zachary . . . I'm pretty sure he's okay, but just in case he's being used, don't let down your guard. And don't mention the warning or Cromwell to him. We don't want to tip our hands, just to be on the safe side."

And with that, she placed the coffee cups on a tray, added a plate of cookies, and headed into the living room. I followed more slowly. A werepuma had been on the porch. Had been at the scene of Cromwell's murder. I still wanted to think it was somebody spying on the freak who'd strung up my cat friend. But Camille made a valid point.

We'd better keep quiet about the matter until we knew more. Which meant keeping my hands off Zachary for the present. Which meant I didn't have to deal with my emerging attraction, one positive side effect from the whole mess.

Fate was guiding us along a dark path this time. And there wasn't much we could do except follow. If we turned away from this situation, we'd always be wondering if we should have followed through. We might also be setting ourselves up as easy targets in the future. This was going to be an interesting trip, there was no getting around that.

Zachary sat in the backseat next to me, while Morio drove. We were in his Subaru Outback. Camille rode in the passenger seat, silent and staring out the window. Morio looked unruffled, as usual. He always seemed to be calm—except when he was in battle, and then he was hell on wheels. More out of curiosity than interest, I wondered briefly what he was like in bed but shook off the thought. A, he was devoted to Camille. And B, well . . . I liked the guy, but he wasn't my type.

I glanced out the window. We were almost to the turnoff

that would lead us to Tom Lane's old place. When we took Tom with us to Elqaneve and left him in the care of Queen Asteria, Smoky had come up with enough money to keep the house running. It made me sad to think that nobody would miss Tom. Except Titania, of course, and those of us who had the chance to meet him. He was lost, long out of time, long out of sanity.

By paying all the taxes on Tom's land and house, Smoky had provided himself with a buffer of protection and, in the process, prevented anybody else from moving in and discovering his secret.

Morio slowed and then turned left at the turnoff. The road was graveled, and huckleberry and bramble bushes with bare runners reached out to snag the car as we drove by. Towering sentinels, stark Douglas firs, kept silent watch over the land, with a medley of other trees crowding in below. The fireweed and flowers were asleep, of course, waiting for spring's kiss to awaken them like so many slumbering princesses. Winter had taken a firm hold, and a thick mist rose along the ground, rolling over patches where the snow hadn't melted off. We were close to the mountain now, and no doubt this land would see a full blanketing of the cold white flakes before many more days were out.

Round the bend to the left stood an old house in front of the circular driveway. Tom's old trucks were still here, rusted and on blocks, but there was an air of emptiness about the place that belied the scattered belongings that dotted the yard.

"Somebody's living here," Camille said, straightening her shoulders. "Look—there's smoke coming from the chimney."

Morio pulled to a stop and turned off the engine. "Smoky, perhaps? He might welcome spending time by a warm fire when he's in his human form."

"Maybe," Camille said, "but we'd better not assume it's him. We go in prepared."

Zachary swallowed with an audible gulp, his face a blank mask with a wash of apprehension hiding just below. "So, do dragons like pumas?" he asked with a slight edge to his voice.

"Uh, you mean do they like to *eat* pumas?" I asked.

He nodded. "Yeah, I guess that's what I'm asking."

Camille turned around and with a grin, said, "Dragons prefer cows for dinner, and virgins for other pursuits. You're not a cow, so you're safe on that account. As for the virgin . . ." She let her voice trail off, and he blushed as she gave him a friendly wink.

"Somehow, I don't think Smoky's your average, everyday dragon." I said, laughing.

Camille headed toward the house. "Yes, well, I doubt if an 'average, everyday' dragon really exists. Okay, let's go see who's inside, folks."

Morio and Camille led the way, readying whatever attacks they had planned just in case we found ourselves facing a less-than-desirable squatter. Since getting between Camille's magic and her intended victim was so *not* a good idea, I hung back with Zachary.

As we approached the house, I noticed that it looked quite tidy compared to when Tom had lived here. Somebody had taken the time to weed out a flower bed that skirted the front of the house, and the porch steps had been repaired. Smoky? Nah, he wasn't the type to play at home improvement. Or was he?

Camille seemed to be thinking the same thing, because she glanced back at me with a puzzled look, then shrugged. As she and Morio crept up the stairs, the front door slammed open, and a funny-looking man appeared, wearing what looked like old-world leggings and a tunic. His eyes lit up when he saw us, and he spread his arms wide.

"It's the D'Artigo sisters, come to visit Georgio! But where is your sister? Oh, that's right, she's sick, she can't come out in the light," he said, bustling across the porch to welcome us in.

"Well, well, well, if it isn't Georgio Profeta!" I beamed him a warm smile. "How you doing today, Saint George?"

Saint George, as he thought of himself, gave us a knowing look. "I've been on dragon watch, of course. He's a wily one, cunning and stealthy. I know he's been prowling around, and someday, when he least expects it, I'll make my move. Until then, I lead him on, allow him to think I don't know his ulterior motive in moving me out here."

Moving me out here? Good gods, what had Smoky gone and done? Georgio Profeta, self-proclaimed dragon slayer, had been after Smoky for several years now, if we understood matters correctly. Of course, he didn't stand a chance in hell of even giving Smoky a broken pinky, let alone "slaying the beast," but Smoky seemed to have developed a soft spot in his heart for the bewildered man who had long ago lost his connection with reality.

Camille and I gave each other a quick look, and she bustled over to him. "Saint George, how brilliant! I'm sure he doesn't suspect a thing. And did you fix up the house all by yourself?"

He shook his head. "No, when my grandmother died last month, the dragon thought to lure me out here, to offer friendship as a guise in order to keep track of my whereabouts. So I'm taking advantage of his guile. He helped me fix up the house and told me I could live here as long as I need to. Of course, he's just trying to keep me where he can see me. I have slain dragons, I've bedded princesses. I've . . ." His attention suddenly wandered off, and he disappeared into a silent veil of thought. It was as if someone had turned off the light switch.

Right about then, Smoky appeared at the edge of the clearing. He was in human form, a good thing since there wasn't a lot of room in the front yard for a dragon. He swiftly strode over to meet us. Tall, with long silver hair and frost-colored eyes that mirrored his milk-white skin, he was gorgeous, timeless in a day and age that ran too quickly. He walked with deliberate, arrogant steps. With a warning glance that was easy enough to read—*Keep quiet or else*—he glanced at us before reaching for Georgio's hand.

"I see Saint George has gone into another fugue," he said, leading the man into the house. Camille and I looked at each other, shrugged, and then followed. Zachary and Morio brought up the rear.

As we entered the house, I could still see Tom's presence in the furniture and decorations, but Georgio had taken over. Prints of Saint George fighting the dragon lined the walls, and draped on a mannequin in a corner of the living room was his plastic-ringed chain-mail armor.

Smoky led Georgio over to a chair and helped him sit down. Then he whistled an odd tune, and after a moment, an older lady came wandering out of the kitchen. She had an apron tied over her floral-print housedress, and her hair was long and gray and braided back in a neat French twist.

"I want you to meet some friends of mine," Smoky said. "Estelle, this is Camille, her sister Delilah, that's Morio and . . . you must be Zachary?" He bowed briefly to Zach, who looked totally nonplussed.

"They dragons, too?" Estelle asked, giving us the once-over.

"No," Smoky said. "They aren't dragons. If they choose, they're welcome to tell you what they are, but that's up to them. Georgio has slipped into one of his fugues again. Take him to his room and make sure he's cared for?"

She grunted as she took Georgio's arm and gently led him away.

Smoky watched until they were gone. "You're right on time. Very good."

"Hold on," I said. "Not so fast. Who is Estelle, and why is Georgio living out here?"

Smoky gave me a long, cool look. "And you consider this your business?"

My blood ran thin. Picture: little kitty cat swatting monstrous beast and realizing maybe it's not such a good idea.

After a moment, he said, "If you must know, Estelle worked for Georgio's grandmother. She's been his caregiver for years. When I found him in the yard a few weeks back, crying because his grandmother died, I took a trip to the city and had a little talk with Ms. Dugan. She agreed to come here and take care of him. His grandmother left him no inheritance, and he has no other living relatives. Since Georgio can't take care of himself, I offered them the use of this house, a small stipend to keep them in food and clothing, and a wage to Estelle that will allow her to save for her old age—what there is left of it."

He motioned to the door. "Let's move. The veils must be parted during the afternoon." As he took his place beside Camille, he looked over his shoulder. "And before you ask, yes, the woman knows I'm a dragon. And no, it didn't faze her." He curled his arm possessively around Camille's shoulder and led us out into the yard. And that was all to be said on the subject. I wasn't stupid, I knew when to stop pushing.

We followed Smoky through the brush.

"Are you sure you want to do this?" Zachary asked, swinging in beside me as we headed into the wood.

"We've come this far. There's no way in hell that I'm turning back now." After a moment, I hesitantly approached what was bound to be a touchy subject. "Zach, I have to ask this, so please don't take offense. How well do you know your fellow clan members? Is there anybody new in the Pride? Would you trust everyone with your life?"

He blinked. "Why? Do you suspect somebody there of not playing straight with us?"

"I just need to know. Trust me in this—it's important." I wanted to tell him about the werepuma energy that had shown up on our porch, but Camille had warned against it.

Zachary stared at the ground, looking worn out and confused. "To be honest? I don't know. I don't know anything anymore. We do have a few new members, distant relatives who came from other clans during the past few months. We don't turn away family. I just wish I knew what was going on. If I did, I could probably answer your question better."

Thinking about our own family troubles back in Otherworld, I said, "Sometimes you may not be able to trust anybody but yourself. Sometimes the world turns upside down, and all you can do is hold on for the ride and try to make it out in one piece."

Zach gave me a quizzical look. "I take it you're having problems of your own?" He stepped over a bramble sucker that had grown out onto the path.

"Trust me, we're all hip deep in shit." I looked around. The trail had become much more overgrown since we'd been out here the first time. Maybe Titania had moved on and left it to grow wild. Or maybe Smoky was encouraging the encroaching forest.

I shook my head. "Don't worry about us. We've always got crap going on in our lives. For now, let's focus on your situation.

You say that you have a few new members. Do you really know everything there is to know about them? Could they have been skirmishing with the Hunters Moon Clan before joining up with the Puma Pride?" I was trying to find some clue that would link the demons, the werespiders, and the attacks on the Puma Pride.

"I don't know. I suppose I can ask," he said.

"We could come out and explain the situation, if you'd like." It occurred to me that if we could meet more of the Pride members, we might be able to get a sense if anyone was collaborating with the enemy. But Zach nixed that idea and sent my ego crashing to the ground in the same breath.

Cheeks flaming, he said, "Delilah . . . uh . . . several of our members have asked that you not be invited back to the compound. Even with Venus's welcome, some have voted against allowing you and your sisters back on our land. I'm sorry. I tried to smooth things over."

"What the fuck did you say?" I stopped and turned to face him. "Let me get this straight to avoid misunderstandings. Do they not want us there because we're strangers, or because . . . we're who we are?"

He wouldn't meet my gaze. "Please don't think I feel the same way, because I don't. But there's been talk going around . . . some of our members think you aren't . . . good influences. They don't like vampires, and they don't trust Camille because she's so blatantly sexual, and . . ."

"Go on," I said, waiting for the final blow.

"Well, they don't like you because you're . . . because you aren't a real Were." He let the rest rush out in a jumbled stutter. "You're only a Were because of a birth defect, so you don't carry the true blood in your veins. I guess they see you as unnatural. Venus and I tried to explain, but some of the guys are older and set in their ways." He screeched to a halt, scuffing the ground in silence.

Stunned by the rejection, I sucked in a deep breath and let it out slowly, surprised to find tears trying to force their way topside.

"I see," I said in the iciest voice I could muster. Anger

swarmed its way to the surface. I wanted to turn around and march back to the car right then and there. Let the Puma Pride clean up their own fucking mess.

"Let me get this straight," I said when I could manage words without tears. "You want our help, but you don't want us around. How generous. How kind of you to allow us to put ourselves in danger for your goddamn compound and yet look down your noses at us. Well, let me tell you this. Knowing what I now know, if I had my way, I'd wash my hands of the affair. You might as well deal with the murders on your own— you've all done such a *great* job so far."

"No!" He looked miserable, and I hoped he was. "I told you, that's not how *I* feel—"

"Oh, right. You're not speaking for yourself, just the rest of your Pride. Your precious family will accept our help because they're impotent, but you won't let us come out to your land because we're trash? Well, let me tell you this—I may watch Jerry Springer, and I may eat Ding Dongs, but I come from a proud family line."

"Delilah—please—" A panicked note filled his voice.

"Oh shut up! As I said, I'd turn around right now and go home *except* for one nasty matter. Your *situation* has become *our* problem. One of my friends, a neighborhood stray cat, was murdered as a warning. He was sucked dry and left for me to find, with a note telling me to back off."

"Don't blame our people for what the Hunters Moon Clan did—" he started to say, but I'd had enough.

"But it wasn't just the spiders involved! There was some heavy-duty cat magic hovering over the whole mess. A werepuma was hanging out with the freak who strung up poor Cromwell!"

My sudden outburst carried to the rest of the group. As they turned to stare, I realized I'd just spilled one of our secrets, but I didn't care. The only thing that mattered now was getting out of this mess with the least possible damage. We had a Degath Squad to catch, and why they were in league with the Hunters Moon Clan didn't matter. What did matter was that we find the demons and kill them.

Zach sputtered, and he reached out to catch my arm. "A werepuma? You didn't tell me this! Is that why you asked me if I could trust everybody—"

I shook him off. Memories of being taunted about our heritage when we were children sprang up, the images and insults all too fresh in my mind. "Go to hell, you and your whole bigoted clan. Once we find out who's been killing your precious members, you can pay us for the job, and we'll never sully your door again."

Smoky suddenly strode over and grabbed both of us by the ears. "You are holding up this little jaunt. Keep your arguments for later. Do you understand?"

I stared up at the dragon. His gaze was a glacial rift in a frozen ocean. Smoky meant business, and I had the feeling he wouldn't hesitate to resort to force if we disobeyed.

"Fine," I said. "Let's go." I pulled away and marched forward. The impulse to transform was strong, but I tried to ignore it. I wanted nothing more than to run off and chase moths and forget about all the stress and tension, but this was the wrong place to let my tabby out to play.

I struggled, forcing myself to stare at the scenery, to think about the Yule tree at home and how beautiful Iris would make it, to think about Chase and how much he cared about me. Anything to distract myself. Finally, with another deep breath, I let my anger go, promising myself that when we got home I'd kick the Puma Pride to the curb.

As we trudged along, Zach tried to speak to me, but I sped up until I was a few steps behind Camille and Morio.

The overshadowing lacework of branches from the giant firs and cedars stretched across the path, forming an interwoven canopy that shut out much of the approaching dusk. Juniper, huckleberry, and salal bushes crowded the trunks, but even they looked worn and ragged. The forest floor was littered with frost-covered leaves and brown needles, and here and there a patch of snow still shimmered where the shade had protected it from melting. The path was rife with tree roots that poked up through the detritus.

As we ventured farther into the forest, the trees grew darker, as if a consciousness had risen to permeate the wood since the last time we were here. The presence felt watchful and ancient, primal in that way Earth's forests had. They were far less welcoming than the woodlands of Otherworld and, as much as I loved being outside, I was always cautious when I walked the back paths here. Even the trails crisscrossing our own land carried that watchful, wary energy.

As we made our way through the woods, I thought I caught a glimpse of some fey creature here and there, hiding behind a moss-covered trunk or a downed limb of deadwood. Each time I'd focus my attention in the direction of the watchful eyes, and there would be nothing to see save for a leaf quivering in the breeze.

Most FBHs confused the Fae with nature spirits. While both sprang from similar roots, there were vast differences. My father's people were more humanlike than nature spirits, who were often queer and unpredictable, born into shapes that left thoughts of humanity long behind. Nature devas often took on the qualities of the plants they were connected to, and most were wary of both human and Fae alike.

I took a deep breath and, forcing myself forward, joined Camille. Smoky was striding ahead, leading the way. Morio dropped back to talk to Zach, and they spoke in soft whispers. I wondered what they were saying, but my pride kept me from asking.

A scurrying sound from the side announced the presence of a dog or coyote, but I could sense no hint of magic. Whatever was out there was four-legged and probably going to stay that way. As we headed deeper into the wood, the temperature started to drop, and I pulled my jacket close and zipped it. A glance at the sky promised new snow.

"Hey, Kitten, chin up."

Camille seldom used Menolly's nickname for me, and when she did, I knew she was worried.

"I just . . . I liked him, Camille. I liked him, and now I find out that all of his cronies think we're trash. It's just like home.

Windwalkers, that's all we ever were and all we'll ever be."
The words cut deep as they rolled off my tongue, leaving a
bitter aftertaste.

"Remember what Venus told you? Don't be ashamed of being a Windwalker. We're daughters of destiny, babe, and that's
not always an easy task. For some reason, we've been singled
out to fight Shadow Wing. Yes, it's terrifying, but we wouldn't
have the courage to face him if we'd had easy childhoods. We
learned to stand up for ourselves because we had to. Now we're
standing up to demons because that's what we're born to do."

She put her arm around my waist and gave me a squeeze.
"Delilah, no matter what, you'll always have Menolly and me.
We'll always be here for you, and we'll always love you. We
are your family, no matter where we happen to live. Father
loves you, too. And Aunt Rythwar. And Iris and Maggie."

I gazed into her upturned face. She could be self-centered
at times, but when Camille spoke from the heart, her convic-
tions bubbled up from a well of passion impossible to doubt. I
leaned down and kissed her forehead.

"You have always been such a role model for me," I whispered. "You take things in stride, you laugh off the insults, and
you have a fuck-you attitude that I wish to hell I could emulate."

"I heard what Zach said." Camille sighed. "If the demons
weren't involved, I'd say screw it and let's go home. But they
are, and so we are."

I tucked my arm through hers. "Damn it, why does everything have to be so complicated? At least Chase respects me.
And that goes a long way in my book."

Camille nodded. "Chase washed up better than I thought
he would. I still don't understand what you see in him, but hey,
you wouldn't touch Trillian with a ten-foot pole," she added,
laughing.

"Make that twenty," I muttered, grinning back at her. "Okay,
let's just shove all this crap aside until we're done here, and then
I'll figure out what I want to do about Zach. If anything."

With that, we came to the edge of the trail and found ourselves looking into the barren lea that held Smoky's barrow.
The trees swayed, creaking as their boughs rubbed against one

another, and the entire meadow glistened with hoarfrost, a tapestry of lacework so intricate I could barely follow the threads of ice crisscrossing the ground.

I looked for signs of Titania, but she was nowhere to be seen, and I decided not to bother Smoky by asking about her. I'd used up my quota of questions for one day, and while we assumed he didn't eat people, he'd never said so directly.

Smoky stopped atop the barrow mound and motioned for us to back off. "I'm going to part the veils between this world and the realm of the Autumn Lord and summon him. He'll come—or not—as he chooses, but if he does, remember this: I have no say over his actions. Don't get near the veil of flame; it will burn you to a crisp if you touch it."

And with that, Smoky gave us a wicked grin and then, even though he was still in human form, all sense of humanity drained away. Like a pillar of ice, he stood, glittering and cold and mesmerizing. I heard Camille gasp as her hand fluttered to her throat as she stood frozen, staring at her lover-to-be.

Smoky threw back his head and laughed, his voice rumbling across the forest. For a moment, I thought he'd been possessed, but then he gave us a piercing look, and his eyes—brilliant as diamonds in the velvet black of the night—flashed, mirroring the aurora that rippled across the midnight sky.

He lifted his left hand to the heavens, and a bolt of lightning flared down his arm, surrounding him with a blue white, blazing aura. Camille fell to her knees, her face a mask of awe and desire, but Smoky took no notice of her.

"*Dracon, dracon, dracon* . . . I call down the fire of the gods, I call down the flame of my fathers, I call down the frozen blade of Hel from the land of the dead. Burn wide the gate. Flame of my blood, open the barrier."

With his right hand, he began to inscribe a cobalt pentagram on top of the barrow. A veil of light began to shimmer in the center of the rune.

"Get ready," he said, and his voice thundered around us. As I gazed at him, his dragon self seemed to surround his body in a vaporous mist, as if he'd simultaneously taken on his natural shape yet remained in his human form.

We huddled together, waiting as Smoky chanted an incantation in an arcane language I couldn't understand. His voice caught hold of the cadence, and like a drummer gone wild, his words beat a staccato rhythm as the flames of the rune began to dance. Melding, blurring, forming a veil, the shimmers of azure and cobalt and sapphire swirled in the gloom-filled afternoon. And then his voice rose, and the curtain of flame parted.

"Lord of the Autumn, I call you forth to this place. Be here, now!"

And then, through the flames, came the flicker of a silhouette. It seemed the Autumn Lord had decided to answer our call.

CHAPTER 12

As he stepped through the veil of flame, first one and then a second stacked-heeled boot appeared. Lustrous, the boots were jet-black and scuff free. With every step, a dusting of frost fell from their heels.

The train of a cloak came into view, a swirl of autumn leaves billowing like a feathered cape. As the Autumn Lord crossed from his realm into our world, I found myself both terrified and transfixed. He stepped down from the barrow in a silence so palpable I could hear the breath of everyone in the meadow.

The Autumn Lord. There was no room for doubt. *This* was the lord of the flames, lord of the autumn winds that shook the windows, lord of pumpkins and tangy soil and decaying foliage. A silent figure, he drove before him the scent of distant fire borne on the northern winds.

He strode toward us, his hair as black as his boots, his face pale and translucent. Twin flames of supernatural fire pierced my shields as he stared at me, leaving me naked and vulnerable. I'd never felt so exposed in my life.

"Back away, dragon spawn." Brushing past Smoky, he held out his hands to me, ten diamond daggers of curving ice pointing in my direction. "You are the one who requires my presence. Come to me, girl, and tell me what you want."

Smoky took one look at the Autumn Lord and backed up. I swallowed whatever was left from my lunch. When a dragon obeyed without question, whoever was giving the orders had to be packing a butt load of power. I forced myself to step forward.

Camille swung in behind me. "I've got your back," she whispered, her voice shaking.

I thought about her journey to Grandmother Coyote and wondered how she'd managed to weather it alone. The gods knew, I wouldn't want to be facing the Autumn Lord by myself. Nope, not going there. Not even remotely brave enough.

I stared at his hands, wondering whether to take them. A little voice deep inside urged me to go ahead. Running on instinct, I clasped his hands in my own.

Fire and ice. The shock almost knocked me over. One hand felt like it was burning up, the other like it had frozen solid. As the two opposing forces raced up my arms to meet at the base of my neck, they sent me reeling toward him. I stumbled into his arms, and he enfolded his cape of leaves around my shoulders and pulled me close.

From within the confines of the cloak I could hear Camille and Smoky shouting and then a noise shook the meadow like thunder, and all was silent. I struggled, but the Autumn Lord's grasp was strong, and he held me so tightly I could barely breathe. I struggled to shift form but couldn't do it. His magic was too strong, so I focused on breathing.

Inhale . . .

. . . the damp odors of decay and mildew, of bonfires at midnight swirled around me. They rode in on a gust of north wind, the boreal wind, murmuring tongues of ice and frost, the chilling touch of autumn.

Exhale . . .

. . . I slowly expelled the air from my lungs, taking with it a hint of the cold. And again.

Inhale . . .

. . . the taste of graveyard dust and dead man's hand on my tongue, and then he leaned down and kissed my forehead, marking me with a burning flame that scorched its way into the core of my being.

Exhale . . .

. . . and as I released my breath the second time, he let go, and I stumbled back, tripping over a loose root and falling on my tailbone. I scrambled away as best as I could, half scooting, half kicking myself along the ground. Camille let out a gasp and dropped to her knees beside me. I glanced up to see the others shaking themselves, as if they'd just woken up. Smoky motioned caution to Zach and Morio, warning them to stand their ground.

I stared up at the Autumn Lord, who stood silent and waiting. As Camille helped me to my feet, I realized that my forehead felt odd, as if something had embedded itself on my brow. I turned to her to ask if she could see anything, but before I could open my mouth, she started, staring at my face.

"Oh, Kitten," she said in a low voice. "Your forehead!"

"What is it? I can tell something happened to me, but I don't know what." Her expression was scaring me. Had I suddenly turned into a frog-girl? Or the creature from the Black Lagoon—who, as it happened, resembled the lemurans, one of our aquatic Crypto races back in OW?

Camille reached out and gently touched my forehead. "Delilah, you've got a black scythe branded on your forehead."

"What? What the hell?" I scrambled to my feet and whirled on the Autumn Lord, who was still standing, a silent figure. "What is it? What did you do to me?" My anger seeped through my fear, and I charged forward.

The Autumn Lord looked down at me—he easily stood six five—and gave me a cunning smile, his lips quirking the tiniest fraction at the sides. "You come seeking information. There will always be a price to pay when you call upon the world builders. Everyone who seeks my help pays me something."

I hesitated, wanting to argue that it wasn't fair, that he hadn't offered me a choice, but one look at his eyes told me it would do no good. What was done was done. There was no backtracking, no turning around, no running.

"What did you do to me?" I asked again.

He gave me the barest of shrugs. "When it's time, you'll know. Now, ask your questions before I get bored and leave." He motioned for us to sit on one of the nearby windfalls.

I hesitated, then led the way, wondering what had happened to me. Would any of us emerge from this unscathed? I took a seat on the mossy log.

The Autumn Lord sat beside me, and I scrunched away as

far as I could without appearing rude. He gazed at me. "It's been awhile since anyone was foolish enough—or brave enough—to seek me out," he mused. "What do you want to know?"

I took a deep breath. Not too deep because I could still smell the smoke and graveyard dust and bonfires raging around him, but enough to steady myself.

"We're looking for information on a group of spiderlings. Werespiders. The Hunters Moon Clan. You rule over all spiderkin, so we thought you might be willing to help. They seem to be in league with demons from the Subterranean Realms, and we're worried they're working for Shadow Wing."

Zachary surprised me. He broke through his fear long enough to speak up. "Do you know why they're killing my people? I come from the Rainier Puma Pride, and the spiders are slaughtering us."

The Autumn Lord blinked, the first time he'd shown any sign of surprise. He pursed his lips, and a cloud of frost came whistling out from between them to form a tablet of snow in his hands. I craned my neck to see if there was anything written on it, but all I could make out were some strange glyphs.

After a moment, the tablet melted away. "You are all in danger. Kyoka has returned to life; he's taken a new body."

"Kyoka?" I asked.

The Autumn Lord cleared his throat. "A thousand years ago, Kyoka was a shaman here, on the North American continent. He led his tribe ruthlessly, and in the end, his greed caused his downfall. He lost sight of the balance and natural order of things and used his magic on his own people to turn them into abominations. I cast him out of my service and named him pariah. He defiled the nature of spiders."

He turned to Zach. "Einarr, one of your ancestors, traveled the seas to the New World and ran afoul of Kyoka."

"My ancestor?" Zachary looked confused but sat up straight and paid attention. Family roots meant a lot to him, that was for sure.

"You are a direct descendant of Einarr of the Iron Hand. When he reached the shores of North America, Einarr lost his first wife and several comrades to the werespiders. So he took an oath to track down Kyoka and kill him. And many years later, he managed to avenge his kin."

"Why didn't you kill this Kyoka, if you knew he was evil?" Zach asked.

The Autumn Lord barely glanced at him. "Why should I? Kyoka disturbed the balance, but so do many creatures and events. If I were to intervene every time the web is broken and rewoven, I'd never have a moment's peace."

Morio touched Zach's shoulder, shaking his head, warning him not to argue. He looked unhappy but kept his mouth shut.

"To continue," the Autumn Lord said, "as a sign of my respect for his bravery, I gave Einarr a gift. I gave him the power to turn into a mountain lion, and all of his descendents who bear his blood are born with that ability and walk under my shadow, whether they know it or not. Puma, panther, mountain lion, they are all my children."

And then I knew—I knew the secret the Autumn Lord hadn't revealed. "And did you give Einarr something else? A pendant perhaps?"

He looked into my eyes, and once again, I felt pulled toward him. I wanted to crawl inside his cloak, to nestle deep and sleep for a thousand years.

"You see too much," he said. "Yes, I gave him one of the spirit seals, but where it is now, I have no idea. It's been over a thousand years. I doubt that the Hunters Moon Clan has a clue as to what they're seeking, but the demons they work for probably do. Of that you can be certain."

I felt like I'd been punched. So the Degath Squad wasn't just out for a little rampage. They were in search of the second spirit seal, and they had a head start. I turned to Camille. "They must believe that the Rainier Puma Pride still has the seal, passed down from Einarr."

"When you're right, you're right, and I wish you weren't." She glanced at the Autumn Lord. "And Kyoka's return was the marshal needed to get the Hunters Moon Clan to work for the demons?"

He nodded and blew another tablet of ice, reading it

slowly. When he spoke, his voice was angry thunder, rumbling through the grove. "Apparently he hasn't returned as one of their own. It seems the demons are more insidious than that. When Einarr destroyed Kyoka, his soul was sent to the depths, down to the Subterranean Realms. And there he remained until Shadow Wing took power. And Shadow Wing has given Kyoka a new body and a mission: rally his people and destroy the descendants of Einarr. Meanwhile, the demons slip in and steal the spirit seal. Kyoka returned in the form of a man. A Were, yes, but not a werespider."

"I knew it!" I jumped up. "The werespider who killed Cromwell and strung him up was accompanied by a were-puma. That must have been Kyoka!" I whirled around, grabbing Zach's shoulders. "He's hiding in plain sight—right in the middle of your compound, Zach. He's trying to find out where the seal is while he kills off members of the Puma Pride."

Zachary paled. "Then that means one of the newcomers *is* a traitor. I have to get back to the compound. What if I'm too late?"

I stared at him, realizing that his panic was going to increase tenfold once he realized just what the spirit seals actually were. As of now, Zach was clueless as to just how bad things were about to get.

"Another question," I said, turning back to the Autumn Lord. "Where can we find the Hunters Moon Clan? Do you know where their nest is?"

He blinked slowly. "Past a city east of where you dwell, where the water falls over rocks, you will find a foothill covered in tall timber. Look for a golden road and follow it back up the hill. There you will find their nest." The Autumn Lord rose and turned back toward the veil of flame, pausing briefly to look over his shoulder.

"You aren't too late. Not yet. But you must hurry. Now go and destroy them. They are abominations, no longer a part of my world, no longer my children." And with that, he vanished through the pentagram, and the barrier closed. We were left alone with our panic.

* * *

Smoky was the first to speak. "The second spirit seal?" He looked at Camille.

We'd done our best to keep him from knowing about the spirit seals, but when he accompanied us to visit the Elfin Queen, he'd found out about them. Our hopes that he'd forgotten were tempered by the fact that a dragon's memories are long and precise, especially when it comes to treasure.

I wondered if he'd turn on us and try to find it himself. He was helpful now, but it wasn't a good idea to forget that first and foremost, dragons were mercenaries, out for themselves.

"Didn't you hear him?" Zach jumped up and pointed to the trail. "There's a traitor living at the compound, and he could be killing off another one of my friends right now! I have to go home."

"Wait a moment," Smoky said. "I'll be right back. Don't attempt the trail without me." He disappeared through a door I hadn't noticed before, leading into the side of his barrow.

Camille stared up at the sky and raised her hand to salute the Moon Mother, who was peeking through the clouds. With a sigh, she glanced back at Zach and then at me. "Zach, we'd better fill you in on what's going down," she said. "You have a right to know what you're up against, but you have to swear to us you'll keep this on the q.t."

He blinked, then glanced at me. I nodded. Mad as I was, I'd have to put my ego on hold for a few moments. "She's right. You can't tell *anyone* what we're about to tell you."

"All right," he said, a touch of hesitance in his voice. "I promise."

"Not good enough," she said. "I want a blood oath. We can't take any chances. You have no idea how many lives could hinge on your secrecy."

Again, the blink. "Let's do it, then."

I pulled my silver knife from my boot. "I'll take your oath," I said. He gave me a questioning look, and I added, "We're both Weres, even if mine is from a *birth defect*."

As he winced, I held up the blade. The edge glistened as

I drew it across his palm. I wasn't squeamish when it came to blood oaths or injuries, just when somebody decided to slurp up the results. A thin line of red bubbled up on his hand, and I squeezed once to stimulate the flow.

Zach grimaced but didn't flinch.

"By the blood of your body, by the blood of your ancestors, do you vow to honor your promises and be cursed if you lie to us?"

"You have my word," he said slowly.

Blood oaths were binding contracts, at least among the Fae and the Earthside Supe communities. If Zach broke his word, we had every right to hunt him down and kill him without any ramifications, unless the police got involved.

"Tell me what's going on," he said.

"Remember, you're sworn to silence." I let out a long sigh. With a little help from Camille and Morio, I filled Zach in on what was happening in the Sub Realms and what ramifications the spirit seals held for Earth and OW. By the time we finished, he was sitting on the ground, speechless. Just then, Smoky strode back out of the barrow, waving for us to follow him.

He'd changed into a pair of white jeans, which showed off one hell of a nice ass, and a pale gray turtleneck. His near-ankle-length hair was neatly braided. I stared at him, suddenly aware of just how gorgeous he really was. I shot an envious glance Camille's way before I realized what I was doing. *Whoa—shut down that train right now,* I thought, *before it becomes a runaway locomotive.*

"Let's go. The trail isn't safe for you after dark," he said. Camille and Morio were hot on his heels.

I grabbed Zach's hand, but before I could drag him along, he whirled me around to face him. Without a word, he pulled me to him, his lips seeking mine.

Caught by surprise, I let him kiss me. The first taste of him was like a dusky port, smooth and warm. Zach growled low and deep in his throat as he pressed against me. He tightened his grip, one hand on my back, the other rubbing my ass. When I realized what we were doing, I pushed him away.

"Zach, no . . . not here. Not now."

He pulled me back into his arms and pressed his lips to my ear. "You want me as much as I want you," he whispered.

"I'm not a *real* Were, so you better just stop this now, before your clan finds out." I swatted him away. "We have to catch up to Smoky. We have to get out of here."

Zach grunted a soft assent and reluctantly let go of me. Unsure of what else to say, I turned and raced ahead, catching up to Camille and Morio. I could hear Zach's steps behind me.

"Delilah! Delilah?" he called, but I ignored him as I hurried through the woods. My body wanted Zachary Lyonnesse. But his comments about what the Puma Pride thought of us were still ringing in my ears, a vicious assault on my ego. I couldn't let them go. Not yet.

As we finally broke out of the trail into the yard near the house, reality hit, and I pushed thoughts of Zach to the side. We were headed home, all right, but who knew whether we were going to be too late to prevent Kyoka and the Hunters Moon Clan from finding the spirit seal? Wherever it might be.

By the time we reached Morio's Outback, all I wanted was a hot shower, a long nap, and a lot of food. Smoky elected to come back to the city with us.

Unnerved by the whole afternoon, I asked, "Should we stop off at the Puma Pride before heading home? It's on the way."

Zach let out a loud sigh. "Shit, I want to go home, but what if we walk into a trap?"

"Did you tell anybody where you were going?" Camille closed her eyes; I could tell she was praying he'd kept his mouth shut.

He let out a long sigh. "Yeah, I told Venus the Moon Child. That's all."

"We may still have a chance then," Morio said. "Venus is no traitor."

"He isn't one of the newcomers to the tribe, is he?" I asked.

Zachary shook his head. "Nope. He couldn't be, not and be

our shaman. But we've had three come in, and they all arrived during the past six weeks. Shannon and Dodge, from the Oregon Cascade Clan. They started out with the Puma Pride, then migrated south some years back, so we know they're safe. And then . . . Tyler."

Tyler? Something rang a bell, and I didn't like the sound of it. "Where did he say he was from? Who gave him references?"

"He came in from the south, from New Mexico. He says he was with the Desert Runners Band, and he did have a letter of introduction. But . . . I'm not sure who checked out the references. I can nose around, try to find out," he said. "So, do you want to stop by the compound first? Or take me back to your house? My truck's still there."

Camille shook her head. "Let's go back to our house. We don't want to tip off Tyler by showing up with you, just in case he's our man. Anyway, we need to figure out what our next step should be."

Morio concurred and slid into the driver's seat. Smoky opened the back door and motioned to Camille, who had moved to sit in front with Morio.

"Get in the back with me. Zachary can sit in front." His voice took on a preemptive tone, and she gave him a dirty look, but he leaned close and whispered something in her ear, and she quickly obeyed. Morio glanced at him through the rearview mirror, but Smoky merely gave him a smug smile, and no more was said.

He draped his arm around Camille's shoulder, and she settled into his embrace. I couldn't tell if she was interested or irritated. Knowing her, probably both. I decided the best way to deal with an imperious dragon was to ignore his arrogance and focus on the matter at hand.

"Okay, it looks like we're ready then," I said. "Homeward bound, Morio, and don't spare the gas pedal."

Morio started up the engine, and we headed out for the two-hour drive home. Three, if traffic was bad. Nobody spoke. It was as if we were all lost in our own worlds.

Zach had to be in shock, and with good reason. I couldn't imagine finding out someone I trusted was turning out to be my clan's worst enemy returned from the dead. Camille looked worn out and in need of a good back rub. And Morio just kept his eyes on the road as he navigated rush-hour traffic. As for me? My thoughts slipped back to the brand on my forehead and what it might signify.

I felt different, but exactly *how*, I wasn't sure. Now that we were in the car, I rooted around in my purse and brought out my compact, flipping it open. Frozen, I stared at the mark on my forehead. A black scythe, much like a crescent moon, glittered in the middle of my brow, shimmering as if a PVC tattoo had melted into my skin. Gently, I reached up and ran my fingers over the brand.

A shiver of fingers ran up my back, and I caught my breath as I was swept back into the cloak of the Autumn Lord's energy. A voice echoed in the back of my head, a hint of laughter flickering through the words. "You belong to me, now. My time is your time."

"What? What do you mean?" I tried to speak, but the words wouldn't come out, and I found myself staring into his eyes again, twin obsidian flames. Lost in those ever-burning flames, I let him take my hand. The tang of freshly turned soil bit deep into my senses. I was standing on the edge of the abyss, ready to leap over the side and fall forever. Suddenly realizing what was happening, I struggled, trying to break away.

He ran his hand over my forehead, then tipped my chin up. With a dark laugh, he said, "Go then, Changeling. You'll return to me. All of my chosen eventually find their way home. Until then, every time you look in the mirror, watch for me. Every time you see a whisper of smoke, you'll remember the smell and touch of autumn, because I am your destination."

And then he was gone, and I was staring at my reflection in my compact. Over my left shoulder, he watched. Faint, a ghost in my memory, but definitely there. I jumped and yanked my fingers away from the mark on my brow.

Camille was staring at me. "What's going on? Delilah, are you okay?" We weren't sisters for nothing—she knew something was up.

"Tell you later," I said, not wanting to talk about it in front of the others. "Listen, have you guys noticed anything that might be the result of our visit to the Autumn Lord? Any . . . visions, or anything?"

Camille gave me a sharp-eyed look and shook her head. "You're right. Those kinds of thoughts are for later when we're safe behind our wards."

"Listen, could you guys keep it down? It's starting to snow hard, traffic's a bitch, and I'm trying to concentrate," Morio said, scowling in the rearview mirror. But his focus wasn't on the traffic behind us. He was staring at Smoky's hand as it looped around Camille's shoulders. So, it was possible to goad the impervious fox demon after all.

When we finally reached the house, we tumbled out of the car like foam snakes out of one of those joke cans. As I glanced around the yard, I saw that Iris had been busy. The front porch was covered with strings of twinkling lights, and a gigantic wreath was hanging on the wall next to the front door. Bound with red ribbons and sparkling gold beads, the evergreen boughs smelled fragrant enough to eat, even from where I was standing.

As we trooped up the stairs, I tried to focus on what the Autumn Lord had said about the Hunters Moon Clan.

Past a city to the east, where the water falls over rocks, back in the foothills.

The city to the east was most likely one of Seattle's bedroom communities that sprawled across the east side of Lake Washington. A single stretch of urban living, one city blended into the next, their economies fueled by Microsoft and Nintendo and dozens of other high-tech software companies. As for the waterfall, I wasn't so sure. We hadn't had time to explore all the natural wonders that made me grateful we'd been posted here and not some desert where water and trees were distant memories. Frowning, I decided to call Chase and ask his opinion.

As we entered the house, Iris hurried out to greet us. She had Maggie with her, and the worried look on her face began to ease as she saw that we were all in one piece.

"Thank the gods you're back safely. We've been so worried about you."

"We?" I glanced around, realizing Chase's car was in the driveway. "Chase is here?"

"Yes, he is, and he's frothing at the mouth for word of your return. He came over as soon as he got off work. Oh, and Trillian's back. It's been an interesting evening, I'll tell you that." The look on her face was worth a thousand words, and I had the feeling that Chase and Trillian had been more than a handful.

"I can imagine the conversation," I said, then stopped. "Is something wrong, Iris?"

"Yes, well, several things have happened this evening." By her tone, the news wasn't good. She stared at me for a moment, then tilted her head to one side. "Delilah, what's on your forehead?"

"More news . . . and I'm not sure if it's good or bad." I pointed to the living room. "Are Trillian and Chase in there?"

She nodded. "I'll hustle into the kitchen and fix you something to eat. Go in and sit down. And don't start without me!" And with that, we were dismissed.

We filed into the living room, and it occurred to me that at least I wouldn't have to call Chase about the waterfall question. It also occurred to me that I'd kissed Zachary and probably should tell Chase. I didn't want to, but I owed him that much. My spirits sinking, I looked around the room for him.

To my surprise, he and Trillian were sitting at the game table, playing a round of chess. Trillian was playing black, Chase, white, which seemed fitting, and they were both so intent on the game that neither one noticed us enter.

Camille gave me a snarky look and started to sneak up on them, but she must have made some noise, because Trillian suddenly jumped out of his chair and grabbed her before she could startle them. He pulled her into his arms and, with a defiant look at Smoky, gave her a long, dark kiss.

"Good to have you home where you *belong*," he said, loud enough for everyone to hear. "Right by my side." He looked directly at Smoky and gave him a *What are you going to do about it?* look.

Smoky didn't rise to the bait, merely moved to the sofa, where he sat, crossing his legs. Morio gave Trillian and Chase a nod and dropped onto one of the ottomans, letting out a long sigh. Zach was staring at Chase. If we didn't do something soon, we'd be in the middle of an all-out testosterone war.

Chase held out his arms. "Baby, I'm so relieved you made it home safe."

What the hell was I going to do? Camille knew how to handle this sort of situation, and her lovers knew they were sharing her attentions. But I didn't.

I sucked in a deep breath and walked over to Chase, giving him a warm, happy-to-be-here kiss. He wrapped his arms around me, a sense of security and safety washing through my frazzled nerves. But were safety and security enough?

As Iris entered the room with a tray of cold cuts, cheeses, spreads, and bread, I motioned for everyone to take a seat. "Where's Menolly?" I asked, glancing at the clock. Dusk had fallen over two hours ago. Where was she?

"Right here," came a familiar voice from the door. I whirled around, and there stood Menolly. "You made it back safe," she said, then did a double take. "Kitten, come here," she said. It wasn't a request. I hurried over to her side, and she motioned for me to bend down. After a moment, her fingers barely touching the outlines of the mark on my forehead, she hissed and moved back. "Who did this to you?"

"The Autumn Lord," I whispered. "Why? What are you sensing?"

Her irises had turned brick red, and when she spoke, I could see her fangs were fully extended. "He's marked you. Territory. What the hell did you do? Promise yourself to him? You're wearing the mark of a Death Maiden, Kitten. And there's no way I know of to get rid of it."

"May the gods have mercy," Iris whispered.

"No," I whispered. "That's not possible. I didn't agree to anything like that. He said he'd exact payment from me, but he wouldn't tell me what it was."

But in my heart, I knew I was screwed. Iris was right: the Elemental Lords were terrifying and lived far apart from human or Sidhe. They played by their own rules, making them up as they went.

Chase shot to his feet. "What the hell is going on? What are you saying? Delilah would never make such a promise!"

Menolly gave him a cool look. "Of course she wouldn't. But understand this, Chase, and listen carefully so I don't have to repeat myself. The Elemental Lords don't care what *humans* think. They don't care what the *Fae* think. Extensions of the very essence of both Earth and Otherworld, the Elemental Lords are encapsulations of primal power. They are who they are, and neither your rules nor ours apply to them. They have the power to bind anyone they choose to their will, and none but the gods can interfere."

Pale, looking almost stricken, Chase slowly took his seat again. "Good God, what's going to happen to you?"

I glanced at Menolly. "I don't know, but whatever it is, I'll do my best to stop it. I think . . . let's start from the beginning. We found out our enemy is a lot more than just a bunch of werespiders under the thumb of a Degath Squad."

Camille silently fixed two sandwiches. She handed one to me, then walked over and hopped up on the desk, dangling her feet over the edge. Menolly floated up to sit on the top of the ladder by the tree. I glanced at the sparkling ornaments but couldn't bring myself to go near them. Iris's spell must be working. I polished off my dinner without tasting a bite, I was so worn out.

With a glance at Camille, I said, "Let's dive in. I don't know how much longer I can hold out before I fall asleep."

She nodded. "I was thinking the same thing." With a quick look at Trillian, she added, "As much as I want to know what's going on at home right now, we'll start with our trip so that Zachary can take off."

Between the five of us, we filled Chase, Trillian, and Iris in on what had happened. I left out the kiss with Zach, as did everybody else, thankfully, but when I came to my vision of the Autumn Lord in the car, Camille gasped and looked over at Menolly, who merely nodded.

"That clinches it. He's claimed you."

"Would you kindly inform me as to just what a Death Maiden is?" My sandwich had become a lump on its journey to my stomach. I'd better hit the antacids before I slept, or I'd wake up with one hell of a bellyache.

"You aren't going to like it," she said.

"Thank you, Ms. Obvious. I already don't like it, and I don't even know what we're talking about. Just tell me, so I can start dealing with whatever mess I've landed myself in." Testy, I wiped my hands on my napkin and folded my legs into the lotus position, a massive headache threatening to join the fray of aches and pains working their way through my body.

Menolly slowly lowered herself to the floor, her face impassive. But her eyes were bright with blood tears, and I knew that whatever had happened to me, it wasn't good.

"Kitten, the Autumn Lord isn't just any Elemental Lord—he's also one of the Harvestmen. I did a little more research while the five of you were off traipsing through the ether this evening. The Autumn Lord collects souls in his palace, and he's served by a contingent of women called Death Maidens. They're similar to Valkyries, and on Samhain Eve, they harvest the souls he's marked for death."

I felt my breath go shallow, and my pulse began to race. The room shimmered as I began to shift. "Then I'm going to die?"

"No, that's not what I mean!" She rushed over and knelt beside me, taking my hands. "Stay with us, Delilah, don't change—it's not like that!"

I struggled to focus on her words, struggled to keep my form, but the cat magic called me. But this time, something was different. My body felt oddly heavy as I slid into a vortex, the nexus where self met self and exchanged places.

The scent of tropical flowers rose heady and thick. All around me, I could see vines and tendrils and trees that grew so high they obscured the night sky. And I was there, crouched on a tree limb, watching below for prey. Something on the path below caught my attention.

A feral pig wandered along the leaf-strewn trail. As I watched the creature, a hunger rose up in me so great I couldn't resist. I stood, all ten fuzzy pounds of me, but within seconds I shifted again. Now my paws were enormous, jet black and gleaming, and a rush of power raced through my body as I leapt out of the tree to land next to the pig. It let out a squeal and began to run. I gave chase, the exhilaration of the hunt coursing through my blood.

A low growl rumbled out of my throat, and I coiled myself to spring, but then a voice intruded, breaking through the haze that clouded my senses. I tried to shake the noise off, tried to focus on the pig, but the voice was so insistent that I finally turned, intent on showering my frustration on whoever had interrupted me.

There, in the glow of the moonlight, stood a golden puma.

"Delilah, come back to us. You have to come back to us. This isn't you, Delilah, not right now—it's not time. Come back," he said, his voice imperative. I wanted to ignore him, to run after the pig, but I couldn't. The puma smelled like an alpha, and I had to listen. Reluctantly, I began to follow him through the jungle.

As my bloodlust died down, my head began to pound, and I swayed, unable to keep my focus. Where was I? What was happening? I started to call out for help but couldn't get the words out of my mouth. The next thing I knew, everything went swirling into blackness.

CHAPTER 13

"Great Mother Bast, what the hell happened to me?" I asked, sitting up, not sure if I'd actually shifted form. I remembered something about blood and a pig and . . .

Iris knelt beside me. When I tried to get to my feet, I lurched, my balance dangerously off. She forced me to slow down, helping me to stand and then move over to the sofa.

I looked around, a frantic feeling rising in my chest. "Zach? Where's Zachary? Is he okay?" Why I was worried, I didn't know, but the fear that something had happened to him was there.

"He's right over there," Iris said as she went bustling out of the room toward the kitchen. At that moment, a large puma came padding out from behind the tree. I swallowed. Hard. It was Zach. He walked over to the sofa, sniffed me, then turned and followed Iris.

Morio followed him. "I'll go with him, just in case he needs any help when he changes back," he said.

Dizzy and unsure just what the hell had happened, I leaned against the seat cushion, rubbing my temples. Chase joined me, his hand on my shoulder, a look of concern filling his face. Grateful for his support, I let him tuck a throw pillow behind my head and closed my eyes as he entwined his fingers with mine, anchoring me to my body. Menolly sat next to him, going so far as to give him a firm nod of approval.

"Here, let's get this on your forehead, my dear." Iris hurried back into the room with a wet cloth in her hand. She pressed it against my brow, and the soothing chill calmed me, clearing my head a little.

"Drink." Camille shoved her water bottle into my hand.

"Finish it off. You're probably dehydrated, and the water will do you good."

I took a sip, grateful the bottle turned out to be filled with Talking Rain berry-flavored sparkling water. Trying to shake myself fully awake, I felt as though I'd entered a fog bank and that the mists had arisen from nowhere to obscure my vision.

Smoky and Trillian were standing near the fireplace, both watching me. Smoky's expression was unreadable; Trillian looked vaguely concerned. Finally, I was able to breathe normally again, and the room quit spinning. I straightened up, trying to make sense of the whole thing.

Just then Morio returned with Zach, who had a wild gleam in his eye. He had changed back into his human form without looking much worse for wear, but the scent of his musk hung thick in the air, and I tensed. Chase glanced at me, then at Zach, but said nothing.

Iris gave us all a long look. "I think I'd better make some tea and haul out the cookies," she said, heading back to kitchen.

Rather embarrassed now that I almost felt normal again, I coughed and stared at floor. "I'm sorry about all this," I muttered. "Did I . . . did I change into my Were-form? I can't remember."

Menolly shook her head, her voice serious as she said, "No, Kitten, you didn't change shape, but you did go into convulsions. Do you remember what happened? Do you feel sick?"

Convulsions? That was news to me, and not welcome news, either. I tried to assess how I felt, but the only answer that came to mind was that I felt conspicuous and embarrassed. My stomach was a little queasy, and the back of my head felt like I'd smacked it a good one on the floor, but other than that, nothing else seemed out of kilter. Nothing except for the fact that I had absolutely no memory of the past half hour. I shrugged.

"Don't think so," I said. I drew in a deep breath, held it, and then exhaled slowly. Nope, nothing. In fact, oddly enough, I felt stronger than before . . . before whatever had happened.

I blinked. "Zachary, what made you shift?"

Zachary looked unhappy as he let out a loud sigh. "I don't know why I changed. I remember you fell on the floor, and there was so much cat magic drifting through the room that I started getting dizzy . . . and then I can't remember anything else until I found myself on the kitchen floor, with Morio standing there over me. I don't like this. I've never lost time when in Were-form."

"I don't like it, either," I said, frowning. "Did I say anything or do anything before I went into seizure?"

Camille glanced at Menolly, then they both looked at me. "Menolly was telling you about the mark on your forehead. About how it marks you as a Death Maiden."

Shit! I let go of Chase and rested my head in my hands. "I forgot about that. I must have had a panic attack or something." While I wasn't prone to hysteria, I felt perfectly justified in losing it over news of this sort. Turning to Menolly, I said, "I probably asked this already, but I don't remember. Does that mean he put a bounty on my head? Am I going to die?"

"I tried to tell you before you phased out. The Death Maidens are mostly Fae, though there are a few FBHs among his harem. Think non-Norse Valkyries. They gather the souls that the Autumn Lord harvests on Samhain Eve and take them to the underworld. The Death Maidens belong to the Autumn Lord, acting as both wives and comrades."

What the fuck? She had to be kidding. "I refuse. I won't do it. I'm not about to let myself be married off to that scary-ass dude, Elemental Lord or not." I stopped, a nasty thought crossing my mind. "Uh . . . just what do you think he can do to me if I don't obey?"

"I'm not sure I want to find out," she said. "From what I know, you have to die first before he can take you into his realm, though I could be wrong. But he's not going to kill you. He just marked you. But for now, I wouldn't let it worry me. We have plenty of time to figure out how to get him to release you from service."

Oh great. So when I died, I wouldn't join my ancestors.

Instead, I'd be handed over like a prize to the Autumn Lord. Spending eternity in his service didn't sound like a load of laughs to me.

"You can tell me not to worry all you like," I said, snorting. "*You* aren't going to die. At least not again."

She shrugged. "We have bigger problems to worry about right now. We *will* free you from the mark. I promise."

I grumbled but sat down. Camille gave me that look she saved for when she had no clue what to do. I frowned back at her. "All right, but I want this taken care of as soon as possible. What if I have some freak accident? What if one of the Degath Squad demons hits his mark? What do I do then?"

Zachary stood up and cleared his throat. "I hate to cut out on this—it's been one hell of a ride so far, but I have to get home and see what's going on. I'll do some digging on Tyler's background and what he's been up to and let you know what I find out." He headed for the door.

I wasn't sure whether to be offended or not. After all, I'd just learned that I was promised in marriage to one of the biggest bad boys of all—a minion of Death. That should rate more than a blink and a see-you-later from somebody who professed to be in lust with me. But then again, the man hadn't yet fully processed everything that had happened. Boy, was he in for a shock once he realized just what he'd gotten himself mixed up in.

I walked him to the door. Outside, on the front porch, I tucked my hands under my arms, trying to keep warm. The rain had turned to snow again, and the temperature was dropping steadily. The air was so crisp it hurt my nose.

"Zachary, will you be okay?" I asked.

He shrugged. "I don't know. I won't be okay until we track down Kyoka and stop him. I'm still not clear about all this spirit seal stuff and the demons, but I understand it's dangerous. Yes, I'm a Supe, but I'm still earthbound, and I realize now that I view the world through an all-too-human frame of reference."

After a pause, he said, "What a different world you and your sisters come from. A world of demons and warring states and kings and queens . . ." Stopping abruptly, he studied the ground.

I moved in a step. He still smelled like puma, and the scent of cat magic set off a longing so deep that I was having trouble ignoring it. I studied him from the feet up, but that was a mistake, too, as my gaze drifted up his legs, which filled out the pair of form-fitting jeans all too well. As his broad shoulders came into view, I let out a little mew. And then, the lion's mane of hair, and those golden topaz eyes.

My pulse was racing as I forced myself to answer him. "Zach, we aren't all that strange. Well, maybe we are, but we want the same thing so many humans and Earthside Supes do. Love, friends, family, peace, to lead our lives without interference. That isn't so very different, is it?"

Maybe I was pleading for him not to push us aside as freaks, or maybe I was trying to convince myself that I wasn't a Windwalker, that I was normal and had a family and friends like everybody else. Whatever the case, Zachary heard me and reached out. I walked into his arms, knowing that now wasn't the right time or place but not giving a damn.

"I don't know what happened in there when I shifted," he whispered, "but I do know that when I returned to my normal self, I had a hard-on you wouldn't believe."

Pressing his lips against my hair, he murmured, "Delilah, I want you. I don't care if you're not a Were by blood. I don't care if you're half Fae, or half zebra. I don't care what my clansmen say. I just want you . . . under me, in my bed, in my arms. I want to see your face when you come, to know that I was the one who brought you to passion. I'm going to leave it up to you when—or if—anything happens between us. But don't wait too long."

And then his lips met mine, and I lost myself in the kiss. He pushed me against the wall, filling every nook of my body with his own. I could feel how much he wanted me; he was rigid and hard and demanding. And yet—and yet, I knew he'd stop in a heartbeat if I only whispered the word. So why wasn't I whispering?

The sound of the door startled us out of our embrace.

I turned to find Chase standing there. I couldn't read his expression, and I wasn't sure I wanted to, but the look of betrayal on his face stabbed me in the heart, and my mother's blood hit home. I stumbled away from Zach as, without a word, he strode down the stairs and over to his truck. As he climbed in the cab, I turned back to Chase.

"Chase . . . we have to talk," I said. "Nothing happened—"

"You call that nothing? Wow, different dictionary than I use." Frowning, he tried to shrug it off. "I should have known better. First time I play straight with a woman, and she screws me over."

His self-righteous tone set me on edge. "*Excuse* me? We've *never* talked about having an exclusive relationship. As for Zachary, I kissed him. Yes. Twice, if you want to know. But that's it."

"Am I supposed to applaud now? Clap my hands that you've only been toying with the guy?" He grabbed me by the shoulders and pulled me into his arms. "Delilah, he can't give you what I can. That guy's trouble, and he doesn't know you like I know you."

I had no desire to deal with this now, especially with all the demon and werespider warfare going on.

"That's enough," I said, shaking him off. "You're right. You *do* know me. You know all about my background and heritage and what it means. And you damned well better know me enough to realize I don't sleep with every man who crosses my path. There's just something about Zachary . . . I can't explain it."

Chase glared at me, then let out a long sigh. "Yeah, I know. I know, but that doesn't mean I have to like it."

I gave him a long look and took a stab in the dark. "What about you? Are you usually exclusive with your girlfriends? Have you ever cheated on a girl?"

He blinked and looked away.

"You have, haven't you? You might tell them you're playing square, but I'm guessing that you've messed around plenty of times."

He huffed. "No, damn it!" I raised my eyebrows, waiting,

and finally he gave me a short shrug. "Yeah, all right, I have cheated a few times. But I never felt the desire to be with just one woman before. I never met the right girl."

Until now. I heard the words as clear as day, even though he hadn't said them.

I crossed my arms and leaned against the railing. "Then how about if we set some rules. Right now? I won't ask you to be exclusive, and you won't expect me to be. But no hiding or lying. If I end up sleeping with somebody else, I'll tell you about it. And vice versa." I waited. It would make life so much easier if humans were just up-front and honest about relationships and sex.

Chase leaned against the railing, staring out at the falling snow. "Okay. For now. But Delilah, if you sleep with Zachary, don't think I want to know all the sordid details. I'm not that liberated. I don't want to know how many times he makes you swing from the ceiling or how big his cock is. Got it?"

He headed for the door. Our relationship had just taken a drastic shift, and I feared it might not be one for the better.

"Got it," I said, following him. "Chase, I hope you know how much I like being with you. Because it's true." But he'd already gone inside.

Trillian was leaning against the desk, staring at the Yule tree, when I returned to the living room. He was ignoring Smoky, who had his arm around Camille. Morio was talking in quiet whispers to Menolly, and Iris was washing dishes. She finished up and came back into the living room, carrying our little sleepyhead, Maggie. Settling into the rocker, she began to lull our girl to sleep.

Trillian let out an exasperated sigh when he saw me. "Are you quite through, now? Do you mind if I change the subject? I have news about your family and the war, and it's vital you hear me out before Menolly goes in to work tonight." He looked so pissed that I decided it wasn't a good time for a snarky comeback. Even if I could have thought of one.

"What's going on?" Camille started to get up, but Smoky

pulled her back down, a faint smile of amusement playing across his face.

Trillian cocked an eyebrow but managed to keep his thoughts to himself. I knew he was scared of the dragon and with good reason. Any jealous boyfriend who forgot that the gorgeous, sardonic hunk of man-flesh was actually a Crypto capable of swallowing him whole was an idiot. And would soon be a *dead* idiot. Trillian knew this, even though it was obvious he was fighting a battle with himself not to stride over there and drag her out of Smoky's arms.

"Your father and aunt are safe, but one of your cousins has been taken into custody," Trillian said.

"Who?" Camille and I spoke at the same time.

Trillian glanced up. "Shamas. He's been convicted of spying for Tanaquar."

Shamas. He was a rabble-rouser, all right, and never listened to a single word of warning that he was playing a dangerous game. A conviction for treason meant that he was lost. Death came slowly to traitors, and by the end, they were usually too far gone to even appreciate it.

Hanging my head, I whispered, "That's it, then."

"He won't suffer," Trillian said grimly. "I promise you that. Tanaquar is kind to her loyal followers. The king of Svartalfheim has provided her with a triad from the Order of Jakaris for the duration of the war."

I looked at Camille, then at Menolly. We knew what that meant. Shamas's fate was sealed. The monks of Jakaris, a Svartan god of death and vice, worked in triads and were skilled assassins. They would trace Shamas through the astral and then—in a quick blaze—stop his heart. He would die. But he wouldn't be in pain. At least not for long.

Chase leaned forward and propped his head on his hands, staring at his feet. Morio frowned, playing with the fringe on the ottoman.

Camille shook off Smoky's arm and paced over to Trillian's side. "That's best, then. Truly," she said, as if trying to convince herself of it. "Shamas won't suffer. He'll die with dignity. Does Father know?"

Trillian gave her a long look, dark and pointed. "Yes, I stopped there before returning through the portal and let both him and your aunt know."

Aunt Rythwar was Shamas's foster mother. Aunt Olanda, Shamas's mother, lived far away in Windwillow Valley, a small community of Fae who embraced an arboreal life.

"What else do you have for us?" Camille played with one of the ornaments on the tree, her hands shaking. She and Shamas had been good friends when we were young, but there was nothing we could do for him now.

Trillian paced over to the window, staring out into the storm-ridden night. "The war is tearing Y'Elestrial apart. Lethesanar is conscripting every male who's barely reached puberty. Families are smuggling their children out of the city, hoping to keep them safe. Officers have been quitting right and left, and in their place, the Queen's appointing her power-mad cronies. The lines of traitors marching to the dungeon are long, my girls. Be grateful your father and aunt fled the city. There are spies everywhere."

"Anything else?" I asked, not really wanting to know. The news was so bleak. Y'Elestrial was a beautiful city, but it would run red with the blood of the enemies before too long.

"Yes," he said, turning to face us. "The OIA has been disbanded for the duration of the war. The portals will stand unguarded."

That brought a reaction, all right. Menolly's eyes flared red, and Camille leapt up, letting out a string of curses that made Chase blush brighter than her crimson lipstick. I stood slowly, unsure of what to do.

"How ridiculous," Iris said. "Makes me glad I'm earthbound. But you girls can't go back. Who's going to keep away Shadow Wing?"

"She's right," Menolly said. "You are telling us that after Bad Ass Luke they're going to just let that damned Soul Eater march in here and wipe out the world? Why haven't we heard word of this?"

Trillian examined his nails. In an offhanded tone he said, "The person carrying those orders never made it through the portal. I delivered the news to Tanaquar, and *she* had a little talk with the director of the OIA."

"The director actually spoke to her?" I couldn't believe it—that was just too bizarre.

"He's a double agent. Don't ask how or why. Just trust me. And he's agreed to a compromise. He'll recall the operatives that Lethesanar would miss. She'll never know that you—and a few of the others who have no love for the Queen—have been left behind. Word's already been sent to them."

A double agent? Our head honcho was working for the enemy? Things must be terribly wrong back home. For a moment, I had the crazy idea that if we could only hurry back, we could somehow make things right, but I stopped myself from even suggesting such a half-baked plan.

With a frown, I asked, "So, how many other operatives are staying? Enough to guard the portals?"

"Not enough, no. And definitely not enough to engage against the demons. I hate to drop this on your shoulders, but it's up to you girls to keep Shadow Wing's Hell Scouts at bay until she can wrap up the war and take control of Y'Elestrial."

Oh delightful. Both the Elfin Queen and Tanaquar were expecting us to keep things nice and tidy. We'd better get really good at what we did, really fast.

Trillian shook his head. "I know what you're thinking, but it really is up to the three of you and whoever you can get to help you. You have my aid, of course. I'll be here as much as I can, when Tanaquar doesn't need me."

"We know you will," Camille said, looking glum. "I just wish we knew who we could rely on and who we can't."

Chase frowned. "From what you say, it might be a good idea to make contact with the other Earthside agents. You could bring in other Supes and humans you can trust."

"That's another thing," Trillian said, turning to Chase. "I hate to tell you this, but you're out of a job. At least with the OIA. All Earthside operatives have been cut loose."

"In case you weren't listening, I figured that out already," Chase said. It looked like they were about to get into it, so I interrupted.

"Bottom line, where does that leave *us*?"

Trillian shrugged. "The way I see it, you should be safe enough here. You bought the house with money from your father, not from the OIA. And nobody from the OIA will be coming through the portals anytime soon. But don't use the Whispering Mirror to contact the OIA or the Guard Des'Estar. And whatever else, don't let yourselves be seen in Y'Elestrial if you return to OW."

All three of us paused. We all knew what was coming next, but nobody wanted to be the one to ask. Finally, Camille whispered, "Why?"

For the first time, I saw a flicker of fear race across Trillian's face. "Because there's a bounty on your heads should you return to the city."

"Then we're under a death threat," I said.

Chase jumped up. "You have a bounty on your heads? What the hell is going on? Is your Queen insane?" Any residue of anger he had left seemed to disappear, and he reached for my hand.

I took his hand. "Lethesanar's lost all sense of perspective. She's never borne an heir to the throne, so there's no princess to take her place. I have a feeling she means to rule for as long as she can."

"But Tanaquar has two daughters," Trillian said. "And she's clearheaded. She can turn things around."

"Where does the portal in the Wayfarer lead?" Smoky said, suddenly breaking into the conversation.

"It's connected directly to Y'Elestrial." Menolly floated up to the ceiling. "We'd better find a way to recalculate its target. And for now, if we return to OW, we have to use Grandmother Coyote's portal, which will take us safely to the outskirts of Elqaneve, the Elfin city."

"So," I said, "we've lost our jobs. What about the other agents over here? Do you have their names?"

Trillian held out a file folder. "I thought you'd want this. I put together a list of their names and where they're staying. One other thing—they know nothing about Shadow Wing. Apparently the OIA never officially acknowledged that the demons are planning to invade Earth, and none of the other agents were told about your encounter."

Well hell. That meant that every OIA agent who had chosen to stay Earthside, other than the ones we knew personally, was in danger. And none of them knew about it.

He handed me the file. "I think they deserve to know what they're facing. When I return to OW, I'll contact your father and aunt to let them know you're safe."

"Thank you," I murmured bleakly. Unemployed except for what we had in savings and what we could earn off our cover jobs, we were alone in a strange land without any hope of support from home. Well, that wasn't exactly true. We had allies, but they weren't available at the drop of a hat.

A sudden thought hit me, and I looked up. "Do you think we could reprogram the Whispering Mirror to contact Queen Asteria's court? That would be so much easier than having to send—or wait for—her messengers."

Camille clapped her hands. "That's perfect! I love the idea. Can we do it, though? My magic isn't good enough to ensure success, and we don't dare take a chance on anything less."

"I'll head out tomorrow first light. My first stop will be Elqaneve. I can convince them to send one of their mages out to work with you." Trillian yawned. "I'm so fucking astral-lagged," he said, wincing.

Frequent or prolonged travel through the portals could cause the system to overload and throw off sleep cycles, metabolism, and all sorts of goodies. Trillian had been hopping between OW and Earthside several times a week since he'd healed from the skinwalker's attack.

Camille took his hand. "Come to my bedroom."

"Gladly, my love." He motioned for her to go ahead, then turned to Smoky. "Remember," he said in a tone that was as calm and deadly as a viper. "Camille is on loan. I don't care whether you're a dragon or a gecko, she's *mine*. Understand?"

Smoky chuckled. "As you wish. I won't interfere," he added, but I wasn't so sure he was telling the truth.

As Camille led Trillian away, Menolly glanced at the clock. "I'd better get down to the Wayfarer." She grabbed her keys and purse, a cute little patent-leather clutch. I had no idea where she'd found the handbag—it was shaped like a bat with wings spread and was probably part of some kid's Halloween costume. "I guess I'll just keep everything we earn from there now."

"Well, you can't send it home anymore," I said.

She nodded. "That makes me think. With the OIA pulling out so abruptly, my guess is that they won't bother to do anything about ownership of the buildings. We'd better find out if there's a monthly mortgage on the bar and the Indigo Crescent. If the OIA is still paying them off, we'll have to make the payments. At least for the bar. There's no way we can let go of the Wayfarer, since it houses the portal."

I grunted and jotted down a note in my book as she headed for the door. "Good idea. The last thing we need is someone trying to foreclose."

Morio stood and stretched. "I'm going to drive Smoky home," he said. "I'll be back, if you don't mind me crashing in the parlor tonight."

"Not a problem," I said. "I'll leave a note for Iris that you're here." The two men left, leaving Chase and me alone. I looked at him and let out a long sigh.

"Things are so messed up," I said, so exhausted I could barely think. So many things were unresolved. I wondered if we'd make it through this. Once again, I longed for the days of my childhood when life had seemed simpler.

Chase said nothing, just opened his arms. I walked into his embrace, and he pulled me close. "I'm sorry," he whispered. "I'm sorry I was such an ass out there on the porch. I know what you are, and I love what you are. I don't want you to change just for me, but it's hard. I've never felt this way about a woman before. I never expected to feel like this."

I wrapped my arms around his waist and rested my head on his shoulder. "My mother and father made it work, Chase, but I don't know if I can. I'm . . . I'm a Windwalker. I don't fit in anywhere. Can you live with uncertainty? Can you live with the possibility that I might sleep with someone else? I'm not like Camille. I'm not experienced enough to know what I want yet. I'm still new at this whole sex thing, but my hormones have woken up, and for the Fae, they're a powerful and driving force."

Chase kissed my forehead, then tipped my chin up and kissed me on the lips. "I guess I'll have to live with it. I wondered how Trillian and Morio could stand sharing Camille, but I think I understand. Being with you part of the time is better than the thought of never touching you again, never making love to you, never kissing you."

I swallowed a lump that rose straight from my heart to my throat. I wanted to tell him that I'd be his. I wanted to make the promises that I knew he wanted to hear. But I couldn't. And I wouldn't lie to him or to myself. So I did the next best thing. I took his hand and led him up to my bedroom.

CHAPTER 14

~⚬⚬~

As I closed the bedroom door, Chase gave me a long, smoldering look. My stomach lurched, and suddenly, the only thing I could think about was screwing our brains out. He usually took the lead, but this time, I wanted to be in charge.

I took two quick steps and, before he could speak, pushed him back onto my big four-poster bed. His eyes widened with surprise as I straddled him, and he gave me a wicked grin that told me he didn't mind being on the bottom one bit.

I unfastened his shirt, one button at a time, leaning over to trail kisses down his chest as I pulled away the material. I let my tongue linger on his salty skin, then kiss by kiss, inched my way down. As I unbuckled his belt, I was gratified to see the impression I'd made. He moaned gently as I slid his pants down.

"Delilah—" he started to say, but I shushed him, slowly licking the length of his cock, using only the tip of my tongue as I worked my way from the root to the head. I couldn't take him fully in my mouth—we'd tried that and lost the battle to my fangs—but I tickled him, fluttering lightly up and down his rigid length. The scent of his lust was heady as he gently reached down to run his fingers through my hair.

Leaning back, I pulled off my turtleneck. Chase stared at me with naked lust, his gaze taking in every movement I made, every jiggle and bounce of my breasts as I unhooked my bra. I pushed myself off the bed, quickly unzipping my jeans and stepping out of them. Chase folded his hands under his head, silently watching as I slid my panties down my hips.

Somehow understanding that I needed to call the shots, he waited. I knelt by his feet and took off his shoes, then helped him out of his pants. As he sat up, I climbed astride his lap, and he wrapped his arms around my lower back, his lips closing around my nipple. The warmth of his tongue on my skin echoed through my body, and I let out a little sigh as he slid one of his hands between my legs, fingering me gently at first. The tension began to build, rippling through my body until it cascaded into a tidal wave.

The sight of him, all sweaty with breath coming hard, pushed me over the edge, and I squirmed, lowering myself onto his hips, sliding down his length with silken ease, nestling him as deep inside me as he could get. Pushing him back on the bed, I leaned down to kiss him.

Chase wrapped his arms around my waist, holding me tight. As our rhythms flowed into synch, I forgot about the Autumn Lord, forgot about the war, forgot about everything except the rocking of our bodies.

As we were lying in bed afterward, Chase changed his nicotine patch, slapping a new one on his shoulder, while I sipped a bottle of root beer. Reluctantly, I brought myself back to the present and our problems.

"Chase, remember I mentioned what the Autumn Lord said about the Hunters Moon Clan?" I dug into my nightstand, looking for a candy bar. Success! A Snickers was hiding right below the notepad that I kept at the ready for any odd ideas that might surface while I was sleeping.

Chase adjusted the comforter—a thick, blue patchwork quilt—so that it covered his chest. "Damn it's cold. Has the snow let up yet?"

"Dunno, but I'll check." I padded over to the window, shivering in the chill of the room. Outside, the snow had picked up, and I estimated there was a good three inches on the roof right now. "Nope, and it doesn't look like it's going to. I think we're in for quite a storm. So, do you?"

"Do I what? Oh, you mean the werespiders. No, not really. I kind of lost track of things when the whole Death Maiden business came up." He finished applying the new patch and dropped the old one in the garbage. "Hey, I'm going down a step tomorrow. I may actually kick this habit because of you, babe."

I gave him one of my happy smiles. Cigarette smoke bothered me so much that I went to great lengths to avoid it. And he'd be healthier when he quit.

"Good for you! I'm proud of you," I said, unwrapping the candy, ready to scarf the entire thing down. He looked at the chocolate bar with those puppy-dog eyes of his, and I relented, handing him half of it. "Why I was asking was this: the waterfall that the Autumn Lord mentioned is supposed to be in a city east of Seattle. Do you know anything about any waterfalls around here?"

I swallowed the last bite of chocolate and jumped out of bed to slip into my pajamas. Contrary to popular belief, the heat in our house sure didn't rise to the top. It just seeped out the cracks. My floor was always the coldest.

Chase thought for a moment. "Yeah, actually, I think I know what he was talking about. The town of Snoqualmie is just east of Issaquah, and Snoqualmie Falls are there. They're beautiful—they were featured in the show *Twin Peaks* some years back. Weird-ass show, though now it seems tame compared to what life's become with you guys around. Anyway, there's a lodge there, very pretty place. And once you hit Snoqualmie, you're heading into the foothills of the Cascades. A lot of undeveloped country out there."

"Foothills . . . that fits. The Autumn Lord said we'd find their nest in the foothills near this waterfall. It's perfect. Close enough to the city that it wouldn't take them long to drive in, yet out where they won't be noticed." I thought about it for a moment. "Chase, we have to hunt them down. Zachary's going to keep an eye on Tyler. If he's mixed up with this, then he's probably going back to the nest every now and then, especially if he doesn't think anybody's onto him."

Chase flinched at Zach's name but let it pass without comment. "I'm tempted to sneak onto the Puma Pride's land and tail this guy the minute he leaves the compound."

I gave him a sideways glance. "I could do that. Or Morio. Or both of us. If I was in my tabby form, or Morio in his fox form, it would be easy enough to hide without attracting attention."

"They know you're a werecat, though, don't they?" Chase

shook his head. "It might be better to send Morio in. I don't like the thought of you trying to fend off a racing puma. Morio can run a lot faster than you in his superhero form, can't he?"

I snorted. "Superhero? That's a good one. I'm going to have to tell him what you said. But yeah, you're right. Morio's greased lightning when he's in fox form. We can send him in, and he can let us know when Tyler's getting ready to leave the compound."

Chase yawned and leaned back against the headboard, playing with the necklace of worry stones I'd bought for him. He used them to keep his hands busy and keep his mind off what it would be like to be holding a cigarette.

"I've been meaning to ask you. What do you think the connections between the murder victims are? I know they're all members of the Puma Pride Clan, so don't even start with that, but what else? Why them? Why were they killed and not anybody else?" He frowned. "It seems so random to me."

I pulled my knees up to my chest and gave a little *purp*. Chase was always good at thinking of the questions that eluded me. Of course, being a detective was his job, while being an agent for the OIA was more of a hobby for me. It's true that I'd been learning the ropes of the PI business, but at home my assignments had mainly been being sent in to rescue someone, or to hunt down criminals and take them out. The OIA wasn't known for its apprehension ratio so much as for its extermination record.

"I'm not sure. Several of them were off the books, if you'll remember. They didn't even try to pass in society and kept to their own kind."

Chase let out a little sigh. "Seems like a lonely life to me. It must have been hard to be an Earthside Supe before you guys opened the portals. They had to hide or pass. I feel sorry for them."

"Humans rule this world, or so they think, but there have been minority groups down through history, Chase. There's always somebody on top, and too often they've gotten there on the shoulders of those who don't have the strength or numbers to protest." I slipped out from under the covers. "Hold on a minute; I'll be right back."

I hurried into my studio, where I kept my laptop, and then scampered back into bed. Plugging it into the outlet by my nightstand, I turned it on and waited for it to boot up. After typing my password in, I pulled up a browser.

"What are you doing?" Chase asked, scooting closer so he could look over my shoulder.

"I'm going to look up my notes on the victims." I pulled up Note One and clicked on the tab labeled Puma Pride, then the section I'd created for notes about the victims. "They had two things in common. One, they were all members of the Puma Pride."

"Not all," Chase said. "Don't forget about the plumber guy. Ben Jones?"

"You're right—okay, but Ben seems to be the lone oddball. Maybe the murderer thought he was a member of the Pride? Anyway, the other commonality is that they were found out by the arrastra in Pinnacle Creek. And that's right below Pinnacle Rock, where we found the cave that the werespiders were using."

I thought about it for a moment. "You know what I think? I don't think there is a pattern other than the werespiders believing they were all Puma Pride members. I think that they just happened to be in the wrong place at the wrong time. But nobody is safe on that land now. The Hunters Moon Clan has to know their cave's been discovered, especially if Tyler's mixed up in this. They won't wait much longer before they start moving toward the houses. They're taking down the entire clan as they search for any sign of the second spirit seal. My guess is that Kyoka's killing off the Puma Pride members for revenge. Wipe out the Puma Pride, get the spirit seal, kill two birds with one stone."

"So Shadow Wing reincarnated this Kyoka as a werepuma?" Chase looked confused. "I don't understand how that works."

"Neither do I, but it's my bet that Kyoka wasn't reincarnated. I think he stole a body. Shamans can do that, if they're strong enough, and Kyoka had to be incredibly strong to turn his tribe into werespiders. With the other two newcomers to the Pride checking out, ten to one it's Tyler. And Tyler's probably the real name of whoever it was that owned that body before Kyoka took possession as a walk-in."

Walk-ins were souls who literally went on body-snatching missions. They either obliterated or possessed a soul, imposing their will over that of the original host. It was a frightening power, and rare, but it happened from time to time. Tyler must have been weak-willed, sickly, or willing to let himself be used. Or Kyoka was just a freakishly strong shaman.

"Walk-ins," Chase said. "I've heard of them but never really believed in their existence. Of course, I didn't believe in a lot of things until you girls came along." He let out a rueful laugh. "Boy, did I have a lot to learn. Looks like I still do. Makes work a blast, though."

"Speaking of work, do you still have a job with the force since the OIA is pulling out?"

"Yeah, though Devins would give his right arm to bust my butt down to the street again. But I've done too much for the department. They'll probably just put me back on a basic beat. Homicide, no doubt."

"Hmmm," I said, thinking. "Who does the OIA officially report to in your department?"

Chase frowned. "Me. Why?"

I grinned. "Good. And who else do they talk to there?" The idea just seemed better and better to me. We could create our own OIA and still have full use of the department's files.

"Just the medics—wait a minute, I think I can see where you're going with this. You want me to go on like nothing happened!" He rolled out of bed and strode toward the bathroom. "That's ridiculous. We're bound to get caught."

"How?" I called out, following him and standing beside the closed door. "Devins doesn't ever ask you what's going on. You, yourself, told me that he doesn't give a damn unless it's something that could make him look like a hero. The medics report to you, and they're all elves. They're not going to pull out. It's perfect. We can remake the OIA the way it should be run. Once we contact the other agents who are staying here, we can include them in the loop. Since they're pro-Tanaquar, they'll be eager to help. I'm certain of it!"

Chase finished peeing and came out of the room, wiping his hands on the towel. I liked that he was clean. He smelled like the wildflower soap I had on the vanity counter.

"You really mean it, don't you?" He stared at the bed, a furrowed line of concentration creasing his brow. "Do you think we can pull it off?"

"If we can't, then Earth is doomed," I said glumly. "Otherworld, too. The demons will find a way in, and there won't be anything left."

Chase let out a long sigh. "I think you're crazy, for what it's worth. But if it works . . . maybe we can pull together a ragtag team. We could base everything out of Seattle and hire our own operatives from the Supe and human community."

"The problem would be how to pay them. We'd have to keep Devins in the dark about the fact that they aren't being sent from OW. And we have to redirect the Wayfarer portal to point away from Y'Elestrial, which might arouse suspicions unless we rig it so it seems to be broken." I sighed. "The logistics are huge, but I don't see any other choice."

"Maybe we can find volunteers," Chase said. "People we can tell the truth to, who would be willing to put in time in order to stop Shadow Wing's attempts. We could use a few medical personnel, especially those who know about Fae body chemistry. And we need somebody really good with computers, because we're going to have to be on top of everybody's whereabouts."

I grinned. Computer programmer, huh? "I might be able to take care of that. I know just the person."

"Let's sleep on it." Chase snuggled under the covers and reached for me. I rolled against him and smiled. He had an erection that wouldn't stop giving. "How about another round of grab and tickle?"

Snickering, I reached down and clasped hold of him. "I'll take care of the grab, you just be sure to take care of tickling me in all the right ways," I whispered.

I wasn't disappointed.

* * *

The raucous call of birds quieted down as I stalked my way through the jungle. Rain splashed out of the skies, leaving diamond droplets on the arboreal canopy that wove together a latticework of vegetation covering the path and everything below.

Dusk had fallen, and soon my enemy would be out to hunt. I paused to listen at every scuttle, every sound of some creature moving through the foliage. The ground was pungent as I silently traced my route, the sour tang of decaying leaves mingling with that of mold that spread like fragile veins through the soil and toadstools popping out of the moss.

My footsteps were silent as I navigated by scent. I could smell my enemies close by, though I couldn't remember exactly who they were or why I was following them. But it was my task to hunt them down, to destroy and purge, to cleanse and send them to the waiting arms of my master.

The plants swayed as I brushed against them, alive in their own right. I could almost hear them whispering in some arcane language used only by the nature devas. But their souls were dark, and I did not stop to listen or intrude. Unlike the trees of the northern forests and the wildflowers of the meadows, the flytraps and corpse flowers would eat you alive if you stopped in their shelter.

And there it was—the turnoff leading to their lair. I veered to the right, pushing my way through the undergrowth, which opened into a shimmering field of light. As I passed through the brilliant barrier, the jungle disappeared behind me, and I found myself standing near a crystalline waterfall that cascaded over the face of a rock wall. The trees here were cedar and fir and maple.

The falls were roaring to the river below, a white sheet of water that glistened like ice, and the rocky shores on either side of the ravine were covered with a light dusting of snow. I paused, wondering where to go from here. As I sniffed the air, my lungs reverberated with the chill, and then I caught it, faint, on the wind. The scent of my prey, leading beyond the falls onto a paved road that wound through the woods.

I took off, looking this way and that, but there was no one

in sight. As I loped along, I began to notice side roads leading into the forest. The snow was cold against my feet, and I shivered as each paw hit the asphalt.

After roaming for what seemed like hours, the smells grew so strong I could taste them. I opened my mouth, letting the breeze kiss my tongue with the flavor of blood, metallic and sweet. Fresh blood. They'd made a kill recently.

I turned onto one of the side roads, but something stopped me. I glanced up at a metal signpost, above which the image of a golden staff appeared.

The urge to hurry was stronger now, and I raced on, following the twists and turns of the road as it wound through firs heavy with snow.

A fork in the road beckoned, and I veered onto it. The path rose steadily, one side flanked by a dirt slope, the other by a ravine. I peered over the side. Below, a stream tumbled along, white-water caps raging at such a clip that they reminded me of spring thaws along the Tygerian River when the ice sheets in the mountains would melt and flood the bottomlands below.

Brambles covered the sides of the ravine, which were sharp and steep. With leaves stripped bare for the winter, their thorns stood out against the snow, promising a quick and painful landing for anyone so unfortunate as to trip and fall. My nose twitched, and I turned my attention back to the road and the scent I was following.

As I trotted along, the snowstorm tapered off, and the clouds parted, letting the moon shine through. A voice, unbidden and unfamiliar, whispered, "Our people used to live in these lands. We were the people of the moon."

Startled, I looked around and saw a shimmering figure. He was not tall, but he was muscular and fit and wore his hair in two long black braids that fell to his waist. He was dressed in a robe of some sort, and I recognized him as Native American. He was also a spirit.

"Good friend, where are you going?" he asked me.

I could not speak—not in words—but I formed a mental impression of the scent and the urge to hunt and thrust them at him. He seemed to understand, because he nodded and pointed to my left, to a cleft in the hillside.

"You'll find them in there, but you can't go alone, not like this. These abominations are defiling our land, so we welcome your help, but you must come back when you're in body. Do you understand, girl? You can't possibly face them like this."

He looked worried, and I thought about it for a moment. I must be on the astral, roaming far from my body. I seldom journeyed out—that was more for the likes of Camille than for me—but for some reason I'd been brought here, and I needed to see whatever there was to see. I decided to continue.

Sending him a thank-you, to which he nodded, I hurried toward the cleft. It was tall enough for a man and wide enough for three to walk abreast. I hesitated for moment. The scent of blood was strong here, and my instincts said, "Follow it, follow it!"

The opening appeared to lead into a cave.

I paused, trying to gauge how safe I was. Then slowly I padded forward, keeping every sense open and aware. As I approached the opening, a hundred eyes, red and gleaming, stared at me from the trees on either side. I paused, one paw still in the air. Something was coming out of the cave.

A man appeared. He looked human, and yet deep in my bones, I knew this was no ordinary man. He was tall and gangly, with gleaming eyes, and when he moved, he scuttled forward. As he said something in a blur of clicks and whistles, his voice stirred an alarm within me that said, *Evil. This man is evil.*

The red eyes gazing forth from the trees began to edge forward, twinkling like fireflies. Grateful I was in the astral realm, I shifted back a step, but as I did, the man looked in my direction. With a slow smile, he moved toward me.

Oh shit! He could see me! What the fuck was I going to do now?

"We have a visitor," he said, and this time his voice rang too loud.

Damn it, he wasn't fully in the physical realm; he was partially in the astral! I backed up again, wondering if I could take him, but right then I saw the first of what seemed like a hundred long, spindly legs emerge from the forest, and I knew that, whatever they were, they were on the astral plane, too. The spirit guide had warned me, and I hadn't understood.

"Why don't we have ourselves a feast, boys?" the man said, and there was sudden movement as at least a dozen shadowy shapes emerged from between the firs. Their bodies the shape of bloated brown spiders, their torsos were those of men—thin and sickly looking. Their jointed legs crooked ominously as they started forward.

I let out a roar and turned, racing back the way I'd come. Ahead, I saw the spirit guide, and he motioned for me to hurry past, then set a blinding light free to blaze behind me. I raced down the road as fast as my four legs could carry me. The shouts behind me told me the spiders weren't enjoying the light show, but I didn't stop to look back. I ran until I reached the sign with the golden rod hovering above it. Panting, I skidded to a halt and looked behind me.

Nothing. Yet. But my intuition told me that I didn't have a lot of time left until the creatures hunted me down. As I hurried back toward the waterfall, the ground below me quaked, and the sky became jet black.

"Delilah! Delilah! Wake up, babe. Delilah?"

Chase's voice cut through the fog holding my thoughts hostage, and I struggled to open my eyes. As I blinked, I saw him hovering over me, the light on behind him. I struggled with the blankets, and he helped me, holding my back as I scrambled to sit up.

"Are you okay? That must have been one hell of a nightmare." He reached across me to the nightstand for the bottle of water I always kept there. "Here, drink."

I gulped the cool liquid, my throat dry and parched. After a moment, my heart stopped racing, and I shook my head. The events of the dream were fuzzy but still there.

"Great Mother Bast, that was bad." I wiped my mouth and scrunched back against the headboard. Bringing my legs up,

I wrapped my arms around them and rested my chin on the top of my knees.

"What was it about, or do you mind if I ask?" Chase pulled the covers up so we wouldn't freeze—by now the temperature in the room was hovering around ten degrees above icicle time—and he put his arm around my shoulders, gently rubbing my back.

"I think I know where to look for the Hunters Moon Clan," I said, trying to make sense of the dream. In it, I'd been a black panther, not a tabby. Wish fulfillment, no doubt, but I knew everything else in it had been accurate. "There should be a road near the waterfall. You said Snoqualmie Falls, right?"

He nodded.

"Okay, we need to look for a road back in the woods near there, and it will lead to a turnoff called Goldenrod Road . . . or Drive . . . or Avenue. There's a cave against one of the foothills, and *that's* where the Hunters Moon Clan makes their nest. And Chase, that man you showed us a mug shot of? Geph . . ."

"Geph von Spynne, the dude Zachary got into it with?" He yawned, then grabbed his pocket-sized notebook and jotted down a few notes.

"That's the one," I said. "He's in charge. Or at least, he's involved, and trust me, he's dangerous."

"And when you factor in Kyoka and the other two members of the Degath Squad . . ."

"We have a very lethal combination." I slid out from under the covers and grabbed the corn chips sitting on my dresser. Normally, I'd go watch Jerry Springer when I woke up in the middle of the night, but my dream was so vivid and the danger so real that I couldn't think about anything except those red eyes that had been staring at me out of the forest. And the spirit guide. Who was he? And why had he helped me?

With more questions than I had answers for, I padded over to the window seat. Chase joined me, and I gave him a gentle peck on the cheek, then he went back to bed and turned off the light while I curled up to watch the snow fall softly to blanket the ground with its white shroud of winter.

CHAPTER 15

~~≈∞≈~~

When I woke up, the world looked a whole lot bigger. I blinked, trying to make sense of things, then realized I was curled up on my pillow next to Chase, who was staring at me with a soft smile. He reached out to gently scratch me behind the ears and then stroke my back. It felt so good I didn't want him to quit and head-butted his hand for another ear rub, then lightly padded down to the foot of the bed and jumped off. Once on the floor, I closed my eyes and willed myself to transform, which went a whole lot smoother than it did when it happened involuntarily.

As I came back to myself, clad in my PJs and feeling decidedly tousled, I looked up at him from where I was kneeling on the floor. Chase started to laugh.

"I think I've almost gotten used to that," he said, climbing out of bed and stretching. "After the first few times, it doesn't seem so strange."

I grinned as I pushed myself to my feet and stretched, yawning. "Good, because it's probably not going to change." About fifty percent of the time when I spent the night with Chase, I woke up in cat form, curled on the pillow next to him. He usually gave me a good rubdown before I shifted back, and I think that my inner cat was so tickled by the attention that she decided to take advantage of him as much as possible.

"What are you doing today?" he asked. "I've decided to go with your idea and see if I can cover up what's going on with the OIA. We need all the time and info we can get, and without the department backing me up, we'd have to kiss a lot of that good-bye."

"Good," I said, glancing at him. Chase kept in shape, that was for sure. His stomach was taut, a six-pack to make any man envious, and the sight of him naked sent my mind reeling in other directions. I looked at the clock. Six A.M. Still early. "Listen," I said, slowly unbuttoning my pajama top. "Why don't we start the day with a workout?" As I slid out of my PJs, Chase's gaze flickered to mine, and there was no more we needed to say.

Iris had breakfast ready by the time we showered, dressed, and headed downstairs. Camille was helping her, and Maggie was sitting in her custom-made high chair, slurping at the bowl of cream, sugar, cinnamon, and sage.

"I'll do that," Chase said, taking the plates from Camille and beginning to set the table.

"Thanks," she said. "You know, you're all right sometimes."

"I'll take that as a compliment. Go sit down and talk to your sister for a while." He grinned at her, but with very little of the continuous leer he used to shoot her way.

Camille settled into a chair and motioned for me to join her. "Menolly left us a note before she went to bed," she said, holding up a paper. "She did a little sleuthing of her own, and I'm happy to report that both the Wayfarer and the Indigo Crescent are paid for in full. We don't have to worry about mortgages. We just pay property taxes and go along like we have been. And they're in our name since we're ostensibly the owners, so there shouldn't be a problem. With a little luck, the OIA—whatever there is left of it—will forget about us."

"Finally, some good news," I said, accepting a plate of hot-cakes, eggs, and bacon from Chase. "Where's Trillian?" Neither of Camille's lovers was anywhere to be seen.

"He took off for OW early this morning. Tanaquar is running him ragged, and he wanted to let Father know what our plans are. And Morio went into town. He said he had something he wanted to check up on." She handed Maggie a squeak toy, and she happily started hitting it against the high chair, making a racket.

Iris finished up at the stove and joined us at the table. "I think it's time we started her on solid food in addition to her cream mixture," she said, attacking her plate. For such a little person, Iris could pack it away, but that seemed true with most of the Fae. We all ate like pigs in comparison to most humans. "I suggest a few ounces of ground meat, once a day to start. After a month, we'll move her to twice-a-day feedings."

"Sounds good. What kind of meat do gargoyles eat?" Camille asked.

"What kind do you have?" Iris grinned. "I almost forgot," she said, sliding off her stool and crossing to the bookshelf that hid the entrance to Menolly's lair. "Wait till you see what Menolly had me get last time I was in OW. Apparently she did some research and found out this was the best book on the subject." She held up a slim volume bound in leather. *"The Care and Feeding of Woodland Gargoyles.* Isn't that just perfect?"

"How do we know Maggie's a woodland gargoyle and not from some other land?" I asked. "Technically speaking, she's a Sub Realms 'goyle if you go by where she was born."

Iris shook her head and flipped through the book. "According to this book, only woodland gargoyles have calico coloring. It's a self-defense strategy to remain unseen in the woods."

Chase cleared his throat. "Like camouflage?"

"Right," she said. "Anyway, the more common black or gray varieties come from the mountains, and the brownish red backs come from the desert. Of course, they can interbreed, but the children tend to follow the mother's coloring. So our little Maggie's ancestors lived in the woods."

"Does the book give us an expected timeline for how she should be developing?" I smiled gently. It had taken Menolly to think of hunting down a book on gargoyle care, which told me a lot about how closely she'd bonded with Maggie.

Iris flipped through. "Well, she's not walking yet, but that doesn't necessarily mean much. This baby stage can last up to five Earthside years before she takes a few steps. Of course, we don't know how old she is. She hasn't said anything yet except for her *moophs,* but again, that all depends on how old she was when you brought her home, and how much she was breast-fed."

Gargoyles' breast milk was very close in makeup to the cream, sage, sugar, and cinnamon mixture we gave her, which is why the formula was recommended for orphaned 'goyles.

"I guess we're just going to have to wait and see." I turned to Chase. "Why don't you tell them about our plan for the Earthside OIA?"

Chase grunted and laid out the plan we'd come up with, while I set about making a list of things to do. For one thing, I needed to touch base with Zach and find out what he'd learned about Tyler and—hopefully—the second spirit seal.

I glanced over at Chase. "You said we need another computer expert for our OIA work, right?"

He nodded. "And you mentioned you have somebody in mind? I think it should be someone who's human, or at least an Earthside Supe."

"Actually, I do know someone," I said. I grinned at Camille. "What do you think about bringing Cleo on board? I know he could use a few extra bucks, and we can afford to pay him a little bit, at least. Or we could give him a free pass at the Wayfarer for drinks and food."

Camille laughed, her voice rich and full. "Oh, that's good. I think Cleo would be an excellent choice. After all, he is taking computer classes to get his degree, and he does love excitement."

"Who's Cleo?" Chase asked.

"Cleo Blanco . . . well, technically his name is Tim Winthrop—he goes by both. Cleo's his stage name. He's a female impersonator by night, serious computer student by day. He's engaged to our mechanic, Jason Binds."

"Is he trustworthy?" Chase fished another piece of bacon off the plate and finished his hotcakes.

"I think so," Camille said.

"Of course he is," Iris broke in. "I've had several long talks with him at the store. He's a good man, and he's a good father to his little girl. I even met his ex-wife once. I think you were out shopping or something," she said to Camille. "He brought her in and introduced her. She's a lovely woman, but it was easy to see the lack of chemistry there. They were polite, though, and I could tell they genuinely cared about each other. I think I saw a diamond on her ring finger, so she's either engaged or married again."

I gave Iris an admiring look. "Good observations, Iris." I made a note to talk to him.

"Sounds good to me," Chase said. "I guess I'd better go home and get ready for work so I can get this charade into gear. Since all of our OIA medics are elves, we won't have any problems on that front." He pushed himself away from the table and pulled me into his arms. "Be careful, honey. I don't want you getting hurt."

I gazed into his eyes. He really did care, that much was obvious. Maybe I'd been underestimating him. I leaned forward, lingering on his lips for a moment before brushing the hair out of his eyes. "Only if you promise to watch your back, too."

He laughed and planted a wet kiss on my nose. "Call me later, babe, and let me know what's going down. I'll start researching the Snoqualmie area and see if I can find Goldenrod Road."

As he shut the door behind him, I told Camille and Iris about my dream. "I'm not sure what's going on," I said. "I know I was out on the astral, but I also know that I wasn't in my normal Were-form. But we have a lead on the Hunters Moon Clan, and I'm betting before the day is out, Chase will have located the road we're looking for."

Camille began clearing the table. "You know, Chase has turned out to be more help than I ever imagined he would be."

A knock on the door interrupted her. I went to answer it, while she and Iris continued to clean up after breakfast. As I opened the door, a blast of the icy winter air hit me full on. The world had turned white overnight.

Zach stood there with snowflakes in his hair. His breath was coming in white puffs, and he looked frantic as he shivered in his jacket, his hands thrust in his pockets against the cold. "Thank God you're home," he said as I hustled him inside. "I was hoping I wouldn't have to go all the way into town to find you." His clothes were grungy, and he looked like he'd been up all night.

"What's happened?" I led him into the kitchen, where Iris took one look at him and began making a pot of tea.

"We've got a situation out at the compound." He dropped into a chair and propped his elbows on the table, clearly exhausted. "We need your help. The Council elders sent me to beg you to intervene. They'll pay anything they can for your aid."

"What's going on?" Both Camille and I took our seats. Whatever it was sounded big and bad, and my hackles were starting to rise. "Start at the beginning."

"I put in a phone call to the clan Tyler claims to be from. According to them, Tyler *died* four months ago." Zach leaned forward, his eyes bloodshot. "His body was stolen shortly before the burial ceremony, and they never found it. It's true that he'd been planning on coming to join our clan, and it's true that they'd provided him with references, but they never bothered to look for the papers when he died."

"And nobody ever called you to let you know he was dead?" Maybe the OIA was bureaucratic, but right now I could see the positive side to red tape.

"We didn't know that he was coming in the first place. Usually, a reference letter is good enough to admit a person to the clan. We're rather informal about that. So when Tyler showed up with papers, we assumed that everything was in order. We didn't bother to call them to check, since he already had his references in hand."

"Doesn't that leave room for imposters?" Camille asked, shaking her head. "Why didn't you guys think of the possibility of fraud before now?"

"Apparently it's never been a problem. Until now." Zach frowned. "I think our admittance policy's going to change."

"Holy crap," Iris said. "Does this mean Tyler's a zombie?"

"Walk-in. It's got to be," I countered. "But Kyoka didn't just bump his soul aside, he killed Tyler for his body. Did they say how he died?"

"No autopsy—Weres don't approve of autopsies. It's against our religious beliefs. I guess he'd been sick with bronchitis, and when they found him dead, they assumed he'd stopped breathing in his sleep."

"Ten to one, Kyoka forcibly drove his soul out," I said. "I'll bet you anything he cast Tyler's essence into oblivion, leaving his body an empty shell. The heart would stop beating, but the body would look like he'd just gone to sleep. With Tyler sick, and the Weres' reluctant to autopsy, it must have been the perfect setup."

"Actually," Camille interjected, "Tyler *could* technically be considered a zombie, but with Kyoka's soul inside the body, Menolly wouldn't be able to pin him as one the undead."

"Undead don't have souls?" Zach asked.

"Some do," I said. "Vampires, for example. When destroyed, they're free to move on like most of the dead. Zombies don't, though, or ghouls. They're not transformed so much as used as puppets. Tyler's soul went to join his ancestors. He's no longer connected to his body.

"That makes sense," I said, darting a look at Zachary, who was squirming in his seat. "Zach, don't tell me that Tyler knows you're onto him?"

He hung his head. "Yeah. He walked in on me when I was on the phone and darted out before I could stop him. By the time I finished my conversation, Tyler had disappeared. I couldn't find him anywhere, so I called an emergency meeting of the Council, but Venus didn't show up. When we went to look for him, his house had been trashed. There'd been a god-awful struggle. We searched the compound and grounds all night but haven't been able to find any sign of either Venus or Tyler."

"Great Mother, you think they have Venus the Moon Child?" This was just getting worse and worse.

He nodded. "There was no sign of a body, and Tyler knows just how powerful Venus is."

"And if anybody in your tribe knows about the spirit seals, it would be Venus," I said, shivering as a goose walked over my grave.

The Hunters Moon Clan and the demons would do everything they could to make him talk. The spiderlings were bad enough on their own, but when aligned with Shadow Wing's minions, the variety and methods of torture available to them were mind-boggling. Unless we could rescue him—and rescue him soon—Venus was a goner, in a very painful way.

"Yeah, I thought of that." Zach leaned back in his chair and took a deep breath as Iris brought him a cup of tea. "Thanks, Iris," he said. "I told the Council everything—not about Shadow Wing trying to take over the Earth, but everything I could to make them believe me that the Hunters Moon Clan is in league with the Demonkin. They said to come to you."

"What's the Puma Pride doing now?"

"The elders are evacuating all the women and children. And we've petitioned the Olympic Wolf Pack for help. They're sending over twenty young pack members tomorrow to help us patrol the borders of our compound." Zach's shoulders sagged. "We don't know what else to do. The Council will be forever in your debt if you can help us out."

We'd need Menolly. And Chase. And everybody we could think of. It was one thing to go up against Bad Ass Luke alone, but with an entire nest of werespiders in addition to Kyoka and the demons, we wouldn't stand a chance without more help.

Camille must have been thinking the same thing, because she said, "Who can we call in? There's Morio. Damn it, I wish Trillian was here—he's good in a fight. Smoky, of course. Anybody else you can think of?"

"Don't forget Chase," I said. "Do you think Grandmother Coyote would help us?"

She shook her head. "I doubt it. She tends to stay out of things unless it suits her fancy. I'm sure she knows what's going on. Maybe Menolly will know somebody from the Wayfarer we can trust."

Zachary cleared his throat. "I can pledge the help of one of our best pride members. She's our most fearless guard." His left eye twitched. "Her name's Rhonda."

"Rhonda?" I asked. "She's a werepuma, too?"

He nodded. "My ex-fiancée, actually. We were engaged until last year."

That stopped me cold. I had been so busy focusing on the current situation that I hadn't even bothered to wonder if he had a girlfriend. Not for more than a few minutes, at least. I felt myself start down that treacherous path of wondering what she looked like but stopped before I got past the garden gate. We were mired in a rapidly escalating crisis, and right now I needed to keep focused on the problem at hand.

"Good," Camille said smoothly. "We can use her." She gave me a look that told me she'd picked up on what I was thinking. "I guess that's it," she said dismally, counting on her fingers.

"What next?" I stretched, feeling antsy. When I was nervous, I needed to move my body. "We can't leave until Menolly wakes up and the rest of the men are here. And what about the shop?"

"Iris, do you mind taking it today?" Camille pushed away from the table.

"Not a problem. Let me go change and get Maggie ready to go." Iris bustled out of the room.

"What are you planning to do until dusk?" I asked.

She let out a long sigh. "I might as well drive out to Smoky's and ask him to help us."

"Just don't get distracted," I said, grinning at her. She paled, and I realized that maybe, just maybe, she wasn't so cavalier about her upcoming duties as dragon-lover after all. "Zach, do you mind waiting in the living room? I'd like to talk to Camille alone for a moment."

"Do you mind if I catch a few winks on your sofa?" he asked. "I'm exhausted."

I shook my head. "Go right ahead," I said as he carried his tea out of the room. "There's an afghan hanging over the back of the recliner that you can use."

When he'd trudged out of the room, I turned back to Camille. "Are you sure you want to go through with this? With Smoky, I mean?"

She snorted. "You think I could get out of it, even if I wanted to? He's gorgeous, and there are sparks when we meet, but . . ."

"But he's a dragon," I said softly.

"That's about the size of it," she said. "I just hope that's not the size of something else. I mean, all I can think about is: How big is he going to be, and will it hurt?" She stared out the window into the backyard. "You think we should put up bird feeders? I think the birds are hungry."

I joined her, and we watched the rapidly growing blanket of white that was shrouding the yard. "Uh, bird feeders might encourage me in the wrong direction, Camille. Think about it."

With a sudden smile that lit up the room, she let out a low laugh. "Ah, Kitten, that's what I love about you; you're always able to make me smile. Don't worry about me. I'll be fine. I'm sure Smoky will be careful. Meanwhile, how are you doing?"

"I don't know. I still don't know how I feel about Zach, other than he pushes my buttons. But I'm not sure . . ."

"What about Chase?"

"We talked. We fought. We agreed that we weren't going to be exclusive for now. But I don't know what he'll do if I end up sleeping with Zach." I played with the fronds of the spider plant sitting on the windowsill. "Never mind all that. We have to focus on this mess with the demons and Kyoka before things get any worse. How long is Trillian supposed to be gone? I'd really like to have him with us when we head out to Snoqualmie."

Camille was about to answer when a sudden flicker caught my eye. I glanced up and saw a brown spider above us on the top of the window, almost hidden behind one of the sweetgrass braids Camille had hung to the side of the sink. I nudged her elbow and gestured toward the arachnid.

Was it a hobo spider? A spy? Or was it just a brown house spider? Just then, Iris came back in the room.

"Maggie's in my room. You should see her playing with—" she started, but stopped when I held my finger to my lips. I pointed at the spider.

She pulled up her stool and climbed up so that her head was actually a few inches higher than mine. As she leaned forward, the spider suddenly scuttled toward the left-hand cupboard, and startled, Iris lost her balance and went tumbling backward off the stool. I leapt to catch her, but too late. With a loud thud, she hit the floor.

"Iris, Iris, are you okay?" Camille knelt by her side while I kept track of the spider.

Iris pushed her way to a sitting position and held out her hand, yelling, *"Piilevä otus, tulee esiin!"* There was a blinding flash and then a blur, as the force of her spell knocked the spider off the wall and onto the floor. Within seconds, the air around it was shimmering.

I recognized that shimmer! The spider was shifting form.

"Great Mother, the thing's a Were!" I'd thought it might be just another one of their sentinels, like the ones in Camille's car trunk. I hadn't expected it to be one of the actual Hunters Moon Clan members. Whirling, I grabbed the nearest weapon I could find, which happened to be one of the kitchen cleavers.

Camille thrust her arms in the air, and I could sense the flow of energy as she called down the Moon Mother's power. I leapt forward just as the spider disappeared, leaving a man in its wake. He scrambled to his feet, too quickly for my taste. He must have heightened reactions for him to move that quick after shifting—especially a forced shift.

He was tall and thin, even a little bony. Dressed in jeans, a black tunic, and a pair of leather tie-up moccasin boots that were popular among the recreationists' groups, he crouched in a fighting stance as I moved in, wishing I had my regular long knife with me. The cleaver was awkward and definitely not balanced for combat.

"Give it up," I said. "You're only going to get hurt. Surrender now, and we'll let you live." It was a lie, of course. I knew perfectly well that we didn't dare let him go. Camille had finally gotten it through my head that we were in an all-out war, and he was on the enemy's side.

"Right," he said, his voice low and gravelly. "I don't think so, blondie." With a movement so quick I could barely follow it, he yanked something out of his boot. Iris was on her feet by now, and she closed in behind me. I heard her muttering some sort of charm but kept my eyes on our opponent.

Just then Camille yelled, "Attack and subdue!" and a blaze of energy shot past my shoulder to strike the man in the legs. Holy shit, she was throwing lightning bolts in the house!

"What the fuck are you doing? You'll blow the place up!" I yelled, but then stopped as I noticed, more to my dismay than relief, that the bolt of energy hadn't done a thing to him. He shook it off like leaves in the wind.

"What the—" Camille said, confused.

The man let out a short bark of laughter and raised his hand to his mouth. Within a fraction of a second I saw rather than heard something go winging past me aimed squarely at Camille. In that same moment, Iris broke her concentration to throw herself against Camille's legs, knocking her to the floor. A solid thud echoed as a dart lodged itself into the wall instead of my sister. A miniature blowgun! Shit.

"Nobody messes with the D'Artigo girls and gets away with it!" I shouted and lunged, sidestepping so I wasn't in his direct line of fire. He turned to meet me, silent in his suede boots, and I could see a gleam of delight in his eyes.

"Come on, blondie, come and get me," he whispered, motioning me in as he lifted the blowgun again.

With no time to think, I body-slammed him. He managed to anticipate my move and was ready, dropping the blowgun and grappling me as I landed square on him. Then he rolled, taking me with him, so that he was on top of me, holding my wrists. The dude was freakishly strong for being as bony as he was.

"Well, this is fun," he said, grinning at me, and I could see that he had fangs that overlapped his front two teeth. They weren't as large as either mine or Menolly's, but they looked capable of inducing way too much pain and damage. He yanked one of my wrists up to his mouth. Damn! The creepy bastard was going to bite me and, from where I was lying, I could see a few drops of liquid glistening on the end of both fangs. *Poison.* Of course; he was a hobo werespider, and even in his human shape, his bite was venomous.

"I don't think so!" I yelled, yanking my knees up to my chest. He wasn't expecting it, and I caught him right in the balls. As he screamed, I threw him off, and we flipped again. This time I landed on top. I sank my knee into his groin as hard as I could, and that put an end to the fight right there. As he writhed, shrieking, Iris calmly hit him over the head with a stainless steel frying pan. Hard. Very hard. I looked at her, taken aback. I knew she could fight but never realized how resilient she was.

"That had to hurt," I said, clearing my throat. "You swing a mean skillet."

Iris beamed. "Hey, you learn to use what's handy. I had more than one skirmish in my day. Back in Finland, I protected the young ones of the family. Every now and then you'd get a bogey creeping in, or a kobold, or some other critter determined to raise havoc." She let out a wistful sigh. "Sometimes I miss those days," she said. "They were good, if a little hard, and I'd give anything to have seen the family live on, but they're all gone now."

While she ruminated on her past, Camille found some rope, and we tied him—hands and feet—to a chair. Remembering our fight with Wisteria a few months back, we also made sure we gagged him.

She picked through his pockets and found a wallet. "Not much here. Ten dollars . . . hold on, here's his identification. Horace von Spynne. *Von Spynne* . . . isn't that the name of the guy Zach got in a fight with a couple years ago?"

"Last name, yes," I said. "Geph von Spynne. They're probably related. They look a lot alike. What should we do with him?"

"For the moment, let's put him in the closet." We carried him to the closet, chair and all, and stuffed him in, locking it firmly. That little storeroom was quickly becoming a makeshift prison. Wisteria had spent some time in there, too.

Camille frowned, staring out into the yard. "I wonder why my blast of energy didn't affect him. It bounced off of him like he had a shield. And how the hell did he slip past my wards without alarming me? I'll be right back. I want to make certain they're still in place."

Iris picked up the skillet with a grunt. It was heavy stainless steel. There was no way in hell we could keep cast iron in the house, so we minimized its presence everywhere we could. The skillet was big enough for Iris to sit in. She had to have some muscles under that demure exterior.

I grinned at her. "I'm so glad you came to live with us. You sure you want to stick around here, though? It gets pretty dicey sometimes."

"Where else would I go?" she said. "With the OIA out of commission and my family in Finland long dead, I'm a free agent. And I like you girls—you're fun, and you make me feel needed."

Her words reminded me of how much house sprites depended on feeling like integral members of the household. Even in this day and age, if you treated them kindly and as one of the family, they would be loyal until the day you died.

"Trust me," I said. "We need you, all right. And Maggie needs you."

"That's good enough for me." Iris giggled. "What do we do with Mr. Eight Legs?" Her gaze darkened. "Delilah, you know we can't let him go. He'd run right back to the Hunters Moon Clan and tell them everything. We can't take a chance on letting them discover what our strengths and weaknesses are. I don't think we have much choice in the long run. He has to be eliminated."

Yep, she was delightful but deadly.

"I know. I don't like the thought of killing him, but I agree with everything you say. Say, why do you think Camille's energy blast didn't work on him? She's gotten pretty good with it, and that particular spell almost never backfires on her anymore. What happened?"

With a frown, Iris peeked in the closet. "Still out cold," she said as she reached out to touch his arm. After a moment, she closed the door again. "He has some sort of natural protection against moon magic, I think."

I held up his weapon and the dart that he had sunk into the wall. "The fact that he had a blowgun and hadn't used it before we saw him pretty much tells us that he must have just sneaked in. Otherwise, we'd all be dead if that poison is as dangerous as I think it is." As I finished talking, the kitchen door opened, and Camille entered, followed by Morio. "What did you find out? Were the wards still armed?"

She shook her head. "No, they weren't. And for some reason, I didn't notice them.

"I can tell you why," Morio said. "I dug around a little in town, talked to a few people, put the pressure on where I needed to. Apparently the Hunters Moon Clan is resistant to moon magic, thanks to their infamous creator. Kyoka worked with the moon when he originally created the werespiders, and it gave them some sort of natural immunity that must have been passed down throughout the years. It also gives them the ability to navigate your wards, since you call on the Moon Mother to set them."

"Fuck," Camille said. "That bites. What the hell am I supposed to do, then? I'm not exactly Wonder Woman in a battle. I guess I'd better haul out my short sword and get in some practice."

"Did anybody else notice that Zach slept through all the commotion?" I asked, suddenly remembering that he was in the living room.

Iris paled. "Nobody should have slept through that racket."

"My thoughts precisely." I raced into the living room, the others close on my heels. Zach was lying half-on, half-off the sofa, looking a little green. I hurried to his side and quickly scanned his neck and arms. Sure enough, there they were, hard to see but not impossible. Two puncture marks on his neck. Tiny, precise, and all too real.

"He's been bitten! Do you think more than one of the Hunters Moon Clan showed up? Maggie!" I turned back to the kitchen, but Camille was ahead of me, Iris right behind her. I listened as Iris's door slammed open. Straining to hear what was going on, I searched for Zach's pulse.

"She's okay," Camille said, returning to the living room with Maggie resting on her hip. "She looks fine. And Menolly can't be killed. Not by poison, anyway."

"No, but they could stake her."

"Oh shit. I'll tell Iris to go keep an eye on her. How's Zach doing?"

His pulse was weak and racing, and I suspected shock. "I need a blanket. Toss me my cell phone, would you? I'd better get Chase and the medics out here right now. They're the only ones who can deal with an Earthside Supe." It flashed through

my mind that we had to make contact with more doctors who
could treat Supes.

While Camille went in search of Iris, I made the call to
Chase and struggled to keep calm. Morio stood behind me, a
cool hand on my shoulder. "What are we supposed to do now?"
I asked. "Fumigate this place?"

He nodded. "Yeah, and it's going to require a pretty damned
big can of Raid."

As I clutched Zach's hand, I prayed Chase would be in time.
And just what could we expect next from the Hunters Moon
Clan? With the demons on their side, who knew what they'd
come up with to make our lives hell? Or to send us there.

CHAPTER 16

"I wish we could stay and help with Zach, but we'd better go convince Smoky to help us," Camille said. "Iris is downstairs with Menolly and Maggie. She's working on a protection spell against the spider poison."

"Just get back here as soon as possible. And try to think of something to do with the closet dude." I desperately wanted her to stay, but there was too much to do and too little time. The Hunters Moon Clan had just upped the ante when they decided to play their warped version of *Home Invasion*.

Camille and Morio were just heading out when Chase and his crew spilled through the door. He'd brought two of the OIA medics with him. One was Sharah, who was one of Queen Asteria's nieces. She introduced her partner. Mallen was pale and thin and barely looked old enough to shave, let alone be a healer, but with elves—even more so than the Fae—looks could be terribly deceiving. He was probably far older than any of us.

"Watch out for spiders," I warned them as they knelt beside the sofa where Zach still lay, unconscious and barely breathing.

"Elves are immune to their venom," Sharah said, giving me a faint smile. "You say he's a werepuma?"

I nodded. "With the Rainier Puma Pride. He was bitten by a hobo spiderling. We have one of their spies in the kitchen, trussed up in the closet."

As I stepped back to get out of their way, Chase wrapped his arm around my waist. "I've got some news about Goldenrod Road and Snoqualmie."

"Wait a moment," I murmured, wanting to hear how Zach was faring. Sharah and Mallen were taking his blood pressure, pulse, and checking out his heart. After a moment, Sharah said something to Mallen that I couldn't catch, and he handed her a bag out of their medic kit. She prepared a syringe and injected whatever was in it into Zach's arm. Another moment, and she gave him a second shot, and when yet another minute passed with no response, she glanced at Mallen, shook her head, and tried yet a third injection.

I was beginning to think that Zach would be the Hunters Moon Clan's latest victim when his arm twitched. He was coming around! But before anybody could say anything, his body stiffened, and he began to convulse. His eyes rolled back in his head as he began to shake, and foam flecked with bits of blood burbled up from his lips, dribbling down the side of his face. He thrashed wildly, and I leapt forward, prepared to help hold him down.

"Get out of my way," Sharah yelled at me, stopping me in my tracks. She turned to Mallen. "Glassophan—give it to him now!"

Mallen ripped open Zach's shirt while Sharah tore the top off of a sealed packet and pulled out a second syringe, loaded full to the top, armed with a terribly large needle. She handed it to Mallen who, swiftly, without the time to be gentle, stabbed it into Zachary's chest. I cringed as Zach gurgled. Mallen bore down on the syringe, pumping the serum into his system, then the horrible shaking began to slow and, abruptly, Zach stiffened and collapsed.

"Oh Great Mother, is he dead?" I stared at him, horrified.

Sharah pressed her stethoscope to Zach's chest, where a pool of blood slicked his flesh. She paused, then shook her head, a look of relief spreading across her face. "He's alive and should come around in a few minutes. I doubt if any spider venom can stand up to Glassophan."

"What is it?" I asked, kneeling beside her to look at Zach's terribly pale face. The foam on his mouth held a faint trace of pink. "Is he bleeding internally?"

She nodded. "The spider venom was extremely potent. If we'd been any later, it would have destroyed something vital and killed him. The Glassophan is something our technomagi have managed to come up with that actually neutralizes neurotoxins."

"Technomagi?" I gave her a questioning look.

She sat back, wiping a bead of sweat off of her forehead. "Queen Asteria appointed several of our mages to learn the ways of Earth's technicians. They've managed to blend our magic with technology, in order to help the few elves that choose to cross through the portals. We call them the technomagi."

They must have created the crystal we used to find the bug in Camille's car. It was a handy tidbit of information to tuck away for future use. I motioned to Zach. "What do you need for him? Blankets, water? Name it, and it's yours."

She felt his forehead as he murmured softly. "Make sure he's warm and stays hydrated. Wake him up every hour to make him drink a glass of water. He needs sleep more than anything. Sleep and rest. He's in no condition to go anywhere," she added, a warning note in her voice. "Keep him from any strenuous activity for the next few days while his internal organs heal from the damage the venom inflicted on them. We'll come back out here tomorrow for a full exam, to see how he's faring."

I groaned. We needed his help with our raid on the spider nest, but one look at Sharah's expression told me that wasn't going to happen.

"Not a problem," I said. Then, because I couldn't help myself, I asked, "Are you staying Earthside to help us?"

She put away her stethoscope and helped Mallen repack their kit. "We talked things over with Chase and decided that yes, we'll stay as part of your new organization. We don't take our orders from Lethesanar. With the situation at hand, if Queen Asteria approves, we'll stay. We sent in our request to her this morning."

"Now that Zach's out of danger, what are you going to do with the spy?" Chase asked me. "Let me see him."

I led him into the kitchen and opened the closet. The man was still unconscious. Iris had dealt him quite the blow with her skillet.

Chase looked him over. "Looks a lot like Geph von Spynne, doesn't it? Maybe a relative."

"Yeah, I wondered about that. What the hell are we going to do with him? We need to question him, but after that . . ."

Without looking at me, Chase said, "Why not hand him over to Menolly? I don't think she'd mind being in charge of his destiny."

That jolted me, for sure. I never thought about Menolly's kills without thinking that at some level she must regret them, pervs though they were. But that was *my* projection. I had no idea how she really felt.

"Did I upset you?" Chase asked. "You look like I just slapped you."

"No, no . . ." I said. "I just . . . I suppose that would work. When Camille gets home, we'll ask her what she thinks." But in my gut, I knew she'd agree, just like I knew Menolly wouldn't have a problem with it.

I wasn't sure how either response would make me feel. Biting my lip, I reminded myself that we had no room for sympathy when it came to Shadow Wing and his minions, be they demonic, Supe, or human. I straightened my shoulders and closed the door on Horace. "We'll question him as soon as Camille gets back. By then, maybe he'll be awake."

There was a knock at the front door, and I opened it to find Trenyth standing there. He was followed by an elf who looked to be about sixty, which meant he was probably several thousand years old. Though he looked as unassuming as a computer geek, the moment I glanced into his eyes, I wanted to crawl under a rock and hide. Power. Sheer power. And brilliance.

Trenyth opened the scroll he was carrying. "Trillian delivered your message about the possibility of retuning your Whispering Mirror to contact the Elfin Court. Her Majesty thinks the idea is worth pursuing. Therefore, to that end, she has sent one of our technomagi, Ronyl, to adjust your mirror." He held out the paper. "You need to sign this so I can return it to Her Majesty."

I accepted the scroll and looked around for a pen. The first one I found was a sparkling pink gel pen, and I grinned, wondering how fitting it was to answer the Elfin Queen with pink glitter. I scribbled my name on the bottom and handed the scroll back to Trenyth.

"Should I show you the mirror now?" I asked.

Ronyl gave me a brief nod, and I glanced at Chase. "Keep an eye on Zach, and keep a watch out for those damned spiders. We don't want any more poisonings."

"Poisonings?" The technomage's voice wasn't nearly as deep as I expected it to be but, rather, a pleasant tenor. "You've been having spider problems?"

"Spiderlings. Unnatural Weres and their pets, and they happen to be hobo spiders, which are poisonous. It probably wouldn't hurt my sisters and me too much, but then again we are half-human, so we can't be sure. One thing is for sure, we have no intentions of playing guinea pig to find out." I nodded at Zach. "Unfortunately, our enemies have a form of souped-up spiders' venom. And since they can transform into regular-sized spiders, it's difficult to spot them until it's too late. They also have a resistance to moon magic. My friend—he's an Earthside werepuma—was just bitten by one. We almost lost him."

Ronyl considered the matter for a moment. "I can help you out with your pest control problem. Before I go, I'll cast a repelling spell on your house, and that should drive out any spiders taking residence, magically enhanced or not. It will last for a good three or four months. Would you like me to do that?"

I almost did a happy dance. "May the Lady Bast bless you," I said. "Do you need anything for it?"

He smiled faintly. "Trust me, girl, I need very little to cast minor spells except the power within my own heart. Now, if you'll take me to the mirror, I'll get to work."

I led him up to Camille's suite and removed the cloth from the Whispering Mirror. He cautiously examined it, running his fingers over the frame and then on the glass itself. "Nice workmanship. Whoever made this knew what he was doing. I can fix it so you can directly talk to Trenyth's office. It won't be activated by a specific voice but by a command word. Will that be acceptable?"

"Go for it." A command word wouldn't ensure as much secrecy, but it would make it easier if Iris, Morio, or Trillian ever needed to use it.

"I require solitude. Please leave." And just like that, he turned as if I were invisible. I could feel the threads of magic starting to build around the mirror and decided it was best to comply. All wizards had their secrets, and I had no desire to see something I wasn't supposed to see. Sometimes a little knowledge was a dangerous thing.

As I rejoined Chase and the others, I noticed that Trenyth was examining Zachary. I knelt beside him.

"He was gravely injured. Only by the grace of our healers did your friend pull through," he said, a grim look on his face. "These creatures you face—they are in league with Shadow Wing?"

I nodded. "We were going to make a report to Queen Asteria but didn't have a way to reach her except for Trillian, and we weren't sure if she'd listen to him because . . ." I drifted off, hesitating to mention the elves' prejudice against the Svartans. Calling them bigots didn't seem very polite, considering all they were doing for us.

Trenyth glanced over at me. "These are dangerous times. Old alliances, as well as old antipathies, must sometimes be set aside for the greater good. Trillian is welcome at our court, provided he behaves himself. You may make your report to me while we wait for Ronyl to finish his work." He pulled out a notebook and smiled at my surprised look. "We learn from others. While we find our own method of making items such as these without terrorizing the environment, we're more than willing to borrow concepts from the humans. Notebooks and pens are very handy devices."

I filled him in on what had happened since we last saw him, leaving out nothing. After I finished, he sat unspeaking, staring at his notes with what almost seemed an awed hush.

"I can't believe you actually invoked the Autumn Lord. You're either a fool or one of the bravest women I've met." He looked up at my forehead. "And now you bear his mark. There is more. Something about you has changed since we last met, Delilah D'Artigo. I can feel it in my bones. You are unrealized, a sleeping lion who has yet to wake and realize how powerful she really is."

I stared at him, wondering what he was talking about. "Are you a seer?"

"No, but I can read energy, which is why Her Majesty employs me as her messenger. I can see beyond the words and give her an accurate picture of what's really going on." He reached for my hand. "May I?"

I held out my hand, and he lightly clasped it in his, then closed his eyes. His touch was like a feather tickling my skin. I wondered if he had a wife, a family, a home. Usually those with positions so vital to the Court and Crown gave up every hope of a personal life and were pledged to the death to protect and serve. What would make someone choose a path like that? I couldn't imagine forsaking my family, but sometimes—as we had found out the hard way—destiny was a cruel mistress.

As Trenyth probed my energy, I linked to him, and a sudden flare revealed his hidden heart to me. He was in love with the Queen. He loved her beyond desire, beyond any hope of being with her. He worshipped her as a goddess, and she was his moon and star.

Overwhelmed by the rush of emotion, I tried to retreat quietly so he wouldn't realize that I'd managed to stumble onto his private thoughts, but his eyes flew open. He paused, then merely said, "You have all the makings of an expert empath. Did you know that you contain two faces, both linked to your soul and both part of you, that are neither human nor Fae? You're a twin, correct?"

"What? What do you mean?" I had no idea what he was talking about.

He sat back, letting go of my hand. "Delilah, twins among Weres seldom occur. And even rarer do the Fae have twins who both develop Were tendencies, but it happens on occasion. Especially with a mixed parentage. You had a twin sister who died, didn't you? And she was a Were like you, correct?"

Huh? I blinked, thoroughly confused. Surely Mother would have told me if I'd had a twin sister. "As far as I know, no. What makes you think that?"

He looked surprised. "Because you have twin shadows within you—one hiding in the darkness, the other out in the light. Were shadows. I assumed your twin sister died. Often, when that happens, the surviving twin inherits the other form. Effectively, the survivor becomes a two-faced Were, able to shift into two different forms."

I jumped up, my stomach flipping as I retreated to the kitchen and poured myself a glass of water. As I stood at the tap, staring bleakly out the window, Chase joined me, resting his hand on the small of my back.

"Is something wrong?" he asked.

"I don't know. What Trenyth said . . . Chase, in my dream I was in Were-form, but I wasn't a tabby cat, and every time I try to remember what I was, I blank out. Could he be right? Could a new form inside of me be trying to work its way free? And what about the convulsion I went into? What the hell was that all about? I've never had anything like that happen before."

"When did all of this start?" he asked.

I thought back. "Since the Autumn Lord marked me. Something's changed, and I can't put my finger on what." I turned to look at him. "I'm scared," I confessed, not wanting to admit it but no longer able to shove the fear aside.

He kissed my forehead gently, then lingered on my lips, teasing them gently with his tongue. After a moment, he pulled me to his chest and held me close. "It's okay. It will all be okay. Do you think your parents would have hid it from you if you had a twin? Sometimes human parents keep news like that quiet for one reason or another."

I tried to put myself in my mother's place but failed miserably. I might be a lot like her, but in this matter, I had to be honest and admit that I had no idea what she would have done.

"My mother was human; maybe she didn't want me to know—didn't want me to feel survivor's guilt. But surely Father would have told me. Or Camille. That is, if she knew about it." I broke away from him and sat at the table, resting my head in my hands. "I don't know what to do. If I do have a second Were nature, when will it manifest itself? And will I be able to control it?"

Chase sighed and joined me, pushing a plate of cookies toward me. "Eat something. As for your parents, well, I have no idea. You should ask your father next time you talk to him. And if you do have a second Were-form . . . I suppose you'll just have to wait and see what happens."

He was right, and I knew it. There was no sense in worrying it like a bone, though that was easier said than done. At that moment, the front door slammed, and Camille bustled in, Morio and Smoky behind her. I stared at them.

"That was fast," I said, glancing at the clock.

"We were almost to the Renton turnoff to SR 167 when who should we see meandering along the road but Smoky himself."

He just smiled with a self-satisfied smirk. "As long as our contract is in effect, I know when you're thinking about me," he said mildly. Camille blushed and stammered, but he held up one hand. "I thought I'd save you part of the trip and meet you partway."

"Are you telling us you can trace Camille's whereabouts as long as she still owes you that week of debauchery you're so happily planning?" I asked. While it smacked slightly obscene, it could also be a very useful tool if anything ever happened to her.

He shook his head. "Not quite. She has to be thinking about me in order for me to pick up on it. Today, she was thinking about coming to get me, and I was able to tune in on her location and save you all some time." He winked at her. "I can't exactly read your mind, but I wish I could."

She shook her head. "You're incorrigible."

"I'm a dragon. For you to expect anything less would be foolhardy." His words seemed to fill the room with the slightest edge of a warning—a hint that he didn't mind playing, but the rules were his to change as he would.

"I suppose so," Camille said softly. "I guess I'll find out, won't I?"

"All in good time," Smoky said, relaxing. "All in good time."

I quickly filled them in on Ronyl and the mirror and Zach's condition. "With Zach out of commission, we're one man down. Meanwhile, before we question our spy, I need to ask Camille something in private."

Chase stood up and motioned to Morio and Smoky. "Come on, boys, let's go check on Zach and the medics." They took the hint and scrammed.

Camille gave me an odd look. "What's going on? Chase cleared them out of here in a hurry."

"I have something important to ask you, and I want a straight answer."

She blinked. "Of course. What is it?"

"Did I have a twin sister or brother? One who died when we were born?" I held my breath, both hoping for—and yet hoping against—a yes. *Yes* would mean my parents lied to me. *Yes* would mean Camille had held a secret from me all of these years. *Yes* would mean that I'd lost a part of myself, in a sense, at birth. And yet *yes* would mean that I carried part of my twin with me, that part of her still lived.

"Did you have *what*? Where did you get that idea?"

"Just answer yes or no." I wanted the truth straight, with no pussyfooting around.

"How about *I don't know*? I don't think so, but I can't say for sure. Nobody ever told me anything about you having a twin, anyway." She wasn't lying, that much I could tell. "Now, how about telling me what this is all about?"

I told her what Trenyth had said, and her expression turned from puzzled to worried. "So I guess my questions are, what is this second nature I've got bottled up inside of me, and did I have a twin?"

The silence in the room muffled my thoughts as I waited for her to say something. As the seconds ticked by on the clock, I thought about my childhood, straining to remember if I'd ever felt like someone was missing. Granted, I'd always felt out of place, but we all had. I'd dreamed of the day when I'd fit in somewhere. But being a misfit and missing a sibling were two entirely different situations. As hard as I tried, I couldn't place my finger on any inborn evidence locked deep within my cells that I'd been born a twin.

Finally, Camille shook her head. "Delilah, I don't know. I can't remember all that clearly before you were born. Oh, vague images of our parents and of home . . . of a few holidays . . . but when Mother went into labor with you, they sent me to stay with Aunt Rythwar. Mother had a hard time with all of her pregnancies due to the mixing of her blood and ours through the placenta."

"I just hope that whatever this second form is, it doesn't jump out and surprise me at the wrong time." I pushed myself out of my chair. "I suppose I'll have to ask Father next time we talk to him."

Camille wrapped her arm around my waist and leaned her head on my shoulder. "And I just hope we're *able* to talk to him again," she said, breaking the silence that bound both of our fears.

I glanced at the clock. "Another ninety minutes, and Menolly will be up. We'd better prepare a list of questions to ask the spy. I have a feeling tonight we're going to be battling more than a handful of spiders, and we might be able to gather some useful information from him."

Sobered by the thought, we joined the others in the living room. The night ahead promised only bloodshed and killing and all the things that made me want to slam the door and lock out the world.

Zach was awake when we entered the living room, and Sharah and Mallen were about to head out. "Keep him quiet, feed him lots of soup and juice and liquids, and don't let him get bitten again. Next time, it could be fatal."

I waved them out, glancing at the sky. Camille peeked over my shoulder.

"We're in for more snow," she said.

"Are you sure?" I looked at the snow piled on the ground. "We already have four inches."

"Seattle may be famous for its rain, but trust me, I can smell it in the air, and I can feel it in my bones. We're due for a storm that will leave the city stranded for a few days. It's coming in, and it's coming fast. I'm glad that Iris didn't go in to the bookstore after all."

"If you're right, we'd better get ready to roll the minute Menolly wakes up," I said. As I turned around, the techno-mage came quietly down the steps and joined us in the living room.

"Your Whispering Mirror now connects to Trenyth's office," he said, nodding at the Queen's messenger. "No one should be able to tell the difference unless they examine it directly, at which point they'd discover elfin magic and know something's amiss. If your city tries to contact you, they'll probably just think the mirror's out of order." He glanced at Zach. "Ah yes, the spider problem. I'll work from outside. It won't take but a moment."

When Camille moved to follow him, he shook his head. "Thank you, but I work alone," he said in a voice that edged on snotty.

"Fine," she said. I could tell she was biting back a snide remark. Not good to make allies mad, even if they did snub you. Thankfully, the phone rang at that point, and she went to get it.

As Ronyl took off outside, I turned to Zach, who had pulled out his cell phone and was quietly speaking to someone. When he hung up, I sat down near him and took his hand. "How are you feeling?"

"Like I was just about to become spider soup. While you were in the kitchen, Trenyth, Sharah, and Mallen checked the room. They found the spider who bit me and squashed it flat."

"We have a spy tied up in the kitchen closet," I said. "The spider probably came in with him. Who were you calling?"

"The compound, to let them know I'm safe." He gave me an almost apologetic look. "And they told me Rhonda's on her way here."

I stared at him, my heart starting to pound. What would she be like? Would she be beautiful? Stronger than me? Had he told her about me? And why the hell did I even care? As I sat there, a smile plastered on my face, Chase knelt down beside me, and I could feel him sizing up Zach, gauging my reaction. I had no idea what in the world I was going to do about either of them.

CHAPTER 17

"Okay, let's drag Horace out of the closet," Camille said as we trooped back into the kitchen.

"Before I do that, any bright ideas on how to make him talk? There's no reason he should." I glanced at the closet, keeping my voice low.

Trenyth and Iris stayed in the living room to watch Zach and Maggie. Just then, Smoky and Chase joined us. Smoky leaned on the end of the table.

"Bring him out. I'll help you find out what you want to ask. Trust me," he said when I gave him a quizzical look.

I dragged Horace's chair out from the closet. He was awake, and the scent of fear filled the air. It was coming directly from him. I was pleased to see that my knots had held—I'd been practicing on Camille ever since we'd had the run-in with Wisteria.

Horace struggled, but mostly he just looked worn down from being tied up for so long and from the clunk on the head Iris had given him. Smoky leaned in and gave him a fierce smile.

"We have some questions for you. Before you refuse to answer, I want you to consider this: we won't kill you if you remain silent. I'll take you home and make you my toy. I can think of lots of games for us to play. And before you ask, you should know that I'm a dragon. Now, are you going to cooperate?"

It was a threat that would have worked on me, that's for sure. Horace took on a decidedly green tinge, and he shifted in his seat.

Smoky continued. "It's your choice. Talk now or later. Either way, I guarantee you *will* speak. Spill your guts here, and I promise, it will be far less painful."

One beat. Two. Three. Horace slowly nodded. Smoky

reached for the gag as the front door opened. Camille, who was closest, yelled out, "Who's there?" but at that moment, Trillian popped around the corner. Before he was free of the gag, Horace began to panic.

Smoky paused, cocking his head to one side. He looked puzzled. Then, with a quick glance over his shoulder at Trillian, he said, "Come here." His voice was so imperious that Trillian obeyed before he had a chance to think about it.

As Trillian entered the room, Horace began to shake and make urgent pleading noises from behind his gag.

Smoky took in the situation immediately. He held up his hand and looked at Trillian. "Hold on. We'll wait a bit before letting you take a crack at him."

Trillian was no slouch in the brains department. He shrugged and stepped back. "Fine, but if he doesn't cooperate, I'd be glad to help out." He tapped Camille on the shoulder and motioned to the living room. "We need to talk."

She frowned, looking at the spy. "All right. Delilah, write down everything he says." Following Trillian, she headed out of the kitchen.

Smoky slowly reached for the gag. As he lowered it, he said, "Any suspect move would be very bad for you right now. Do you understand?"

Horace nodded. "Yeah, I understand. Just don't turn me over to that creep from Hell," he said. "I'd rather be your boy toy any day. I know what *they* can do, and I don't want any part of their games."

Curious. What had happened to make him so afraid of Svartans? He was an Earthside Supe. It should be a long shot that he even knew about them.

"Your name is Horace von Spynne?" Smoky motioned to me, and I picked up a steno pad and pen.

"Yeah, yeah it is." He spat out the words.

Chase leaned back, arms crossed, as he eyed the spiderling closely. "Are you related to Geph von Spynne?"

Horace nodded. "He's my cousin."

I stepped up. "Were you here at our house before, with Kyoka?"

By the gasp he let out, it was apparent he wasn't expecting that question. "How do you know about him?"

"That's not your concern," I said, leaning down to stare him in the face. "We know a lot of things. We know all about Kyoka, and we know about the demons who are helping the Hunters Moon Clan. You realize you're pawns in Shadow Wing's game to take over this world? And that he won't leave you alive, no matter what he's promised?"

Horace blinked. "The Jansshi demon promised. And Kyoka won't let us down."

"He's already let you down," Smoky said. "He sent you on a suicide mission. You really think he doesn't know we're onto him? He's out for himself now, and the Hunters Moon Clan is just a tool to get what he wants."

I began to understand Smoky's strategy. Make Horace think Kyoka had sold out to the demons, and he might tell us everything we wanted to know.

"He's right," I said. "Kyoka knows that we're after him, and yet he sent you into danger, without a hope or prayer of surviving. What did he promise you in return for completing this mission? Money? Long life? Power?"

When Horace flinched, I knew I had hit a sore spot. "What happened? Were you in line for leadership of the clan before he returned? Did Kyoka yank away that dream?" When he didn't answer, I motioned to Smoky. "Might as well call in the Svartan and let him take our friend here away. Horace, I hope you're ready to face your worst night-mare—"

"No! I'll tell you," he shouted as Smoky headed for the door. "I'll tell you everything. I know what Svartans can do. Lianel is bad enough. Don't sic another one on me."

Lianel? Who the hell was Lianel? "All right, but you'd bet-ter spill everything you know, and you'd better do it quick." I forced as much menace into my words as possible, and Hor-ace let out a shudder.

"What do you want to know?" he whispered.

"Why don't you start from the beginning?" I picked up my pen, and he opened his mouth.

* * *

Ten minutes later, he'd emptied his conscience. Horace was sweating buckets by the time he was done. He should be. If we didn't kill him, Kyoka surely would. I told Smoky and Chase that I'd be back and went into the living room where Trillian and Camille were talking to Zach.

"Trillian, we got some news out of the spy that you might want to take back home as soon as possible. There's a renegade Svartan who's helping Shadow Wing. He may be connected to the war, though I'm not sure. His name is Lianel—"

"Lianel?" Trillian jumped up, interrupting me. "Did you say Lianel?"

"Yeah, I'm pretty sure I did," I said, hopping out of the way as he barreled forward. "Why? Who is he?"

"He's wanted for murder and rape back in Svartalfheim. He kidnapped one of the King's nieces, raped her, and then slowly cut her to bits, one piece at a time. She was still alive during his . . . surgery. He killed her bodyguards, too. The girl was . . . young," he said, looking vaguely ill. "Very young. Lianel worships Jakaris."

That was enough to make me squirm. The Svartan god of vice and cruelty—we were keeping delightful company, it seemed. "Well, he's running with Kyoka and the Jan5shi demon. That's why we've had such trouble getting a bead on things this time. The Degath Squad only has one actual demon in it."

"Lianel's worse than a demon. He knows more ways to torture a man than ought to exist." Trillian dropped into one of the chairs, shaking his head.

"What else did Horace say?" Camille asked.

"He confirmed the location of the nest and gave us an approximation of how many werespiders we can expect to be fighting. And he also verified the fact that they have Venus the Moon Child trapped out there. So when we go in, we'll have to be careful, or they'll use him as leverage. *If* he's still alive."

Camille glanced up at the clock. "Menolly's due to wake any minute. Get everyone out of the kitchen, would you?"

As I herded everyone back into the living room, including

Smoky, who had replaced Horace's gag and stuck him back in the closet, Ronyl chose that moment to appear. He was covered with snow but looked proud of himself.

"Spider wards are set up. You should have been out there to see the mass exodus from around your house. I'm not sure how many were actually hobo spiders, but there were several hundred of the creatures in all. Those should hold for a few months. I suggest investing in a fly swatter." He glanced at Trenyth. "All right, we should be getting back."

Trenyth nodded. "Yes, I know enough to tell the Queen what's happening. And I'll contact you through the Whispering Mirror tomorrow to find out how your raid goes."

"You have a lot of faith in us," I said.

He grinned. "That I do. But then again, look at what you've accomplished so far. Have faith in yourself, or you'll handicap your battle."

As he and Ronyl headed out into the growing dusk, I found myself wishing that they'd volunteer to stay and help us fight. But they had a war of their own to cope with. I was shutting the door behind them when Menolly appeared, blinking furiously. Iris and Maggie were right behind her.

"Who have you got locked up in the closet?" she asked. "I can smell his fear a mile away, and it's making me ravenous."

Uh-oh. She needed to feed, that much was obvious, and we had a ready-made TV dinner in the kitchen closet.

"Sit down," Camille said. "We have a lot to go over and not much time."

While Menolly floated up to the top of the Yule tree—she seemed to have taken a shine to hovering by the glittering ornaments—we filled her in on what had gone down, punctuated by her bursts of "I wish I'd been awake!" and "Really, we can use the Whispering Mirror to call the elves now?"

After we finished, she said, "So what do we do with him?"

"I suggest you have yourself a good meal," Trillian said as casually as if he might be suggesting she make herself a roast beef sandwich. I cringed, but Camille nodded.

"That's the best way. We can't trust him. If we lock him up somewhere, chances are he's going to get out and do us damage. He'd sell us out to the highest bidder if he had the chance. We learned that lesson with Wisteria."

They were right, and I knew it, though I still grappled with my conscience. But images of the victims his people had already claimed flashed through my thoughts, and I knew we couldn't afford to let compassion rule in this case. The Hunters Moon Clan wouldn't make that mistake, and they were out for blood.

After a moment, I raised my head. "Menolly, do you need help?"

She shook her head. "No," she said, giving me a look that was almost sorrowful. But a flicker in her eye told me that all of her regret was aimed at me, not for von Spynne. "We're soldiers, Kitten," she said softly. "Just like Father . . . and sometimes we have to do things we don't want to."

As she headed into the kitchen, I shook it off and turned to Zach. "How long will it take Rhonda to get here?" I said.

"Not long. She should be here soon," he said. "You'll like her, I think."

I wasn't so sure about that. There was the brief sound of a scuffle from the kitchen, and I decided now would be a good time to change. "Time to get dressed for the trip. Camille, you should, too. We're going out into the freezing night. We need to be warm and to blend in. Come on."

She followed me up the stairs. As we reached her floor, she turned. "I know how much this takes out of you," she said. "It wears on me, too."

I swallowed the lump rising in my throat. "I just hate that we're mixed up in all this killing. I hate that we can't go home because the same damned thing is happening there, only the stakes aren't quite so high. I hate that our father and aunt are in danger."

"Speaking of family, Trillian told me that the Jakaris priests reported that Shamas—"

"Right, he's dead," I said flatly.

She shook her head. "No! That's what I wanted to tell you. The monks were about to stop his heart when he—and I have no idea how he did this—but he managed to take control of their spell. He used it to . . . well . . . to vanish. They don't know if he's alive or dead, and nobody can figure out where he went."

"Holy crap." I stared at her. That was the first good news we'd had in ages. "You don't think he . . . uh . . . imploded, do you?" The thought made me queasy, but it was a possibility. Yanking the threads of somebody else's magic away and warping it to work for yourself was risky, at the very best. Then again, he hadn't had much to lose.

Camille grimaced. "That is a distinct possibility. The gods know it would probably happen to me, but to Shamas? He had a lot of power, though I don't recall what specific gifts he inherited from Aunt Olanda and Uncle Tryys. Whatever his powers are, they must be doozies, because he used them to get away. Lethesanar was furious when she found out. Trillian said that his informant told him the scene in the throne room was hideous. The Queen flew into such a rage that three servants and the messenger were dead by the time she was done. She ripped out their hearts."

"Oh, Great Mother." Lethesanar had it in her. We all did—our father's race was not a docile one. But the thought still turned my stomach. "I imagine that's the last time anybody ever volunteers to take bad news to her."

"Yeah, isn't that the truth?" Camille shrugged. "Here's hoping Tanaquar can vanquish her. Let's get moving. I'll dress and meet you downstairs. As soon as Zach's friend gets here, we'll head out. We have to end this. Tonight."

I nodded, taking the stairs two at a time up to my suite. Camille was right. It was time to put a stop to the Hunters Moon Clan. We might not be able to thwart Shadow Wing by taking out this latest Degath Squad, but if we could get to the spirit seal before they did, we'd be another one up on the demon lord. And *that* would truly be reason to rejoice.

I slipped on a pair of tights, then a pair of jeans. Under a hunter-green turtleneck, I was wearing a cotton camisole. Layering was good; it wouldn't impede movement as much as a thick parka, and yet it would keep me warm.

I dug around in my closet until I found a black suede jacket that was warmer than my unlined leather one. Along with gloves, a black bandanna over my head to keep my ears warm, and a pair of light hiking boots, I figured I could withstand the weather and still make it through the bush. I studiously kept my mind off of Rhonda while dressing. Some thoughts were unnecessary torture.

Camille shocked the hell out of me. Rather than her usual long skirt, she'd opted for a pair of winter leggings and a heavy cowl-neck tunic over the top. The tunic clung to her thighs, molding to every curve. She was wearing a pair of lace-up ankle boots and leather gloves, and she slipped her short spider-silk cape over the top. Even geared up for the outdoors, she still looked like an ad out of *Vogue*, albeit much more curvy than the typical model.

"I've never seen you dressed so . . . *functionally* before," I said, grinning at her. "It's a change."

"I'm not thrilled with it, but hey, we're facing spiders, and they bite. I don't want to tempt them by leaving too much skin exposed," she said, rolling her eyes. "Let's get this show on the road."

When we entered the living room, Rhonda was there. I stopped dead in my tracks. She was a bombshell. Gorgeous, regal, and dominant. Shorter than me, she was athletic and sleek. Her mane of golden hair had been braided into a long French braid, and her outfit was perfectly pulled together, but her build screamed that she was far more than just a ski bunny. She'd be one tough cookie in a fight; that much was obvious. But it was more than her exterior that floored me. It was the way she held herself—as if she were queen of the pride. And maybe she was.

She held out her hand, and I reluctantly shook it. Her grip was firm and warm. Involuntarily, I drew closer, wanting to be part of her circle. But one step too far, and I felt the dividing line—a reserve not born of snobbery but of the inborn sense that she stood a few rungs farther up on the social ladder than I did and that she always would.

I pulled back, and we locked gazes.

"We're so glad you're here," Camille said, stepping in front of me and extending her hand. She paid no attention to Rhonda's glamour, and the werepuma seemed disarmed for the moment.

"Yes," Menolly said, joining us. "Thank you for coming. We can use the help." She, too, ignored Rhonda's demeanor and abruptly, after a quick shake, turned her back on her and went into the kitchen.

Rhonda looked over at Zach. "Will he survive?"

I nodded. "We called the medics in time to neutralize the poison, but he can't move much for a few days. He's stuck here tonight, and there's no chance he can go with us."

"Have the boys filled you in?" Camille asked.

Rhonda nodded, her gaze flickering over to Trillian, who stared back at her, cool and aloof. After a moment, she looked away, blinking. I had the feeling Rhonda was used to being the center of the party, and tonight, not everybody was playing the way she had expected.

I stood up. "Okay, before we get moving, let's come up with a rough plan. Camille, since moon energy doesn't work so well on the werespiders, what are you going to use for a weapon?"

She patted the sheath on her belt. "Short sword. And I know a few spells that don't rely on the moon's energy. I might be able to summon up an Elemental to help us—perhaps a wind or an earth Elemental. Of course, if they're pissed, they may decide to help the spiders, so . . ."

"Let's leave that as a last resort," I said quickly. "I'll go in fighting, as usual. Chase, what are you bringing to the table?"

"I have my gun, of course, and nunchakus," he said, holding up the fighting sticks. "Silver bullets only work on lycanthropes, so I didn't bother bringing them."

"Good. Smoky, Trillian, Morio?"

Morio arched his eyebrows. "My repertoire includes a number of spells and illusions. And if all else fails, I can let loose my true form and have at them. I'm not such a pretty boy when I let the demon out to play." He said it so calmly that I had to smile until I remembered that none of us had ever seen Morio when he was in *full* demon mode.

Smoky snorted. "I'm a dragon. I'll do what I do best."

Trillian held up a serrated blade, then carefully sheathed it again. That was all he had to say.

"Well, if we're done, then let's get moving," Smoky said, standing up.

Iris entered the room. She carried a tray holding a bowl of chicken soup and a sandwich. Maggie was curled up on the end of the sofa by Zach's feet.

"You all be careful. I don't want to have to come rescue anybody," Iris said.

Camille gave her a hug. "We'll be back as soon as we can. Menolly will be back by sunrise, in any case. If something happens and you need help, use the Whispering Mirror to contact Trenyth."

Iris nodded as we herded out the door. "Understood. Please, girls, don't take any unnecessary chances. It only takes one mistake . . ." Her voice trailed off, and she waved as we clattered down the porch steps, our boots scrunching over the newly fallen snow.

We split into two groups. Chase, Rhonda, and Menolly rode with me in my Jeep, while Camille, Trillian, and Smoky rode with Morio in his Subaru Outback. Rhonda insisted on sitting next to me rather than Menolly, and I grudgingly agreed. I preferred having Menolly ride shotgun but didn't want to start a ruckus.

As I put my Jeep into gear and pulled out onto the road, I wondered if we'd all be alive by the end of the night. And would we be able to find Venus the Moon Child and the second seal before Shadow Wing got to it?

To get to Snoqualmie from Belles-Faire means driving over the 520 floating bridge, the world's longest pontoon bridge, which separates Seattle from the greater Eastside, then taking the 405 freeway to the exit leading to I-90 East. Once on I-90, it was a relatively short jaunt to reach the exit for the town of Snoqualmie.

By eight o'clock, rush hour had finally ended, and the roads were fairly clear, meaning plenty of traffic but not high volume. The ice and snow had slowed things down, but there were still a lot of drivers who assumed their SUVs gave them a free ticket to reckless winter driving, and twice we passed one of the big-ass cars that had skidded to the side of the road.

The snow fell steadily, muffling the world in a blanket of crystal. Something felt odd about this storm, almost magical. If we were still in one piece after our sojourn tonight, maybe I'd ask Camille to tune in and see what she could find out from the weather imps. The creatures usually ignored mortals of any kind, preferring to interact with only Elementals, but they made an exception for witches who could use weather magic.

I took the I-90 East exit and watched to make sure Morio followed me. As we curved under the overpass, I merged onto the freeway, and we were headed toward the Cascade Mountain Range. Of course, we'd stop long before we got to the top of Snoqualmie Pass, but even in the darkness I could feel the difference. We were headed toward still-active volcanoes and ancient mountains, towering peaks born from the heaving movements of great plates under the land. Earth's growing pains.

The traffic was light. Most people were shopping for the holidays or cozying up at home. We had the road pretty much to ourselves as we sped along.

"So what's our objective again?" Rhonda asked.

"Pretty simple," I said. "Find and eradicate Kyoka and the werespiders. Save Venus the Moon Child."

"So you don't *really* have a concrete plan of action?" she said, sniffing.

I kept a firm grip on the steering wheel. Her tone grated on my nerves, but I had no intention of letting her disrupt my thoughts. "We're lucky we even found the nest at all. We don't know what we're going into, and there's no way of finding out till we get there, so we just go in and fly by the seat of our pants. If you have a better idea, I'd like to know about it, because, babe, your people are running out of time."

She shut up. I knew I'd offended her, but I didn't care. The closer we got to Snoqualmie, the more I could feel the web that the Hunters Moon Clan had spun around the area. It was like a shadow growing in the mists that would take hold and root deep if we didn't clear it out. My senses clicked into high alert.

Chase directed me to turn off on Parson's Creek Road. The road was two lanes, and as my Jeep sped over the ice-encrusted pavement, I let myself slide further into trance. Menolly had remained silent in the backseat, but she suddenly stiffened and leaned forward.

"Demon scent. I don't know how long ago, but a demon's passed this way," she said.

I glanced in the rearview mirror. Her eyes were shining red, and her fangs were extended. She gave me a feral smile and winked.

"Jansshi demon," she said. "They're scavengers. They'll eat whatever you throw at them. This squad of Hell Scouts is probably led by Kyoka. Both Lianel and he have to be smarter than the Jansshi, who's primarily a thug wrapped up in brimstone."

Rhonda coughed. "I've never faced a demon," she said, sounding less sure of herself than she had a few minutes before.

"We have." I gave her a quick smile. "They can be terrifying, but in this case, I think we face more danger from Lianel and Kyoka than from the Jansshi. And don't forget the spiderlings. When I saw Geph von Spynne in my dream, he wielded a tremendous amount of power, *and* he can see out onto the astral. Of that I'm sure."

"The turn's a half mile up the road," Chase said. "Goldenrod Road."

My blood quickened, and I focused on driving. The scenery was looking familiar. I caught my breath. Shit, this was going to be bad.

"They're in a cave, mind you. We don't want to walk into a trap, but I doubt they'll welcome us at the door. We're going to have to go in after them. And that means danger."

Chase pulled out his cell phone and dialed. After a moment, he started speaking. When I glanced at him in the rearview mirror, he covered the mouthpiece and whispered, "It's Camille. Just coordinating."

I concentrated on driving. And there it was—just as I'd

dreamed, a signpost that read Goldenrod Road. In my vision I'd been coming the other way, but that didn't matter now.

I took a shuddering deep breath and turned left, Morio right on my tail. As we bumped along over the rough drive, I tried to remember how far it had been before the turnout leading to the nest. The S-curves seemed more precarious now that I was driving, especially with the packed snow and ice clinging to the road. And then, before I was ready, there it was—the turnout. I pulled to the side and killed the motor.

"We're here," I said. "See that dark spot there between those two fir trees? That's our path." Reluctantly, I unbuckled my seat belt and climbed out of the car. The others followed suit, and Chase pulled out our supplies that we'd prepared before leaving. As I slid my backpack on and made sure my long knife was fastened firmly in my boot and that my wrist blades were secure, Camille pulled to a stop right behind my Jeep.

They tumbled out of the car, and we gathered by the edge of the road.

"Everybody have everything you need?" Camille asked. We all nodded. She glanced up at the clouds and closed her eyes. "Moon Mother, be with us. Great Mother, watch over us."

"Lady Bast, guide and protect us," I added my own prayer. "See us through the coming battle, strengthen our magic, and enchant our blades."

I looked up. It was time. "All right, let's go." The second seal hung in the balance. We couldn't wait any longer. I swung onto the path, slipping between the fir trees that towered over us. As a gust of wind billowed past, setting the trees to creaking, the mark on my forehead tingled. My blood surged and, like a river raging in its banks, a current of fire rolled through my veins. Shaken but feeling stronger than I'd ever felt in my life, I straightened my shoulders. Somebody had heard our prayers, it seemed, but a little part of myself wondered just *who* had decided to answer.

"Okay, boys and girls, here we go," I said, and plunged into the brush, the others following in a silent line behind me.

CHAPTER 18

As we headed into the bush, my vision shifted, and I found myself seeing everything as clearly as if I were wearing night-vision goggles. Startled, I stumbled, and Camille, who was right behind me, braced me from falling.

"Are you okay?" she asked, keeping her voice low.

I blinked. Sure enough, I could see almost as clearly as if it were daylight, in an odd, colorless sort of way. "I don't know," I said, quickly filling her in on what was going on with my eyesight. "At least whatever this is seems to be in my favor. Where's Menolly?" I added, looking around.

"Look. Up there, see her?" Camille pointed to a low-flying bat. Menolly was slowly but surely learning to use her own powers to shift, although she couldn't stay aloft for long.

"Wow, she's starting to get the hang of it," I said. "Though she won't be able to stay up for long. I don't think she's managed a transformation for more than ten minutes yet."

"Well, at least she's trying, and this is a good place to give it a shot. She might be able to hide in a tree when we get to the cave. She could be our surprise element." Camille did her best to sound lighthearted, but her expression told me she was anything but that. She knew as well as I did that a lot was riding on what happened in the next few hours.

As we hiked along the inclining path, we came out into the patch looking down into the ravine. Just as I'd dreamed it. Peering over the edge, Camille and I stared into the raging water as it poured along the channel.

"I wouldn't want to get caught in those blackberry bushes," she said, pointing to the thorny mass covering the side of the dirt slope.

"What's up this hill?" Chase asked from the other side of the road. "Did you have a chance to explore at all?"

We crossed the path to join him. Smoky was staring at the hillside, frowning. He shook his head and said, "I don't think it's a good idea for any of you to go up there. I could without worrying, but I won't."

"What is it? What do you know?" I asked.

"This area was inhabited by Native Americans. They called themselves the people of the moon, and I think they have sacred burial grounds near here. I can feel spirits moving," Smoky said.

"My guide! He said something about his people being *the people of the moon*." As I spoke, there was a flutter on the wind, and a hush settled over the area. A translucent figure took shape in front of us, his aura gleaming in the night. It was the spirit I'd met in my dream. He looked quizzically at Smoky, Morio, and Trillian.

I bowed, hoping that was the proper way to show respect to a land guardian. "We meet again." Great, I sounded like some melodrama out of the forties.

He cocked his head to one side. "Have we met?" he asked, and then a smile flooded over his face. "Oh yes, I remember you. But you were your animal self that night."

I nodded, not wanting to admit that I wasn't sure just *what* animal I'd transformed into. "We've come to clean out the werespiders. Will you help us?"

With a shake of the head, he said, "I can't leave this place. But go, my friends, and may the spirits be with you." And with that, he faded out of sight.

"What do you make of that?" Rhonda asked.

"I don't," I said. "I've learned not to bother trying, because it's just a waste of time. Come on, we've got to get in there."

As I led them through the undergrowth toward the cleft in the hillside below, the snow picked up, and the wind howled down from the other side of the hill to sweep past us. Menolly landed nearby, abruptly shifting back into herself.

"Winds are too high for me to fly in bat form, and I can't

hover up there either," she said. "I'm not going to be much use when it comes to aerial tricks. Give me a good solid wall, and I can climb it, though."

"Well, it was worth a shot," I said. "I don't see anybody around, do you?"

"We could shine a light in the forest and see if any eyes reflect, but that would give us away." Chase scooted up next to me, squatting as we hunkered down behind the huckleberry bushes that had grown wild through the area. "It's your call, Delilah. What do we do?"

I glanced at Camille. She shook her head. "Chase is right. You're the one who was here in the dream state. You're in charge."

Shit. I'd been hoping she'd volunteer to take over. Camille was good at being in control. Me—not so much. But one look at her face told me she meant business. I sucked in a deep breath and looked around.

"We can't all charge at once; that would put us all in danger in case they've developed some sort of large-scale weapon—"

"Like an AK-47?" Chase said.

I glared at him. "Like an area spell that might catch us all in its effect. Menolly, you can't fly right now, but you're silent and you don't let off any heat. Why don't you creep through the edge of the woods and see if there's anyone hiding outside the cave? There were plenty of them when I was here in my dream."

"And if I find any?"

I gave her a hard stare. "Take them out as silently as you can."

"Right," she said, and took off.

I frowned. "Smoky, you're with me in front. Trillian, Chase, and Rhonda, fall in behind us. Morio, can you cast any invisibility spells? If so, you and Camille can sneak in ahead of us and scout around."

Morio scratched his head. "Yeah, I can pull that off. Come on, Camille, let's get out of the way so I can see if this works. Remember, we'll still make noise, so try to be quiet when we head over to the cave. It won't last long, but it should be enough to get us inside without a problem."

They stepped off to the side and as we watched, Morio muttered a few words. After a moment, he and Camille faded from sight. Relieved that something was working right, I waited a moment to give them time to get inside, then motioned to the others.

"All right, let's go," I said. "Don't ask questions. Don't take prisoners. We're looking to accomplish two things: rescue Venus the Moon Child and destroy Kyoka, Lianel, and the Jansshi demon."

Slowly, trying to make as little noise as possible, Smoky and I crept toward the cave. So far, nobody had showed up to stop us. I was beginning to get suspicious when we neared the mouth of the cleft, but a noise coming from within caught my attention, and I motioned for the others to stop.

Two men appeared at the mouth of the cave, both looking very von Spynne–ish. Tall, scrawny, and gangly seemed to be the trademark look among the Hunters Moon Clan.

They stopped, staring at us as if we were clowns at a black-tie formal or wearing fur coats to a PETA meeting. I decided that taking advantage of their surprise would be a good thing. Pulling out my long knife, I started to race forward, but Smoky was in front of me and with one grab, he caught both men around their necks and knocked their heads together.

He examined them quickly. "They're just unconscious. I suggest you finish the job."

Shivering, I stared down at them. Trillian seemed to sense my hesitation, because he shoved me aside and knelt down, quickly slicing their throats.

I stared at the spreading blood, at first in horror and then with fascination as the scent crept up to tweak my nostrils. A deep longing rose within me, a power that was as old and dark as the hills. Frightened, I hurried inside the cave and caught up with Smoky.

The entrance to the tunnel was large enough for three men to walk abreast, and rounded, like a tube. I flashed back to the specials I'd seen on *Animal Planet* about trap-door spiders.

Yep, it looked remarkably like that. Kyoka must have played demented geneticist as well as mad magician.

The passageway led far back, with openings along the way, both to the left and to the right. I could still smell the tang of blood from outside, but now other scents crowded in, flooding me with an intoxicating array of sensation. The pungent swirl of sweat and urine and feces made me cringe. Sex was in the air, too, and the smell of decay and food long gone bad. My stomach lurched as I reeled, trying to focus.

"Delilah? Are you okay?" Chase grabbed my elbow as I swayed.

"Yeah, I think so." I forced myself to concentrate. One step at a time as we entered the nest. We were almost to the first side tunnel when a shriek cut through the air. I clasped my hands to my head in pain, noticing that Rhonda was doing the same.

"What the fuck was that?" Trillian said, pushing by me as he raced ahead, Chase and Smoky right behind him. I started to follow, but something caught hold of my elbow, stopping me.

"Delilah? It's me," a disembodied voice whispered in my ear.

"Camille?" There was no answer, and I frowned. "If you're nodding, remember I can't *see* you."

"Oh yeah, right!" She sounded flustered. "Listen, Morio and I are going up ahead to check out a room where we can smell cat magic coming from. You want to come with us?"

"I can't see to come with you," I said, but just then, a shadow disengaged itself from the wall. "Holy crap, what's that?"

"Hush, it's me," Menolly said, slipping into view. "I'll lead you. I can hear Camille and Morio walking. My ears are sharper than yours."

I looked over at Rhonda. "Come with?"

Her eyes were filled with fear, but all she said was, "I've got your back."

As Menolly hurried down the hall, leading us, shouts erupted from the passage into which Smoky, Trillian, and Chase had disappeared. An unfamiliar voice screamed for help, and all we could do was hope our boys were all right.

We passed two more passages before turning to the left. As

we entered the narrow tunnel, I caught a fleeting glance of men racing down the hall. Probably in answer to their comrades' screams.

The passage we had entered led into a large room. The walls were rounded and had been chipped out by hand. They were solid rock, polished to a high sheen. The ceiling was at least twenty feet high, and as I peered into the darkened heights, the faint shape of spiderwebs draping one onto another formed a canopy across the entire room. I swallowed, trying not to think about what might be hiding up there. Several exits opened into what looked like yet more tunnels, leading far into the mountainside.

And then I noticed the dais in the center of the room. No wonder Morio had smelled cat magic. Next to what looked like a large egg on the dais, Venus the Moon Child hung cuffed by his wrists and ankles to a circular stone that stood upright. He was slumped over as far as his chains would allow, and he was naked. A latticework of bloody welts and burns crisscrossed his chest, ridged and still oozing. His nose had been broken, and both eyes were swollen and black. I swallowed hard, unable to look away.

Three men were standing around him. One wielded a whip. Another was heating a poker in a stone fire pit nearby. The third leaned against a stalagmite, looking bored.

Menolly let out a little growl. Her eyes took on a crimson glimmer as bloody tears leaked down her cheeks. She stared at Venus for a moment and then, without a word, launched herself at the man holding the poker.

I looked at Rhonda. "They know we're here, so let's get to work!"

She whipped out a wooden baton and raced in as I unsheathed my knife and followed her.

"What the fuck—" the dude with the poker said when he saw Menolly heading toward him. She was in kill mode, her teeth fully extended, and he whirled around, swinging the poker at her. Without missing a beat, she grabbed the branding iron by its glowing end and yanked it out of his hand, tossing it in the air so that it landed on the other side of the room.

"Holy shit!" He screamed, but she was on him before he could get out another sound, and within a second, his head lolled to the side, and she tossed him on the ground. Straight for the kill. Do not pass Go. Do not collect two hundred dollars.

Meanwhile, Rhonda engaged Mr. Bored while I moved in on the one with the whip. He gave me the once-over and, leering, tossed the whip back and forth between his hands.

"Who's your daddy, little girl?" He smacked his lips. "Be good, and I might just give you a good fucking before I teach you not to meddle in the affairs of men."

A low growl emanated from my throat, rumbling through the room. What the hell? Where had that come from? My opponent looked a little disconcerted but raised the whip anyway.

"You like pain, *pussy*cat?" he whispered. "Come play with the master."

"Big talk for somebody who's standing on the other side of a boulder." *The perfect setup. Now, if he just stayed where he was.*

I gathered myself and then raced forward and leapt onto the rock, using it as a springboard. A back flip in the air, and I landed directly behind him. Very Bruce Lee, I thought. Before he could whirl around, I thrust my blade into his left side, angling so that it struck through the heart. He had time enough to mutter something that sounded vaguely like "Fuck you" and then collapsed as I yanked my knife free.

"Thanks for the help," I said, wiping my blade on my jeans. Whatever I'd expected to feel, it wasn't the intense sense of satisfaction that swept over me. Taken aback, I glanced over at Rhonda, but she had managed to dispatch her opponent, too. Menolly was up on the dais, where she ripped Venus's manacles out of the rock wall. He slumped into her arms, and she carefully laid him down on the rock platform.

"He'll live," she said grimly. "He's been trained to handle pain, but he's going to have some pretty nasty scars." There was a catch in her voice, and I suspected that she was reliving her own bout with torture. Some scars fade. Others never disappear, even if you can't see them. Menolly's—both her physical and emotional ones—were eternal.

Rhonda raced over to his side. "I'm a certified nurse's assistant. Let me have a look."

"Where did Camille and Morio go?" Menolly asked, looking around.

"I'm right here," Morio answered, now visible as he stepped out from one of two exits leading off to the left. "Camille and I split up to find out what was down these two passageways. There's a bunch of spiderwebs and egg sacs down this hallway. I think we should torch them," he added.

"So you just left us here with those maniacs?" I looked around, searching for any sign of Camille. I could smell her perfume, so she wasn't that far away.

"We figured you could take care of those goons by yourselves." He caught my gaze. "Delilah, where's Camille? Isn't she back yet?"

I shook my head. "No, and I'm starting to get worried." The sounds of fighting echoed from the main passageway. Apparently the boys had managed to start a full-scale skirmish. Among the shouts, one of the voices sounded like it belonged to Chase, and I prayed he was safe.

"Something's happened to her, I know it," Morio said.

"What about Venus?" Rhonda asked, frantic.

"We'll get him on the way back," Morio said. "Until then . . ." He leaned over the unconscious shaman and said a few words, then blew on his face. In another moment, it looked like Venus was a pile of rocks. "That illusion should hold till we get back." He ducked into the tunnel down which Camille had disappeared. With a glance back at the main hallway, the rest of us followed.

This tunnel was narrow and cramped, tall enough for Menolly to walk through unhampered, but I had to hunch down to make it without scraping the top of my head on the ceiling. We followed Morio and the faint scent of Camille's perfume, which was growing stronger, until the passage opened out into another chamber, this one half the size of the main room.

Halfway across the room, the cave ended in a drop-off.

I peeked over the edge. Stone steps led down the cliff, cut into the side wall. Even with my heightened sight, I could barely see the bottom. There appeared to be an underground pond or river or creek down there.

I turned to Menolly. "Can you hear the sound of running water?"

She closed her eyes, and we kept as still as we could. After a moment, she nodded. "Sounds like a loud creek. I don't think it's big enough to be a river."

I sniffed the air. Yep, Camille had been here, but where was she now?

"Let's try down there," I started to say when a crash interrupted me. As we whirled around, three figures stood at the entryway. One of them was Geph von Spynne. The other was a Svartan, and he had his arm wrapped around Camille's waist, holding her so tight it looked like she was having trouble breathing. I'd thought Trillian looked dangerous, but this Svartan had a glint in his eye that made my blood run cold. *Lianel.*

Geph darted forward. "I know you," he said, waggling his finger at me. "I know you from somewhere!"

I raised my knife, but Lianel shook his head. "I wouldn't do that, not if you want to save your sister." He pressed his nose into her neck, and she struggled, but he tightened his grip, and she froze. "Oh, she's ripe, she's so ripe. I wish we were back in the temple at Svartalfheim. We'd have a high old time there, we would, my brothers and I." The longing in his voice oozed like the scent of a rose long decayed. Rotten, through to the core.

Unsure what to do, I looked at Menolly for guidance.

She was fuming, so tense I could see the muscles in her neck tighten. "What do you want?"

Geph gave his companion a smug grin. "I believe they're ready to negotiate," he said. "Too bad they didn't try it first before launching this ridiculous attack on our nest."

Lianel was about to respond, but he had barely opened his mouth when Camille took advantage of his inattention. She launched herself backward, throwing him off balance and landing square on him as he toppled over. She was at the ready, thrusting her elbow hard into his stomach as she rolled off and came up crouching. Before he could move, she'd clasped her hands and brought her fists down square on his nose, putting a stop to his fighting for the moment. Geph leapt at her, a knife with a rusty blade at the ready.

"No!" Menolly shouted, but Rhonda was closer. She launched herself at him, and he whirled as she swung her wooden baton, connecting directly with his stomach. He doubled over with a loud groan.

Then everything went to hell.

Geph managed to recover as Rhonda raised her baton for another blow, leaving her chest open and vulnerable. Lightning fast, he plunged his knife deep into her left side. She screamed, and the baton dropped from her hand to land with a ringing thud on the floor.

Menolly and I raced to help her, but before we could get there, the light in her eyes faded, and she fell backward, his knife stuck in her side.

Morio started forward but stopped when Camille swung around toward Geph, her hands held high, a look of fury on her face that I'd only seen once before, when she'd been fighting Bad Ass Luke.

"Mordentant, mordentant, mordentant," she yelled, and a faint beam of light shot from her fingertips.

This wasn't moon magic. Even I could feel the difference. No, this was something else, older and darker and far more dangerous.

Morio leapt to her side, and the energy from their hands merged, hitting Geph square in the chest. A look of surprise washed across his face—one that said, *But this wasn't supposed to happen,* and he let go of his knife and collapsed.

Morio broke off the attack and gave Camille a quick smack across the face. Startled, she dropped her hands. "You can't take him to the finish," he said hoarsely, and I wondered what the hell they were talking about. "It's not safe. You don't know how to retreat from it yet."

Lianel was struggling to pull himself along the ground. He

had barely made it three feet when Menolly put a quick stop to his not-so-hasty retreat. He slumped and was still.

I knelt beside Rhonda's side and felt for a pulse. Nothing. There was no breath, no sign of life in her eyes. She'd gone out like a light turned off at the end of the day. I stared at her for a moment. Zach had loved her and, at one time, he'd wanted to marry her. When he'd asked for her help, she'd given it willingly, walking into a dangerous situation with people she didn't know. And now she was gone. All my petty jealousy flew out the window as I whispered the prayer for the dead.

"What was life has crumbled. What was form now falls away. Mortal chains unbind, and the soul is lifted free. May you find your way to the ancestors. May you find your path to the gods. May your bravery and courage be remembered in song and story. May your parents be proud, and may your children carry your birthright. Sleep, and wander no more."

Soft voices joined me, and I looked up to see Camille and Menolly standing by my side, praying along with me. After we finished, I stood and brushed past them to where Morio was keeping watch over Geph. He looked on his last legs. Whatever spell Camille and Morio had cast, it had mortally injured him.

I motioned for Morio to move aside and leaned down to stare Geph in the face. "You've taken too many lives."

His eyes grew wide. Feeling colder than I'd ever felt before, I felt something within me struggling to shift, struggling to get out. I was transforming, and yet it was different than usual. As I arched my back, trying to free whatever it was that wanted loose, Geph gurgled, and his head lolled to the side. I let out a roar, loud enough to vibrate against the walls, and then the pressure died away.

Menolly raced to my side. "Kitten, are you okay?"

I shook my head. "I don't know. But we don't have time to muck around figuring out what's happening to me. We'll come back for Rhonda's body, but right now we have to find the others and make sure they're okay."

My thoughts turned to Chase; he was an FBH, the easiest

target by far. Gripped by sudden fear that he'd become another victim of Kyoka's insane clan, I raced toward the tunnel. We reached the main room again just in time to see Trillian, Smoky, and Chase race in from the main hallway. Smoky looked pissed. Chase and Trillian just looked terrified.

"What? What is it?" I asked.

"About two dozen members of the Hunters Moon Clan are on our heels!" Chase added, panting. He skidded to a halt by the dais. "What the hell?"

Morio waved his hand, and the illusion hiding Venus broke. "We found him. He's been terribly hurt, but he'll live."

"Well, that's good, but I'm not sure we'll be able to say the same for us in a few minutes," Smoky said. "I can't change underground. There's just not enough room, although maybe . . . in this chamber . . ."

Trillian looked around. "Where's the girl? The puma?"

I let out a long shudder. "Dead. As are Lianel and von Spynne. They tried to take Camille hostage."

Trillian strode over to Camille's side. "Did that motherfucker put his hands on you?"

She shook her head. "He managed to catch me but didn't have a chance to do anything to me."

"I'll see his soul in hell, all the same." Trillian shook his head and turned back to our approaching adversaries. "Let's hope they don't all attack at once. Too bad the opening is so accessible."

That gave me an idea. "It doesn't have to be! Smoky, if you change in here, there will be just enough room. You won't be able to fight, but you'll fill up the space, and they won't all be able to fit in at once."

"Oh, delightful. You want me to become a giant paperweight. All right," he said. "Stand back. I'll try not to hurt anybody, but no promises."

As we fell back, the sounds of our enemies grew louder. Before they could make it through the door, a haze of glittering mist rose around Smoky. I covered my eyes and backed away, Chase by my side. The sound of breaking rock echoed in the room, then more crashes, and when I finally peeked,

there was Smoky in all of his dragonly glory. And just in time.
Three men popped through the door, but they took one look
at the dragon and screamed, retreating as quickly as they'd
come.

I was about to let out a sigh of relief when another movement caught my eye, this time from behind. Whirling around,
I was just in time to see Tyler-turned-Kyoka enter the room
from the cave where we'd left Rhonda's body, with the Jansshi
demon right behind him. We were in for it now.

CHAPTER 19

~~~

Kyoka's eyes were glowing like a rabid dog caught in head-lights. He glanced up at Smoky, then back at the Jansshi demon. "He can't hurt us without hurting his friends."

The Jansshi demon nodded. Tall and spindly, he had a bloated stomach and looked like a caricature of a human, with greenish skin and long claws that dripped with what I could only assume was venom. When he opened his mouth, I could see the gleam of his sharp, serrated teeth. He moved with a lurching gait, his knees bent. No wonder the werespiders liked him—he was one of their homeboys.

I caught my breath. The Jansshi actually worried me less than Kyoka. A thousand years hanging out in the Sub Realms must have given him a whole new perspective on how to make life miserable. His powers had probably grown during that time, and he hadn't been keeping the best of company. No doubt Lianel had given him a number of pointers.

Camille, Trillian, and Morio were closest to the Jansshi, and they formed a semicircle, waiting for it to make a move, while Chase, Menolly, and I reluctantly faced Kyoka. Smoky kept watch on the entrance to the hall. There were a lot of spiderlings out there, but they knew what a dragon could do to them, and they kept out of his reach, which meant that he kept *us* out of *their* reach.

In every battle comes that one moment of quiet calm. It only lasts a fraction of a second as force assesses force, estimations are made. Then the flag falls, and the journey into hell begins. And so we stood poised on the brink, waiting for that indecipherable moment when the muse whispers, "Go."

Kyoka raised his arms and, as if waking from a long dream, I lunged forward, sword out. To my left, Chase whipped out his gun and fired, but it was useless. Kyoka inhabited the body of a man already dead. There was no heartbeat to stop. When he saw that nothing happened, Chase went for his nunchakus.

To my right, Menolly sprang into action. Kyoka spun toward her and muttered something. She froze in midstep, paralyzed as if she were porcelain. Cripes, he knew spells that worked on the undead! I lashed out with my blade, catching him across the upper arm, but he just laughed and spun into a dropkick, landing a blow in my stomach that propelled me back a good three yards. I landed hard, scrambling to my feet just in time to see Chase move in.

Camille and Morio were conjuring some force together, their hands joined as they focused on the Jansshi. The demon was trying to engage Trillian, but he danced back, pulling out some shooting stars and firing them quickly. One of them caught the beast in the forehead. The Jansshi let out a loud yowl and yanked the star out of its brow, tossing it on the ground. Camille and Morio took that moment to fire off whatever it was they were conjuring, and a shower of sparks flew from their hands, daggers of light aimed directly at the Jansshi. It screamed, rubbing its eyes as it stumbled around.

"It's blind!" Morio shouted. Trillian whipped out his blade, dashed in, and gutted the creature, ripping it from stomach to throat. A grotesque pile of intestines flopped out as the demon flailed and toppled over backward.

Back on our side of the battle, Chase had moved in on Kyoka, expertly whirling his nunchakus. If we hadn't been in the middle of a life-or-death fight, I would have stopped to watch.

Kyoka frowned and raised his hands. He was getting ready to try another spell. I grabbed a rock and lobbed it at him, hitting him square in the shoulder. That was all it took to break his concentration, and startled, he jerked around. Whatever he'd been planning on doing went out the window, because Chase seized the opportunity and let fly with a blow that hit him in the head.

The shaman lurched backward, but then a noise caught our

attention, and we all turned toward the dais where Smoky sat. The egg that rested behind him began to crack, and before we could stop him, Kyoka raced toward it and jumped, landing next to it as it broke open in a cloud of dust and smoke. With a loud screech, he slowly fell to the ground, his body decaying before our eyes like time-elapsed footage on some forensics show.

What the hell? Was he dead? It couldn't be that easy, could it?

And then, as the dust cleared, a creature stepped out of the remains of the stone egg. A nightmare straight out of my dream. With the torso of a man and the body of a spider, he was gloriously terrifying. Hair as black as night drifted down his shoulders, and his eyes glittered, but the rest of his body was bloated and huge, with jointed legs that ended in sharpened points. His laughter reverberated off the ceiling, and a crazed light filled his eyes. Kyoka had truly returned in all his former glory. And more.

"Shit, they grew a new body for him!" I stumbled back, terrified and yet knowing that we couldn't stop yet.

Smoky let out a roar as the mad shaman looked at him and said something I couldn't catch. Within seconds, Smoky shifted back into human form and collapsed. Shit! Kyoka had the power to dispel a dragon?

"Toto, I don't think we're in Kansas anymore," Chase muttered. I glanced back at Menolly, who had managed to come out from under the statue spell. She took one look at Kyoka and backed away. We quickly joined her.

Camille whispered something to Morio, who shook his head. "It's our only chance," she said. "Just do it. We have no choice."

They clasped hands again and began the chant Camille had been using against Lianel. *"Mordentant, mordentant, mordentant, mordentant . . ."*

Trillian and Menolly stepped in front of them in order to deflect Kyoka's attacks while they built up their energy. A chill raced down my spine. Now I knew what kind of spell they were casting: *death magic*, one of the most ancient and dangerous kinds of magic to use. Slowly, as the energy built, Kyoka moved forward, an impassive look on his face. Out of the corner of my eye, I saw that his warriors—the werespiders—were now in the form he had taken. They were edging into the room. We had to do something, and we had to do it now.

A wave of dizziness rushed over me, rising from the depths of my soul. An ancient stirring began to awaken. It had tried to waken before, only this time there was nothing to stop it. I let go and surrendered to the transformation, only it wasn't my tabby self I was changing into. Whatever this new form was, she was huge and fierce and imbued with a power beyond the natural world.

My head dropped back, my neck rolling as bones shifted and skin stretched, fur sprouting from every pore. I dropped to all fours, arms growing as legs shortened. Hands and feet became paws, huge and black with pads that were thick from running in the jungle. A sharp, painful tug, and my spine lengthened. Claws and teeth grew, sprouting long and sharp, and my already heightened sense of smell intensified.

The mark on my forehead blazed, and I could feel *him* nearby. He was standing there, in a cloud of smoke and fire, the wreath of leaves around his head burning like Lucia's candles. His cloak swept his feet, and with every step, he left a trail of frost and flame.

I glanced up and saw myself reflected in his eyes, a massive black panther, sleek and muscled, with eyes as emerald as the shimmering forest.

The Autumn Lord leaned down and touched my head. "Complete the task I set forth for you," he said. "Destroy the shaman and send him and his children to the grave for good. I give you the power to act with this form."

And then I was back in the room again, but the only other person there was Kyoka. Everyone else had vanished. Kyoka moved toward me.

"So, he's sent you to do his dirty work?" Kyoka said. "The first time he sent a Viking, and now he sends a panther? Come

then, my pretty pussy. Let's play." He motioned for me to
bring it on.

I let out a roar that shook the room, then hunkered down
and sprang.

Kyoka shot a stream of energy directly at me. It hit my side
but passed through as if it were nothing more than vapor. Startled, he let out a cry. "What the hell—why didn't you—"

Before he could finish, I was on him, trying to avoid those
sharp daggers he used for feet. I let loose with a swipe from
my claws. Kyoka lurched and fell onto his side. It was as easy
as dropping a shoe on a spider.

Flash. I caught him across the chest, and he began to bleed
as I raked, slashing through his flesh. The smell of blood set
off a hunger so deep that I knew I could never quench it.

Flash. He grabbed for me, catching me around the throat
as his hands formed a vise. He twisted my head, trying to
break my neck.

Flash. I leaned back, then lunged, bringing my fangs down
to rip at his face. The taste of blood filled my mouth, warm
and sweet, and teasing me on.

Flash. He managed to reach up with one of his jointed
legs. Pain lanced through my left back leg as he punctured it,
and I let out a yowl. Furious, the fire of the Autumn Lord fuel-
ing my heart, I gathered my strength and bit once more. This
time, my teeth went through his shoulder, into the soft flesh of
his neck, and I snapped my jaws shut. The killing bite.

Kyoka shuddered as the room swirled.

I blinked and found myself in a field of mist, in my normal
form. My left leg was bleeding, and I was standing in front of
Kyoka's spirit, which hovered above his dead body.

As if I had done so a thousand times before, I held out my
hand and touched the ghostly presence. Visions of fire and
anger swirled through my thoughts. Men dying under torture,
women being ravaged for use as breeders, children not true to
the new form being offered to the young spiderlings as food.

All of these images passed through me like a silent movie, flickering in an abandoned theater. Kyoka's memories, they were of his life as a shaman when he had created the unnatural Weres and perfected their new form.

My stomach rolled, and I thought I was going to vomit, but a force stronger than my own will steeled me up, and I straightened my shoulders.

"Kyoka, in the name of the Autumn Lord, I charge you with the Death Maiden's curse: the final death. Go and be cleansed from this world and from all worlds. Return to oblivion. Return to the pool of fire and ice from whence we all emerge. *Be no more.*" The words were unfamiliar to me, and yet they were mine to say. As I spoke, my core froze, and I aimed the icy line of frost directly into his spirit. Like a snowflake melting on the pavement, he vanished.

Kyoka was dead. Truly and forever dead, consigned to oblivion.

As the presence of the Autumn Lord began to fade, I heard him say, "You have done well. You will be the first of my living emissaries. My Daughter of the Grave." And then he, too, vanished, and I found myself standing in the middle of the room, and my friends were scrambling, shouting my name.

"Delilah? Where are you? Good gods, there she is!" Chase was closest to me and, as I collapsed, he caught me and lowered me to the ground. My leg burned like a son of a bitch. I blinked as they crowded around me.

"Are you all right?" Camille dropped to my side. "Delilah, say something. Where were you? What happened? Where's Kyoka?"

I glanced around. There was no sign of the shaman. His body had vanished. Smoky was awake again, guarding the door, though the rest of the spiderlings seemed to have beat a hasty retreat.

"How long have I been gone?" I managed to ask.

"A good fifteen minutes. Kyoka vanished when you did."

She looked at me closely. "Great Mother, the mark on your forehead!"

"What? What is it?"

Menolly joined her. The men hung back, more out of respect than lack of curiosity, I thought. "It's swirling—all gold and black and red."

I reached up and lightly skimmed it with my fingers. My brow tingled, and I could feel the presence of the Autumn Lord, barely out of reach. "I think what just happened activated its power."

"Tell us everything," Camille said, a worried look on her face.

And so I did.

"We have to get medical help for Venus," Camille finally said when I'd finished. "And we need to return Rhonda . . . Rhonda's body to her family."

I nodded, silent. Trillian went into the other room, and when he returned, he was carrying Rhonda over his shoulder. Smoky picked up Venus, gently like he might carry a child, and Menolly gathered the Jansshi demon and Lianel. We'd return their remains to Elqaneve, just as we had the first demons.

Morio and Camille torched the eggs and webs in the other passageway. I leaned on Chase's shoulder as we made our way out of the cave. Nobody bothered us. In fact, there was no sight or sound of a single living thing in the cavern, and I wondered where the rest of the enemy had scattered to. Perhaps the Autumn Lord had killed them. Perhaps they'd recognized defeat. Whatever the case, they were gone for now.

We silently trudged through the snow, back to the road. As we passed through the firs guarding the path, the spirit guardian stood at attention, nodding silently as we filed by. I glanced at him, and his face crinkled into a knowing smile, but he didn't speak.

Back at the cars, we piled in, putting the demon in one trunk and the body of Lianel in the other. Rhonda, we covered

with a blanket, and I sat next to her while Chase drove. Smoky
and Trillian sat in the back of Morio's SUV, Venus spread
across their laps. When we were ready, we headed out into the
icy night.

I gazed down at Rhonda's body. What was I going to tell
Zach? At this point, I was so numb that I couldn't even think.
I leaned back and closed my eyes, drifting as we headed down
toward the freeway. After all we'd been through, after all we'd
seen and done, there was nothing left to say.

By the time we arrived home, Venus had come around. His
wounds were nasty, but he'd live. Smoky carried him into the
bathroom.

"Chase, would you and Morio help Venus? Clean him up
and tend to his wounds?" I asked. They nodded and followed
Smoky.

Menolly unloaded the demon and Lianel and put them on
the back porch for the time being, while Camille and Trillian
made the rounds to check on the land and wards. My leg had
stopped bleeding. It would need a good cleansing and some
rest, but if Kyoka had tried to envenomate me, it hadn't
worked. I'd be okay.

I joined Zach in the parlor, closing the door behind me. He
was resting. I sat beside him and took his hand in mine. "I
have to tell you something," I said, not knowing how to start.
"We found Venus. He's hurt, but he'll live. But the fighting got
rough. There was a death . . ."

Zach looked up at me, his eyes full. "Rhonda?"

I nodded, feeling like I'd just stabbed him in the gut. "She
died trying to save Camille. She was a true warrior to the end.
We brought her body back so that you can take her home."

His face crumpled. Desperate to wipe away the pain—
there had been so much pain—I leaned down and kissed him
lightly on the lips. He slid his arms around me and pulled me
close, and I let him. He'd suffered so much over the past
weeks, I couldn't pull myself away.

"She was good . . . too good for me. We just weren't ready

to get married, but I never stopped loving her," he said, his voice breaking.

I wanted to ease his pain, wanted to put to rest the confusion and fear in my own heart. So much had happened, so much *was* happening. It would take a long time to sort everything out, and I wasn't sure we had that time. The second seal was still at large, and we had to find it before Shadow Wing did.

Zach shifted and reached under my blouse, fumbling for my breast.

"I'm grimy, I'm covered in blood," I whispered, but he shook away my protests. Unwilling to reject him, I let him unzip my jeans and slide them down over my hips. He rolled me over, easing himself between my legs.

"You have to be gentle with yourself," I whispered, but he just kept shaking his head, and finally, I opened myself up to him as he covered me in kisses. Desperate to find a touch of life in the midst of so much death, I shivered gently as he plunged inside me, driving deeper with each stroke, pushing away thought and memory and dark visions.

"Delilah, I need you," he whispered. "You're the first woman I've wanted since I broke up with Rhonda. Love me. Make love to me."

I held on, my hips moving against his hips, my breasts aching with a need so deep I thought I'd explode. He leaned down, took one nipple in his mouth, and sucked, the fire of his tongue driving me toward the edge. Everywhere I looked, there was fire and ice, flame and glaciers, passion and death.

"I can't love you," I said, gasping as I matched his rhythm. "As much as I like you, I can't give you my love." As I spoke, I finally broke through and heard what my heart was whispering. Somehow, beyond all sense, I'd fallen for Chase. I felt safe with him. I felt *home*. My body didn't care at this moment who wiped away the ache and pain, but my heart belonged with the FBH who had given me some sort of roots, as fragile as they might be.

"Then give me this," Zach said. "This one night." And with one final thrust, he drove home to my core, pushing me to the edge. I hovered for an instant, then let go, giving in to the passion, giving in to the feral energy that rose between us—puma and panther, puma and housecat, Were and Fae. Biting back a scream, I arched as I came, a shower of sparks racing along my body leading me to blessed release.

When it was over, I paused for a moment, then gently pushed him away. "I need to get up, Zach. I need to get dressed." I quickly stood and adjusted my clothing, desperate to collect myself before Chase stumbled in on us.

"It's your detective, isn't it?" Zach asked, leaning back, his hands behind his head. "You've fallen for him, and you're afraid he won't understand."

Startled by his insight, I nodded. "We've talked about it before, but when push comes to shove, I'm not sure if he can handle me being with anybody else. Please, don't say anything. I'll tell him, but . . . but let me do it in my own way."

Zachary nodded. "Whatever you like. But Delilah," he said, "don't think you can manage a relationship with him. Don't even hope. It won't work in the long run. You need more than he can give you, even if you don't believe that now. I may not be the one you need, but it's not him. Trust me."

I wiped my mouth and winced as the wound on my leg opened again. "I'm hurt. I've got to go tend to my leg," was all I said.

As I closed the door behind me, I dreaded the coming days when everything was sorted out and when I'd have to tell Chase what I'd done.

CHAPTER 20

~~~

Menolly, Camille, and Trillian were sitting at the kitchen table, hot tea in hand. Iris held Maggie, her eyes wide as Camille filled her in on what had happened. I dropped down beside them.

"Zach knows about Rhonda," I said, looking up to find Camille staring at me. She didn't say a word, but I knew we'd be having a long talk later on. I glanced at the clock. It was almost seven. The sun would be rising soon, and Menolly had made her way to bed.

"When should we contact Queen Asteria—" Camille started to say when Morio, Smoky, and Chase returned with Venus in tow. The shaman looked pretty beat up, but he definitely looked better than he had when we first found him. They helped him into a chair.

"We thought you'd want to hear this," Morio said.

Venus leaned forward, gratefully accepting the mug of tea that Iris pressed into his hands. "I'll thank you all for saving me in a bit, but first, we have more important matters to discuss." He wrapped his hands around the warm mug and shuddered, then took a long sip of the tea. "That's good, so good," he said, shuddering again. "Listen, I know what you're after. The same thing the demons are after. I can tell you where to find it."

"The second spirit seal?" I whispered.

He nodded. "Yes. It's been a symbol of our clan down through the ages since Einarr the Iron Hand found it."

"He didn't find it," I spoke up. "The seal was given to him by the Autumn Lord as a reward for destroying Kyoka the first time."

Venus looked at me and blinked, staring at my forehead.

"Oh my girl," he whispered. "You know him, then." He stretched out his fingers and barely grazed the swirling scythe on my forehead. "During my training as a shaman, I underwent a ritual of death and rebirth. During that journey, I met a man who walks in flames and frost. I never knew his name, but he touched my soul, and that's when I came into my power."

I nodded. "We'll talk more when the sun shines and the seasons turn and death isn't in the air. But for now, where's the seal? We have to take it away from this world, to hide it from the demons before they gain control of it."

"When the old shaman died and passed his staff to me, he gave me the seal." Venus pushed his chair back from the table. He held out his leg, the one with the limp. "He told me how to hide it. All these centuries it's been passed down in the same manner, and the tribe has been left unaware of its existence. The shaman has been the only one who knows about the seal, and it's from where we gather most of our power. This is the only way we could ensure its protection: When I give it to you, we will be left open and vulnerable. Perhaps it's time we stood on our own."

Before we could say anything, he pulled up his pants leg and ran his hand over his calf. An incision opened up, raw and bleeding, but clean. Inside, a small cabochon sparkled with red and gold set in bronze. He motioned to me, and I gingerly reached into the open wound and pulled out the fire opal. Venus the Moon Child ran his hand over the cut, and it sealed again, leaving a ridged scar.

I stared at the glowing gem. The pulse of energy washed through me like a cleansing wave, and my pain and anger fell away. I let out a long sigh and looked up to see the others do the same. Venus closed his eyes and turned his head. All these years he'd possessed the gem but never directly used it. He'd been its home and protector, as had his master before him, and so on back through the veils of time.

"The Degath Squad could probably sense you'd been around the jewel, but they never realized it was right inside you," I said.

"It's a good thing they didn't use that lash low enough to open me up there," he said, his eyes sparkling with tears.

"So that's the seal?" Zachary eased his way into the kitchen, still looking shaky. "I wondered where you got that limp," he told Venus. "I guess all of our shamans had a limp, then?"

Venus nodded. "It was always thought to be one of our traits—a trade for accepting our powers. I guess, in a way, it was."

I laughed then, suddenly feeling like a burden had lifted. "We'd better use the Whispering Mirror and call Trenyth to warn them we're on the way."

Camille and I headed upstairs to put in our call. The mirror worked like a charm, and we found ourselves facing not Trenyth, but Queen Asteria herself.

"I'll send someone to get the demons and the seal," she said. "In fact, I'll dispatch them as we speak." She turned and said something over her shoulder, and we heard Trenyth acknowledge the order. "You have to be careful coming back to Elqaneve right now," she continued. "It's not safe for you."

"We know about Lethesanar's death threat—" I started to say.

She cut me off. "It's not that. Although that alone is reason enough to take care. No, something else has happened."

Camille glanced at me. I could feel it, too; bad news rode ahead of itself on the wind, and whatever this was, it was bad. I swallowed my instinct to turn tail and run. "What is it?"

The Queen looked like she'd rather be doing anything but having this conversation. "There's no easy way to tell you this, so I'll just come out with it. Wisteria escaped. We don't know how—she must have had help—but she managed to kill her guards and escape from her cell."

"Well, hell. She's probably going to try to contact Shadow Wing." I looked over at Camille. "Looks like we don't have much of a reprieve this time."

"It's worse than that," Queen Asteria said. "Informants tell us that she's joined up with the Elwing Blood Clan."

"Holy crap, that's the clan that—"

"Yes, that tortured your sister Menolly and turned her into a vampire." The Queen took a long, shuddering breath. "Until we find her, or find out for sure that she's left the city, you shouldn't come here. Instead, travel to Aladril through Pentangle's portal. Go to the City of Seers and look for a man named Jareth. He knows the history of the Elwing Blood Clan and might be able to provide you with some useful information. For now, though, meet us on your end at Grandmother Coyote's portal."

"The City of Seers? Jareth? Who is he?" I asked.

Queen Asteria stared at my face for a moment, and when she spoke, it was only to say, "I see you are now walking a dangerous path, child. The Elemental Lords are not for the weak of heart. But I doubt you chose this journey. Go now, and bring the bodies to our meeting point. We'll take it from there."

Trenyth, Ronyl, and several hefty guards met us outside Grandmother Coyote's grove. They took the seal and bodies away. Camille and I watched as they disappeared back through the portal.

"What are we going to tell Menolly?" Camille asked, shaking her head. "That her old enemies are aligning themselves with Shadow Wing? That the creatures who tortured her and turned her into a vampire may be next on our list to hunt down and destroy?"

"I don't know if she'd mind that so much," I said. "She's always wanted revenge, and I don't blame her."

We wandered back to the car where Trillian was waiting. Chase had opted to go home to rest, and I hadn't had a chance to talk to him before he left. Morio was on his way toward Mount Rainier, driving Zach and Venus back to their home. They were taking Rhonda home for the last time.

We'd been invited to the burial ceremony, which would be held in a few days. Of course we'd go, although our hearts ached at the thought. Rhonda had laid down her life for us.

We wouldn't miss the chance to say one last thank-you and good-bye.

"It's hard to believe that tonight is Yuletide. Midwinter, already. And tomorrow night is Sassy Branson's party. I don't really feel like going." Camille brushed past a low-hanging branch, and the snow slid off, showering us with a sudden flurry.

"We promised," I said. "Besides, I think we need some cheering up. We need to contact Cleo about the computer position with our new-and-improved OIA. He'll be a blast to work with." I hesitated, then gingerly proposed a thought that had been running around in my head since we'd talked to Asteria. "Say, what do you think if we hold off on telling Menolly about the Elwing Blood Clan until after Sassy's party? We deserve a couple nights away from worry."

Camille stared at me. "I think she'll kick your butt. Menolly, that is."

At my pleading look, she let out a long sigh.

"Oh, all right, but it's on your head if she gets pissed. All I know is that I've had enough of spiders to last me a lifetime. There's the car! Come on, Iris will be waiting. She wants us to hurry back for a holiday brunch." Camille ran forward and threw herself into Trillian's arms. He blinked, but he picked her up and whirled her around, kissing her soundly before we headed for home.

CHAPTER 21

Late that night after we'd rested, my sisters and I followed Iris as she led the way down to Birchwater Pond. The path through the woods had been lined with luminarias, the candle flames flickering softly from within their ivory holders. Trillian, Chase, Morio, and Smoky followed a respectful distance behind. They were our family now, and we wanted them to celebrate with us.

We'd dressed up in our holiday clothes that we'd worn to the winter festival last year, back in Y'Elestrial. Woven from the finest spider-silk, the gowns were as warm as they were beautiful. That had been our last holiday at home; we'd come Earthside a month or so after that.

Camille's gown mirrored the color of the moon, silver and shimmering, faceted quartz beads shifting color with every step she took. And mine reflected the sun, golden and warm. A belt of topaz and citrine rode low on my hips. Menolly was clad in night-sky black. Intricate cabochons of onyx and obsidian dangled from her ears, and her lips were bloodred.

Iris was also dressed to the hilt in a silk gown as blue as glacial ice, and she wore a cloak trimmed with wolf fur. It was the outfit I'd picked up from Pike Place Market for her. Maggie snuggled asleep in the crook of her arm.

The men were also in their finest, although Chase looked a little uncomfortable in the leggings and tunic that Trillian had loaned him. But they were both in a good mood. Trillian's bid on a house had come through, and he'd be moving within a few days, with a mortgage to die for.

All of us, even our calico wonder, were wearing wreaths around our heads, woven with white roses and red carnations, interspersed with baby's breath and soft fern fronds.

We glided through the falling snow, following the path to the water's edge. The pond had frozen over, and we gathered at the edge.

"The winter's colder than it should be," Iris whispered. "There's something behind this weather, but I'm not going to even try to guess what."

Camille nodded. "You're right. It's not natural." She looked around. "Shall we get started? Menolly, you've got the best voice. Will you lead us?"

Menolly threw her head back as a swirl of snow danced around her, and she caught a flake on her tongue. She let out a low laugh. "Of course."

As we began the tradition that stretched back a thousand years and a thousand more, her voice rose into the icy night, a chime of quicksilver on the wind. Camille, Trillian, and I joined in the familiar chant, echoing her in a call-and-response. We sang for our ancestors, we sang for our homeland, and we sang for our mother's world as well.

When we segued into the invocations to honor the Holly King and the Snow Queen, my thoughts began to drift. I glanced over at Chase. He looked radiant, thrilled to be included, even though he wasn't sure just what was going on. What was I going to tell him? He meant so much to me. Would he run when I told him about Zachary? Would he be angry? And what would he think if I spilled my secrets and told him what was really hiding in the corner of my heart? Yet, surely it was far too soon to tell him that I thought I loved him? Hell, I wasn't even sure I knew what love was.

So much had changed. Everything in my world was shifting, and I didn't know who I was anymore. I might have a twin sister who died. I was now a Death Maiden for the Autumn Lord. I needed to explore what was happening to me before I invited anybody else to share my life.

I shuddered, trying to keep my thoughts away from those final moments with Kyoka when I'd turned into the panther, but they crept up to haunt me and, with a little cry, I dropped my candle in the snow as the world shifted again.

A vortex of color and a blink of the eye later, I was sitting on the ground, staring up at my sisters and Iris. My golden fur quivered in the wind. Comforted, I let Camille pick me up and rest me on her shoulder. Her scent was familiar, and I snuggled into her hair, purring, happy to be where I was.

Maybe we *were* trying to keep the floodgates to Hell closed, but in the meanwhile, we'd live to the fullest. After all, a life spent in fear was no life at all. Whatever dark shadows lay in our path, there had to be sunny days ahead, too. And nights as crystalline and pure as this one.

I brought my attention back to the ritual, and eventually, when I'd calmed down enough, I returned to my normal form, no worse for the wear. The hours wore on as we wove the magic of our father's ancestors. For one perfect evening, everything was brilliant and beautiful and shining as we stood sentinel through the longest night of the year, waiting to greet the reborn sun.

And now . . .
an excerpt of the next book
in the Otherworld series
by Yasmine Galenorn . . .

DARKLING

Available from The Berkley Publishing Group!

CHAP†ER 1

"McGregor, if you think you're going to toss your cookies all over my clean counter, think again. Get to the bathroom now, or I'm going to toss you outside and teach you the meaning of roadkill."

I wiped my hands on one of the crisp white rags that we used to clean the counters of the Wayfarer and carefully draped it over the railing behind the bar while keeping a close eye on the goblin. I didn't like goblins.

Not only were they conniving little sneaks, but goblins in my bar posed a potential threat for my sisters and me. The goblin bands were in league with our bitch-queen back in Otherworld who had effectively exiled us by means of a death threat. Until the civil war was over and she was vanquished, we either had to stay Earthside or head for parts other than Y'Elestrial, if we decided to go home to OW. One loose tongue—and goblins were squealers—and Queen Lethesanar might know we'd stayed Earthside.

The elves had helped us rig the portal leading from the basement of the Wayfarer so that it now pointed into the shadowed forests of Darkynwyrd instead of our home back in Otherworld, but that only eliminated the immediate threat of the Queen's guards coming through. Now we had to cope with goblins, shades, and other skulking creatures wandering through. But we didn't dare close the portal permanently. We needed access to Otherworld.

I wouldn't have minded the occasional goon poking his head through my doorway, but the elfin guards watching the other side were lazy. This week alone I'd been in four fistfights with miscreant Fae, taken out three kobolds, put the kibosh on a touchy-feely gnome, and barely corralled a butt-ugly troll who'd somehow managed to sneak through.

"Try an' make me leave, dolly . . . I'll show you jus' what women are good for." The goblin thrust his pelvis toward me with a lewd grin and grabbed his crotch. He was plastered all right. He had to be, or he would have slunk out of there, shaking in his boots. By the look on his face, I figured that I had about five minutes before his supper paid him a return visit.

"No, let *me* show *you* what women are good for," I said softly as I leapt over the bar. His eyes went wide as I landed silently beside him. I could smell his pulse, and the beat of his heart echoed in the back of my mind. Even though you couldn't pay me to touch goblin blood unless I was starving, my fangs extended and I gave him a slow smile.

"Holy shit." He tried to scramble away but only succeeded in wedging himself between his stool and the next one. I yanked him up by the scruff of his collar and strode over to the stairs leading into the basement, dragging him behind me. He struggled, but there was no way he could squirm out of my grasp.

"Chrysandra, keep watch on the bar for a minute."

"Sure thing, boss." Chrysandra was my best waitress. She'd been a bouncer over at Jonny Dingo's for a while, but got tired of being harassed by sleazeballs for minimum wage. I paid her more, and my patrons knew better than to harass the help. At least most of them did, I thought, looking down at the goblin as I hauled him toward the basement and picked him up to carry him down the steps. The goblin squealed, kicking the hell out of my stomach.

"Can it, dork. You can ram your size fours into my midsection from now until doomsday without making a dent," I said, hissing.

He blanched. "Oh, shit."

"Yeah, that about sums it up," I said. Being a vampire had its perks.

As I entered the basement, Tavah looked up from her post. She glanced at the goblin, then at me. "I didn't think he was supposed to be here . . ." She let her words drift off as I tossed Mr. Unlucky on the floor.

"No way can we allow him to go back through the portal. I suggest you take an early lunch," I said.

Tavah blinked. She wasn't as picky about where her meals came from as I was. "Thanks, boss," she said as I turned to go back upstairs.

The goblin let out a startled cry behind me, cut off in mid-shriek. I stopped for the briefest of moments. The basement was silent except for the faint sound of Tavah, lapping gently. I quietly shut the door and returned to the bar. There was no sense in taking a chance the goblin might run back to Otherworld—and to Y'Elestrial—and spread tales. Neither the Queen nor the OIA—or what was left of it—knew we were still here. And we wanted to keep it that way.

The Wayfarer was rocking. When I'd first been assigned to work the bar, I resigned myself to serving a bunch of drunken sots and sad-assed streetwalkers. But to my relief and surprise, most of the Fae who came to the Wayfarer drank enough to have fun, but not enough to cause problems.

The humans—FBHs as we call them—were pretty good sorts as well. They spent good money to fritter away the evening in the presence of various Fae and Earthside Supes. All except for the Faerie Maids, that is, and they only irritated me because they were cheap. Cheap as in, buy one drink and nurse it half the night while taking up valuable booth space. They were there for one reason and one reason only: to be noticed by some pussy-hungry denizen of Otherworld.

To be honest, I felt more pity for them than irritation. It wasn't their fault they were vulnerable to Sidhe pheromones. And if anybody should exercise restraint, it was my father's people. We knew what could happen when sex worked its way into the mix, but a lot of the full-blooded humans didn't.

However, I'd learned to keep my mouth shut. On the rare occasions when I tried to dissuade a love-struck Faerie Maid from her quest, I'd been met by disbelief. A few times, by outright anger.

With the goblin taken care of, I returned to the counter just in time to see Camille and Trillian wander through the door. My oldest sister, Camille, was gorgeous, with long raven hair and violet eyes. She was curvy and buxom, and dressed à la designer BDSM, decked out in a leather bustier and flowing chiffon skirt. Trillian looked like an escapee from the Matrix with his black suede duster, black jeans, and black turtleneck. His clothing and skin blended together in one long silhouette, while his silver hair hung free to his waist. It had a life of its own, that hair. As a couple, they turned heads, that was for sure.

I waited until they chose a booth and then wiped my hands on the bar rag and tossed it to Chrysandra. "I'm taking a break," I said, heading over to join them. I could do without Trillian, but I needed to talk to Camille. She glanced up as I slid in beside her and gave her a quick squeeze.

Trillian flashed me a brief smile. As usual, I ignored him. "What did you find out?" I asked her.

She leaned back, shaking her head. "They've disappeared. Trillian looked all over but couldn't find any sign of either Father or Aunt Rythwar. The house was deserted, everything gone."

"Shit." I stared at my nails. They were perfect, and they always would be. "Anybody have any idea where they went?"

Trillian spoke up then. "No. I checked with all my usual sources without any luck. Then, I managed to scare up a few who weren't happy to see me—they owe me big and were hoping to stay hidden a little bit longer. But nobody seems to have any idea where your father and aunt went."

"You don't think that Lethesanar found them and killed them, do you?"

I grimaced as Camille asked the question, but she was right—it needed to be asked.

"You know that she wouldn't be able to resist parading them around the Court. She loves to flaunt her victories over her enemies. She'd schedule public executions at the very least. No, I think they just found a damned good place to hide and are waiting it out."

Trillian leaned back, draping his arm around Camille in an

easy way. Someday, I'd have to come to terms with the fact
that they were back together and likely to stay that way. I
might not be happy about it, but there wasn't much I could do.
And he was helping us, I had to give him that much credit.

I thought about this for a moment, then decided to ask another question I really didn't want to ask. "What about our
other problem?"

"No word yet," Trillian said.

Camille let out a long sigh, the violet of her irises flecked
with silver. She'd been running magic and running it heavy.
"Queen Asteria's guards can't pick up any sign of Wisteria,
and the Elwing Blood Clan seems to have disappeared from
the radar. They aren't anywhere near their usual haunts, and
nobody's heard anything about what's going on. But they're
up to no good. We know that much."

"I know what they're capable of." I closed my eyes for a
moment, pushing away the memories that haunted me if I let
myself dwell on them for more than a moment. At least during
the night, when I was awake, I could shake off the memories.
"So," I said, meeting her eyes. "What do we do next?"

Camille shrugged. "I don't know what we *can* do. I suppose we watch the portal, watch the news, and hope to hell the
elves have better luck in their scouting missions."

"Asteria told us to visit Aladril, the City of Seers, and look
for a man named Jareth." I wanted to do something. Sitting
around, waiting for something to happen, it was anathema to
me. Surprise the opposition before they have a chance to surprise you. That was my motto.

"I know, but what do we say? How can we expect him to
give us answers when we don't even know what questions to
ask." Camille tapped her foot on the floor. I could feel the vibration of her leg.

"I don't know," I said after a long moment. "But we'd better think of something soon. Wisteria's not going to wait forever and, with a clan of rogue vampires on her side, she could
do a lot of damage if she makes it back Earthside."

"You really think they'll listen to her and not just drain
her?" Camille frowned, tracing a spiral with her finger in the

condensation that dripped to the table from her glass of Blossom Wine.

"Oh, they'll listen to her, trust me. Psychos tend to stick together, and the Elwing Blood Clan is run by a sadist. Aren't we the lucky ones?" I glanced over to the bar where a sudden rush of customers appeared. The movie across the street must have let out. "I've got to get back to work," I said. "I'll meet you at home. Just be careful. Something's going on . . . I can feel it."

Camille lifted her face, letting the lighting bathe her in a golden glow. She blinked. "Yeah, I can smell it on the wind. We're in for a bad jolt. I just don't know what." She motioned to Trillian. "Come on, let's go. Delilah and Iris are probably waiting for dinner."

As they bustled out of the booth and headed toward the door, Trillian lingered behind. "You're right," he said. "The Elwing clan will take to Wisteria like a duck to water. Keep watch as to who comes through the portal."

I nodded as he turned to go. As I said, I might not like the Svartan, but he had a good head on his shoulders. I swiveled back to the bar and surveyed the room. The place was packed. Over the past month or so, the Earthside Supes had discovered the Wayfarer and were making their way out of the closet in droves.

In addition to several run-of-the-mill Fae from Otherworld, I spotted two lycanthropes whispering in a corner booth, a werepuma who was reading a copy of Daphne du Maurier's *Rebecca*, a half dozen house sprites engaged in some sort of drinking game, and a couple of FBH neopagans who were taking divination lessons from one of the Fae seers who'd taken up residence Earthside. There were also four Faerie Maids, all looking for a fuck. They'd been here two hours and had bought two rounds of drinks.

I was headed over to shake them down when the front door burst open and Chase Johnson strode through, a nasty ketchup stain covering the front of his shirt. About to make a snarky remark, I stopped cold when my nose picked up the fact that it wasn't ketchup after all. Chase had been splattered with

blood. Swept under a sudden wave of dizziness, I forced myself to close my eyes and count to ten.

*One . . . two . . . don't even think of attacking. Three . . .
four . . . remember that you ate before you came to work.
Five . . . six . . . Chase is Delilah's boyfriend—hurt him and
you alienate her. Seven . . . eight . . . push the temptation to
the side. The blood isn't coming from Chase, it's merely on his
suit. Nine . . . ten . . . take a deep breath even though you don't
need to breathe. Let it out slowly, loudly, send the tension and
thirst with it to be cleansed and negated.*

As the last of the air left my lungs, I opened my eyes. Each
time, it got a little easier. Each time, I felt a little more control
returning to my life. During my hunts, if I wasn't out scouting
for pervs but instead had to drink from someone who was just
an innocent bystander, I made use of the technique. It kept me
from doing permanent damage I'd regret, although I'd given
up retraining my psyche to view the process as nutrition, not
pleasure. It always felt good, and it always would.

"Chase, what's going on? Are you hurt?"

His eyes widened as he met my gaze, but then he shook
his head and nodded toward the door. "Across the street, at
the theater. We got reports of some sort of fight going on. By
the time we got there, we found four dead—two men, two
women."

"What happened?" Chase knew better than to come around
the bar all bloodied up. With Earthside Supes and denizens of
Faerie hanging out here, it was sort of an unwritten rule: If
you are sporting a nasty laceration or if you're a woman in the
middle of a heavy flow day, don't come to the Wayfarer unless
you want to risk setting somebody off. Blood was an aphro-
disiac to a number of Supes. There must be something going
on to make Chase break convention.

"Vampires," he said. "They were drained of blood but with
no obvious cuts or wounds. Sharah examined their necks and
sure enough—twin punctures on every one of them. They
were up in the balcony, near the back, where nobody else was
sitting."

Vampires? Of course there were other vamps in Seattle, but

ones who would resort to attacking humans in a theater? That didn't track right. I shook my head. "Did you catch them?"

Chase frowned. "We couldn't find any sign of them. We thought you might be able to help—the wounds are fresh, the vamps are probably close by. If anybody can find them, you can."

I groaned. "You want me to play Buffy? Give me one good reason why I should go staking my own kind?"

Chase gave a rough laugh. "Because you're part of the OIA. Because you're on the right side. Because you know what they did was *wrong*. Hell, you can dress up in drag and call yourself Angel, for all I care. Just help us."

Great, just great. This was the price I paid for being nice to my sister's boyfriend. But as he stared at me, pleading for my help, I couldn't say no. I untied my apron and tossed it on the counter.

"Chrysandra, I'll be back in a while. Watch the bar for me." I hurried to follow Chase out the door, into the dark January night.

My name is Menolly D'Artigo and I used to be an acrobat. In other words, I was damned good at getting into places and spying on people. Or rather, most of the time I was damned good. I happen to be half-human on my mother's side, half-Fae on my father's. The genetic mix leads to trouble, and whatever powers a half-Fae, half-human child is born with tend to get swallowed up in a mix of uncertainty. My sisters Camille, a witch, and Delilah, a werecat, learned that lesson only too well.

During a routine spying mission, thanks to faulty wiring and a random roll of the dice, I slipped up. It was the last mistake I ever made. The Elwing Blood Clan took me down, and they knew how to play dirty. The torture seemed to last for an eternity, and now—I will. After they killed me, they raised me into the world of the undead, turned me into a vamp just like them. But I refused to let them win. Nobody ever gets the last word with me, especially a son of a bitch like Dredge.

My sisters and I work for the Otherworld Intelligence Agency, which went bust a couple months ago. Civil war broke out back in Y'Elestrial, our home city in Otherworld, and the Queen recalled all operatives. We opted to stay Earthside, especially since there's a death threat out on our heads at home.

Now, we're in a race against time and a powerful demon lord named Shadow Wing. He's big and he's bad, and he's currently ruling over the Subterranean Realms. Together with his hordes of Demonkin, Shadow Wing intends to raze both Earth and Otherworld to the ground. We do have allies back home in Otherworld. The Elfin Queen is giving us all the help she can, but it isn't much. Together, my sisters and our ragtag group of friends are all that's standing in Shadow Wing's way. And that's a scary proposition, at best.

The Delmonico Cinema Complex is an older theater in the Belles-Faire district of town, where the Wayfarer is located, and was still outfitted with the original décor complete with squeaky chairs and a balcony right out of the fifties where lovers used to grope and fondle their way to celluloid ecstasy. The Delmonico had seen better days, but held nostalgic charm for the Seattle suburb, and hearkened back to a time of ushers who actually did their jobs and real butter on popcorn and monster movies on Saturday afternoons.

The theater was empty; the moviegoers had been questioned and had gone home. I doubted there had been many. There wasn't much call during the week for late shows unless it was a cult classic, like *The Rocky Horror Picture Show* or *Plan 9 from Outer Space*. A young woman, the ticket taker by the looks of her uniform, and two food-stand attendants were sitting on a bench, waiting for Chase's team to give them the go-ahead to leave.

Chase led the way up the threadbare carpet-covered stairs, and I followed. Luckily, I had enough control to keep my instincts reined in. I shook the smell of fresh blood out of my thoughts and focused on what he was saying.

"We received an anonymous tip about an hour ago. The call came directly to me, so somebody knew this was a case for the FH-CSI," he said.

The Faerie-Human Crime Scene Investigations unit was Chase's baby. He'd created it when he was first accepted by the Otherworld Intelligence Agency, Earthside Division. The team responded to all law-enforcement matters dealing with the Fae or Earthside Supes.

"Direct to your office, you mean? Is your number public?" For some reason, that seemed odd to me.

Chase shook his head. "No, but it doesn't take much to find, if somebody wants it bad enough. Thing is, caller ID was blocked and whoever it was sounded pretty damned sure that the FH-CSI was necessary. But when we got here, it took a few minutes to realize that the victims had been attacked by vampires. A cursory glance wouldn't have shown anything out of the ordinary. If you can call any murder ordinary. So whoever called me had to know they were killed by somebody other than a FBH."

It was odd to hear the term FBH come from Chase's lips, especially since he was one, but it made sense. The acronym was easier than constantly saying "full-blooded human, Earthside born," which is what it really meant.

"Were the bodies moved? Could someone have checked to see if they were alive and in doing so, noticed the punctures?" I stared at the victims. The OIA medical team was still looking them over. Well, they'd been an *official* OIA medical team until a few months ago—now the OIA was our baby, and we were calling the shots.

"Nope. Don't think so. Sharah said that while there's a lot of blood, the patterns indicate they're right where they were when they died."

"Speaking of blood," I said slowly, gazing at the four bodies that, until earlier this evening, had been very much alive and—probably—happy people. I was no angel, that was for certain, but I chose my victims from the lowest of the low, which kept me in the clear as far as my own conscience.

"Yes?" Chase tapped me on the shoulder. He looked a little worried. "Menolly, are you okay?"

"Yeah," I said, shaking off my thoughts. "I'm fine. I was just going to say that there's something else odd about this massacre. There shouldn't be this much blood. There shouldn't be much blood at all unless we're dealing with one incredibly sloppy vamp, and even the grimiest bloodsuckers I know are usually fairly neat and tidy. That's why vamp attacks have generally gone unnoticed over the years. Unless . . ."

A thought ran through my head, but I didn't want to entertain it. There had been a lot of blood when I was turned, and I had the scars to prove it.

"Unless what?" Chase sounded impatient, and I didn't blame him. He still had to think of something to tell their next of kin. We weren't passing on information about the demons, nor were we in the habit of telling people that their loved ones had been killed by vampires and Earthside Supes. There were enough locos in the world who would gladly go hunting anybody or anything who even remotely resembled a Supe if they got word that we'd been responsible for somebody's death.

"Unless they either wanted to hurt these people, or . . . leave a calling card. Are there any scars? Any signs of torture . . ." As I glanced up, Chase returned my look, and I tore my gaze away when I saw the pity in his eyes. I quickly turned and strode over to the bodies, searching their expressions for some sign of pain, of anger.

Sharah was finishing up her notes. She and her assistant, an elf who barely looked old enough to shave, were getting ready to bag the bodies and take them back to the morgue for closer examination. Sharah's gaze flickered up to catch mine, and she softly nodded.

"I don't know yet," Chase said. "There doesn't appear to be extensive damage, but we'll know more when we fully examine them."

I studied their faces. Mainly, they looked surprised, as if they'd been simultaneously attacked. One last surprise for the night. For life.

With a sigh, I stepped out of the way and let the medics get on with their work. Over the past few months, I'd worked closely with Wade, the brains behind Vampires Anonymous, and we'd managed to enlist promises from at least fifteen vamps who lived in the city to avoid taking blood from the innocent. Or at least to avoid killing or hurting them in the process, if they had to drink from someone just passing by.

We'd developed quite a following, and were contemplating the next step, which would be to take control of vampire activity in Seattle and run it like an underground police force. Those who didn't cooperate would have to leave or face punishment. We hoped to inspire other groups in other cities, until vampires could walk among the living without fear of being skewered.

"Wade needs to know about this," I said. "I'll contact him, and we'll see if we can find out anything on our end."

Chase nodded. "I appreciate it, Menolly. I really don't know how to go after vampires, except with a butt load of garlic and a wooden stake. You said crosses don't work . . ."

"No, they don't. Neither do pentacles, ankhs, or any other religious symbol. All claptrap made up to give hope to the country dwellers who lived in fear of vampire activity. Of course, sunlight's a sure cure. Fire's not too welcome, either, but not nearly so dangerous. There are a few spells to ward off vampires. Camille knows a couple, but no way in hell will I let her practice on me, so the gods only know if she can work them right."

He snorted. "It's a crapshoot every time she gets it into her head to cast a spell."

I couldn't help but grin along with him. "Not necessarily— she's getting better at offensive magic, though her defensive and household magical skills leave a lot to be desired. Don't write her off, Chase. She could still do a lot of damage to you if she wanted."

Chase relaxed then and gave me a full-blown smile. "Yeah, I know. And so could Delilah. And I already know what you could do to me. But I trust you girls. *All* of you," he added.

Recognizing the significance of what he said, I accepted

the compliment graciously. A month or so ago, Chase still jumped whenever I entered the room, and I used his fear to play him to the hilt. We still didn't like each other. Much. But I'd developed a sense of respect for the tall, handsome young detective who had wooed Delilah's heart. She may not know it, and I was pretty sure Chase didn't know it, but the two of them were falling in love. I wasn't about to be the one to tell them. They'd find out soon enough on their own.

I silently made my way to the steps leading down to the main entrance of the Delmonico. "I'll get back to you when I've talked to Wade. Meanwhile, I suggest you think of a good excuse for why these four died. We can't possibly let the truth out. Too much chance for mayhem. Call me when you know more."

"Right," he said, sighing and turning back to the crime scene. "As if we didn't already have enough mayhem to deal with."

Silently agreeing, I left the theater and returned to my bar. The night was a frozen wonderland, but all I could smell was blood.

Don't miss a word from the "delightful...series
that simmers with fun and magic"* featuring
the D'Artigo sisters, half-human, half-Fae
supernatural agents.

By **Yasmine Galenorn**

Witchling

Changeling

Darkling

Dragon Wytch

Series praise:

"Pure delight."
—MaryJanice Davidson

"Vivid, sexy, and mesmerizing."
—*Romantic Times*

penguin.com

*Mary Jo Putney